SEQUESTERED

THE NEW DAWN: BOOK TWO

VALERIE J. MIKLES

Cover Design by James, GoOnWrite.com

Editing by Bob Greenberger, bobgreenberger.com

Proofreading and Layout by Frostbite Publishing, frostbitepublishing.com

Dedicated to those who feel trapped

1

"Sir!" Deputy Arman cried.

Constable Channing Mace groaned and squinted as blood poured from his split temple and stung his left eye. Adrenaline pumped through his body, compelling him to keep running. It took him a moment to realize he was lying flat on the ground.

"After him!" Mace choked, pointing at their target. Two other deputies were already in pursuit, and though Arman hesitated a moment longer, he obeyed, leaving his fallen commander behind.

Over the past few months, four men and one boy had died in mishaps at Rocan's chemical plant. They were testing new technology to facilitate production, but the mechanical failure rate was too high for Mace to believe that the mishaps were accidents. Mace hadn't understood the chief engineer's explanation, but he understood the word saboteur, and he'd finally found a lead worth chasing.

Forcing himself to sit, Mace cradled his left hand to his chest. His wrist was broken—snapped when he'd hit the pavement. The target was Thomas Gate, a product runner in his late twenties. He'd worn the gray coveralls of a plant worker—a stolen resource. Sabotage, theft, assault. Staggering to his feet, Mace tried to rejoin the chase.

"Which way?" he hollered to the onlookers. They'd been drawn from their shops by the deputies' shouts, but they were riveted by the Constable's beaten appearance. He shouted again and several of them pointed toward the water treatment plant. It was a gray building, clean and shiny on the outside, though rarely did anyone cross the threshold. The front door swung on rusted hinges and Mace bolted through, nearly ripping it off.

The plant smelled of metal and water and had minimal lighting, since all of its functions were automated. Mace heard scuffling sounds from overhead and when his eyes adjusted sufficiently to see the staircase, he charged up the stairs. The cross-hatched metal rattled loudly, the stairs splitting off to the right and encircling a water tank. Arman, Miller, and Grimes had followed the target onto the tank itself. It was difficult to assess the situation in the darkness. Miller was completely still and likely unconscious. Mace circled Miller, making sure the man wouldn't fall to his death.

Arman shouted and Grimes launched toward Gate, club raised, but Gate slid clear, catching a release that crashed a pair of crates onto the tank. The first crate splintered and went up in flames. The explosion punched a hole through the tank sending the remnants into the water supply.

"No!" Gate cried, seeing his precious bounty in flames. If the second crate exploded, they would lose a third of the city's water supply. And their lives.

Damping the fire became Mace's first priority. Screaming as he pulled his jacket over his broken hand, Mace charged the burning crate, and knocked it into the tank, dousing the flame.

"There's a child! Mace, there's a child in there!" Gate shouted, pointing to the crate.

Arman and Grimes had finally flanked Gate, but Gate's word stunned them all. Grimes acted first, diving into the water, but he could not support the crate alone.

"Arman, save the child!" Mace shouted. Arman growled threateningly at Gate, but then dove into the water to help Grimes. With his captors occupied, Gate slid down the opposite side of the tank. Before Gate could escape, Mace pulled a knife from his boot and chucked it at the man, hitting just below the rib cage. Gate slid off the side of the tank and fell to the lower level. Even if he survived the fall, he would bleed out before help arrived. No one would question Mace for the killing. Any man who would threaten the life of a child would have been put to death.

2

Douglas Hwan sipped the gin from his flask and sat on the front steps of the hospital, building the courage he needed to face his ailing mother on the anniversary of his father's death. Time was supposed to heal the wound, but all it did was exacerbate his mother's mental illness to the point where she barely recognized him some days. His father's death had taken but an instant, his mother's had been a slow fade over the last ten years. They'd taken her from home and forced her to live in the asylum, in a dark room with no windows.

Folding his flight jacket over his arms, he hugged the worn, brown canvas. He'd outgrown it before he'd worn it out, but he carried it with him always. It had arrived by messenger just two days after his father's death—a gift from his father to commemorate the flight.

"Maman, please remember," he whispered, sucking in his emotions and hiding the jacket under his shirt and striding through the front door. He didn't want the Resource Manager to take it from him. Clothing was a rationed resource, and the jacket should have been redistributed years ago to someone who could wear it. Douglas had tried giving it to his mother, but the asylum wouldn't allow it. When she wore it, she remembered her husband, and she spoke coherently. It was a memory of love, but it felt more like magic every year.

Asylum was on the east side of the second, third, and fourth floors of the hospital, and the need for space grew every year as more and more people succumbed to the trauma of living in a dying Dome. The hospital lobby was dimly lit and lined with hand-carved, stone benches. There used to be cushioned seats in here, but part of dying was losing luxuries, and part of surviving was filling the void with artistry. Douglas' stenciled jacket, and dyed-red hair were expressions of that cry to feel alive.

"Where are you going?" Dr. Amir Frank barked, intercepting Douglas by the stairs. Frank was a stout man whose ruddy complexion and double chin made him appear too unhealthy to be in the medical profession. His position at the top of the social ladder afforded him first pick among the fabrics, and Douglas suspected him of hoarding significantly more than the six sets of clothing issued every other man.

"Seeing my mother," Douglas replied, his voice cracking under the haze of alcohol. Dr. Frank oversaw the resources and medications allocated to women in asylum, and Douglas had learned to be civil for his mother's sake.

"No, you can't. Not now," Frank replied, directing Douglas back toward the benches.

"Why? She's not dead, is she? Is she?" Douglas asked, his heart rate climbing.

"She is beyond help," Frank said quietly, pushing Douglas' shoulder to make him sit. "We are letting her go."

It was a euphemism. They were giving her food and water, but not the medication she needed to recognize it or keep it down. They were letting her die.

"Then can I take her home?" Douglas asked. He knew this

day was coming, and he petitioned every year to bring his mother home.

"It would only distract you from your work. Which you should be getting back to," Frank said sternly, raising his bushy, white eyebrows. "You leave now on your own, or I will report you for skipping work."

Douglas shuddered. Bad things happened to men who refused to go to work, no matter how pointless the work was. "I'm not leaving until I see her," he said, swallowing hard. It was the anniversary. If she was to die, then he wanted her to hold the flight jacket one last time.

"Hwan—"

"I can get her to eat. I can get her to take medicine. I can get her to be calm. Whatever you want, I'll help her," Douglas insisted, charging past Dr. Frank, flying up the stairs. He made it into the common area of the asylum, where the in-patients pretended to be social.

"Maman!" Douglas hollered. Two orderlies intercepted him, dragging him back into the hall.

"Hush! You'll frighten the residents!" Frank warned, bustling from the stairwell, panting for breath. Constable Mace was a few steps behind him, favoring a broken hand. The orderlies held Douglas down and Mace reached under Douglas' shirt, pulling out the jacket.

"That's mine!" Douglas cried.

"Can you wear it?" the Constable challenged. He was a dark-haired man with angled features and a menacing scowl, and despite their strained relationship, Douglas felt safe with him. Even angry, he exuded peace. It was hard to believe he'd killed a man in cold blood less than two weeks ago.

"My father gave it to me. It's all I have left of him. The Resource Manager claimed everything else," Douglas sniffled, wrestling one arm free and snatching the jacket. "They took everything that was my mother's. They took everything. I need to see her. It's the anniversary. I need to—"

"Dr. Frank?" Mace asked.

"There is nothing he can do for her but prolong her suffering," Frank sneered, red-faced. "She is being given basic resources."

"Can't basic resources include human contact?" Douglas pleaded, rolling to his knees, hugging his jacket. "She's my mother!"

"It is not a good day for her," Frank said, his arrogance melting just enough for Douglas to believe his intentions sincere. "Trust me, Little Hwan. You should not see her today. I will send a messenger if her condition improves. Your place is the yard. Go to work."

"But—"

"Hwan, this is your only warning," Mace said, yanking Douglas up by the elbow.

Douglas hugged his jacket and ran, fighting back tears. When he made it out of the hospital, he downed the last of his gin, but it would take more than a flask to drown Dr. Frank's words.

Choking back emotion, Douglas hurried to the mechanical yard. The yard was a multi-story complex, with thirteen bays. Every gliding door in Rocan that could be salvaged had been moved here to protect the general population from the volatile engine work that occurred inside. Of the thirteen bays, only three spanned the entire height of the building. There were eight smaller bays on ground level, and two upper-level areas with workstations for hand-held products. Douglas charged up the stairs to his workstation on the second floor, pulled a gin bottle from a box under his desk, and drank directly from the bottle.

The light in this area came mostly through a skylight in the ceiling. Douglas' workstation had a lamp, a magnifying glass, a tool chest, and a box of trinkets collected from around the Dome, whose purpose had yet to be identified. When Douglas needed a break from the mundane people, he rooted through the box, trying to identify what the trinkets did, and what parts could be salvaged from them. He picked up a blocky one with inset circles, and set it under the light, making himself look busy in case anyone came by.

"Douglas? I didn't expect you in so soon," McGill Lefevre called, pulling up a stool across the workbench. McGill was lean and tall, with rounded facial features. His hair was naturally strawberry blonde, but he dyed it dark brown because he didn't like it. He didn't like his name either, but the town was so small, everyone knew it and called him by it no matter how he introduced himself. "The Intendant is here about the Coureur." The Coureur was Rocan's only motorized vehicle, built by Douglas' father. "Ramsey is giving him the overview. I was about to head out to the processing plant to troubleshoot some issues with engine output—Douglas, what's wrong? Is it your mother?"

McGill put a hand over Douglas', sliding it up his arm as he moved around the table. He and McGill had been close once, but their relationship had dissolved when Douglas' mother went into asylum. Douglas couldn't remember the last time he'd let McGill close enough for a hug.

"Where's the Intendant?" Douglas asked, wiping the tears from his face and pushing McGill away. The Intendant was the only one with the power to overrule Dr. Frank.

"Bay 3. Douglas—"

Douglas charged down the stairs and crossed the hall into Bay 3. It was a larger bay, used both for storing refined fuel and Coureur maintenance. There were a few metal pieces collected for the chassis of the new Coureur, barrels for the fuel, and a gliding door leading outside. His father's glider had been built in this bay. Most days, Douglas loved being in here, but today—the anniversary—it hurt.

Intendant Hubert's deep-base voice echoed through the tall chamber, giving a lashing to Ramsey—an older engineer with a heart for building, but shaky hands.

"Nine months and this is all you have!" the Intendant ranted, his bright red face contrasting his stark white, neatly combed hair. "A couple pieces laid out. Not even attached."

Ramsey jutted his pointed chin, looking down his nose at the Intendant. "With limited resources and no paper to convey design—"

"You have fifteen men working on it!" the Intendant countered.

"Most of whom have never driven the old Coureur, let alone dismantled it," Douglas interjected, strutting confidently into the conversation. "The designer my father worked with—"

"The woman, you mean," the Intendant seethed. "You are not bringing a woman into a building with refined fuel."

"Her name is Zoe, and she is brilliant," Ramsey snarled, his voice and temper rising.

"So is he!" the Intendant snapped, pointing to Douglas. "Your designer is perfectly capable of using documents and schematics."

Douglas shivered, feeling the weight of his father's legacy bearing down on his slumped shoulders. The men in the yard had been so kind, apprenticing and training him, but Douglas was no mechanical genius, and being put in charge of the projects here made him feel like a failure and a fraud. "I am not my father. I am still learning what he knew."

"Which would be easier if you actually showed up to work," the Intendant huffed. "Where were you when I came?"

"Visiting my mother," Douglas said, his insides quivering despite the dulling power of the gin.

"The invalid," the Intendant groused. "She is on basic resources, but I will kill her faster if that's what it takes to get this Coureur done."

Douglas paled and stumbled back a step, nearly falling on Ramsey. "If you want me here, restore her access to medicine," Douglas threatened, his fist clenching. "If I lose her, you lose me."

"I want you, but I don't need you," the Intendant sneered.

"The Coureur will work as promised," Ramsey interjected, putting a hand on Douglas' back, moving his thumb just enough to show he wanted to impart comfort, but not show weakness. "We know what needs to be done now. We just need time to put the pieces together. It may be another year or more before we have the frame together."

"Will this Coureur move faster than the last? Will it be able to get to the mountains to search for new resources?" the Intendant demanded.

"There have been so many catastrophic failures this past month, we may not have any engines left by the time the chassis is ready," Ramsey shrugged.

"Constable Mace has found the saboteur. That should put a stop to the failures for a while," the Intendant replied, crossing his arms, pacing over the chassis pieces they had, looking ready to kick them.

"Did he say why he did it?" Douglas asked. He'd reported the sabotage to Mace, but hadn't expected someone to be found so quickly.

"We weren't able to ask," the Intendant sighed. "The man was a Sequesterer. And he is dead."

Ramsey gasped, and Douglas hung his head, aching inside.

"There are no engines in the yard right now," Ramsey tried. "If we could just bring Zoe to help direct the design, we could move so much faster—"

"You are not bringing a woman into the yard! Ramsey, if you put a breedable woman in harm's way, you will not live to see tomorrow," the Intendant growled, turning on his heels and stalking out of the bay.

"Intendant!" Douglas called, chasing after him. "About my mother—"

"She will continue receiving basic resources so long as I see progress," the Intendant grumbled, closing the conversation with a flick of his wrist. Douglas stood in the hall connecting the bays, feeling tiny, insignificant, and overwhelmed.

"It'll be okay, son. Your Maman is strong," Ramsey said, giving Douglas' shoulder a squeeze.

"We need Zoe," Douglas whispered. He had a knack for machines, but he couldn't do this on his own. He didn't want to.

"The old Coureur is outside. We can design off of that for now," McGill said, coming down the stairs, screwing the cap onto Douglas' flask and handing it back to him. The show of familiarity was strange, but at this point, Douglas needed comfort more than normalcy. He peeked at his old friend—the blue eyes that he'd once adored gazing into were looking back at him with love and support. It wasn't the same now. They were older, and had spent too many years as cool, distant colleagues. Douglas always suspected that McGill's testimony had been instrumental in having Kinley locked in the asylum. No one besides John had known the details well enough back then.

"John," Douglas whispered, crying out for his adoptive father. Ramsey and McGill huddled protectively around Douglas.

"Did something happen to your mother?" McGill asked again. "I can send a messenger to John."

Douglas shook his head. Bad things happened to men who didn't work, and Douglas didn't want John coming home to cry over this.

3

The hospital in Qu'Appelle, the southern district of Rocan, was the primary care facility for all of the citizens of the city, and as the population declined through the years, wings were shut down and consolidated. Of the ten floors, only six were still in use and two were committed entirely toward medical research to save the children. Where once the Dome housed half a million, now the population was down to twelve thousand. Every effort they made to cure the Malady seemed to make things worse.

Don Yale, the Administrator of the Geneculture Registry, came to the hospital daily. He was kept apprised of every woman who conceived and he visited those lucky enough to give birth. He returned for the naming ceremonies and witnessed as each child went home to their adoptive families. A few generations ago, one man could not have handled the task load, and Don hoped he'd live to see such times again.

The hospital lobby was clean, but not bright. They had begun rationing lights when they realized they had no way to replace them. The supply that remained came from the upper floors and from LeTroy's hospital on the north side, which now had only one floor that remained open for emergent care. When Don reached the nurses' station, it was unmanned, so Don helped himself to the records he needed. Since the electronics started breaking down a year ago, they were switching to hard copies, but paper was not an infinite resource either, and the doctors had developed a short-hand to save resources. As it was, they'd spent too many centuries taking for granted the fact that everything worked and not enough time learning how. There were those like the Hwans who seemed to have a knack for reverse engineering and fixing things, but the work could get dangerous and Don could only hope that the eventual benefits would outweigh the human cost.

"Dr. Yale!" Dr. Andre Louis said, quickening his pace from the patient hall to meet Don at the nurses' station. Louis was Chief of General Medicine, handling injuries and illnesses not related to birthing. The combination of stress and middle age had brought out crow's feet around his eyes, but he still looked younger than his years.

"Dr. Louis, the Exceptions are large this time around," Don said, sighing as he perused the list of ineligible breeders. Every three months, they did a large draw from the general population, and Louis was responsible for declaring individuals healthy enough for breeding. Don was responsible for pairing breeders.

"Yes," Louis said, shrugging out of his white coat and hanging it on the rack. "Doctor Frank's latest interventions have markedly decreased the number of early term miscarriages, so there are fewer women recovered from the last round."

"I hadn't heard," Don said, feeling a bit of relief. "This is good news."

"Not yet," Louis sighed, pulling up a stool and sitting across from Don. "Late term miscarriages and stillbirths have increased proportionally. The net live birth rate remains the same."

Don's shoulders slumped, realizing why the news hadn't been shouted joyously from the rooftops. "It is still progress."

"In the wrong direction," Louis said sternly. "The danger is higher for the women and since the birth rate remains the same . . . this round we will resume our previous methods."

"We had to try," Don said, shuffling the records he had and looking at his hands. "Is there any additional information on our young Sequestered that Constable Mace rescued?"

The change in topic brought forth an uncharacteristic smile in Louis. "We are treating the little girl's injuries. She is social and playful. The nurses adore her."

Don shook his head and chuckled. Louis was not easily endeared to anyone. "I have heard. Already three families of them have petitioned to adopt her, including Deputy Arman."

"Really?"

"It surprised me too," Don said. Reginald Arman and his wife Colleen were both decent breeders, but as a pair they'd never been able to conceive and they'd never requested to raise a child in their home before. Don's heart twisted with nervous hope at the thought of the couple finally having a child of their own, but he feared that if he ever found the girl's birth family, Colleen would reject the child. "Has she told anyone her name?"

Louis shook his head. "She hasn't said a word. There's no apparent damage to the vocal cords, but she's mute. As with other Sequestereds, I'm not sure she's familiar with language. In light of her disposition, I've named her Felicity."

Don laughed again and nodded. "My Andre, I think you are under her spell."

"She is the youngest Sequestered we've ever found," Louis pointed out, letting a small smile emerge for a microsecond before resuming his stern mask.

Don nodded thoughtfully. "Do you ever wonder if the live birth rate is significantly higher than we imagine, but more children are being hidden?"

"I would rejoice at the first, but also pray that those hidden from us are kept better and safer than those we have discovered," Louis said gravely. There was a strong overlap between Sequesterers and child abusers. Every man, woman, and child they'd rescued to date had suffered some kind of emotional and physical abuse that went beyond social isolation and confinement. "Dr. Yale, I wanted to speak to you about young Hwan."

Don nearly dropped his papers at the mention of Douglas. "Is he injured? Please tell me you aren't Excepting him."

"Nothing of the sort." Louis slid a document across the table to Don. "It is a petition for custody of his mother. It is the sixth Dr. Frank has received in as many years and it is a disruption every time."

"He is of legal age to ask. That is what the Intendant would say," Don pointed out.

"Kinley Hwan was driven to madness after the loss of her husband and the Intendant knows I cannot release her to her son unless Douglas is relieved of his duties at the yard—a condition which the Intendant has no intention of granting," Louis said, dropping his voice to an intense whisper so he wouldn't be overheard. "It is cruel to continue to build false hope in the boy by allowing the petition process to continue."

"Doctor, I merely work for the Registry. I do not have the Intendant's ear," Don said.

"But you have the ear of his adoptive father," Louis persisted. "The boy grows more destructive every year he is denied."

Don hung his head and closed his eyes, not knowing what to do. He knew John Harris had had an exceedingly difficult time raising Douglas and counseling the boy through the loss of his family. Unless they found some way to temper Douglas' moods, his fighting could lead to catastrophic injury that would make him unbreedable. His mother kept him alive.

Don looked helplessly at Louis. "You would have me tell him to give up hope?"

4

The landing gear crumpled as the small pod crashed in the barren tundra where Sky had been forced to land. Chase had promised her that this *Bobsled* would revolutionize inter-dome travel. What he failed to mention was that its practical range was limited to the ten square miles around Quin city. She'd done modifications to extend the range, using a focused gravity beam to hover instead of relying on traditional rocketry. The small wheels were designed for smooth-paved spaceports, not rocky landscapes. When she hit an ice patch, the *Bobsled* spun out of control, flipping tail over nose. The craft landed upside down, jarring her against the safety restraint, stealing the breath from her lungs. Blackness closed in, followed by an assault of future visions.

"Spirit!" Sky screamed, using the sound to fight Spirit and ground her mind to consciousness. Spirit, that infectious being that had plagued her with visions and dreams since she was a teenager, tortured her with images and sensations of violent deaths, clouding her mind whenever she was in darkness. She'd come north to escape the densely populated Domes of the middle continent, but she felt the live city when she flew overhead. Something drew her into this valley—something she felt most prominently on Terrana, and occasionally in places with high concentration of the other-realm energy spirits fed on.

Sky was a spirit-carrier. Some non-physical alien being shared her consciousness—or rather, her unconsciousness. When humans first came to this solar system, the mystery of a lifeless water planet was overshadowed by the joy of finding something habitable. They'd colonized the planet and both moons before the spirits first revealed themselves. The spirits communicated as reliably as ghosts, and most people didn't believe them real. Sky hadn't believed until one infected her family. The ethereal being's attempts to communicate had driven her aunt to insanity, and after killing her, it jumped into Sky's cousin. It choked, it killed, and it moved into the next nearest host. Spirit was a psychopath.

Sky had fled the feeding ground of souls and lived between Domes, skipping between civilizations and cultures, surviving Spirit's assaults for decades. As near as she knew, Spirit was immortal, and so long as it kept her, so was she, more or less. She thought Spirit had killed her a dozen times over, but then he came—Hawk. He was a man with feathered wings and a golden face and a hawk tattooed on the breast. Sky never figured out his place in the visions Spirit plagued her with, but whenever she saw him, she could breathe again.

Hawk descended on her, filling her lungs with air with the swish of his massive wings. She had to move fast.

Freeing herself from the safety harness, she fell hard on her shoulder. Her jaw clacked and she tasted blood on her tongue. The *Bobsled's* oxygen tank hissed, leaking air into the cockpit. One spark could set the whole pod on fire. No time to dawdle!

Sky wiped her face with the back of her hand, smearing blood and ash across her forehead. The cut on her brow was shallow, and the pod was in far worse shape than she was.

According to her Virp, the air outside was breathable. It was the UV index that worried her. The sun had barely peeked over the horizon and already it was dangerously high.

Sky held her breath and pressed the hatch release on the pod. The dry air was cold in the long shadows cast by the mountain, and the perma-frosted ground crunched under her feet. The glow of dawn tinted the sky, silhouetting the mountains in red. Stars were still visible in the darkness to the west, but her UV monitor chirped in warning. The Ozone was depleted here. The pressure suit would slow her down, but it was the only protection she had for her skin.

Spirit could feel a Dome full of souls as clearly as Sky felt the sun's heat on her skin. There could be other spirit carriers here, half-breeds, or hybrids. The half-breeds were immortal, like the spirits, but hybrids were humans with spirit-like abilities. They lived, aged, and died like humans.

Sky cried out as she pulled the glove over her hand. Her fingers were cut and her elbow was sprained. Spirit would heal her body with the same power it used to slow her aging. It did not want to die here. Neither did she. She dabbed the cut on her forehead, rubbed her nose, drank water from her canteen, and took one last breath of fresh air. This far north and in the dead of winter, the daylight may only last a few hours.

Following the pull of the strange energy concentration, she walked across the ridge of the valley, and saw a Dome. There was a covered tunnel leading out the other, stretching for a few miles, then disappearing into the ground.

"What is it with half-breeds and tunnels?" she muttered. The wind gusted in response nearly bowling her over. Any shelter would do for now.

The road to the Hudson mine was three miles long, barren, and coated in winter frost. The midmorning light streamed into the covered road, creating a greenhouse effect that barely countered the subfreezing temperature outside. In the summer, the condensed water fell from the ceiling making a false rain, and children liked to play in the water. The aged road was ground to gravel in some places and twice daily, the city's lone ethanol powered Coureur made the journey to the mine.

Douglas Hwan dug his fingers into the steering grip of the Coureur, muttering obscenities while straggling miners along the path jumped into the rear cabin, taking advantage of the unscheduled ride. The flatbed carried men as easily as mining equipment.

"Watch the bumps, Little Hwan!" one of the workers shouted when a pothole nearly threw him from the bed. Glowering, Douglas hit the accelerator, imagining the Coureur breaking through the wall and charging past the mountains that isolated Rocan from the world. The tragedy of his father's death had driven his mother to madness, and as much as Douglas denied it, the madness was in him, too—the odd hallucination haunting his hours.

As he pulled up to the mine, the workers that were topside looked up, wondering what had prompted the Coureur's arrival. Celio Ferreira, the recently appointed Overseer of Raw Mining, rolled his eyes at Douglas. Glancing at his flight jacket on the seat and clutching his gin flask, Douglas hopped out of the Coureur.

"Have you seen John?" he asked one of the miners. Douglas couldn't remember the man's name. Perhaps if he could, he'd have a titled position like Celio.

"He's already down below," the miner answered. "He's shift lead today, so he got here early. Do you want me to get him?"

"No," Douglas said, taking a swig of gin. The drive had

calmed him some and there was nothing his adoptive father could say that would change anything.

"Hwan!" Celio shouted. "That Coureur's not supposed to be here."

"Celio," Douglas grunted, capping his drink and tucking the flask into his pocket.

"Overseer," Celio corrected. "I have a title here."

"Taking the Coureur for a test drive, *Celio*," Douglas growled. He hadn't thought about an excuse for bringing the Coureur, but he was too upset to stay at the yard.

"The Intendant commissioned you to build a second Coureur, but you can't do that if you're taxiing people about in this one!"

"Don't tell me how to do my work," Douglas shouted. "I may not have a fancy title, Overseer, but I know my job."

His rage seemed to make the air catch fire, and Douglas turned sharply on his heels, fists clenched, eyes seeing red.

His Coureur was engulfed in a fireball!

"Celio!" Douglas warned, diving to the ground, taking Celio with him. There was no heat with the fire, but an exploded ethanol engine could easily collapse the entrance to the mine.

"Kerf! What is wrong with you?" Celio hollered, kicking Douglas off and charging toward the Coureur. "Hey! You by the Coureur! All new workers are required to interview first!"

Douglas groaned and rolled to his feet. He'd long ago accepted that he didn't see the world like other people did. He'd learned to ignore the visions—the onset of the madness he'd inherited from his mother—but he'd never seen a walking fireball before.

"Shift has started! Get to work!" John Harris ordered, blustering out of the mine, pushing through the crowd of men surrounding Douglas and Celio. He grabbed Douglas by the shoulder, nearly knocking him off his feet. "What trouble are you stirring now?" he hissed.

Douglas' jaw flapped, the morning of grief surging. His adoptive father was weathered and hard, and his skin smelled of the solvent they used to extract potash from the rock. Douglas felt calmer now that John was here. There were no free-floating fireballs or winged angels racing through the sky. He blinked away the phantom memory and saw Celio's new worker shoulder deep under the open the hood of the Coureur!

"Hey! Get away from that!" Douglas shouted, charging over and tossing the worker aside, sending him flying backwards. Scanning the hood, Douglas assessed the damage. He had intuitive understanding of the design when all the pieces were in place, but now the belts were mucked.

"Hawk?"

The voice was soft-pitched like a young, messenger boy, but there were no messengers at the mine. His face getting tight, he glanced at the worker and froze. Sprawled on the ground, clutching his precious flight jacket, was a woman! *Kerf all. I'll be hanged for this.*

The woman rolled into a crouch, drawing a knife. Her sweat-soaked blonde hair clung to her burned and bleeding face, but the fire in her eyes and the blade in her hand warned that she was not defenseless.

"Keep back! Weapon!" Celio warned, herding the other workers behind him. "Tamar, Kris, get some rope and send a messenger to the Constable!"

"Celio, you kerf!" Douglas shouted. "You can't tie up a Sequestered!"

Sequestered! The whispered word was repeated among the men and the woman whipped around, her fist pumping on the blade.

"I can tie up a violent one," Celio said.

"What violence? Aside from ripping out the pump belt on the Coureur, what has she done? She's scared," Douglas said. He kept seeing flickers of the fireball consuming her, confusing his perception.

"But who is she? Why is she here?" John asked, taking a step closer. "Madame—"

The woman whipped around, snarling. Her blue eyes glittered in the morning light. John stared, mesmerized, but Douglas cut behind him, pulling him back to safety.

"Hawk," she said, stepping toward them, laughing when she locked eyes with Douglas, as if they were sharing an inside joke.

"She knows a word," Douglas commented, hiding behind John. "That's more than most Sequestereds."

"Whatever that means," Celio grumbled.

"Is that your name? Hawk?" John asked.

The woman smiled at him and lowered her knife. She had to stand at least six feet tall—taller than Douglas and only a few inches shy of John. Her eyes wandered toward Douglas, her fingers tracing the pattern on the stolen jacket. Then she tapped her chest and spoke three short sounds.

"Say again," John said. "I didn't catch that."

"That's Trade language," Celio said. Trade was the ancient language agreed as the common language between Domes, and was passed from generation to generation in the hope that someone would come to save Rocan. "She's speaking Trade! Those are numbers. One, twelve, and, um . . ."

"Six-hundred sixty-eight," Douglas finished. His father had taught him Trade. They used to practice as a family, while they sat in the glider and dreamed of the world outside. "It's a date. She's reading the date on the jacket."

It was the day his father died. And today was the anniversary. Douglas rubbed his cheek on John's shoulder, blotting his tears.

John turned just enough to offer sympathy, but he couldn't pull his eyes off of the woman.

"If she reads, she's not a Sequestered. And whoever she is, she doesn't belong here," Celio said.

"At least she speaks," John said. "Do either of you remember enough to tell her she is among friends? Maybe ask her name."

Celio blustered forward, offering a greeting.

Exploding in motion, the woman swung her fist and knocked Celio flat on his back. She stomped on his chest and raised her nine-inch, steel knife. Celio screeched. John dove in, tackling the woman, rolling on the ground. Douglas stumbled back, keeping his eye on the knife.

The woman squealed and Douglas couldn't tell whether she was laughing or sobbing, but by the third roll, she'd fainted in John's arms.

"Is everyone all right?" Celio checked. "The woman?"

"Still breathing," John said, cradling her and checking her injuries. She had dark bruises all over. "We need to get her to the hospital."

"I can take her. I speak Trade," Douglas said, kneeling down and rifling through her jacket pockets until he found the Coureur's pump belt. "Good, it's still in one piece."

"You're more worried about your machine than her!" Celio accused, rubbing his bruised cheek.

"Am not!"

"Thinking when you get to asylum, you can trade her for your mother."

"Hey!" John warned, putting a hand on Douglas' leg to keep him from running into Celio's fist. "Overseer, I will help Douglas get the woman settled in the Coureur. I'll be down shortly. Douglas, fix the Coureur."

Douglas shifted foot-to-foot, staring at the woman's blood staining the collar of his precious jacket. "John, I need to talk—"

"She's waking," John whispered, cradling the woman's face.

"John—"

"You come to my place of work and pick a fight. You're not even supposed to be here!" John seethed. "You fix this machine and you get her to the hospital. And whatever your problem is today, you work it out on your own."

"Hawk," the woman hummed softly, her eyes drifting open and shut, her bleeding fingers tracing the bird stenciled on the jacket. Douglas felt like he was watching his father die all over again, but he took out his flask, and dampened the feeling with his drink.

5

The taste of ash, dust, and blood coated Sky's tongue. Her elbow throbbed, the injury agitated by the fight at the mine. The cabin of the tiny vehicle felt claustrophobic, and Sky leaned her face against the window, trying desperately to hold on to consciousness.

There was something off about the people in this town. They didn't feel like normal people. It was hard to pin down what was different, and it wasn't a bad thing. But it was more unsettling because it was so peaceful. The wooziness was lifting now that they'd left the crowd, and Sky could feel Spirit reviving.

"Are you still with me, bébé?" her young escort asked, rubbing her shoulder. "You can lie down if you need."

"I'm fine, Hawk," she murmured, her gaze wandering over him. He was a gold-skinned man with long, red hair that was not by any stretch of the imagination a natural color.

"Hwan," he corrected. "Douglas Hwan."

"I found you," she murmured, touching his hair. He didn't have feathered wings, but she'd seen his face a thousand times, and she'd always assumed he was a figment of her imagination, drawn to protect her from Spirit's vicious attacks. Now, she wondered if Spirit had brought her here intentionally, to meet her protector. It was the jacket she recognized first. The bird stenciled on the breast was the reason for his name. "I call you Hawk."

"And what's your name, bébé?" he asked.

Hawk's shoulders were hunched over and he gripped the steering wheel with both hands, keeping a straight path despite the obvious smell of alcohol on his breath. His eyes were half closed, and Sky couldn't tell if it was natural or if they were swollen from weariness. It looked like he needed her protection now.

"Hey, stay with me," he said, catching her when she pitched sideways. It could be the head injury making her woozy, not the natives. *Spirit, don't you hurt him.*

"I'll take you away from here. Far, far away," she promised, absently running her fingers along his arm.

"Far isn't an option. This Coureur runs from the mine to Qu'Appelle," he sighed. "But I'll dream with you. Tell me a story."

"Qu'Appelle," she repeated, laughing at the strange cadence of Hawk's language. His Trade was thickly accented, but he was fluent in it.

"We'd be there by now if you hadn't messed up my Coureur," Hawk said. "You could have been sitting in a warm bath while I made lunch."

Sky laughed at him and laid her head on his lap. The vehicle was bumping around and his clothes smelled weird, but she'd literally met the man of her dreams. The man who saved her in every dream. When Spirit was at its most violent, he came and shielded her. He was not as comforting in real life, but he tried, combing his fingers through her hair, shielding her face so she didn't hit the steering wheel every time they hit a bump.

"Do you have a name?" he asked again.

"You called me *Es—sequesere*?" she said.

"*Séquestre*. That's not a name," he said, his body twitching, his expression going cold.

"What does that mean?" she asked, lifting her head.

Hawk nearly swayed off the road. Tugging the tips of his hair, he cleared his throat. "It translates as Sequestered. A Sequestered is a woman whose family hides her from society, keeping her from a normal life. Someone isolated and abused."

"I am not Sequestered; I am not from here," Sky told him.

"You certainly talk more than most Sequestereds. Did you have a lot of people to talk to growing up? Where are you from?" Hawk asked.

"Nowhere in particular."

"Were you born in a cave?" Hawk laughed.

"Yes. But it was a very nice cave," she said, scooting away from him and leaning against the window. Spirit had forced her to leave home decades ago, but she'd learned never to trust anyone with the secret of Spirit's existence. She had to remind herself that regardless of the energy that had drawn her here, Hawk was no more benign than any other man.

"What will happen to me in Qu'Appelle?" she asked.

Hawk took a drink from a flask and increased their speed. "I'll take you to the hospital first, then Geneculture. They'll trace your lineage, figure out which cave you crawled out of."

"Why is that so important?" Sky asked.

Hawk shrugged. "For breeding—"

Sky sputtered and pulled a gravity gun from her satchel, pointing it at his head. "Stop the Coureur."

Hawk glanced sideways at her, his eyes widening. "No."

"Do it, now!" Sky insisted, biting her lip. She'd never felt qualms about shooting anyone before, but a part of her worried that she wouldn't see him in her dreams anymore if she killed him.

"Kerf, I hate it when Celio is right," Hawk muttered, slamming the brakes. "Why are you threatening violence?"

"I am not here to breed!" Sky growled, blood rising to her sunburned cheeks. Hawk reached past the gun, putting a comforting hand on her arm. She would have shot any other man. She should have shot him.

"Calm down, bébé. It's not happening today," Hawk said. "My mother was Sequestered as a child. She told me things. I won't let anyone hurt you, I promise."

"Hawk," she murmured, piteously.

"Hwan. Why is that so hard for you?"

Her finger twitched on the trigger of the grav-gun. If she knocked him out, she'd be nowhere. She needed shelter, supplies, and either a way to fix the *Bobsled* or a way to replace it.

Hawk cocked his head, his hands hovering over the dash.

"Something is wrong," he said, stepping out of the vehicle. "I think you damaged more than I realized."

Not one to miss a golden opportunity, Sky slid across the bench into the driver's seat. The hand controls seemed straightforward enough, though her first attempt to start the vehicle resulted in a loud revving of the engine. Hooking her elbow, Hawk reached across her to pull the key.

"Get out. Something is wrong with the engine," he said, his attention focused more on what he was hearing than on the fact that Sky was trying to steal his Coureur. With his hand hovering over the body of the vehicle, he circled to the front.

"Is that smoke or steam?" Sky asked, sliding out of the vehicle. She couldn't hear what he heard, but she saw the thin wisps of smoke leaking out of the Coureur and jumped out. Hawk touched the hood of the vehicle, hissing and pulling away.

"What do you see?" Hawk asked, turning to her, then squeezing his eyes shut. "My vision is hazy."

"Because you've been drinking too much," Sky commented, smacking his arm.

Pressing his lips together, he pulled the sleeve of his shirt over his hand and reached for the latch on the hood where the smoke leaked out. Launching toward him, Sky grabbed his shoulder and yanked him away from the vehicle, but not before he'd tipped open the hood. The smoke met a fresh wave of oxygen, and the ethanol caught fire.

Hawk is on fire! Sky's instincts screamed at her to run—to live—but she tackled Hawk to the ground, rolling back and forth in the dirt until the fire on his body was extinguished. His body seized as he went into shock.

"I knew you were too good to last," she cried, brushing his red hair away from his face, willing him to open his eyes again. Then she whispered a quiet goodbye and left him on the ground.

6

Paints and dyes made from plants were among the unregulated resources in Rocan. With no surplus resources for canvas, the walls of buildings became the medium of choice. So long as the medicinal gardens weren't trampled in the process, the art was encouraged. In the central square, the walls were painted and repainted frequently, sometimes with personal messages of congratulations, most times with pictures.

Constable Channing Mace strolled the illustrated walls in the mornings, checking for signs of inappropriate content or vandalism. Most people respected the art, but every generation seemed to breed at least one new troublemaker.

Jotham Gate, a golden-skinned man in his twenties, sat by the wall, facing a mural painted by his brother Thomas. The work was half-finished, and blocked off for protection, pending the completion of Mace's investigation into the Sequestered. It was a fantasy image of a winged angel harnessing the lights of the Aurora.

"You killed my brother," Jotham said when Mace approached. His chin dropped, his curly hair falling into his eyes. This was the first time Mace had seen him out of the house since the incident. He'd questioned other members of the household, but Jotham had been so grief-stricken, it was pointless to talk to him.

"He Sequestered a child," Mace pointed out, keeping his distance. He had a good deal of strength on Jotham, but he also had a broken hand.

"He wouldn't do that," Jotham whispered, tears rolling down his cheeks. He ran his hands over the multi-colored swirls in the painting, as though trying to harness its energy.

"Then why did he know where she was?" Mace probed. Of all the places to run, hide, and escape, Thomas had run directly to the girl. He wanted her to be found.

"He had a gray uniform. Where did he get it?" Mace tried.

Jotham touched his own blue coveralls, his brow furrowing. "He didn't have . . . he wouldn't steal."

"He sabotaged three engines!" Mace growled. "You two were inseparable. You called him your twin. You're telling me you have no idea how he did all this. I'm surprised I wasn't chasing the both of you!"

Jotham touched the mural again, his jaw quivering. He was confused—unable to rectify what he knew about his brother with the events that had unfolded.

"Did he ever take you to the water tower?" Mace asked.

Jotham nodded.

"Why?"

"Stories." His hands traced the wings. "We were birds, perched atop the world. Safe from . . . safe from Geneculture."

"When he took you there, did you see crates suspended above the water?" Mace asked.

"Something's burning." Jotham wrinkled his nose, backing away unsteadily.

Mace sniffed, then rubbed his finger under his nose. Since the day he rescued Felicity, everything had a charred sent. He saw the smoke before he smelled it, leaking in wisps from the tunnel junction.

"Fire! Sound the alarm. Fire in the tunnel!" He heard the cry repeated almost instantly by messengers on every block. An air horn blasted from the clock tower, the noise summoning fire repression. There were more firemen in Rocan than police. Any area that still received heat and electricity was susceptible to sparks, especially in the winter.

Jotham ran for the tunnel, but Mace hooked his arm, throwing him back. "Wait, Jotham. You can't go in there!"

"Kyrn. He was waiting for me by the rain," Jotham panted. Kyrn was another Gate brother, a little older than Jotham, but adopted in at the same time. Kyrn's first family had died in an electrical fire.

"And help will get to him," Mace reassured. "Even if he's trapped on the other side of the fire, he's not alone. We'll get to him."

"Mace, you gave the first call?" a fire chief questioned, hanging back while the other men suited up and accessed the fire.

"We saw the smoke. Don't know how far in it goes," Mace replied. "There may be a runner in the tunnel."

"Keep the crowd back." The chief hurried forward to relay the message and Jotham rushed to follow.

"Jotham, go home," Mace ordered, hooking the boy back again, the fight agitating his injured hand. "I will send a messenger as soon as we have Kyrn."

He let go of Jotham, testing to see if the man moved, then gave a whistle, summoning any deputies and officers within earshot. The roar of panic spread, and smoke poured into the Dome faster and faster. Jotham disappeared into the mob, but Mace didn't have time to track him now. Officer Grimes wove through the gathering throng.

"Keep these people back. Fire rescue and equipment only," Mace ordered. "Has the Resource Manager been contacted?"

"Yes. Hospital is standing by," Grimes reported.

"It's the Coureur. The Coureur caught fire!" someone shouted. Mace glanced at the clock tower. The Coureur wasn't meant to be in the tunnel at this time of day. A rumble overpowered the noise, followed by a plume of black smoke and a gust of frigid air.

"Tunnel collapse!" the fire chief called. "Mace, I need this block evacuated!"

Mace felt the collapse cascade through his body. He prayed for the light and protection of the Aurora. He couldn't tell Jotham Gate that he'd lost another brother.

Colleen Arman groaned and pounded the pillow as she stirred from a weird dream. It was barely ten in the morning and after a long bartending shift last night, she had wanted to sleep in until lunchtime. Her internal clock never cooperated with those plans.

"Colleen!" Her husband's cry for help dissolved the last vestiges of weariness. "Colleen, quick!"

"Reg, what's wrong?" Colleen called out, grabbing her robe and charging down the stairs. Her police deputy husband met her half way up the stairs, carrying a little girl in his arms. It was the Sequestered one that he'd saved from drowning. "What—why do you have that girl?"

"No time to explain!" he cried, shoving the girl toward Colleen. She wore a plain green, sleeveless jumper dress, which revealed the white bandages on the right side of her chest and down her right arm to the fingertips. The burns on her neck and face were sufficiently healed to not require bandaging, but the wounds were highlighted by her unevenly singed hair. She clung to Reg, her eyes pressed closed.

"There's smoke coming from the tunnel. I need to get down there," Reg said, peeling the girl's arm off his shoulder, but it only made her cling harder.

Colleen dashed down the stairs ahead of Reg and blocked the front door. "You're not going anywhere until you tell me why you have that girl."

"Long story short: she's ours now," he said.

"What?" Colleen's skin turned to ice as she finally looked at the frightened little girl. The doctors named her Felicity because she was so delightful. She wasn't smiling now.

"Just take her, okay," Reg insisted. "I have to—"

"You're scaring her," Colleen cried. "You're scaring me. There are plenty of police and first responders in this town. There's one of you and if she is ours, you are going to stay here and give me the long story."

"Colleen!"

"Reg!" Colleen blocked the door. "Sit or I'll make you sit. This little girl is your first priority. Why is she here?"

Felicity darted up the stairs, but Reg scooped her around the waist, being careful of the slow-healing burns on her skin. Colleen didn't know if it was fear or pain that prompted the tears streaming down her cheeks.

"Our petition for custody was granted. Dr. Louis wanted her to develop her language skills with her family," Reg said, sitting her on his hip and fussing at the tears.

"So they just send her here? No warning? No supplies?" Colleen said, sinking onto the couch. "Good thing we didn't ask for a newborn. We don't have a bed for her. We don't have clothes."

"There is a fire in the tunnel, Colleen," Reg explained. "Dr. Louis thought it might be better to get her out of the burn ward."

"Stop looking at that door, Reg. You have a new child. No one expects you to work today," Colleen snapped, then she rubbed her hands over her face, thinking about her bar. "A lot of people will be needing drinks, though."

"True. Maybe we can stop by the bar on the way to the library. Dr. Louis recommended a book on sign language," Reg said.

"Sign language?" Colleen repeated. "She can hear us, can't she?"

"She was on fire and she never screamed. She never made a sound," Reg said, settling on the couch, sitting Felicity on his lap. "It's better to teach her a real language than let her get caught up in gestures."

"Oh," Colleen said, feeling the numbness spread from her heart to her limbs. They'd only had an hour with Felicity at the hospital, but Colleen had never wanted a child so badly, and she agreed to the petition for custody the moment Reg asked her. Now she just felt scared. She loved her bar; she was great with customers. This child had less vocabulary than a blackout drunk.

Colleen studied the girl's burn-scarred lips, her trepidation growing. She could hear the sniffles and the gasps for air, but Felicity had no voice with which to cry.

"Do you want to hold her?" Reg asked.

"No. I'm still working through shock and I have a panic attack scheduled immediately after," Colleen replied, wringing her hands. "How is your head on straight?"

"Remember five minutes ago when I was telling you I needed to run into a fire?" he huffed, putting his arm around her. Felicity wriggled out of Reg's arms, her eyes wide with fear. She circled the family room, tracing a labyrinth mural that Colleen had painted on the wall. Her right hand was so damaged by fire, it would be useless for sign language.

"Felicity, do you want me to show you around? Are you hungry at all?" Colleen asked, squeezing Reg's hand. Felicity reached the edge of the wall with the mural, then turned the corner and pressed on the swinging door that led to the kitchen. The door swung back, nearly knocking her over, and she ran back to Reg, squatting on the couch, cowering against his shoulder.

"That's right. Papa will protect you," Colleen encouraged.

Reg's eyes misted, his breath quickening as the realization struck him. He was a Papa now. "Thank you. Thank you for letting me keep her," he whispered.

7

John Harris' skin tingled. Inside the Hudson potash mine was a mixture of blinding work lights and black shadows. The mineral fertilizer had a distinctive smell and the dust coating every surface and piece of equipment could choke a man if he weren't wearing the appropriate mask. Every vat of potash John moved, every bead of sweat on his face, even the rub of his clothes against his skin agitated the tingles, making his body both icy cold and boiling hot. Ever since he'd touched the woman—ever since she'd fainted in his arms—he felt the tingles, starting at his fingertips and working through his body.

"Harris, we need to speak," Celio Ferreira said, tapping his shoulder.

John shivered, but kept pushing his load to the collection room. "Overseer. Is there news on the woman?"

"It's Hwan. Come with me."

"You are two grown men, Ferreira. If you have issue with him, work it out on your own time," John grumbled, crossing his arms. His chest tightened and he scratched his sternum, the move finally bringing relief to his over-stimulated skin.

"Come with me," Celio repeated.

"Ferreira!"

"Harris," he whispered, the plaintive plea chilling John to the core. "There was an accident with the Coureur. Please come to the surface with me."

John slumped against the vat, his chest aching. Celio caught the load and set the break, giving John a moment to find his feet. Taking John's elbow, Celio guided John out of the mine. A few concerned workers asked if they needed help. John could barely hear them.

"We've been cut off from the city for almost two hours now," Celio explained, stopping just inside the mine. "It's safer and warmer underground right now so I'm keeping the men down there, but when the product runners don't show for the mid-morning run, they'll know something is wrong. Did the woman ever tell you her name before the Coureur left?"

"No," John murmured, his teeth chattering.

"Okay," Celio said. "The tunnel has collapsed, but a rescue team has created a path and Mace will escort you through the debris."

The Constable trotted into the mine, decked in fire gear, black soot covering his clothes. He carried two heavy coats, which he handed to John and Celio.

"Thank you, Constable," Celio said. "I have eighty-seven men accounted for. I was expecting six more today, but they hadn't checked in at shift start. Also, no runners on this side."

"The runners are accounted for. Kyrn pulled Douglas away from the explosion," Mace reported. "Who is on this side?"

Celio rattled off a list of names for Mace to memorize. John's mind circled around the last conversation he'd had with Douglas. He'd sensed Douglas' pain, but had lashed out in anger.

"We didn't know the woman's name," Celio finished.

"Woman?" Mace repeated.

"There was a woman in the Coureur with Douglas. A Sequestered, possibly. He was taking her to the hospital," Celio said.

"We didn't find her. You're sure she didn't come back here?" Mace asked.

"I doubt it, but I'll have the men search the mine," Celio said. "She may have ventured into the valley."

"Put that coat on, Harris," Mace said, giving him a shake. "Let's move."

The tingles in John's skin turned to shivers. He felt sick and numb.

The first mile was quiet and cold. The wind picked up as they approached the collapsed section. A layer of frost coated the black soot along the wall. The smell got worse the closer he came to the Coureur. It seemed Douglas' fate was to die in flames just as his father had.

"Did he suffer?" John asked.

"He wasn't burned, but the blast knocked him out. The fire kept him from freezing until help arrived," Mace said, picking his way across the rubble.

"He's alive," John murmured, tucking his hands into the sleeves of his coat.

"Yes, but unconscious," Mace said, touching his elbow. "Shield your face. The ceiling has collapsed and the sun is bright today."

John's heart skipped at the site of the burnt out shell of the Coureur. Tears stung his eyes, burning from a mixture of ashes and emotion. Mace pushed John around a bend, past a heavy drape. The Rocan side of the rupture was hot and bustling with rescue activity—builders and medics. Someone reclaimed his coat and John was directed to the hospital. After a few dazed steps, he took off running.

The last two miles were harder than the first. More of the

smoke had come this way, and the polluted air burned his lungs. There was a crowd by the gate, but the police and emergency personnel kept the path to the hospital clear. They shouted questions at him, but he had no answers. The hospital was only a few blocks from the entrance to the tunnel.

"Where?" John cried, bursting into the hospital, panting too hard to complete the sentence. His shout turned heads, and within seconds, Doctor Don Yale hurried down the hall calling his name.

"Where is he? Where!" John cried. Don was an old friend and had been nursing Douglas' wounds since childhood.

"Calm down, Johnny," Don said, grabbing John by the shoulders.

"Is he all right? Is he—"

"Johnny, listen to me," Don insisted, slapping him across the cheek. Shock from the blow temporarily overrode the panic and John took a long, shuddering breath.

"I need to see him," John begged, clinging to his friend.

"And you will. Please listen," Don said, pushing John against the wall. "He has a concussion. I'm not sure how bad. By the time anyone knew he was awake, he'd snuck over to asylum to be with his mother."

John clambered for the stairs, but Don snatched the back of his shirt, getting dragged along. "You must be calm and quiet for Kinley. She's been attacking the nurses; that's why Dr. Frank didn't let Douglas see her this morning."

"They didn't let him see her!" John exclaimed, picking up speed, his guilt compounding. He dashed up the stairs to the asylum, blasting by the sign-in station. Don leapt on his back, wrestling him to a halt outside Kinley's door.

"Don't startle her," Don whispered, his restraining shoulder lock relaxing into a hug. "She's been good since Douglas arrived."

"Of course she has," John panted, wiping tears from his eyes, leaning into Don's embrace.

Kinley sat at the head of the single bed and Douglas lay on his side, nestled to her thigh, one arm draped over her lap. Kinley's long, delicate fingers stroked up and down his arm. Her head was cocked to one side, and she kept singing the same line of a song over and over. Her brown eyes stared into space, her mind a million miles away, and yet she reacted every time Douglas' body trembled.

"Come in with me?" John whispered.

"I don't want to crowd the room," Don sighed, rubbing John's arm. "Don't rush him, but he needs a head scan. Concussion. You know the drill."

"I know the drill," John sighed, bracing himself for an outburst, but Kinley didn't seem to notice when he entered.

"How many heart attacks do you plan on giving me today, boy?" John said, his knees wobbly. Douglas shushed him. He relished these tender moments with his mother, broken as they were. The rhythm of the song had her rocking slightly.

Tiptoeing across the room, John knelt in front of the pair, breathing in comfort at the sight. He was relieved to see Douglas awake and reactive. Douglas' eyes were open, but heavy lidded with sadness. The skin on Douglas' face and neck was pink from heat exposure and his hair was singed, but overall, he'd made a lucky escape.

Kinley gripped Douglas' arm hard and glowered at John for a split second before turning her wrath on some other phantom in the room, all the while singing the same line of that song.

"I feel sick," Douglas moaned, reaching out to John. His hands were smooth and clean, free of engine grease and abrasions. Kinley grabbed his wrist, and Douglas clasped her hand.

"I'm not surprised," John said, folding his hands to show

Kinley he meant Douglas no harm. "You checked yourself out before the doctor could take a look at you."

"I'm not checked out. I'm checked in. I belong in here now," Douglas sniffled, rubbing his cheek against his mother's hand, his face twisting in self-loathing.

"Douglas, it was an accident," John said sympathetically. "Sometimes engines fail. There's nothing you could have done. It's no reason to check out of the world."

"I'm seeing things that aren't there," Douglas whined. "There's black smoke coming out of my hands. It's all around me."

"If there are spots in your vision, you need to see a doctor right away," John said, touching Douglas' cheek. "You have a concussion."

"I'm not seeing spots. I'm seeing . . . I'm seeing walking fireballs, and wings, and people in the sky," Douglas said, his glassy eyes turning to the ceiling.

"People in the sky," Kinley echoed, lifting Douglas' hand, using his fingers to point. "One, two, three . . ."

John squeezed Douglas' hand, then carefully wove his fingers under Kinley's. "Kinley. I need to take Douglas with me."

Kinley's song resumed and her face twitched, her eyes darting from John to Douglas. John wrapped his arms around Douglas, moving slowly for Kinley's sake. Douglas dry heaved when John lifted him; his body curled into a fetal position against John's chest and he shivered uncontrollably.

"Don't close his eyes," Kinley said, standing on the bed, grabbing for her son. "Don't make him close his eyes, John."

"Don't worry, Kinley. I'll keep him awake," John soothed, his heart somersaulting at the sound of his name on her lips. It had been almost a season since she'd said anything directly to him. He was so thrilled, he wanted to hug her.

"You would see it too, if you only open your eyes, John," she ranted, her volume rising. "It's dangerous, walking blind. Open your eyes! They're up there! They're stealing our light!"

"My eyes are open, bébé. I can see," John assured.

"Papa, I don't want to be sick in here," Douglas moaned, his body heaving again. John hurried out of the room, telling the nurse that Kinley needed help. They could hear her cries echo through the hall, becoming more hysterical.

"Help me close my eyes, Papa," Douglas whispered between dry heaves. "I don't want to see what she sees. Help me."

Douglas Hwan was hydrated and hopped up on painkillers, but his stomach still wasn't settled. He lay in bed, mesmerized by his fingers. The smoke wasn't oozing through his skin anymore, but now they presented a different mystery. The fingerprints he'd worn off through years of metalworking had returned, and his fingernails were long and healthy, free of cracks or engine grease. No amount of scrubbing had ever gotten his hands this clean.

John took his hand and tiredly rubbed Douglas' knuckles against his stubbled cheek.

"John, go home," Douglas murmured. "Take Maman. They're not giving her medicine anymore. She should come home with us."

"I know you want to take care of her, Douglas," John said. "But you can't."

"That's the thing, John. She doesn't need caring for," Douglas explained. "If I can be fine, so can she. She just needs someone to tell her what's real and what's not. When she knows the difference, it won't distract her. She doesn't need the medicine. If I can do it, she can do it."

"You are on a lot of medicine right now, son," John chuckled. "You're delirious."

"Go home, Papa. Get some rest," Douglas sighed.

"Papa? I've never heard him call you that," Don Yale said, peeking into the room. "Johnny, you have to go home."

"Get out of my room, kerf! It's not time for breeding." Douglas spat, kicking off his sheets, scrambling to sit. His stomach knotted and acid burned his throat.

"Calm down," John said, planting a hand on Douglas' chest, giving him a push.

"You're not breeding this round, My Douglas. Your Exception has been filed," Don said, backing away respectfully. "Excuse me, Johnny. I don't want to upset him."

"Don't leave, Donny," John said, his nostrils flaring. "Douglas, you do not talk to my friend like that. Donny has been good to you your whole life. Apologize."

Douglas twisted and buried his face in the pillow, his body twitching with dry heaves, white sparkles exploding in his vision. After Douglas' father died, Don used to come over all the time to help John. It wasn't Douglas' first breeding that destroyed their family, it was the loss of his first child. The cold look on Don's face, telling him he couldn't legally name his still-born baby girl.

"Douglas!" John warned.

"Let it go, Johnny. I came for you; not him," Don said, slouching behind John.

"Apologize, Douglas!" John insisted, shaking Douglas' shoulder.

Douglas yelped and rolled off the bed. "Oww!" he cried, darting to the window, cradling his hands to his chest. His body went flush, but he paced back and forth, huffing and staring at his arms.

"Are you hurt, my Douglas?" Don asked, rushing around the bed, going into doctor mode. "Tell me what hurts."

"Nothing. I'm fine," Douglas said, running his hands over his arms, forcing himself to breathe. After seeing the walking fireball that morning, he wasn't sure which fires in his memory were real. "I'm not burned. I'm not hurt."

"Your arms," Don insisted, walking his fingers over Douglas' hands. "Tell me what you feel. Is there pain?"

"It's fine. But it doesn't feel right that it's fine."

"Your skin looks rejuvenated," Don marveled, pressing Douglas' finger tips, watching the color change.

"It stings underneath the skin. Ash on raw flesh. I was on fire. The skin wasn't there before," Douglas touched his fingers, then ghosted his hands over his arms, neck and face. "She healed me. The angel. She's magic."

"She was just a woman," John said, directing Douglas back onto the bed. "Just a lost, confused, and remarkably beautiful woman."

"My Douglas, you must be careful with words like that," Don warned. "You don't want to wind up in asylum."

"Even if I belong there?" Douglas whispered, pressing the heels of his hands to his eyes.

"I know you want to be near your mother, but this is not the way," Don said. "You would be separated from her, for her protection and yours. You wouldn't get medication, except for breeding, and you wouldn't get to build anymore. If you need help, I will try to help you, but please don't lie about what you see to get closer to your mother."

Douglas looked at his perfectly clean fingernails and cried softly.

"You're not lying?" Don asked. "You see things you know aren't there?"

Douglas shook his head, bitter fear rising in his chest.

"That's what I thought," Don said sternly, probing the lump on Douglas' head.

"Breeding doctor," Douglas muttered.

"Yes, I am. It is a position that has allowed me to see and help far more people than you realize. Has the pain in your hands subsided?" Don asked, touching Douglas' hand. Douglas jerked away, then looked at his hand, confused.

"There's no pain. Just the memory of pain," Douglas said, shaking off the tingles and taking John's hand. He felt calmer when John touched him. "I don't need to be here. John, let's go home."

"You can't leave," John said, leaning his elbows on the bed. "You were in a coma earlier. Or did you forget?"

Douglas frowned. "You need rest, John."

"Stop trying to take care of me."

"Well somebody's got to," Douglas retorted. His eyes flashed, ready for a fight, but the pain in his head flared and the white spots returned.

"Do you have a headache, my Douglas?" Don asked.

"No, it's nothing," Douglas said, tugging the tips of his hair, rubbing his cheek with the heel of his hand.

Don cradled his cheek and pulled back his eyelids. "You were caught in an explosion. Even a nothing headache is concerning. Let's do a head scan."

"But we have to get John home," Douglas protested.

"How about this," John said, enveloping Douglas in a warm embrace. "When they put you on the gurney for the scan, I'll nap in your bed."

His body was warm and his presence calming. It was like a cloud of peace enveloping him. "Okay, Papa," he sighed, closing his eyes. "Okay."

8

The Dome lights flickered sporadically for the first hour of the morning and in some parts of the city, they didn't come on at all. Sky climbed down from the rooftop where she'd spent the night, her limbs shaking from exhaustion. The empty parts of the city were too dark for Spirit, and the full parts kept Spirit terrifyingly quiet. The energy that had drawn her here seemed to move with the people. The hybrids and humans mixed together, and if any of them had the ability to sense her out through Spirit, they hadn't done so.

The Virp on Sky's wrist buzzed and she blinked in confusion. The *Bobsled* was transmitting a distress beacon, but she was pretty sure there were no receivers in Rocan. There was no way the signal would make it out of the valley; she'd have to escape on foot. Unless there was another Coureur.

Where are you?

The text appeared on her screen, and Sky ripped the device from her hand, her heart pummeling. She blinked away fresh sweat and paranoia, frantically typing to source the message, but the fact that it was written in Lanvarian told her that it wasn't local. The gray moon Terrana was overhead today; it was the only place she knew that could get a signal to the *Bobsled.* She needed to get a message back before the power died on the transmitter, but she didn't know if the *'sled's* beacon could send messages.

"Where am I?" she muttered. "Lost? Trapped? Stranded with a bunch of hard-up men wanting to make babies?"

It wasn't unusual to be told 'women aren't allowed in the mine.' Plenty of cultures were protective of their women. But if Sky was to survive this culture, she needed to find the women and figure out what they were allowed to do.

She smoothed out her white clothes, and then added Hawk's jacket. The worn garment would help her blend. She observed nearly an hour before she identified a woman among the masses of people going about their lives. There was a short, brown-haired lady wearing a rainbow-colored dress that was stretched out from wear, but still fitted enough to show her hourglass shape. A little blonde girl clasped her hand, tripping as her mother tugged her to their destination.

The two entered a corner restaurant in the main square, and when they turned on the lights, the glass walls seemed to glow. A bilingual sign on the door advertised Trade conversation classes in the afternoon. When Sky entered, the woman was bent over a booth, talking quietly to the little girl. The woman popped her head up and greeted Sky in Rocanese.

"Do you speak Trade?" Sky asked.

"Yum," she hummed. "Um. I mean, yes. I can't believe I translated that. What brings you to my bar, gorgeous?"

"You," Sky smiled flirtatiously. "Is the kitchen open?"

"Not this early," the woman said, leaning against the booth, squeezing her arms to her side to accentuate her breasts. "The cafeteria down the street serves food all day. Or are you here practicing your Trade conversation?"

"I'll wait," Sky said, taking a seat at the bar, licking her lips. "I'm just glad to finally see another woman."

"We are rare," she laughed, then frowned and pulled Sky's jacket to see the design on the breast. "That's Little Hwan's jacket, isn't it? You must be very special to him. I've never known him to part with it."

"He was special," Sky murmured, pinching the hem. "We only just met, though."

Colleen did a double-take. "Dressed in white, speaks Trade. You were at the mine yesterday, weren't you? What's your name?"

Sky kissed her hand. "I'm called Sky. And you?"

"Colleen," she replied, though she didn't react to the flirting now that she knew Sky wasn't a local stranger. "The men have been searching all night for you, but no one knew what name to call. Your sketch doesn't do you justice. Stay here. I'll send a messenger to let them know they can stop looking."

"I don't want to be found yet," Sky said, tugging Colleen's hand. "Can you tell me about being a woman here."

Colleen looked doubtful, then retreated behind the bar, pouring a drink. "I suppose I could answer a few questions before the men come to interrogate you. I want Felicity to get to know the bar before it fills."

"Thank you," Sky smiled. "Where are the other women?"

"Not many come through here, unless they want a bunch of laborers fawning over them," Colleen said, sliding the drink over to Sky. "When my father left me this place, I set out to change things, but there just aren't enough of us left."

"Why are there so few women left?" Sky asked, taking a sip. It was a non-alcoholic berry juice, and it needed to be sweeter.

"Science was never my thing, darling," Colleen said, opening a refrigerator and pulling out some raw greens. Tearing off a few leaves, she tossed them in a bowl and added a dressing. "No doctor has ever explained to me why my sons live and my daughters die."

"But isn't that your daughter over there?" Sky asked, pointing to the little girl. The girl hadn't moved from the booth; in fact, it seemed she hadn't moved in the booth. She stared forward, as though in a trance.

"Um," Colleen stammered, fumbling a fork and sliding the salad dish over to Sky. "Oh, um, adopted, yes. She's the Sequestered that my husband rescued two weeks ago. He brought her home yesterday. It was a surprise. I mean, we petitioned to adopt, but I never expected it to go through, and I'm not ready to be *Maman* yet, but Reg has wanted to be a father for so long and Felicity seemed so lonely. And I shouldn't be telling you this, but I really needed to tell somebody and men congratulate me and women are jealous and no one asks me how I am."

Colleen took two steps toward the booth where Felicity sat, then two steps back. She raked her fingers through her hair, then poured herself a shot of vodka.

"You're married?" Sky asked.

"Yes. Hence the blushing at my inadvertent flirting," Colleen rambled, adding a splash of vodka to Sky's juice. "Your hands are shaking, darling."

"I've been through a lot since yesterday, too."

They smiled at each other and Sky relaxed. She didn't feel the same shroud of exhaustion around Colleen as she did around the men, but she should have picked up that Colleen was married.

"I should send that messenger now," Colleen said, wiping her hands, checking on her daughter before poking her head out the door. She gave a loud whistle and a teenaged boy showed up a moment later to take her message. Sky moved her Virp from her wrist into her satchel. These people didn't have basic communication devices. They relied on oral messengers.

"How did you get to the mine?" Colleen asked, coming back to the bar.

"I'm a traveler," Sky shrugged. There were many travelers and wanderers on Aquia, moving the vast distances between Domes, blending in where they could. Sky could beg, borrow, and steal her way through any city, and she was always on the lookout for technology that would help her move farther and survive longer between Domes. She tried not to repeat a Dome visit given her long life, although she was tempted given who she left behind now and then. "The covered road was the easiest way to get into the Dome."

"I don't think you have the hang of travel stories. You're supposed to talk about breaking out, not breaking in," Colleen said. "Unless it's not a travel story to you."

"Hawk—Little Hwan—told me the people here are bred like animals," Sky said.

Colleen shook her head and gave a fake laugh. "He wouldn't say that. And I won't have talk like that in my pub, even if you are a Sequestered."

"Do you worry about your daughter being bred?" Sky asked.

"I am scared for her," Colleen confessed, sliding into the booth next to Felicity, wringing her hands. "Felicity—she doesn't speak. I'm not sure she even understands what's going on. But when she comes of age, they'll breed her either way. All Geneculture sees is her womb. I can't prepare her. I can't explain that it will all be okay. And when things aren't okay, how is she going to tell me?"

"You've had her one day. There's still time," Sky pointed out.

"I've had her a day, and six different people have suggested I close my bar so I can school her privately. Three have criticized me for not having a few hand signs mastered. One man called her rude because she didn't return his greeting. Even after two weeks, having doctors working with her every day, she doesn't know to wave or smile or anything like that. And I'm afraid to teach her to trust, because for all I know that's how she wound up trapped in a box, unable to scream, getting lit on fire by her Sequesterer!"

Colleen hid her face and squeezed the girl, but Felicity barely seemed to register the interaction. Felicity was bandaged down one side and burned worse than Hawk had been. She leaned into the hug, favoring her injured side, but her attention was on a bowl of cereal, and she clumsily loaded her spoon with her good hand.

"When I came to this planet, I didn't talk to anyone for two months because I didn't know the language. I didn't even know the right sounds to make," Sky said, sliding into the booth across from them. She felt a strange shadow over Spirit when she touched the girl—not as strong as what she felt next to Hawk or John, but there just the same.

"From another planet?" Colleen sniffled. "That's a travel story I'd like to hear."

"Perhaps I used the wrong word," Sky smirked. She appreciated that storytelling was so ingrained in the culture that she could get away with slip-ups. "When Hawk called me Sequestered, I didn't understand his fear. Is this why there are so few women?"

"I hope not," Colleen said, fussing at Felicity's unevenly singed hair. "That evil Sequesterer had her in a box, in the dark, and the cold!"

"It hurts to eat, doesn't it?" Sky asked the girl.

"She doesn't cry, so they don't give her medicine," Colleen whispered, crying into the girl's hair. "We don't even know her real name."

Sky touched the burns on Felicity's jaw, gaining the girl's attention, and Felicity mirrored the move, her rough, little hand feeling along Sky's jawbone.

"Maybe you speak Lanvarian," Sky suggested, trying out the other most common language of the continent. Nomads were known to leave children behind in affluent Domes if they couldn't be cared for.

Felicity's tongue peeked between her burn-scarred lips. She heard the sound, but she seemed to look through Sky, not at her.

"Do you understand that I'm trying to speak to you?" Sky asked. She tried a few more greetings, bouncing between regional dialects, on the off chance that one might be familiar. Getting bored, Felicity went back to her cereal and licked her spoon, avoiding contact with her lips.

"Why don't you tell us a story about your home planet," Colleen said, her fingers sliding toward Sky, her loneliness tangible.

"In my home, 'hello' sounds like this," Sky said. She made a click and two pops with her tongue. Felicity's head popped up, like she understood. Or perhaps the sounds had surprised her.

Sky repeated the greeting with a smile. "So you see why it took so long to train my tongue on Trade."

Felicity clicked her tongue, scratching her neck, and then she squeaked, forcing the sound from her throat. When she did, the darkness around her seemed to break and Spirit seeped into the cracks.

"Kerf, it's happening," Colleen murmured, her face going white. Felicity clicked her tongue, a wheeze following every articulated sound. "That's it, little darling. Talk to us."

Sky said 'hello' again, slower so that Felicity could mimic the sounds in rhythm. The more Felicity tried to speak, the easier it was to be next to her.

"What is it? What is she saying?" Colleen asked.

"She's not saying anything, yet," Sky laughed. "But she's trying. And it's only been one day."

Douglas Hwan hadn't had a dizzy spell in hours, but the foot of the stool jabbing into his chest still floored him. Kinley Hwan screeched, dropping the chair when John wrestled her arms to her side.

"I'm okay. Don't take her away," Douglas said, rolling onto his stomach, clutching his shoulder.

"Eyes!" Kinley screeched, kicking at John. "You promised not to close his eyes!"

"Stay there, Douglas," John ordered, forcing her from the asylum's common area and back to her room.

"John, I'm okay. Bring her back!" Douglas cried, righting the stool and climbing onto the seat. The meal he'd brought for his mother was untouched, the shatterproof dishes spared her wrath. She was angry with him because he was visiting, not checking in to count the phantoms. After Don's warning last night, Douglas could not allow himself to admit he belonged here.

Abandoning the meal, Douglas staggered out of asylum, down the hall, leaning on the wall as a fresh dizzy spell hit.

Don Yale bustled past, then paused and looked back. "My Douglas, weren't you having lunch with your mother?"

"It's not a good day," Douglas whimpered, tugging the collar of his shirt.

"For her or you? You look ill," Don said, coming closer.

"She didn't mean to hurt me. She did, but—don't touch me. I'm fine on my own!" Douglas cried, shoving Don's hand away from his face.

"I don't have time to fight you, Douglas. I have errands of my own," Don said, crossing his arms. "When you take John home later, tell him he has to stay with you. I can't look after you this afternoon. He has to take a day off work."

Douglas laughed at first, thinking it was a joke—John taking off work. "Was there a baby born?" Douglas asked hopefully.

"Not since last week," Don said, grinning conspiratorially. "I've received word of a strange woman at the Glass Walls who only speaks Trade. Your angel has returned. Dr. Frank and I are going—"

"The asylum doctor!" Douglas cried, leaping to his feet.

"He is a skilled physician and he speaks Trade. If your angel is in need of a doctor—Douglas!"

Douglas took off running, swaying into the walls, but fighting through the vertigo. If his angel was at the Glass Walls, that was where he needed to be.

9

"It was this tiny Dome on the eastern continent, fiddling with grav-tech because they had nothing better to do," Sky gabbed to her audience of men at the bar. She leaned back on her stool, taking a sip of her vodka-infused berry juice, crossing her legs, taking note of which men responded to her sexuality. "I said to myself: the people of Terrana need this! It was made of moon-slate after all. Terrana's the little moon. The gray one. So I entertained the inventor, and while he was in a wine-induced snooze, I stole a handful of grav-sources and hightailed out of there!"

The men who understood Trade laughed, the others joining in once the words were translated to Rocanese. The truth was she'd slept with the guy, but based on what she'd learned about breeding, she didn't think it was safe to casually mention.

"There you go, darling," Colleen said, tapping her shoulder and sliding a plate of food across the table. "Let me know if it gets too rowdy for you out here. I have a private room in the back."

"Tell us about the moon, Madame!" one of the men called.

"You tell a story, Jude. Let the woman eat," Colleen retorted.

"Thank you," Sky whispered, squeezing Colleen's hand. There weren't any menus. Or meat dishes, apparently. The lunch plate consisted of grilled vegetables and seasoned grains.

Jude started a story about space travel, building fictions off of Sky's notion of artificial gravity. Like all the stories the locals told, this one veered toward finding a cure for the Malady that afflicted their daughters and kept the birth rate so low.

"Sa-ai!" Felicity wheezed, climbing onto the stool next to Sky.

"Can you say 'lunch'?" Colleen asked.

Felicity ran her hands over the bar, not seeming to hear.

"Felicity?" Colleen called, tickling the girl's chin. "Do you hear me?"

Felicity giggled soundlessly, folding over the counter, gasping. Then she pointed to Sky's food.

"Try this one, little darling," Colleen sighed, handing her a bowl of boiled peas. Felicity glanced up, as though only just noticing Colleen, but she smiled and held her hand open so that Colleen could help her grip the spoon. The little girl's hands shook with effort, but once Colleen massaged her fingers into place, she was able to command the utensil. She brushed the back of the spoon over the peas, then licked it, wrinkling her nose at the taste.

"Doh-meh," Felicity said, tapping Sky on the shoulder.

"Dome?" Sky asked. "I've told you half a dozen stories already. Ask someone else."

Felicity cocked her head, looked back to her mother, then looked into her bowl, smashing the green and yellow peas under her spoon.

Sky wolfed down her own meal, invigorated by the sustenance. She could feel Spirit prowling in her soul, its claws closing around her throat. The aftershock of the crash had passed, and Spirit was back to its old, demented tricks. Trapped in a Dome like this, Spirit would kill every person in this town until only one was left and that one it would possess and torture until it found a way out of this valley.

"Colleen, do you have anything with caffeine?" Sky asked.

"I'm afraid I don't know that word, darling," Colleen chuckled.

"A drink to wake me up?" Sky rubbed her neck and glanced at the door. Normally, when she needed sleep, she'd go to the middle of nowhere. Spirit wouldn't kill her if it was just the two of them. But outside this Dome was all tundra

"Would you like to try some fruit?" Colleen suggested. "Maybe you should go to the back and lie down."

"In a bit," Sky agreed, scanning the streets for signs of other women. People seemed to come in clumps, and even then, the groups were sparse.

"Hawk," Sky murmured, seeing Hawk outside the glass walls. He came in and stumbled into the first high-top table, pale-faced. Sky rushed to him, embracing him, and he broke into tears, hugging her back.

"You have my jacket. I thought I lost it in the fire," he sobbed, running his hands over the sleeves. "Are you okay?"

"I am," Sky said, shrugging out of his flight jacket and resting it on his broad shoulders. "How are you?"

"It's not a good day," he whimpered. "My head hurts."

"Come sit with me," Sky said, putting an arm around him, sitting him on her stool. "Colleen, a drink for my friend."

"Hello, Little Hwan," Colleen greeted, pouring a glass of berry juice for him. "Didn't expect to see you today."

"Hi," Hawk sighed, taking a sip, his emotion dulling with the drink. "Is that Felicity? I didn't realize you'd brought her home."

"Well, you were in a coma," Colleen teased. "And how did you know she was even coming to me? I didn't know until she showed up."

"Don assigns families. Don talks to John. I hear things," Hawk shrugged. "Hello, Felicity."

Oblivious to him, Felicity slid out of the chair, taking her food with her. She went to one of the booths in a quieter corner of the restaurant and tapped a man on the shoulder. Sky's stomach twisted.

"Is it something I said?" Hawk asked. "How are you doing, Colleen? Are you getting along with her?"

"At times, she sees me. Then she seems to forget I exist," Colleen said, her eyes misting, her voice getting tight. "She spoke to Sky."

"Sky?" Hawk said, smiling at Sky again. "So that's your name."

"If you can believe anything she says. Her storytelling rivals your father's," Colleen said. "Excuse me. I need to catch my daughter." She chuckled at the word daughter, but a warm glow lit her face.

"Let's get out of here," Sky said.

"I'll get in trouble," Hawk said. "I'm just glad I found you first. There's a man coming—Dr. Frank. He's in charge of asylum, where my mother is. Remember, I warned you that stories can get you locked away? Be careful."

"All the more reason to leave," Sky said, sliding off her chair.

"And go where?" he asked, getting half-way off his stool, then deciding he wasn't stable enough to stand. "Dr. Frank doesn't want to hear travel stories. You can tell them, but don't pretend to believe."

John's heart raced as he came into the Glass Walls. He arrived with Dr. Frank and though the bar was crowded for lunchtime, there were a few empty tables near the door. All eyes were on the angel, standing by the bar, her smile as bright as the sun.

"That's her," John said breathlessly.

"Hmm," Frank frowned, furrowing his bushy, white eyebrows until they were touching. He was one of the oldest doctors in the Dome, and he'd seen more Sequestereds than anyone.

"Johnny, I am so sorry about Douglas," Don Yale said, approaching from the side, hooking John's elbow, and pulling him into one of the empty booths. "Dr. Frank, I'm glad you could make it. How is Kinley?"

"Restrained," Frank sighed, standing in front of the booth, blocking John's view. "Little Hwan's visit bought her a few hours of peace yesterday and now we seem to be paying for it. How long have you been observing . . ."

"Sky," Don finished.

"Sky," John exhaled. He finally knew her name.

"Twenty minutes. Douglas got here first," Don reported, giving John a nudge.

"You're the idiot who told him she was here," John laughed. "Where is he?"

"Standing right next to her. Or were you too focused on her to notice?" Don teased, pointing to Douglas. Douglas sat in a low chair next to the bar, his cheek resting on Sky's knee. She was a good surrogate for Kinley and John didn't know whether to feel grateful or worried.

"John Harris, there will be no ogling of women in my bar," Colleen clucked, strutting over to their booth, Felicity in tow. "Amir Frank, that goes for you, too."

"I apologize. Her attire is striking," Frank mused, mesmerized by Sky's spotless, flowing tunic. He touched his own, high-quality garments, which seemed like rags next to Sky's. Her pristine, white clothes draped beautifully over her figure, leaving her blue eyes as the only sparkle of color. "What is that fabric? I've never seen its equal."

"You could ask her," Colleen Arman suggested. "But you might not get a clear answer. She's been liberal with storytelling. Poor darling is exhausted, though. Likely to keel at any moment."

Felicity groaned, shaking her arm to loosen Colleen's grip. "Sah—" she croaked, leaning toward Sky.

"Did you hear that?" Frank exclaimed, his doctorly manner springing to the forefront.

"I did," Don smiled, rising from his seat.

"Yes, she's made a few sounds today. But now she's resting her voice." Colleen directed the last command at Felicity, but the girl didn't seem to understand.

"May I?" Frank asked, kneeling in front of the girl, pressing his fingers along the sides of her neck. "Open your mouth, little one."

Felicity stared blankly, her gaze drifting until her cheek found Colleen's elbow.

"Her understanding comes and goes," Colleen apologized.

"Most little girls her age have selective hearing," Frank shrugged, touching the top of the little girl's head, and standing, as though he hadn't expected Felicity to obey. "And what of the Sequestered?"

Their eyes turned to the beautiful woman at the bar, and John felt a twinge of rapture.

"She's selectively deaf to Rocanese," Colleen murmured. "Speak Trade."

"Yale?" Frank said, motioning to Don.

"I prefer to observe at this stage," Don said, folding his hands, his expression souring. "I'm sure Douglas has already instilled in her a fear of Geneculture."

"Donny," John warned. John tried to encourage Don to push

past Douglas' obstinance, but Don shrugged it off as one of the pitfalls of working for the Registry.

"She did ask a lot of difficult questions about breeding," Colleen agreed, her face twitching.

Frank shrugged it off, and went to the bar to introduce himself.

"Is that his father's jacket?" John asked.

"Sky had it when she came in," Colleen said, tickling the back of John's neck. "She cracked you."

"Yes, she did," Don laughed. "I've rarely seen such a profound case of infatuation outside the teen population."

"Will you two stop. I don't know her," John carped, biting his lip. "We've barely even said hello."

"If you want to know her, you'd better brush up on your Trade," Colleen teased.

"Oh, he is. He fell asleep with his face in a Trade primer last night," Don gossiped, patting John's arm. "Said he was too worried about Douglas to sleep."

"Stop it," John growled, guilt rising with the shame. "So she intrigues me. So what? I made a vow to be celibate, and we'll never be more than friends. I'm here for Douglas."

"We believe you, Johnny," Colleen crooned, ruffling his hair. "Here, tell Felicity the story of how you and Sky met. I'll get you two something to drink."

John shifted, making a space for the little girl, but when Colleen left, Felicity followed, clinging to her elbow.

"She keeps looking at you," Don chuckled, more as an observation than a taunt.

"Because I'm familiar," John said, scratching his arms. He felt jealous just seeing Sky talk to Dr. Frank. His skin was tingling, the sensation spreading more rapidly than before.

"Johnny, you have got to relax before you give yourself an aneurism," Don said, pinching his shoulder.

"How can I? I can't stop looking at her, but the more I look, the more angry and jealous and . . ."

Their eyes met across the room and she raised her chin, giving the slightest pucker to her lips. The world seemed to stand still. He waved her over with two fingers, and she gave him a wink. John exchanged a giddy grin with Don, then licked his lips, watching Sky's every move.

"Don't bring her over here," Don said.

"Are you really so afraid to meet her?" John asked. Don crossed his arms, his frown deepening. John pinched his cheek, forcing a grin. "She'll love you."

Sky inhaled sharply, her wooziness increasing with the crowd size.

"Sky, meet Dr. Amir Frank," Hawk said, tapping her shoulder, turning her toward the newest arrival. "Dr. Frank—"

"Where did you get your clothes? I heard you were wearing a miner's coveralls," Frank interrupted. His clothing and adornments set him at the top of the socio-economic ladder, though from the stories Sky had heard, the economy was likely communistic.

"Hawk," Sky whispered, pulling the front of Hawk's flight jacket closed. She usually liked when men stared at her, but Frank was looking at her clothes, like he wanted them for himself.

"She means me," Hawk laughed, keeping his head down. His submissiveness toward Frank confused Sky and made her uneasy.

"I gathered," Frank harrumphed, pulling back the collar of the jacket. "But this white shirt—what kind of fiber is it?"

"It's a synthetic fiber," Sky said, slipping off the jacket, pushing her shoulders back.

"It's so clean." He licked his lips, but Sky could tell he was more turned on by the shirt than the body filling it.

"I could be doused in engine grease and it would bead right off. I've been wearing this same shirt for twelve years," Sky explained, running her finger up Dr. Frank's hand. He wore a ring and a gold-plated timepiece—something none of the other men had.

"Where did you get it?" Frank asked, his patience practiced but insincere. "Can you show me?"

Pressing her lips together, Sky weighed the truth against possible lies. All of her truths thus far had been dismissed as fairy tale, and Frank wanted something believable. Normally, she could mislead and misdirect flawlessly, but Spirit was rattled and distracting her. Wrapping her arms around her middle, she mustered a few fake tears, then leaned forward and let one roll off her nose.

"No. No, I can't go back. It's not safe," she whispered.

"You're safe here, bébé," Hawk said, his hand immediately on her back.

Frank eyed her skeptically. "Tell me about the place, then. What about your situation was not safe?"

Sky grimaced. As romantic as she could make traveling sound, she had far more stories of the unsavory and brutal cultures. Unbuttoning her blouse, Sky pulled back the fabric for a few seconds, giving Frank a peek at the bruises on her torso. Spirit was healing the injuries so quickly that most had faded, but she'd slammed hard against the safety harness when the *Bobsled* crashed and in a civilization that had only had one (blown-up) Coureur, it'd be an unfamiliar injury.

The bar went silent a moment, then whispers spread like wildfire. The word 'Sequestered' was repeated over and over.

Frank reached out to trace the bruise, but Sky pulled her blouse shut and averted her eyes.

"You were restrained?" Frank asked.

"Sky, you should do this in private," Hawk whispered.

"I'm tired of stories," Sky said flatly, sliding off the barstool. She met John's eye again across the room, and walked towards him. He wasn't whispering to his friends or staring aghast. At the mine, it had been so peaceful resting in his arms. She could feel the comfort of his touch from here. Then someone plowed into her from behind. Someone short.

"Sa-ai!" Felicity screeched at the top of her lungs, squeezing Sky tight around the waist.

Sky felt a surge of fire from Spirit, and then the chilly pull of the other realm—the feeling of being sucked through space. Felicity was a hybrid! Whipping around, Sky scraped Felicity off her body, her own cries choked by Spirit's surging presence.

"No, Sky, no," Douglas groaned, rushing to Felicity's aid. The force with which she handled Felicity stirred up the crowd. Sky raised a barstool and Douglas jumped on the other end, wrestling it from her hands before she could swing.

Two men grabbed Sky by the elbows, but Sky threw one to the ground, then grabbed Felicity by the hair and tossed her aside. The outright violence against a child turned more men against Sky. Felicity wheezed and whined, rushing back into Sky, her voice coming and going. Douglas wrestled to get Felicity from Sky, but Sky was blind to his help, seeing everyone as a threat now, and she kicked him. The force sent Felicity flying out of his arms.

"Mercy!" Sky cried, fighting against the three men holding her back. "Mercy!"

"Sky!" Douglas cried. "Sky, stop fighting."

"Sequesterer!" Sky screeched. "Let go! Sequesterer!"

Concentrating on the men holding her, she flipped one over her shoulder, laying him flat, then reached behind the bar, finding a knife to defend herself.

"No!" Douglas shouted, throwing his arms around her. "Stop fighting and listen! No one is trying to Sequester you."

"Hawk, get me out of here!" Sky begged, locking her arms around Douglas. Brawls were breaking out everywhere as men took sides in the fight. Someone's foot connected the small of Douglas' back, knocking him into Sky and sending them toppling over a table. He barely had time to cradle Sky's head against his chest before he landed on the floor on top of her. His head cracked open against the corner of the table, and blood spilled through his hair, dripping onto Sky's cheek.

"Why are you dying again?" she asked, touching his face. "Why did you draw me here?"

Then he heard Colleen shouting over the crowd.

"Close your eyes," he warned Sky, pressing her face to his shoulder and squeezing his eyes shut. A flash of light and loud banging sound went off. The room erupted in a blinding light, and the crowd fell silent.

10

Sky screamed. She wrestled against Douglas, gasping and keening.

"Sorry," Douglas apologized, trying not to panic at her hysterics. "Help!" Douglas cried.

Dr. Frank plowed through the fallen tables and threw Douglas aside. Douglas slammed against the floor, sparkles exploding behind his eyes. Sky's body bowed in seizure, then she went limp in Frank's arms.

"Madame, can you hear me?" Frank called, forcing Sky's mouth open, clearing her airway. Her lips were blue and the sporadic convulsions in her body slowed.

"She's not breathing!" Douglas cried. "Help! She's not breathing!"

"Yale!" Frank hollered, rolling up the sleeves of his beer-soaked shirt.

"Were her eyes open when the flash went off?" John asked, hustling over and cradling Sky's head. Sky's body seized again and she inhaled, her bloodshot eyes glistening with tears. She gripped John by the wrists and frantically climbed up his body, making labored sounds that Douglas could only guess were meant to be words.

"Not so fast, darling," Frank said, tugging her shoulders. Sky whipped around, her fist clipping Frank's cheek, knocking him on top of Douglas.

"Sky!" Hawk squealed, curling into a ball.

"Hawk!" Sky gasped, burrowing under Frank to get to him. She pulled his hands away from his bleeding head. "No, no, no. Don't die. Don't die."

"Sky, darling, you should lie down," Frank insisted, pulling her off of Douglas.

"Hawk's bleeding," she cried, writhing.

"I'll be okay," Douglas assured, even though he felt ready to vomit. He reached out a hand to her, saw the blood on his fingertips, and got dizzy.

"You're bleeding." Sky coughed and wheezed.

"Sky," John whispered.

"Madame—"

"Help him!" she cried, latching onto Frank's hand and putting it on Douglas. Her body quaking, she moved Frank's hand over the bleeding wound. "Help him. Please. I can't watch him die."

"I'll help him," Yale said, kneeling next to Douglas with a handful of dishrags and a mug filled with water. "Sky, let Dr. Frank help you."

Sky bowed over, resting her head on Douglas' stomach. Her cries choked off and her face went white, her breath coming in short gasps. Frank pressed a stethoscope to her back, listening to her lungs. Sky jerked up, but this time, John caught her fist.

"What are you?" Sky cried, banging her head against John's chin. "You're not human. Not hybrid. What are you?"

"He doesn't speak Trade, Madame, and I'm afraid I don't understand what you're asking him. I'm not going to hurt you.

I'm listening to your breath," Frank explained, his voice and motion so gentle it almost lulled Douglas to sleep. "Has it happened before? The sensation of your lungs closing?"

"No. Yes. Every time I close my eyes," Sky said. She closed her eyes and leaned against John's chest. "But not when John holds me. That's strange."

"Then you keep holding on to him," Dr. Frank said, reaching over the bar and pouring a drink. Sky's fist tightened on John's shirt, and she murmured in another language. "You nearly asphyxiated over something. That's not a typical response to a flash bomb."

"Don't be scared, Sky," Douglas said, pillowing his head on his arm and closing his eyes.

"Looks like you gave your concussion a concussion, my Douglas. Fortunately, it doesn't require stitches," Don decided, pressing a wet rag to Douglas' head. "Ambulatory assistance will be here soon to take you both to the hospital. Sky, he will recover. Now I have to help the other men who were hurt."

Douglas winced on Sky's behalf, checking Frank for a reaction. The severity of the fight would determine her punishment, and harming Felicity assured a few days in confinement already. Frank massaged his jaw, his fingers dancing around the bruise on his cheek.

"Don't confine her, Dr. Frank," Douglas begged. "It didn't help my mother and it won't help her."

"And if she turns violent again?" Frank asked. "She overpowered three grown men!"

"She was afraid they would Sequester her," Douglas said. "I tried to explain—"

"Kerf! Stop arguing. You'll frighten her!" John hissed. "Dr. Frank, she passed out again."

"But she's still breathing," Frank observed, feeling for her pulse.

"That's the second time she's fallen asleep on me," John said.

"That's worrying," Frank commented, shaking her shoulder. Sky grunted and he immediately smoothed his motion, soothing her back to sleep. "Holler if her breathing changes. The Constable has arrived. I need to speak to him."

Douglas scooted closer to John, trying to figure a way to rest his head on his father's lap without getting him all bloodied. John put a protective hand on his shoulder, massaging away the fear and anxiety.

"Don't worry, Sky," Douglas whispered, petting Sky's hand. "I won't let him lock you away. I'll take care of you."

"Colleen!" Deputy Reg Arman called, charging into the Glass Walls. The bar looked worse than he'd expected. The tables were righted, but the fallen drinks told him that many had been overturned in the brawl. A few contrite men mopped the mess and swept up the spilled, wasted food, taking orders from Colleen; others were medicating their injuries with ice and gin. Felicity clung to Colleen's arm, keeping her eyes covered, stumbling occasionally.

"I'm fine. We're fine," Colleen said, her expression softening at the sight of him. "Reg, you'll never believe—"

Reg vaulted over every obstacle between them and knelt down, coaxing Felicity's face toward his. Her gaze wandered, finding focus and losing it. "You covered her eyes?"

"Of course. Reg, listen—"

"My little darling, you must have been scared," Reg gushed, touching Felicity's cheeks and hair. Felicity wriggled out of the embrace and tugged her mother's sleeve, tapping her chest urgently. The tiniest cry escaped with a sob, and Reg's heart stopped. Felicity had made a sound!

"I know your voice hurts, little darling," Colleen said, bending down to be at eye-level with the girl. "Let it rest. It'll come back, and then you can tell Papa he's being an ass."

"Her voice? She's talking?" Reg asked.

Colleen stood straight, her expression stony, her eyes forward. "She makes sounds. It comes and goes," she said, putting a hand on Felicity's head.

"So a flash bomb is not the most exciting thing to happen today?" Reg smiled, sitting on the floor to be close to his daughter.

"Kerf, no."

"Colleen, language!" Reg admonished, not wanting his daughter's first word to be a curse.

"Don't talk to me about language," Colleen snapped, her fists clenching. "You weren't here. You didn't see Sky throw her across the room. Felicity just wanted to talk."

Colleen sucked her cheeks in, but put a hand on her stomach, going pale, then green. Reg jumped to his feet and gave her a hug, but he knew she wouldn't break down here in front of her patrons.

"Let me take you home," he whispered in her ear.

"No. No, I want to stay here," she said, running her hand through her messy, brown hair. "I can't leave this mess in my father's bar. Take Felicity."

Felicity bounced on her toes and pounded her chest.

"Did you recognize your name, Felicity?" Reg smiled, ruffling her hair on the side where it still grew.

Felicity burst into tears, wheezing with every breath, scratching at her throat until she had red marks on her skin. Reg gripped her hands, then lifted her off the ground, putting her arms around his neck.

"Do you think she's hurt?" Colleen asked, biting her nails. "Do you think she'd be able to tell us if she were?"

"Good, you're here," Don Yale said, bustling toward them.

"Hello, Don," Reg greeted, bouncing Felicity in his arms. The message that reached him at the Bastien was garbled, but he was glad that Yale had summoned him.

"Can you take them both to the hospital, please?" Yale said, going behind the bar to rinse off the rags he was using to minister to wounds.

"Donny, I'm fine. I want to stay here," Colleen insisted, going behind the bar to help. She was shaking, but she hid it by keeping one hand on the bar for balance.

"Colleen, you're due for a breeding follow-up anyway," Yale whispered, giving her a look. Colleen glared back, and Yale rolled his eyes. "In the next day. Please. But Felicity does need to be checked now."

"Stay away from her, Donny. She doesn't need a breeding doctor. She's a child," Colleen growled. It was strange seeing her hostile toward Yale, but the doctor seemed to understand her stress, and he took his rinsed out rags and left to treat someone else.

"Is the Sequestered woman over there?" Reg asked, noticing Mace towering over one of the side booths. John Harris and Douglas Hwan sat in the booth with the woman. There were a number of things surprising about this scene: the first was that Douglas Hwan did not have bruised fists. The lack of offensive wounds and the wet napkin pressed to Hwan's head indicated he was a bystander. As if that weren't strange enough, John Harris had the blond woman snuggled to his chest, fast asleep. Harris never let women hang on him like that. He was cautious, polite, and morally opposed to baseless flirtation.

"Her name is Sky," Colleen said, sympathy warring with her disapproval. "She panicked when Felicity ran at her. You could see the trauma of whatever was done to her. She was fighting for her life. Their screams filled the room."

"Felicity ran to her?" Reg asked, cradling he daughter's head. "She hardly even runs to us."

"Maybe I should give up my bar," Colleen murmured, leaning her head on his arm.

"I won't let you," Reg said, taking her hand. They'd talked about trying for a love child when they were younger, but so much had changed since then. They were settled into their lives and their work, and making space for a child, especially one like Felicity, was more than they could handle. It was only a matter of time before someone noticed, and took her away from them.

11

The Glass Walls had never felt so peaceful, and Douglas wasn't sure if it was the concussion or John's arm around him that made it so. John often worked hard and came home exhausted, and when he didn't have work, he was busy running errands and fixing the house. If it weren't for Sky sleeping on him, he'd have found an excuse to leave.

"Aren't you hungry?" John asked. Even now, he wouldn't give into the peace of the moment. He wanted to practice speaking Trade so he'd be ready when Sky woke. Douglas translated the phrase for him and John laughed, tickling his arm. "No, son. I mean aren't *you* hungry. You haven't touched your food."

"Queasy," Douglas said, picking at the grilled vegetables on the plate Colleen brought him. He nibbled on the green beans, testing whether his hunger overrode the nausea.

"You can take the next ambulance," John suggested, moving his thumb over Douglas' shoulder. "Let Sky sleep a little longer."

"I have to stay with her. I promised," Douglas said, picking up another bean. Now that he'd started, he felt ravenous. "I can ride with Sky. She won't hurt me."

There were two other men with head injuries, and they'd

gone in the first ambulance. Constable Mace had questioned them about the incident, and his officers had cleared out most of the patrons, but Colleen refused to go.

"It's my bar. If you don't want her near me, get her out," she'd said snippily, although she'd been corralled behind the bar. Her husband had taken Felicity to the hospital, much to Felicity's dismay. The girl didn't want to leave her mother's side, and Douglas couldn't help crying for her. She was a Sequestered with no voice, and her parents weren't making the effort to understand.

"The ambulance is here," Dr. Frank announced, standing up from his table by the window and finishing his drink. His clothes were spotted with spilled drinks and blood. It was the messiest Douglas had ever seen him, and the least repulsed he'd ever been by the man. Seeing him act as a physician in an emergency, as opposed to mercilessly incarcerating Douglas' mother, humanized the man just a little. Douglas still bristled when the old doctor came over to check on Sky.

Sky groaned at the light touch, her body tensing for a fight.

"Perhaps we can move her without waking her," Frank suggested, looking to John. Despite his stature and apparent strength, John had been getting weaker the past few years, but it wasn't something he'd admit. When Douglas asked, he'd say he was just getting old. Douglas would have helped carry Sky, but his head still ached.

"What happened?" Sky groaned, her body lengthening until her head fell off John's shoulder. "It's quiet. My ears?"

"The place emptied out while you were sleeping," Douglas explained, tugging her hand until she flopped back against John. John laughed, enjoying the apparent game, but Sky didn't seem as comfortable.

"Sleeping? My eyes were closed?" she asked.

"Nearly an hour," he replied.

"An hour," she repeated, tears glistening in her eyes. "I'm not dead. I'm still breathing."

"Yes," Frank interjected lifting her chin. "These two sat with you the entire time to make sure you didn't stop. You seem to be breathing well now."

"It's over. You saved me. I'm not dead," she whispered, tears overflowing as she processed her newfound freedom. She leaned forward to give Douglas a hug, and only then seemed to notice how entwined her limbs were with John. A smile rising to her lips, she dropped her head back on his shoulder. "Did you do this?"

"You sleep on me," John answered, employing his refreshed Trade skills, delivering his words with the toothiest grin Douglas had ever seen.

"It's hard to keep my eyes open," Sky sniffled, fingering his lips. "Hay nah! I haven't slept in years."

"You did. And we kept you safe," Douglas assured, shifting away from them so Sky could get up. The movement came with a rush of sparkles to his vision.

"Sleep on me," John repeated. Douglas wasn't sure what he was trying to say, but Sky gave him a light peck on the lips and he blushed like crazy. Turning in John's lap, she hugged him, resting her forehead against his, taking slow, concentrated breaths.

"Sky, it's time to go," Dr. Frank huffed impatiently.

Sky's eyes drifted open, and she looked up at Dr. Frank then past him to the others in the bar. "Who are they?"

John looked questioningly at Douglas.

"That is Constable Mace, Officer Blayze, and Officer Grimes," Douglas introduced, pointing to the three encroaching officers. "They're going to escort us to the hospital."

"Okay," Sky agreed, shaking and clinging to John.

"Can you walk or do you need help?" Frank asked.

"Yes. Yes," Sky murmured, shifting to the edge of the booth, then collapsing against John again. "No," she whimpered, putting her arms around John's neck, her limbs shaking like she could barely lift them. "I'm old."

"You haven't aged that much in the last hour," Frank chuckled, rubbing Sky's shoulder, his compassion surfacing. "Maybe you've exhausted yourself."

"But I will, right?" Sky asked, a high-pitched innocence to the question. "I'll grow old."

"I'm not sure I understand," Frank said.

"She's free," Douglas explained, making the connection based on his mother's stories. "She was afraid her Sequesterer wouldn't let her grow old."

His mother had told him that she was kept in a room with a dim lamp that never got turned off. There was either too much heat or not enough, and she knew she'd die before she had a chance to grow old. She'd been told that she was being protected from a life far worse. When she'd first been found and subjected to the bright lights, the loud noise, and the invasive medical exams, she felt guilty for doubting the intentions of her Sequesterer.

"I'm free. It's over," Sky whispered over and over, scooting with John out of the booth. "I can go home."

"Where is home?" Frank asked.

Sky gave him a look, her mouth opening, then closing when she realized she didn't have an answer. "Wherever I want. Hawk? Where's Hawk?"

"Right behind you, bébé," he said, reaching around John to get a hand on her shoulder. "I'm riding with you to the hospital."

"It's over," Sky repeated, sobbing against John's chest.

"That's right. You're safe now. You're free," Douglas said, his stomach knotting because he knew the journey still ahead of her. "I'll make sure you stay that way."

Sky sighed, absorbing Hawk's warmth, relishing every pain free breath. She wanted to laugh, but tears of joy overwhelmed her. She thought her life would end when Spirit left her. Maybe it had shown her Hawk all these years because it knew this was their end. It found what it needed to escape and let her live.

The ambulance was a spectacle of sorts. It was a bit like the med-wagons they had on Terrana—a glorified wheelbarrow. The wheels were soft stone, and there was no 'suspension' to speak of. The young man hauling it seemed excited by the job, and he kept glancing back at Sky. John, Frank, and the police officers were walking next to the ambulance. It was a bumpy ride, and a distance Sky would rather have walked, but it was difficult to keep her eyes open.

The city looked beautiful now that she saw it as a haven. There were hand-painted signs over the buildings, and gardens at every corner. Sky recognized some of the flowers, but it wasn't until she saw someone crack open an aloe leaf that she realized their purpose was medicinal.

"When we get to the hospital, ask for a woman doctor," Hawk warned, keeping his voice low, putting an arm around her as though offering simple comfort. "Maman always said it would have been better if she'd seen other women from the start."

"Okay," Sky whispered. She was so overwhelmed by the loss of Spirit, it was difficult to believe any human danger could be so threatening. But there were hybrids here. Leaning over the edge of the wagon, she flagged Dr. Frank.

"Problem, dear?" he asked. "Is the ride making you sick?"

"I want a woman doctor," Sky said.

Frank frowned.

"You must give her one if she asks," Hawk added. "The Intendant ruled that any woman who asks must be granted the request."

"The Intendant's rule didn't account for women who engaged in bar fights," Frank scowled, his eyes narrowing.

Sky sat back in the wagon, not caring to argue, figuring it better to act as though things were already decided.

"Don't give them your clothes," Hawk advised. "Don't give them your bag. Keep everything that's yours with you. They'll tell you they want to inventory, but they'll take it all away. And maybe you don't care now, but someday you'll want to see and remember where you came from. Remember what you survived and what you overcame."

"They're not getting my bag," Sky said, putting a hand on her satchel. In it, she had a medicine kit and a weapon. It was all she carried with her. Everything else could be improvised. "Will we be separated?"

"For a little while. But if you want, you can come home with John and me after they release you. I know he would be happy to spend more time with you," Douglas smiled. "Although, if you don't like his attention—"

"I do," Sky smiled, imagining sharing a bed with John. Not just having sex, but sleeping next to someone for the first time, falling asleep in his arms. "Do I just tell them I'm going home with you?"

"I'm not sure," Douglas said. "You have to convince the Constable that you won't get violent again, and Dr. Frank not to keep you in asylum."

"I'll be charming," Sky smiled, sitting up when she felt the ambulance trundle to a stop. The hospital was surrounded by gardens, each section of plants labeled with a list of Rocanese words. They used the same alphabet as Lanvarians, but there was no recognizable root language she could discern.

"Carry you, bébé?" John asked, coming to the edge of the

wagon and taking her hand. She felt a fresh wave of peace and she crawled into his arms, letting him carry her. He was warm and intoxicating. They took her to a room with a wide bed and fresh linens. It did not look like a hospital room, and Sky worried this was the Geneculture that Hawk had described.

"Hawk?" she asked, lifting her head, getting woozy again. "Where is he?"

"Head doctor," John said, setting her on the edge of the bed, then backing away, leaving her cold. If there were springs in the mattress, Sky couldn't tell. It felt like the thing was stuffed with leaves. "You are doctor here."

"Your Trade needs practice," Sky grinned, testing her balance, then sauntering toward him. "I'll help you with that tonight." She licked her lips, but he backed away, covering his lips.

Taking advantage of her slowly clearing thoughts, Sky circled the room, checking the exits. There was only the one door, no window, and only a tiny ventilation shaft. John leaned against the wall, giving her space, managing to gaze at her without ogling.

The old, wooden door swung open and Frank entered, pushing a cart with a boxy computer wired to a scratched and dirty screen. Officer Blayze came next, hand on his baton. He had natural reddish hair, dark freckles, and lines indicating middle age.

"Is she calm?" he asked in Trade.

"Calm enough. Bring her in," Frank replied.

Blayze motioned and made space for a woman to come next to him. Her skin was bronzed, her eyes lidless, just like Hawk's.

"Sky, this is Dr. Edwige Song," Frank said, motioning to the woman.

The woman crossed her arms, highlighting the ill fit of her dull, white coat.

"You are golden," Sky observed. At the Glass Walls, she'd heard a story about the goldens—how they'd arrived in Rocan a hundred years ago to save Rocan from the Malady and wound up trapped here. Parts of it seemed like it could be true, but the people were so brainwashed into believing they were the last survivors on the planet that it became nothing more than a fantasy. Hawk said he didn't like the story, because it made him feel like he didn't have a place in Rocan.

"Is that a problem?" she grouched, tipping her head so that her smooth, black hair fell over her dull eyes. Her Trade was passable.

"No." Sky smiled disarmingly, but the woman slouched against the wall. "I haven't seen many women or many goldens, and you are both. Why would that be a problem?"

"Some find it difficult to look at her," Frank interjected. "Given your affinity for young Hwan, I didn't think it'd be a problem."

"Also, among women in the medical profession, I'm considered expendable," she muttered.

"Dr. Song!" Frank admonished, taking Sky's arm, leading her back to the bed. "Per your request, Madame Sky, a female doctor is present. Let us begin."

Dr. Frank donned a stethoscope, but Sky scurried away from him, pulling John away from the wall to hide behind him. Cluing into her discomfort, John turned, but Sky stayed at his back.

"Sky," Frank whined, puffing his fat cheeks.

"Is this woman a doctor or isn't she?" Sky demanded.

"She is protected and you have shown yourself violent," Frank snapped, reaching around John. John intervened, pushing Frank back, but being diplomatic about it rather than aggressive. He asked a question in Rocanese and Frank sneered a response. Blayze took a defensive stance, guarding Edwige, but all the while, the woman slouched by the door, unengaged in the antics.

"They don't trust you?" Sky asked her.

Edwige tucked her hair behind her ears, revealing puffy, tired brown eyes. "They don't trust you. They're arguing about my safety."

Frank paused, looking suspiciously at the two.

"So you're not expendable," Sky taunted, stepping around John, but keeping her distance to show Blayze she wasn't a threat. "Are you anything more than a womb to them?"

"You demanded to see a woman," Edwige pointed out. "Am I anything more to you?"

"You are a glimpse into how I will be treated if I stay," Sky offered.

"If you stay," Frank sputtered, blustering between them. "What are you going to do? Go back to your Sequesterer?"

Sky sucked in her cheeks, mustering a few fake tears before deciding they would be worthless on Frank. Lifting her shirt, Sky showed off her bruises again. Spirit had done a number on her, making her pass out in mid-air when the *Bobsled* flew over the Dome. The most striking bruise was the crisscross of the harness that went across her torso, down her sternum, and across her hips. Her hands and arms had impacted the console and the low cockpit cover. She had a few minor burns and scrapes from the Coureur explosion, but she'd used her medicine kit to heal Hawk, trusting Spirit to take care of her. Edwige raised a brow and studied Sky's face. When Frank reached out to trace the bruise on her hip, she pulled back and averted her eyes.

"Oh, Sky," John murmured, covering his mouth and squeezing his eyes shut.

"Are you ready to tell us what happened, Sky?" Frank persisted.

Edwige pushed off the wall, circling closer to Sky, keeping her arms crossed. "Dr. Frank, gentlemen, will you excuse us? Sky deserves privacy. I can handle this examination on my own." She repeated the request to John in Rocanese. Blayze didn't seem happy, but Edwige stood taller and more confident. The ensuing argument in Rocanese resulted in Blayze forcibly dragging Dr. Frank from the room. John waited for them to leave first, then gave Sky one last pitiful look. Edwige pressed the door closed behind him, then turned quickly.

"They may only leave us for a few minutes. I have so many questions," she said, her face coming alive. "Where did you come from? How did you get here? And don't tell me you were Sequestered. I'll never believe that."

"Never?" Sky asked, relieved to find someone finally believed in a world beyond Rocan.

Edwige shook her head. "Two weeks ago, my son was stillborn. After three healthy babies, I expected the streak to continue, but—they took him. They wouldn't let me name him. I'm not exempt from breeding this round for grief, but for physical recovery. That's how you will be treated if you stay. Now tell me, where can we go?"

"What happens if you fight?" Sky asked, overwhelmed by the influx of information.

"You are drugged, tied down, and bred anyway," Edwige growled. "You're not from Rocan, I can tell. And you weren't Sequestered—not the same way the other Sequestereds have been in the past. You hold your head too high, speak with too much grace, and you picked a fight in a bar. I don't know where you came from, but you should go back now. You will not find a better life here."

"Then I need to find Hawk," Sky said, her skin growing cold. She needed to get a message to Quin and fast. "I need . . . parts. Machine parts."

"You'll have to be more specific," Edwige rolled her eyes.

"Hawk," Sky said, pointing to the jacket. "Hwan."

"Sit here. We'll do this exam quickly and get you out." She motioned to the bed, rolled the machine over, and handed Sky an aged mask. "Put this over your nose and mouth and breathe normally. Or as normally as you can."

Sky wrinkled her nose at the dusty mask. "You need to patch this leak if you want meaningful readings."

"You know how this works?"

"I'm a hundred years old. I've seen a lot," she grinned.

"Nobody lives that long anymore. Not in Rocan, at least. You don't look a day over thirty," Edwige sighed, pushing the mask toward her face. "Do people live past a hundred where you come from?"

"Quite often. Do you have any kind of medical tape?" Sky asked, craning her neck and hopping off the bed. There were no supplies in the room, and only a limited kit of bandages and salve on the cart with the computer and breathing machine, all of which looked used and worn. Sky used one of the bandages to clean the mask and another to patch the tube. "You don't use this much."

"Breathing problems are rare among the adult population. The weak tend to get weeded out in infancy by the Malady," Edwige said. "Why do you speak Trade?"

"Why do you?" Sky countered.

"Boredom, mostly," she shrugged, placing the repaired apparatus over Sky's mouth. "We learn and we practice to stave off the feeling of isolation, uselessness, and boredom. There's a hidden medical history to this place. Not just the Malady. The population decline began before the Malady became apparent. Some people thought it was a curse from the gods—to punish us for trying to leave the Dome after the skies cleared. People worship the Aurora as the protector of Rocan—those lights in the night sky. It's funny, even when you know it's not real, you still want—you hope there's something out there watching over us. Something that can save us."

"You tried to leave this valley?" Sky asked, hacking on the stale air.

"Breathe; don't talk," Edwige said, clamping the mask in place. "A few expeditions left and never returned. We launched rockets to show we had survived, but no one responded. That was almost two centuries ago. Those things aren't permitted anymore. We can't afford to lose the supplies. We barely had enough cold weather gear to furnish a rescue when the tunnel collapsed.

"Now, we send men to the mine every day, not because we need the potash, but because if we don't they will die of boredom. Our most abundant resources don't give us what we need. We need to get out of this valley, but all we can do is paint the walls over and over, and try to convince ourselves we've found some place new. Run away. Take what you need and run. I've never known a Sequestered that understands language well enough to heed a warning like this before she is bred—"

The door swung open and Dr. Frank poked his head in. "Not done yet? What's taking so long?"

"Sky was fixing the machine," Edwige said, glancing at Sky. "She is mechanically inclined. I didn't even tell her how it works. She knew by looking at it. I think she would do well in engineering design. Perhaps even in the yard with Douglas Hwan—"

"You stupid girl—" Frank grumbled, crowding Edwige aside. Sky dropped the mask and punched him in the nose. Blayze charged into the room, but Sky jumped to her feet, standing on the bed, her fingers itching to draw a weapon. She had them if she needed, but she didn't want to cross that bridge yet.

"Hawk. I want to see Hawk now!" Sky demanded.

"Sky, sit!" Edwige ordered. "Dr. Frank, I told you to let me handle her. Now you've startled her again."

Sky looked warily at Dr. Frank, but she obeyed Edwige to diffuse the tension. Edwige motioned the men out of the room, and when they left, she covered her mouth, fighting to hold back a smile.

"What you need is in the yard," Edwige whispered. "That's where your mechanical parts are. Women aren't allowed there, but Hwan can get you what you need."

"Thank you," Sky smiled, kissing the other woman.

Edwige flinched in surprise, then ducked her head. "Where did you come from?" she begged. Sky could tell by her tone that casual kissing was not prevalent in the culture.

"Originally or recently?" Sky smiled. "I flew in from the south. It's warmer there."

"Is there breeding?"

"Depends on the city," Sky confessed. "But from what you've told me, there are plenty of places better than here."

"If you find a way out, take my children," she said. "I don't want them to grow up here."

12

There was a machine in Douglas Hwan's room that was meant to monitor blood pressure and heart rate. Over the past few years, the screen had more and more horizontal lines, and today the screen went black. Douglas had tried fixing it a few times, but in his opinion, it was better to replace the display with an analog technology, since there was no way to replace the screen. In the hour since he and Sky had separated, only Don Yale had come to check on him, and told him to sit tight until John came to take him home. Douglas had removed the cover of the machine and separated as much of the inner circuitry as could be done by hand. He had a basic sense of how information transferred from the cuff to the display, and a few ideas for the analog dial.

There was a clatter in the hall, and Douglas rushed to cover the machine and hide the sundries he'd extracted. A tired grunt had him rushing to the door to find the source of the noise. John stood in the midst of a spilled rainbow hash dish.

"John?" Douglas called, stepping into the hall.

"It slipped," he whispered, looking at his hands, dazed. He

bent down to clean the multi-colored vegetables, hissing as his fingers touched the steaming hot potatoes.

"No, leave it. I've got it. Come here," Douglas said, taking John by both hands and guiding him back to the hospital room. "You haven't slept a wink since yesterday. Lie down."

"I want you to eat something," John said. There were dark circles under his puffy eyes and sweat beading around his hairline. It wasn't the glow of excitement Douglas had seen when John was next to Sky.

"You're not my nurse," Douglas chided, pushing John's shoulder until he laid down, then covering him with a blanket. John was well past breeding years, and if he was deemed unfit for work, he'd stop receiving any kind of medicine that wasn't freely taken from a street garden.

Hurrying to the hall, Douglas cleaned the spilled food, using a fork to scoot the food onto the plate again. He was hungry, and considered eating the hash regardless of the contamination. It was still hot. Giving a quick blow to get the dirt off, he loaded the fork with sprouts and took a bite while walking back to his room.

"Close your eyes, John," Douglas ordered, scooting next to the pillow.

"Hand me my book," John murmured, rolling over Douglas' lap, nearly knocking the plate out of his hand.

"No," Douglas insisted. "No, you're going to rest. Papa, please."

"You only call me that when you want something," John sniggered, pumping his fingers. The joints were swollen stiff and the tips of his fingers turning purple. Setting his plate on his lap, Douglas took John's hand and massaged gently, trying to coax warmth back into the shaking limbs.

"I want you to rest," Douglas said.

"You're supposed to be resting. Sneaky boy, working on little projects while in the hospital," John laughed. The more he pretended to be brave, the more Douglas worried about him.

"Don gave me a little something to stop the headache. I'm just waiting for you and Sky to be ready to go home," Douglas laughed. There was a knock at the door, and Douglas quickly hid John's hand so the doctor wouldn't see.

"I thought you were the one injured," Edwige Song quipped. She was half-golden, like him. They had twins together several years ago. It was his second breeding, but first live birth, and though they rarely crossed socially, she still updated him on occasion, even painting portraits of the little ones on scrap wood or fabric. She painted them with fair skin, but he knew that they looked golden, too.

"Hi Eddie," he said, greeting her by the nickname that he'd known her by in their youth. "I was just—well, he hasn't slept —and I—"

"You're worried," she finished, shoving her hands in her pockets. She had a watch with a second hand, like most practicing doctors, and it seemed to gleam with her intent to diagnose. Douglas hedged, worried about confessing anything. When she approached the bed, he slid off the side, standing between her and John. His eyes flickered toward the machine he'd dismantled, a new worry layering over the old. Douglas wasn't cleared for work. This whole room was an indictment of resource abuse.

Edwige pursed her lips, a pink tint rising to her cheeks. "Are you up for a visitor?" she asked.

"No. We're waiting for someone. The Sequestered."

He leaned against the bed, and Edwige gave him another scan, using her thumb to peel back his eyelids. He'd never seen her at work, and was surprised by the matter-of-fact attitude, but he adored her strength.

"You mean Sky," she smiled. "She said you told her to ask for a woman. Did you expect them to assign me?"

"Never even occurred to me," Douglas murmured, seeing Sky by the door. Officer Blayze was behind her, keeping a hand on her shoulder. "Is Sky okay to walk home with us?"

"She's so happy, she's dancing," Edwige answered in Trade, giving Sky a wink. Douglas cocked his head, surprised to see her so playful, but then, he'd rarely interacted with Edwige outside of breeding.

A ruckus erupted behind them as John rolled off the bed and grabbed his Trade primer book. "Hello. Hello. How are you?" he said in Trade, blurring the words together like a song.

"Hello, again," Sky giggled, swishing past Douglas, crawling over the bed until she was nose to nose with John, closing her eyes and exhaling, then cradling his chin like she intended to kiss him.

"*Non*," John stammered. "Sky, must tell."

"Sky, not everyone here will respond well to kissing," Edwige warned, taking Sky by the shoulders and pulling her away from John.

Sky bit her lower lip, her gaze locked on John. "Sorry."

"*Sorry*?" John repeated the Trade word, flipping to the glossary at the back of his book for a translation. Douglas translated the apology, and John stammered, getting more flustered than Douglas had ever seen him.

"Forgiven, bébé. Forgiven," John gushed in Rocanese, turning to the book again to find the word. His hands shook, the adrenaline surge fueling his initial reaction to Sky already fading.

"You have books here?" Sky asked, coming around the bed to stand next to John. Her hand fell to the small of his back, and John squirmed.

"We have one library left," Edwige said. "It gets smaller each year. We rely more on recitation and oral stories now."

Sky squeezed her eyes shut, leaning a little more on John. "I need your help."

"Help her, Douglas," Edwige whispered in Douglas's ear, her cheeks tightening.

"Help what?" Douglas asked, leaning his elbows on the bed. "Help her read?"

"Home," John said, pointing to a page in the book. "Come home with us. We can take you home."

Sky's eyes sparkled, and she took the book from John, frowning at the page, reading the Rocanese words with Trade pronunciations, creating a phrase so butchered Douglas couldn't figure out what she was trying to say. She sat on the bed, the book in her lap, and John snuggled next to her, tossing words back and forth, smiling and laughing.

"Huh," Edwige said, leaning against the door. Douglas sidled next to her, leaving John and Sky to muddle through the conversation they seemed intent on having.

"When she came in, I guessed her in her thirties, but now I see them together, and she looks older," Edwige whispered to him, crossing her arms.

"She doesn't know her age?" Douglas asked. He was so drunk before the explosion, he couldn't recall much of the details of his conversation with Sky.

"A hundred. That's what she said," Edwige laughed, then frowned, then pulled the front of her lab coat closed. Her body was puffy from her recent pregnancy, her eyes shadowed with sadness, and the shadows deepened every year he saw her.

"I'm surprised you're already back at work," Douglas said. He knew about her loss, because every time a baby died in this town, Don Yale showed up looking for John. The man didn't have any other shoulders to cry on.

"I was called in to meet with Sky," Edwige said, sniffling and ducking her head. Her lips twitched as a mix of emotions surfaced. "And I'm glad I came. I'm going to arrange for her release. Take her home with you. Give her what she's looking for."

"What is she looking for?" Douglas asked.

"The same thing you are," Edwige said. "The same thing you have been since I met you. I'll have resources allocated for her. Be careful with her. She gave Frank a black eye," Eddie said, laughing at the last bit.

"Eddie—"

"Doctor," she corrected. "Doctor Song. I earned the title, and it means something. Sky reminded me of that. It means I can decide these things without Dr. Frank looking over my shoulder."

She pushed off the wall abruptly and hurried out of the room, covering her mouth as though she were sick. Douglas exhaled, his mind in a whirl. Douglas had never seen John talk to a woman, but he was infatuated with Sky.

"Papa. It's time to go home now," Douglas said, kneeling on the bed.

"Papa again?" John said, his brow furrowing with worry. "Douglas, what's wrong?"

"I don't know," Douglas said, scratching his face, then his arms. He looked at his hands, remembering the feel of them burning. Douglas dreamed of escaping Rocan, but what he was searching for was a way to belong here.

Sky shivered, her stomach churning as John pressed in beside her. She batted her eyes at him, flirting as much as he seemed able to handle. Of all the people she'd met in Rocan, he seemed most eager to be taken by her, and the more she fostered his interest, the more use he would be. Hawk was attached to him, but the parent-child relationship that had seemed so obvious before seemed to have flipped, with Hawk worrying over John.

"Let us see Cannington Arts," John said, linking her arm, pulling her right once they exited the hospital.

"John, *non*!" Hawk countered, stamping his foot, yanking Sky by the other elbow. They argued in Rocanese, John bouncing like a horny teenager, Hawk scowling like a reluctant parent.

"Sky, there's a song group performing in the gardens. John would like you to go with him," Hawk grumbled, his sour glower making Sky laugh.

"Do they perform every day or just today?" Sky asked, linking each man's arm, standing between them. She could see John's energy tanking, despite his excitement. "I'd like to clean up and rest. And stay away from crowds for a few hours."

Hawk translated, and John's smile grew. "Come home. Have bath!" he said, his hand tightening on his Trade primer, though he waited to see if she understood before he opened the book to check.

"That sounds divine," Sky crooned, her body relaxing at the thought. She raised her chin and kissed his cheek, making him blush.

"Thank you," Hawk whispered, trudging in the direction of home. John chased after him, getting under his shoulder, helping him walk, resuming the roll of caretaker. He fussed over Hawk, pausing to rest every half a block.

"Hawk, do you need to go back to the hospital?" Sky asked.

He shook his head. "It's not a concussion. They kept me up all night and I haven't slept since yesterday. John hasn't slept either. When we get home, we'll all have a place to lie down."

Sky smiled, relishing the thought of sleep in a bed. It would be scary, but Hawk would be there to protect her. If she could sleep in a bar, she could sleep in a bed.

Once away from the hospital and industrial buildings, the houses and cafeterias were intermixed. The steps of Hawk's porch were crooked and broken on one side. There were no numbers or markings, but there was a different mural painted on every door. Hawk's door had a picture of a glider plane flying toward an Aurora. John let himself in without use of a key. They entered a medium-sized room with yellow-orange walls, faded red furniture, and mostly empty shelves. It was bland compared to the artistry outside. There was no noticeable technology in the room whatsoever, and Sky's heart sank.

"Bath or food?" John asked, setting the Trade book on one of the barren shelves between a sunken couch and equally sunken chair.

"Sit. Both of you," Sky ordered, directing them to the couch. "You're exhausted."

Hawk didn't need any prompting before flopping on the couch and covering his face with his hands. John muttered a few more words, then turned through another door.

"John," Sky admonished.

"He's getting drinks," Hawk sighed, tipping sideways and throwing his legs over the arm of the couch. "I'm hitting that crossover point where sobriety hurts more than this cut on my head."

Brushing her fingers through his hair, Sky checked the gash on his head, an internal war igniting. It was a minor wound, but still red and glistening. He may have rescued her from Spirit, but he didn't have power to heal quickly like she did. She wanted to understand what was so special about him, but if Edwige was right, she didn't have the luxury of time. She pulled a small rod from her satchel and waved it over Hawk's head.

"What is that?" Hawk asked, perking up.

"Um." If it had a name, Sky didn't know. "It's a wand. I picked it up in a place called Cordova."

"Can I touch it?" he asked, running his finger along the unassuming black rod. "How does it work?"

"Let me use it first. Hold still," she said, pressing his shoulder down. It was a strange piece of technology that gave no indication that it was working. Sky didn't understand its power source, but in the last fifteen years, hadn't had any issue with it.

"What's it doing?" Hawk asked, his heels tapping, his fingers rapping against his thigh.

"I'm not sure. It always seems to know what to do. But I think, it's helping the blood flow even out," Sky replied. The redness faded and Hawk's wound shrank. She didn't want to make it disappear entirely, because that would arouse too much suspicion, so she cut short her last pass and dropped it back into her satchel. "Feel better?"

"Yeah," he smiled, running his hand over the back of his head.

John returned from the kitchen, using his shoulder to push through the swinging door. He carried three mugs filled with a deep, purple liquid. Sky had seen the berry juice at the bar, but Colleen mixed it with alcohol. Sky and Hawk both hopped up to help, each taking a mug, but then Sky took John's arm and led him to the couch. His grip on his drink was tenuous, his joints enlarged from arthritis. Sky could heal that, too, but she didn't want to burn through all the resources in her medicine kit, and she didn't have the same lack of restraint around John that she seemed to have for Hawk. She sipped the juice, then set it aside, turning John away from her.

"What are you doing?" Hawk asked.

"Helping him relax," she replied, massaging John's shoulders, forcing him down on the couch. He tried to protest, but Hawk sandwiched him in from the other side, massaging the joints on his hands. John groaned and mumbled something, and Hawk laughed.

"He says if we keep doing this, he'll fall asleep," Hawk translated.

"I can stop," Sky said, stilling her hands, her first instinct being that sleep was a bad thing. John relaxed and sank back into her, closing his eyes, resting his head on her chest. She dared close her eyes too, feeling the peace of Spirit-free existence. It was both disconcerting and wonderful, and time seemed to stand still. John's weight on her increased as his breathing steadied.

"Lie him down," Hawk instructed, shaking out a threadbare blanket.

"He's sleeping," Sky said. "Will he stop breathing if you let go?"

"No. Why would he?" Hawk asked, putting the blanket over John's legs.

"Still paranoid, I guess," Sky murmured, sliding out from behind John, but keeping hold of his hand while Hawk tucked the blanket around him. She let go for a second, waiting for a reaction, but John didn't stop breathing. She backed away one step at a time, feeling her own calmness diminish with every step.

"Where did it go?" she asked.

"I don't understand," Hawk said, motioning her to follow him. He took her down the hall to a washroom with a large stone-carved tub. The stone had a few chips in it, but it was big enough to lie down in.

"When you freed me from my Sequesterer, where did it go?" Sky asked. She was beginning to think that was just the Rocanese short-hand for a spirit-carrier, and it felt like Spirit had isolated and abused her. "Does it just exist here, feeding off the other realm energy? I can't sense any of that anymore. It's quiet. It's empty. It's terrifying."

"It may be a while before you stop jumping at every sound, expecting your Sequesterer to return. It is terrifying how empty this place feels. Rocan is dying," Hawk said, plugging a drain, then running his hand along a silver spigot to initiate water flow. Sky frowned, frustrated by his avoidance of her question, but also knowing that if she hadn't seen him in her dreams so often, she wouldn't have had the courage to speak them aloud. He didn't recognize her the way she did him.

"Do you use scents in the water?" He asked. There was a cup next to the tub, and Hawk picked out a few dried leaves, sniffing each before handing them to Sky.

"Is there a water limit?" Sky smiled, her body warming with anticipation.

"Water limit?"

"A limit to how much we can use?" Sky asked.

"No, the water comes from ice lakes just past the mine. We just warm it up," he explained.

"Is there a limit to the warm water?"

"No, silly," Douglas laughed. "We may not have towels, but we have all the water we want. You can bathe all day and all night if you wish."

Sky squirmed with delight, finding another redeeming virtue in this hellish city. She hooked Hawk's face, and kissed him gleefully. He pressed his lips together, his body remaining tense even after she let go.

"You kiss everyone, then?" he stuttered, his face getting pale.

"Not *everyone*," Sky laughed, rubbing her lips.

"Please don't kiss me like that again. It's confusing." His calmness was forced, and his head dropped in submission.

Sky frowned. A lot of the folks she kissed seemed unaccustomed to the level of intimacy, but he was the first to look hurt by it.

"You don't like kissing," she asked, dropping her clothes and stepping into the tub. He wasn't fazed by her nakedness, the way he was by the kiss. He dropped a few dried leaves into her water, and a strong, floral scent filled the room.

"I like kissing, I just prefer to do it with men," he mumbled, sitting by the tub, separating his jacket from her clothes. Sky chuckled, realizing that he didn't intend to leave her alone in the bath.

"Hmm. You kiss John?" she teased.

"No! He's my father," Hawk balked, splashing the water at her face. "My second father. He adopted me after my mother got sick."

"You didn't have a father before that?" Sky asked, folding her arms on the side of the tub.

"I did. My first father. My genetic father. He died." Hawk touched the date on the jacket. "Ten years ago yesterday. I was their love child. They weren't breeding partners; they had a love union. They chose me. We were a beautiful family until he died."

"How did he die?" Sky asked, combing her fingers through Hawk's hair, watching for tears.

"Engine exploded. Like what happened to us, I guess," he murmured. "He was flying into the aurora."

"Flying?" Sky repeated. "Like the picture on the door?"

"Yes. I had it done for the anniversary, but I usually can't bear to leave it that way more than a day. He, um . . . we built a—I don't know the Trade word. Air, glide, glider," he decided on the word, then hugged the jacket again.

"You built a glider to go over the mountains?" Sky asked, her toes curling with excitement. "The one he flew, is that the only one you made?"

He looked at her guiltily, then down at the jacket in his hands, nodding.

"Can we make another?" Sky persisted. "I can help make it safe. Do you have the resources to build another?"

Shuddering, he reached past her and turned off the water, then stood to go.

"Hawk, listen. There are worlds out there—thriving cities, with medicine and towels and people," Sky urged. "Edwige said that I need to go to the yard."

"No way. We'll be hanged!" Hawk exclaimed, his cheeks getting red.

"Then can you bring what I need here?" she asked

"*I'm* not even allowed in the yard right now," he retorted, his fists clenching around the jacket. "Unless you want to explain to the doctor you healed me with your magic wand from Cordova."

"I've healed you twice, and still you doubt me? Cordova is a Dome beyond the mountains. I flew there," Sky said carefully.

Hawk closed his eyes and shook his head. "That's what Eddie meant, then? She thinks together we can dream our way over the mountains?"

He stalked out and Sky sighed. She needed to stop treating him like an outsider desperate for escape and tread more carefully. She had the Trade primer. She could learn their language tonight, and tomorrow, find the help she needed to escape.

13

Don Yale came out of the second floor hospital room, leaned against the wall, and pinched the bridge of his nose. They'd been so close this time. A healthy pregnancy, a hand-knitted pink blanket . . . and a stillborn. It was this woman's third miscarriage in as many tries, and to lose a child so late, Don was beginning to think her unbreedable. No matter how many he dealt with, it never got easier. The parents wanted a name and all Don was permitted to give them was a number—a tally on the breeding score sheet for the month. What the Intendant didn't know was that Don kept their names. He couldn't write them down in the official record, but any parent that dared defy the code of conduct and confide in him their chosen name, he remembered. He etched the names onto a stone and added the stone to his garden. At the end of every year, he would read all the names and remember. Paige was this girl's name.

Heading down the hospital stairs, Don switched off lights where he could. The number of working bulbs in the city was dwindling and the few adept engineers in the village had limited success manufacturing new ones—at least ones that were safe. He paused when he saw Colleen at the end of the corridor. She sat hunched over, elbows resting on her knees, picking at her fingernails.

"Colleen," he said, changing direction to check on her. "You always do check-ups in the morning. Were there some after effects of the flash bomb?"

Colleen glanced at him, then back at her hands. She picked at her nails more agitatedly and chewed on her cheek. "I didn't want to bring Felicity here."

Don sat down next to her, and she scooted over, leaving a space between them. He knew from the moment he saw Colleen at the Glass Walls that she was pregnant, and though she needed immediate medical attention following the brawl to check on the baby, he couldn't insist without revealing her pregnancy to everyone at the bar. Given how tenuous pregnancies were in the early stages, it would not have been right to reveal her.

"I'm sure everyone here would have loved to see her," Don said tenderly. "How is the little one? Recovering from this afternoon, I hope?"

Colleen's sullen pout resolved into a weak smile, eyes still focused on her fingers. "She hasn't made a peep since we got her home. Reg keeps trying to make her speak and it's driving me crazy, because I know she has it in her to call him 'Papa,' and she's stopped seeing us again."

Don frowned, worried that Colleen was so focused on Reg's connection to the girl. He knew Colleen hadn't been connecting with Felicity as well as they'd hoped when they granted her custody. His concern grew when Colleen buried her face in her hands and groaned.

"Knowing I can love a child that's not ours . . ." Colleen trailed off, swallowed hard, and looked sullenly at her hands. "I keep seeing the four that I gave away. Every time, Reg asked if this was the one we were taking home and I said no. It wasn't ours."

Don pressed his lips together. He knew exactly who Colleen's children were, but telling her they were happy in their adoptive families wouldn't help. "There's no sense in sitting here brooding alone. You have a little girl of your own now who wants to kiss you goodnight. Come on, I'll walk you home."

Don stood up from the bench and tugged Colleen's elbow.

"You don't have to do that," she mumbled.

"It's on my way," Don said. "I need to check up on Johnny. He's got Sky with him."

"You need to go home, Donny," she sighed, standing and smoothing her clothes.

"Are you my mother now, too?" Don teased. "If you don't want me to walk with you . . ."

Heaving a sigh, Colleen shook her head and shuffled down the hall. "Tell Johnny his crush owes my daughter an apology."

Don chuckled, not sure if the comment was meant to be an invitation. Then Colleen stopped and turned around.

"Did you see how he blushed? I have never seen Johnny like that with a woman," Colleen said.

"I think even if he'd been fluent in Trade, he would have been stumbling for words," Don commented, laughing and joining her. He wasn't sure what to hope for John, especially considering how little they knew about Sky. But he was glad to be able to smile with Colleen.

The couch wasn't comfortable, but it was better than the floor, and John had given his bed to Sky for the evening. He heard her prowling around the house, and when she disappeared into the kitchen, he listened for sounds of running water or whirring appliances. After half an hour of silence, he worried she'd either passed out or run out the back door.

Yawning and stretching, John rolled off the couch and padded to the kitchen. Sky was seated at the table, fiddling with an electronic device, munching on a plate of beets and sipping at berry juice. John didn't imagine that food combination tasted too great.

"Do you only sleep in noisy bars?" he joked, taking the seat next to her. His mirth faded when he saw what she'd done. "You've dismantled my toaster."

Sky held up a thick wire and said something in Trade that he didn't understand, then she held the wire to the end of the device.

"You want the wire? I want my morning toast," he retorted, taking the wire from her. The metal had been ripped and the edges of the wire were frayed. *Does Douglas even know how to fix this kind of thing?*

Sky made a face and reached for the wire, but he shooed her away.

"No, that's enough for tonight. You need to rest," he said, lifting her from her seat and then massaging her shoulders as he directed her out of the kitchen. She glared, but then her face softened and she rolled her shoulders back into his hands, humming.

"I knew you'd like that. You can't understand a word I'm saying, can you?" he laughed. Giving her a push, he steered her down the hall to the bedroom. Sky let him lead, but when he opened the bedroom door, she planted her feet and refused to enter.

"Come on," he said in Trade, motioning toward the bed. She laughed at him, then started mimicking the hand motions.

"Don't mock me, lady. Do I have to tuck you in or something?" he teased, taking her hand, and leading her into the bedroom. She seemed more willing to follow him inside than go alone, and standing behind him, she started massaging his shoulders. John groaned, and then leaned over to pull back the bed covers for her. Suddenly, he felt her body pressed flush to his backside, and her hands snaking across his hips and cupping him through his pants.

John twisted out of her hands, but the only way to avoid knocking her over was to fall onto the bed. Sky took that as an invitation and straddled his lap. Her lips were wet and parted in a voracious smirk. Her eyes were dark and hungry. Her hands dipped under the hem of his shirt and raked over his chest.

"No, Sky. This isn't why I brought you in here," he said in a panic, trying to pull her hands out of his clothes. *Is this why she was so reluctant to go into the bedroom?* "Sky, no," he pleaded as she rubbed her body against his.

Sky stopped just as suddenly as she had started and pulled her hands out from under his shirt, but still tugged at the hem, looking at him uncertainly.

"Just for fun. I teach you," she said. Her Rocanese was as broken as his Trade, but he caught her meaning well enough.

"No," he said firmly.

Sky got off his lap and sat next to him on the bed, hands in her lap, eyes on her knees. A part of him felt disappointed, but mostly he was glad she understood and respected his request. He reached out and took her hand, wanting her to know that he forgave her. She turned his hand over in both of hers, kneading his palm.

"Sorry," she said.

John crossed his arms, aching to touch her—to at least feel the comfort of holding her, but a part of him was screaming, warning him that he would never get to keep her. He didn't even control what happened to himself.

"There's a principle to it," he explained. "There is no fun

watching the person you love summoned for breeding. Carrying someone else's child. Losing that child. How can a few moments of pleasure take that pain away?"

Sky cradled his face and kissed the side of his mouth. She didn't understand his words. Lust taking hold, John latched his lips to hers. For a split second, the pain was gone. Then it hit harder than before, taking his breath away.

"I am sorry," Sky said, her finger brushing his cheek, smearing his tears.

John thought his heart was going to explode. He hated his life; he hated his world. It wasn't fair. He had vowed never to enter a love union until the breeding stopped, and for the first time, he felt cheated.

"You should sleep," he told her. When she looked at him blankly, he tried the phrase again in Trade.

"Safe in your arms?" she asked hopefully, hugging his hand against her chest.

"Safe in bed," he corrected. He stood to leave, but she tugged his hand, turning him around.

"Please, don't go. I won't touch bad," she said, fumbling through words. She ran the backs of her fingernails over his cheeks. His lips parted, but no protest managed to form. He gazed helplessly into her crystal blue eyes and she studied him with that gentle, amused smile she seemed to reserve only for him.

"That's the problem, Sky. I want you to touch me. I want you so much," he confessed.

"I am afraid to sleep alone. Not safe. Never safe," she said. "If you not stay, then I go."

John didn't want her to be afraid, but he didn't like being forced into bed either. Sky pulled back the blanket and made him lie down. John obeyed, wanting to submit and hating the submission. She pulled the blanket up to his chin and wiped tears from his cheek that he hadn't realized had fallen.

"I am on couch," she said, leaving and closing the door behind her. Regret and confusion mingled together, and John licked his lips, savoring the lingering taste of Sky. He wanted to hold her, protect her, and sleep next to her. He'd fallen in love with her, and even though she was willing, it hurt.

14

The tunnel leading to the Hudson mine was buzzing with repair activities and the natural sunlight beamed through the fractures left from the Coureur explosion, melting the ice that had formed in the cracks overnight. Constable Channing Mace wished for the warmth of a coat, but only those on the exposed side of the tunnel were allocated cold weather gear.

"Intendant Hubert!" Mace called, scanning the faces that popped up in response. The Intendant knelt over a line of studs, drilling holes so that the workers outside could more quickly frame the new structure. There were several white-haired men among the workers, but the Intendant had the warmest jacket and the reddest cheeks.

"You seem to be making good progress," Mace said, stepping around the stacks of materials. The seals blocking the mine were expected to be lifted by mid-day, so that the men would have a way to return to work.

"Well, there's something new and necessary to do. Even I'm drawn to sign up for that kind of work," the Intendant replied, handing off his drill, and rising to meet Mace. "Mon Ferriera has been helpful in locating roofing."

"I scavenge Caswell often. The mine needs similar materials to keep from cave-in. It's amazing how much disintegrates the moment it touches natural sunlight," Celio Ferriera spoke up. He was on his feet, acting as overseer of construction rather than getting his hands dirty, but he had a puffy snow coat on, meaning he was spending time in the direct sunlight orchestrating action. "Have you come to lend a hand?" Celio asked.

"I'm afraid one is all I have," Mace replied, holding up his splinted hand.

"Ah, yes. I heard the little one spoke yesterday." Intendant Hubert said, searching for pockets in his jacket, and when he found none, tucking his hands into his sleeves.

"She made some efforts in the Glass Walls, but went silent the moment Deputy Arman carried her out of there," Mace reported. Arman's heartbreak at the renewed silence had been evident the moment he trudged into the Bastien that morning. Mace sent him home to see to his family.

"That is a shame," the Intendant grumbled insincerely. "The other one—Sky—you arrested her?"

"No. She's a victim," Mace explained. "After the fight, she went to the hospital."

"After she attacked the girl," the Intendant pointed out. "What about Dr. Frank? She attacked him, too."

"And me," Celio spoke up. "Though that was before we knew she only spoke Trade."

"She cannot begin a brawl, putting women and breeders in danger, with no repercussions," the Intendant persisted. "Where is she now?"

"Staying with Hwan and Harris," Mace said, getting colder the longer they stood still. "Dr. Song released her to Harris' custody and had resources sent there—clothing, bedding. Sky seemed soothed by him."

"Harris, huh?" Celio muttered. "So I shouldn't expect him to help build?"

"He's tasked with caring for his son today," Mace grimaced. There was no need for additional workers. There seemed to be people standing around already, waiting to be given something to do.

"Are you sure it's wise to leave her with them?" Celio remarked. "They could be the ones that Sequestered her? Harris has denied companionship his entire life, and maybe now we know the reason. He's had a woman, Sequestered. Hwan stole the Coureur that morning, maybe just to capture her before she could be discovered."

He pointed to the charred, warped metal frame that remained of the Coureur. When the engine had exploded, shards of glass and metal had gone flying, and were embedded in the ground and surviving wall of the tunnel.

"She knew Douglas. She went right to him," Celio continued. "She went right to the Coureur."

"Frank said she fixed that breathing machine in the hospital," the Intendant added. "The woman has skills, language, and the capacity to defend herself. She could be a danger to them both."

"They could be a danger to her," Celio added.

"She trusted them. She panicked at the Glass Walls, but she trusted them," Mace said. "If any of your twisted theories are true, she's still innocent in this as a Sequestered."

"Hardly," the Intendant huffed. "Sequestereds are given a pass on violent behavior only if they lack language and social adjustment. This woman had the entire bar eating out of her hand."

"Intendant—"

"I don't care if she only speaks Trade. She understands!" the

Intendant snapped loud enough to draw attention from the others.

"She doesn't know anything about the rules of this culture," Mace pointed out.

"Then explain it to her," the Intendant growled. "I want you to find out where she came from, who kept her, and whether she is competently able to take responsibility for her actions. She will have a hearing in two days, assuming there are no further assaults. One more indiscretion, and she will be committed to asylum."

Sky frowned when she saw the first person walking past the kitchen window down the road that lead to the town square. The lights in the Dome were rising. She'd been awake all night, and she thought she'd be more tired. Maybe it was the residual energy from carrying Spirit so long. Yesterday at the Glass Walls, she could barely keep her eyes open to weep for joy. She didn't feel the same peace she felt last night, and it bothered her.

The kitchen was Sky's favorite room in the house, outside of the bath. The appliances cooked food with varying degrees of efficiency, but every one of them was capable of leaving sear marks on food—even the ones that weren't meant to heat. There was a table and two chairs shoved into a corner, and the chairs were covered with the same ugly, red upholstery as the living room furniture. There was evidence that the two men ate here often, but rarely entertained.

"Mon Kerf! What did you do!?" Hawk cried, stopping dead in the doorway, nearly getting whacked in the face by the swinging door.

Sky had dismantled a few pieces that looked like they might be controlled by circuit board. The *Bobsled* was beyond repair, but that message had made it from Terrana, and she was going to build a way to answer.

"You said we couldn't go to the yard, so I was looking for supplies in here," Sky smiled.

He was shirtless, hair askew, wearing only pants that sagged on his narrow hips. In this light, she could see scars and burn marks spattered across his body. The skin of his arms, where she'd healed his burns, was obviously smoothed over. The skin was so clean and perfect, that it looked as though his arms had been severed and new ones attached in their place.

"You broke it. You broke everything!" he shuddered, his face clouding with anxiety at the betrayal.

"I dismantled a few things." Putting her hands on his shoulders, she steered him to the table and pressed him into one of the wobbly chairs. "I also cooked breakfast."

Going to the oven, she pulled one of her masterpieces of the small hours. She set a plate of fruit pancakes in front of him. It took her fifteen batches to get it right, but there seemed no shortage of fruit or flour here. The fruit was meticulously placed with blueberries in the center, a red buffalo-berry, and a banana slice on the perimeter, so that it looked like Aquia, Caldori, and Terrana.

"You cook, too?" he asked, looking up at her, then poking at the warm plate. "Why did you run away from wherever you were? Why come here?"

"To meet you, apparently," she said, taking the seat opposite him, lining up the bits of metal and wire she'd extracted over the course of the night. "Hawk, when I leave, will I still be able to close my eyes? Will I still be able to sleep? Am I free, or is it just this place that makes things quiet?"

Hawk gave her a look, and Sky felt the truth sinking in. Spirit was still with her, dormant. She hadn't escaped anything

"I don't understand what you're asking. I'm not using any

special magic, Sky. I'm just trying to be here for you," he said, taking her hand, and then plucking the wire from it. Finding the casing of the toaster, he pulled that close, too, evaluating the damage. "What are you building?"

"From these parts? Nothing useful," Sky sighed. Just because it was this place subduing Spirit didn't mean she had to live here. Even the people that did live here wanted to leave. "I need to go to the yard. Edwige said you could get me what I needed from there. Do you have circuits? Things I can use to broadcast a signal to the moon?"

"Sky—"

The door swung open again, and John breezed in, smelling of bath scents, dressed in clean clothes, his thin, brown hair combed back.

"Good morning," he said in Trade, his accent making it sound like a song.

"Good morning," Sky said in Rocanese. She'd passed much of the night going through the primer, and seeing it written, decided it was decently close to Trade in root structure. "Sit. I cook."

"You cooked or you are cooking?" John asked. She recognized the different Rocanese tenses once he said them.

"She cooked," Hawk muttered, shuffling to one of the lower cabinets next to the refrigerator and pulling out a bottle of liquor. John glowered in disapproval, and Hawk only added a tiny splash to the juice cup next to his plate.

"You look terrible, Douglas. Did you have trouble sleeping?" John asked.

Sky stiffened. "Is it normal? Trouble sleeping?" she asked.

"No, Sky. I slept fine. I woke up to this," he grouched, motioning to the table, speaking in Rocanese so John would understand.

"Yes, I caught her last night with the toaster," John apologized, rubbing his smooth-shaved chin. He glanced at Sky, then looked away again. "She's going to have a stream of visitors today. You know that, right?"

"I'll be at the yard," he groaned, pushing the pancakes away and getting up from the table.

"You're not cleared to work," John reminded him, catching his wrist before he could escape. "Day of rest. One more follow-up head scan."

Hawk pouted and left anyway, slamming the door to his bedroom.

"He didn't eat," Sky murmured.

"Give him space," John sighed, rubbing his face, pulling the pancake plate in front of himself and eating with his bare fingers. "Oh, that is sweet," he choked, grabbing the spiked berry juice to wash it down.

Sky turned her gaze back to the window. The foot traffic was picking up and she heard the gong of the clock tower sounding the first hour of the morning. The first shift, the locals called it. They all could have been hybrids and spirit-carriers, their nature subdued by the energy of this place.

"Do you sleep?" Sky asked.

"Everybody sleeps," he chuckled, reaching around her to fill a glass with water from the sink. He was perfectly evasive about his spirit side.

"When I close my eyes, I see . . . nightmares. Do you?" she asked.

"What kind of nightmares do you see?" he asked, his eyes meeting hers.

"You first?" Sky said, looking away. John touched her cheek, twirling her blond locks around his fingers.

"I can never seem to remember when I wake up. I feel like there's a whole chunk of my life missing. That I only remember in dreams. I remember I was happy, but I don't remember what happy feels like. Except when I'm with you, I kind of do," he sighed, running his finger down her arm. Taking a deep breath, he leaned over to kiss her.

"Don't," Sky said, pushing him away, feeling a rush of loneliness. "You have principles. You will . . ." Sky paused, racking her brain for the Rocanese words. "You will hate you. You will . . ."

"Regret," John offered. "I regret taking on a life-long chastity protest. It's not helping anyone and the only person it's hurting is me."

He dropped his chin, but squeezed her hand again, his face contorting with conflict.

"Do you want me to leave?" Sky asked.

"No," he sighed, looking at her again. "Tell me about your nightmares."

Sky's skin went cold, her instinct telling her to lie. But she felt safe with him. His desire to protect her was rooted in something deeper than sexual desire. "I see the future. I see people dying," she said, shifting closer. Their hands clasped, and he kissed her knuckles.

"Tell me that Douglas outlives me," he begged, squeezing his eyes shut.

Sky's heart sank. By the tone in his voice, he'd dismissed her confession as fairy tale.

15

'What is it like being a woman in Rocan?' Sky had asked.

Colleen closed her refrigerator and slumped into a chair at the kitchen table, nauseated by the sight of food. Felicity wouldn't eat anything that required chewing, and Colleen was too tired to mash up the vegetables.

What was it like? It was being pregnant when she didn't want to be. It was having so many miscarriages, that she started lying to her husband and saying a breeding failed, because she was tired of seeing that heartbroken look on his face. It was being tired all the time. Being lonely. Wanting to find someone she could talk to about everything that was going wrong, and at the same time, not wanting to talk at all.

Sky seemed the same way. She had hard questions and needed answers, but was happy to tell fantastical stories and smile and flirt, so that they could escape the pain of the truth she asked about.

"Morning, darling," Reg said, guiding Felicity into the kitchen with a hand on her shoulder. Ever since he'd taken her to the hospital yesterday, she kicked and fought when he tried to carry her. She didn't scream, though. Sky hadn't appreciated how significant even an incoherent scream was from Felicity.

"She still hasn't forgiven you," Colleen teased, caressing the girl's face. Felicity turned her head, following Colleen's hand, letting herself be guided into a hug. Reg pulled a plain bread loaf from the breadbox, and prepared a plate for Felicity. There was an ongoing fight over the lack of nutrition in the loaf, but it wasn't one Colleen wanted to have today.

"That looks good," Colleen hinted. Biting back a smile, Reg sliced some for her, too.

"Maybe we should take her to see Sky," Reg said, bringing the plates to the table.

"Why? So Sky can lash out at her and throw her across the room?" Colleen grumbled, chomping on the bread. Reg brought some jam to the table and gave her a look. He'd expected Felicity to eat the bread dry, but not her.

"I thought she'd talk to Sky," he said, sitting next to Felicity. "Maybe we can learn why Sky is so important to her. Maybe she can convince Sky to tell us."

"Do you think she's Felicity's mother?" Colleen asked.

When Reg didn't answer right away, Colleen knew he had been thinking the same thing. The thought had crept in yesterday afternoon, when the Constable had interrogated her about Sky's behavior, Sky's interest in Felicity, and the conversations the two had.

"No. Blond hair is not uncommon," Reg said, spilling out the rationalization when he realized he'd waited too long. "And Felicity doesn't know Trade any better than she knows Rocanese."

Felicity wrapped her fist on the table, like she was knocking on a door. She did it twice, looking directly across the table at Colleen, summoning her attention. Then she tapped her chest.

"Does something hurt?" Colleen asked, springing up from

her chair and hurrying around the table. “Does your chest hurt?”

Felicity shook her head and Colleen shivered. Felicity had responded directly to a question! She clicked her tongue and forced air past her lips.

“Who? Who?” she wheezed in Rocanese.

Colleen glanced at Reg, aghast. “Who . . . are you?” Colleen guessed.

“You’re Felicity,” Reg answered. “We named you that, and we adopted you into our family because you needed a home.”

Felicity shook her head, sending her blond locks flying into her face.

“No?” Reg asked, putting a hand over hers. “You remember your home? Do you remember your name?”

Felicity shook her head again, tearing up.

“Of course not. That’s why you’re asking who you are,” Reg chided himself.

Felicity nodded. Even yesterday at the bar, their communication hadn’t involved this much back and forth. Felicity either said ‘Sky’ or ‘Dome’ and she didn’t respond to questions.

“I’m sorry, little darling. I don’t know,” Reg said, his voice cracking. “But I will do everything I can to find out for you.”

Colleen looked away, seeing the heartbreak on his face that she hated so much. If he found Felicity’s family, her name, or her past, they would lose a piece of her. Wiping away her tears, Felicity seemed to notice her bread plate anew and stuffed a piece into her mouth.

“Felicity, do you remember Sky?” Reg asked.

Felicity chewed, her eyes tracing the patterns on the wall.

“Dome?” Colleen tried. “Do you want to hear a travel story?”

Reg got up from the table, turning to the wall to hide his emotions. Colleen came behind him.

“Doh-meh?” Felicity wheezed, knocking on the table again.

Her eyes lit up and she watched Colleen expectantly. Colleen had listened to so many travel stories while tending bar, but she was usually serving drinks rather than taking notes.

"There was once a Dome filled entirely with birds. Do you know what birds are?" Colleen asked.

Felicity watched her mouth, but gave no indication of understanding the words. It didn't matter. She was trying. In three days they'd gone from silence, to sound, to answering yes-or-no questions. Felicity would get better.

Sky's breakfast had infused John with more sugar than he could handle. He leaned over the sink, swishing water in his mouth to clear the taste of her pancakes. After a whole night to mull on regret, John was more eager to take down the walls he'd put up to protect himself. Sky grinned and nodded, walking her fingers up his arm and tickling his neck, making him spit the water. Catching her hand, John tickled her back, laughing when she squealed. Then it ended. The laughter faded into a mirthful silence and they stared at each other.

"Fun?" John prompted, hoping Sky understood his meaning. All John had ever known of physical intimacy was a little discomfort and a lot of awkwardness. Sky knew a different truth about everything it seemed.

"Regret?" she challenged. Sky tilted her head, inviting him to close the distance. She wasn't going to do it for him.

John ran his tongue over his teeth, tasting the sweetness of the pancakes she'd made. He kissed her clumsily, but the way she hummed boosted his confidence. John had never been kissed before—not like that. It was not demanding like the way she'd come after him last night, nor was it the polite, apologetic kiss of a breeding partner trying to distract his brain long enough for his body to become aroused. Her hands didn't wander. Her lips were soft and inviting, and her fingers lightly stroked his jaw, coaxing him in until he was lost in her. When she pulled back, he chased instinctively, wanting to keep their lips connected.

She moved to the counter, parting her legs, drawing him to stand between them. Her touch was loving and intimate—something he had mimicked and forced for the benefit of his breeding partners, but had never felt in its true form. She moved slowly, keeping her hands above the waist, but hardly chaste. She peeled off his shirt, exploring his chest with her lips. In breeding, he had never removed his shirt—it was an effort to stay disconnected. With Sky, he was free. His body responded naturally and eagerly to her touch, and the delight on her face told him he had no reason to be ashamed.

Tentatively, he slid his fingers under the hem of her shirt, and she leaned back, raising her arms so that he could remove it. Had he not already seen her bruises, he would have panicked, but Sky didn't seem bothered by them. She placed his hands where she wanted, gently nudging him away from the tender and ticklish spots. He played with the ticklish spots to make her squeal, and she returned the favor mercilessly, wrestling lightly, all in good fun. *Fun*. That word, she repeated over and over.

"Johnny, are you in here?" Don asked, breezing into the kitchen, stopping short when he saw John and Sky shirtless. "Oh."

"Good morning, Doctor Don Yale. Come eat. I cook," Sky smiled, sliding off the counter, her breasts bouncing when her feet hit the floor. John scrambled to find his shirt and pull it on.

"Um," Don stammered.

"Cooked. I cooked," John corrected, wrangling her under her own shirt and pulling it over her head. "She has trouble with the past tense."

"But she speaks Rocanese now?" Don asked.

"I am learning at night," Sky said, sliding her arms into the sleeves of her shirt. "We have fun."

"I see," Don said slowly, still standing in the doorway, like he wasn't sure he wanted to be there. "I saw Douglas go out the window."

"Hawk is gone? To where?" Sky asked.

"The yard," John sighed, rubbing his chest. His body ached from the interruption, but at the same time, he was glad for the break to process what had just happened. "He'll brood for an hour, until he forgives you for breaking all his father's gadgets.

"Oh, this is her doing. I thought Douglas was making projects for himself," Don commented.

"He has plenty now," John commented.

"Johnny, you are in trouble," Don warned. "Dr. Frank will not keep quiet if she resists breeding, considering she is so comfortable with you. He's on his way. So is Mace. I wouldn't be surprised in the Intendant stopped by."

"I am not for breeding. I choose. I am comfortable to all I choose," Sky said, stepping into Don's personal space, looping her arms around his neck, pressing her hips against his. John bristled jealously, but the sour look on Sky's face said she was proving a point, not soliciting a response.

Don shuddered and closed his eyes, his hands instinctively rising to Sky's waist, before his face contorted in pain. "No one is comfortable with me."

"She is more than a potential breeder. Donny, I can't even begin to tell you—" He did try to say no to Sky, but Don was right. It didn't matter what Sky wanted, or even what he wanted. They didn't control their bodies. "What do I do now?"

"You've crossed a line, Johnny," Don said, sidling away from Sky, half-sinking into a chair, then deciding he didn't want to sit. "If this is what the two of you want, you need a license."

"What is that word?" Sky frowned, returning to John, and leaning so that her backside pressed against him.

Don translated into Trade and Sky's frown deepened. She questioned Don further about the license. In Rocan, it was an affirmation of consent and protection, more casual than the bond of a love union, not binding in the slightest. If anything, it was a way for Geneculture to track fertility outside of legally mandated coupling, and to prevent inadvertent cousin-coupling.

John listened for a moment, losing track of the Trade conversation, getting distracted by Sky's closeness. Running his fingers up and down her arms, he studied the soft, white fabric protecting her skin. There was no visible seam anywhere. It was a like a piece of fluid poured over her. She tilted her head to one side, and his lips gravitated toward her neck. She giggled when he made contact.

"Johnny!" Don cried, finally sinking into his seat.

Sky turned in his arms and laughed against his face. "I have troubles. I am not here to breed. I kiss you later."

"I am in so much trouble right now," he chuckled, wrapping his arms around her and pressing her body to his. He loved kissing this woman.

Douglas slipped outside of the Qu'Appelle gate. Every section of the city had its own little window to the outside world, and they opened occasionally to the brave 'explorers' who dared run ten feet to a degrading pagoda. Weather-watchers were the most common visitors. Douglas came out once a year to commemorate his father's life. Kneeling on the cold, stone floor of the pagoda, Douglas set out a fat, hand-made candle, diminished by years of remembrance. He laid his jacket over his knees, running a hand over the bird. Then the shadow of an intruder fell over him.

"Do you imagine your father coming out of the ice caps? Is that why you come outside the gate?" Celio Ferriera sneered. Sometimes Douglas swore Celio was stalking him. The man had been taunting him since their school days and his promotion to Overseer at the mine had fueled his ego.

"Please be quiet. I'm honoring the dead," Douglas said, closing his eyes and folding his hands.

"Traitors have no honor."

"Fathers are honored. Dead are honored. It is my right to honor him here." This was where he'd watched his father's glider explode in midair. After that day the small group that had protested the venture grew, blinded with fear of the dangers of crossing the sky-gods. They cried 'hoarder' and claimed his father had stolen valuable resources from the people for a pipe dream.

"He neither died here, nor is he buried here," Celio pointed out.

Douglas clenched his fists. "It is my right."

"You are not like him," Celio said, a manipulative hum in his tone. "Surrender that engine you've got wasting away in a glider that will never fly, and let us use it for the new Coureur. This is your city as much as mine, Hwan. Get your head out of the clouds and claim it."

Douglas whirled around. Celio wasn't supposed to know about Douglas' glider. It was a hodge-podge of scraps, scavenged from Caswell over many years, pieced together in secret. Celio must have happened upon it by accident, and it was beyond belief that he hadn't gotten Douglas in trouble for it already.

"Everything I do is for this city," Douglas said.

"Because it is yours. Let go of the engine. Show the Intendant you can do that, and he might consider releasing your mother."

Pinching his nose, Douglas fought to maintain composure. Celio was implying that the Intendant knew, and he was dangling before him a dream even more impossible than flying across the mountains. His mother was sick. As much as he wanted her to come home, he knew it would never happen. Yet, he couldn't let go. "That glider was my father's dream for me."

"Yes. And it killed him," Celio said.

The cruel words shredded Douglas' yearning for redemption. Howling with grief and anger, he leapt to his feet, decking Celio. The man quickly sprang up, grabbed Douglas' shirt, and threw him against the wall of the pagoda, but Douglas pushed back, tackling him, and they rolled out into the tundra. Gaining the upper hand, Douglas pressed his knee into Celio's rib and cocked his fist, but then decided better of it, and made a dash for his glider, leaving Celio in the cold.

The Coureur his father had built was gone. The one the Intendant wanted would likely never be finished. With every engine explosion, Douglas lost one more piece of his father. It was almost worth it to surrender the engine in his dilapidated glider, just so he could hold on to the rest of the pieces a little longer.

———

When John left, Sky felt the first hints of Spirit waking inside of her, leaving tingles in her chest. It was nothing painful; it was just normal. Never tired, never hungry, never human.

"I am glad your suffering is over, Sky. We will protect you," Dr. Frank had promised, his words making Sky cry. Frank assumed she was overcome with gratitude. He and Dr. Song had arrived shortly after Don. In private, Edwige quizzed her about her progress in leaving, begging again for Sky to save her children.

"Where is John?" Sky asked Don after the other doctors finally left.

"It's best for him to separate himself," Don repeated every time she asked. "Don't become too reliant on him, Sky."

"I'm not reliant. He's not hurting me," she protested, pacing the kitchen. "Am I hurting him? Am I? I don't mean to. I'll leave. I'll leave and never come back. I'll go right now."

Slinging her satchel over her shoulder, Sky walked to the back door, pausing when Don didn't protest. His eyes were down, and he had no intention of stopping her. Like Edwige, he seemed to think Sky would have a better life elsewhere, but he wasn't brave enough to say it out loud.

"Should I hit you?" Sky asked.

"Pardon?" He said it meekly, like he was used to being struck.

"So that you can say you tried to stop me," Sky explained, returning to the table.

"No, my darling," he chuckled, wiping lines of fear from his eyes. "That would only make the Constable chase you."

There was a knock at the front door, and Spirit settled into silence.

"John?" Sky murmured, bursting through the kitchen door to see. But Constable Mace was standing there, eyes narrowed, hand on his baton like he expected danger. Sky paused, head cocked, blinking slowly, but not daring to close her eyes for too long. Spirit was silent.

"John's brother?" she asked, stepping closer. Sky felt a blast that chilled her from the inside out, like the darkness that had consumed her the first time John touched her. She'd learned to move through it, like moving through a bog, but the bog felt thicker around Mace.

"What?" Mace relaxed and stood straight.

"I felt you. From all the way in there," Sky said. He and John had the same spirit-scent. "What are you? What's going on?"

"Sky, what's wrong?" Don asked, coming from the kitchen with John at his shoulder. It felt like a trap. John had been testing and honing the quelling power, but with Mace, he had reinforcements, and they could easily overtake her.

"Where's Hawk? Where is he? I need him," Sky whined, her head spinning.

"Sky, I'm here. Don't be scared," John said, his voice getting garbled by the ever-thickening bog in the spirit realm.

"It's too strong. You're too strong. Hawk!" she cried. The world went black, but then there was a light in the arena, and a whoosh of ethereal wings. Sky saw Hawk's red hair and his tattooed chest. His thumb traced her temple and he sang softly in Rocanese. The dream image that used to rescue her had merged with the person she now knew. She woke up on his dusty couch, in Hawk's smelly living room, with his petal-scented fingers tracing her lips.

"What happened Sky? You just dropped," he asked in Trade. She was on her back, covered with a light blanket, her head resting on a pillow on his lap. "Maybe you should've slept last night."

"They radiate sleep," Sky groaned, rubbing her head. "And both of them together, it was too strong. I couldn't fight it."

"I don't understand," he murmured, offering her a glass of juice. Sky lifted onto her elbows and took a drink. Hawk wasn't like John. The psychic scent he radiated would amplify John's, but by himself, it didn't affect her the same way.

"There's always so much noise. All the time, wading through the chaos." Sky took another drink. "When it's gone, there's nothing to hold me up."

"I do know that feeling," Hawk sniffled, hugging his knees to his chest as soon as she lifted her head.

"Where did he go?"

"John's over there. So is the Constable," Hawk said, pointing down the hall. "You kept calling my name, so they made me sit with you."

"Am I hurting you?" Sky asked, scooting to the other side of the couch. The way he spoke, it sounded was like she was violating him. "Am I hurting you by being here?"

"You destroyed my kitchen," he sighed. "My father—he built those things. He made that place for us and you ruined it. I don't know how to fix it. I can't do it."

"I can," Sky reassured, putting a hand on his foot, inching closer. "There's nothing I took apart that I don't know how to fix or that I can't turn into something better. I'll show you. There's something important I need to build."

"Cordova," he said, showing her his greasy, nicked hands. "Use your magic?"

Sky had a salve in her satchel that would heal his cuts, but she didn't want to risk falling into another trap.

"You see. She hasn't raised a hand toward him," John said in Rocanese, coming to the end of the hallway. "She is very protective of him."

Mace scowled. "Sky—"

He asked a question, but the Rocanese words weren't simple enough for her to follow.

"Translate," she said, keeping a light hold on Hawk's hand. The two men were blocking her avenue of escape, and she felt dizzier the closer they encroached.

"He says the Intendant has summoned you for a hearing regarding the incident at the Glass Walls," Hawk translated. "Sky, this isn't good. They could take you to asylum."

"Then I need your help," Sky said, taking both his hands. "I need you to take me to where you built the Coureur."

"Sky—"

"I didn't mean to hurt Felicity. But I felt something strange about her. Like she could touch a spirit-plane of existence," Sky confessed. "Like she was supernatural."

Hawk shrugged and squeezed his eyes shut. "So are you. Aren't you?"

"What do you mean?" she asked.

Hawk rocked forward. "I mean, you glow sometimes. Unless there's something wrong with my eyes."

"Am I glowing now?" she asked.

"Maman says my eyes are closed."

Sky panted and dropped her head back to the couch. He could see something of the other realm when he looked at her, but he didn't understand it. "Hawk, I've never been around anyone who can do to me what your people do. You have to help me get out of here."

Hawk clenched his jaw, his stomach knotting. "Can you keep a secret?"

"Yes. Tell me later." Sky kissed his forehead, then pried the gin bottle from his hand, handing it to John. "Now, I need to understand about the danger. The Intendant. Can you help me talk to the Constable?"

Hawk groaned and shook his head, curling into a ball, cuddling the broken toaster.

"Come with me, Sky," Mace said in Rocanese, venturing closer to the couch.

"Trade," Sky said. "Tell me in Trade."

If he wanted to arrest her, he was going to speak a language she understood.

16

"Is the Intendant a forgiving man?" Sky asked Hawk, leaning on the counter, munching on some bitter beets. He sat at the table, reassembling his toaster. They'd taken it apart and put it back together a dozen times already, and every time, he got faster. The thing would still short out, because the heating filament was flimsy.

"No. Not at all," Hawk mumbled, wiping his nose with the back of his hand. "He took my mother and he won't give her back. He's going to take you, too. I know it."

"He can't take me if I'm gone," Sky said, pursing her lips. "So, what's your secret? Do you have another Coureur?"

"Shh!" Douglas hissed. "Wait until John's sleeping."

"He is sleeping," Sky said. "I tucked him in an hour ago. He's out like a light."

"His light broke?" Hawk asked.

"That's not a literal statement."

"Then we can go," Hawk said, scooting his chair back and slipping his shoes on. Setting her plate by the sink, Sky slung her satchel over one shoulder.

"It's going to be cold," he whispered, handing her his flight jacket and putting on a coat of his own. "Quiet. Follow me."

They tiptoed until the door closed behind them, then Hawk took off at a run. The dim Dome lights did little to help them navigate, but Hawk stayed close to the center of the streets where the road was least broken.

"Quick and quiet," Hawk whispered. "You can't tell anyone. No one."

"I understand," she whined. The lights were almost completely out, and Spirit stirred in the darkness. "Hawk, I can't see."

"Trust me," he said.

Sky gasped for breath and switched on the flashlight of her Virp. If Hawk could share his secret, she could share one of hers. The device she wore was not a decorative glove.

"Will you show me how that works?" Hawk laughed, taking her hand, accidentally shining the light into his eyes. He covered the light and looked around. "We don't want to be seen."

"I can make it less bright," she said.

"We're almost there," Hawk promised. "Can't you—"

"I need light."

"Then point it down," Hawk instructed, guiding her at a slower pace, tripping over his feet because he couldn't stop staring at the Virp.

Sky smiled when he hopped the broken barrier dividing the populated part of town from the rest. Beyond that point, lights were sparse and parts of the buildings had been meticulously cut away. Even pieces of the street had been sheered, like the old town was being dismantled.

"This is where we need the light," Hawk breathed.

They wound through a few streets, then approached a silver building built into the Dome wall. It was one of the few places on the street that still had a door, and as soon as they were inside, Hawk turned on the lights.

The hanger held a single-engine glider, disconcertingly hacked together from spare parts, bearing on its shield the same hawk symbol as his flight jacket. It looked primitive, like the builder had seen a picture of the earliest flying machine and mimicked it. The top wasn't enclosed, and even if it had enough fuel to reach the mountains, the engine would stall out at that altitude.

"It's beautiful," Sky said, dropping his hand and circling the glider. "You built this? Without help?"

"I brought fuel from the yard this afternoon," Hawk said, running his hand over the wing. "I tried to leave once, but I didn't. That's when John started to get sick. I don't know if the gods were punishing me for trying to leave him or being too much of a coward to fly out on my own."

"So it's ready to fly," she said, climbing up to get a better look at the mechanics. The inside was as hacked together as the outside, the pieces painstakingly welded together with tools obviously meant for smaller jobs. She scanned a few with her Virp. "How many times have you tested this engine?"

"Only the one time. The biofuel is a renewable resource, but we don't stock much in the yard because it's explosive," he said, climbing into the cockpit and running his hand over the console. "I don't have a navigation panel. I was using the Coureur as a test bed, but I guess I don't have the hang of how all the gauges get calibrated or I would have known it was about to explode."

"I think metal fatigue was a serious factor in that," Sky said, showing him the command screen of her Virp. Her control panel wasn't in Trade, but the virtual keypad piqued his interest. "Where is the steering?"

Hawk moved a few levers, demonstrating the system. "The rudders were the easiest part."

"So it's just the details now," she said.

"Details matter," he said, fiddling with exposed wires where the gauges should have been. "My father spent years working the details and I haven't done half what he did."

"Then let's get to work," Sky said, rubbing her hands together. It was chilly in this part of the city, but it wasn't as drafty around this gate as the Qu'Appelle one. "Do you have tools?"

"You're not going to break it, are you?" he asked. "Like you did the kitchen?"

"Nothing was broken," Sky huffed. "Does it fly?"

"I think so," he whispered, his face getting pale.

"You put fuel in it, so you had to have some confidence," Sky pointed out.

"I had confidence in the Coureur, too," he said, wringing his hands. "I put you in there, and then . . . You looked inside it. Could you tell it was going to explode?"

"I wasn't paying attention," Sky shrugged. Now that she understood John's effect on her, she realized she'd passed out at the mine. She thought she'd just swooned for a second because she never stopped breathing. "I was overwhelmed by John. Like I said this afternoon, he radiates sleep. Fogs things up."

"I see things differently around him, too," Hawk confessed, lifting up one of the worktables on the perimeter, revealing a storage compartment in the support structure. He laid out a few wrenches, a mallet, and pieces of a compressor tool. "That's why I come out here to work. I see things more clearly. I look at the parts, and they talk to me."

"Talk to you?" Sky repeated, lifting the other tabletops to see what tools were available.

"It's not a literal statement," he said, sitting on the ground, assembling his compressor tool. "There is something wrong, though. With me."

"Am I glowing?" Sky teased, sitting across from him.

"You're red. You're fire." His breath hitched and he winced, keeping his eyes down.

"Take a look at this," Sky said, showing him the Virp embedded into a band on her forearm. "It's called a Virtual Projection Network Device. Virp for short."

She projected an image of her scan of the engine and Hawk flinched again. "It can scan the metal for fatigue. Acts as a two-way communicator. The other day, I got this message." She switched the translation to Trade.

"Where are you?" Hawk read, touching the words. His fingers penetrated the projection and he jumped back. "There's nothing there."

"It's a projection," Sky laughed, running her fingers through the image as well. "But the message is real, and I need to answer. I don't want to take this glider apart, but I do need parts. Like what you would need to finish the gauges and dials. Would those be in the yard?"

Hawk nodded, squatting down to see under the projection and pressing his finger against the Virp mount. "Can I hold it?"

"Only if you're going to help me," Sky said, springing to her feet and returning to the glider. Hawk followed, curiosity overwhelming his hesitation. Sky put the Virp onto his hand and showed him how to use the imaging feature to scan for weak points on the glider. Every time the results projected, he jumped, and after the third time, he gave the device back to Sky and climbed into the cockpit.

"The story of the goldens," he began, his voice shaking.

"I heard that one already," Sky said. He was nervous about sharing his glider, seeing her on it—seeing her as fire.

"Not the way my father tells it," he said, running his fingers over the flight controls. "The goldens came in a rocket from far away. They crashed into Caswell, and that's why this part of the city died. That's why no one can live here."

"Doesn't look broken to me," Sky commented. The hanger was built to incorporate the gate and the Dome wall, and that structure didn't have a crack in it.

"Because there are magic people, and they conjure materials just by thinking," Hawk said, glancing at her as though for confirmation. "They made it look like everything was still okay. To most people. But the other magics could see and remember everything that happened. Some choose to forget, but some aren't able. Those that remembered kept reminding everyone of the truth, and that's why they are Sequestered. So the magics take the voices of the Sequestered so they can't break the spell. That's why they don't talk when we find them. That's why they get sick, like Maman, and see things others don't. That's why she tells me to open my eyes—because it's wrong to hide the truth. But you don't make sense. You're magic and you don't see those things."

"I'm not magic, Hawk," Sky groaned. "Ready for a test flight? I'll show you how I got here. How I traveled from another city, no magic necessary. How this message got to me."

"We're going over the mountains?" Hawk asked.

"That gate goes outside, right?" she asked.

"No, no, no!" he cried, leaping from the glider, blocking the door. "It's the middle of the night. In the dead of winter!"

"That's why we have coats. You probably need a blanket," Sky said, finding a dirty drop cloth and wrapping it around his shoulders.

"I have blankets," he protested, twisting out of the cloth. "Everything I need to run is in the glider. But I'm not ready to run!"

"You brought me here for this," she said.

"What about John? We're not going to say good-bye?" he asked.

"We're not going over the mountains tonight," Sky assured. "The engine would stall at that altitude. I just want to show you what we can do."

Sky yanked open the Dome gate, letting loose a shower of caked dust. The chilled air cut through her borrowed coat. The moons were gone, but the starry sky was filled with pink and purple light.

"The aurora!" he whispered, his face changing.

"Beautiful, isn't it?" Sky grinned, swinging into the cockpit again. The controls were similar to the Coureur. The engine choked. "Hawk, I need you to fly this thing."

"Sky, if the glider is trapped in this valley, we shouldn't waste resources," Hawk said. "I should give Celio the engine."

"Don't you dare," Sky warned. "I'm taking off now. Stay clear of the propeller."

"But you're coming back?" he checked, climbing in, crowding her out of the pilot's seat. He started the engine, and stared at the gate, his shoulders tensing, his fingers pumping on the yoke.

"Go, before we run out of fuel!" Sky laughed, leaning over him, pushing the throttle to start them moving.

Hawk gasped.

"Do you want me to fly?" Sky offered. "I can show you how."

Hawk shook his head and swallowed hard. "If anyone is flying my glider tonight, it's going to be me."

The takeoff was choppy, and Hawk made jittery sounds as he fumbled the controls under her guidance. He flew the glider in a practice loop around the Dome, the small victory bringing tears to his eyes.

"Take me west about four miles."

"There are no gauges," he said, choking on emotion. Lining himself up with the Dome, he turned and headed straight for the streak of light where the aurora disappeared behind the mountains.

"West is that way," Sky said, pointing over his shoulder. "Don't waste fuel."

"There's something else I need to see first," he said. His eyes were dark and sad, belying none of the tension or nervousness she'd have expected. Shivering, she leaned forward, putting her hands on his shoulders to keep the wind from beating against her chest. Hawk banked the plane, circling around a shell of blackened land with a lump of ruins in the middle.

"What is that?" she asked.

"That's where my father died."

Douglas had been waiting his whole life for this moment. He was following in his father's footsteps, taking off toward the aurora, the cold air blasting against his face, making his cheeks numb. Whatever he'd expected, he wasn't prepared for the flood of emotion that came with seeing his father's wrecked plane from the air. He'd made it this far without suffering his father's fate, and while a part of him wanted to land, a part of him wanted to keep heading for those mountains and make the entire forty-mile loop his father had mapped out ten years ago. Sky's hand on his shoulder and her gentle words coaching him through landing were the only things that kept him together. It wouldn't have taken more than an hour to get here in the Coureur. It seemed so close now.

There was more left of his father's glider than he thought there'd be. The back half of the plane was intact, its red skin weathered, but clean. The tip of the hawk's wing was still visible on the shield, though the color was bleached. Everything from the wings forward was charred. The engine had taken out the forward cockpit when it exploded. What stopped Douglas in his tracks were the bones.

"It looks like someone has been here," Sky observed. "This wreckage was scavenged."

"Fire," Douglas murmured, shaking with the memory of the plane bursting into flames. He could still see the plume of black smoke rising toward the pink aurora. The black soot covered the bones. His fingers ached. "Sky, my hands are on fire."

"You're not on fire. You're freezing cold," she said, putting a blanket around his shoulders.

Douglas hiked the blanket up to protect his face, and climbed onto his father's plane. When he touched his father's bones, he felt a jolt, and the air caught fire, the red embers lighting the wreckage. He looked back at Sky, his throat tightening when he saw the long, scaly fingers closing around her throat. Sky wasn't the fireball; the clawed creature was.

"Is that your Sequesterer?" he asked, nearly falling off the glider. There were bits and pieces of dragon limbs, moving Sky like she was a puppet. It had to be a hallucination.

"Soon I will convince you that I'm not Sequestered at all. I am a traveler," she said, her voice crystal clear. He was seeing things that weren't there. He needed to check himself into asylum, whether he'd be near his mother or not.

"I need help," he whispered.

"I'm helping you." Sky hugged him, but he couldn't really see her anymore. His tears froze on his eyelashes. She took the bone and set it aside, and once it was out of his hands, he could feel the blanket around his shoulders again.

"I tried to leave before," Douglas whispered. "The glider is packed. The fuel was waiting. I've run before. Why can't I leave?"

"Well, for one thing, that little engine in your glider can't get you over the mountains," Sky said. "You have your father's eyes, don't you?"

Douglas shuddered. "You didn't know my father."

"He saw that the world didn't end at the Dome wall," Sky said, rubbing his arm. "You see it too. It doesn't end at these mountains. It doesn't end at Aquia. There are worlds beyond ours."

Douglas' father used to talk like that. Other Domes and other worlds were never treated like fantasy when Douglas was younger. Now, he wasn't sure what to believe. Sky had more perfect answers to his questions than an imaginary friend. Ever since she'd shown up, nothing had been quite the same. John was different. Rocan was different. Douglas felt like he had one foot in asylum already. Maybe the only way to get back to reality was to fight her. Fight Sky and the fairy tale she offered.

"Do you want to take the bones back to Rocan?" Sky asked, patting his arm. He was so cold, his body felt brittle.

"No," Douglas said. "No one can know we came out here."

Sky studied the bones. When she held them, she didn't glow. "Then lay him to rest here."

"How can he rest here? All he ever wanted was to leave this valley, and here we are. Trapped by mountains too high to fly past. Sequestered."

Hawk lay on the frozen tundra next to a pile of stones covering the dozen bone fragments they'd wrestled from the wreckage. There were no tears in his eyes. If anything, Sky saw peace in him.

"The sun is rising," she said, touching his skin to make sure he hadn't gone hypothermic. The blankets covering him were frosted stiff.

"Who will take care of Maman if we go? Who will take care

of John?" Hawk asked, his teeth chattering, his fingers turning over a pebble that he couldn't seem to leave on the grave.

"I think he'll manage," Sky said. "Doesn't he have six wives?"

Hawk half-laughed, half-cringed. "Did he tell you that?"

Sky shrugged.

"I'm not sure 'wife' is a valid translation for a breeding partner, but yes, I think six is right. More than that, if you count the pairings that didn't yield conception," he answered. He furrowed his brow and took one of the smaller stones from his father's grave. "I have several myself."

Tucking the stone in his pocket, he retreated to the glider.

"I thought you only kissed men," Sky asked, trotting to keep up.

"Breeding partners are a special consideration," Hawk muttered, climbing into the cockpit, not offering to help Sky up. He switched on an electric box, letting the engine warm so he could start it.

Sky climbed onto the wing, resting her arms on the lip of the cockpit. "Colleen says your people 'breed the love out of families.'"

"We distinguish between unions of love and unions for breeding as a necessity. Before John's generation, too many men of strong stock were left unmarried and childless, while the ill begat more ill," he said. "The reason John is paired so often is that his children survive. He has fourteen, all living. All. His prior partners request him even beyond their breeding obligations, and no petition is denied when the probability for live birth is so high."

"No wonder he feels used," Sky said, feeling her temper flare. Hawk cringed. "And you? Do you have children?"

Hawk nodded. "I'm not their father. They have parents who love and care for them. And John—he wasn't a father until he took me. There's no reason for you to be jealous of his breeding partners. He has no attachment to them. But he hasn't put down that Trade primer since he met you. I've never seen him more desperate to have a conversation with a woman."

"Hawk, do you think John would leave Rocan?" Sky asked.

"I can never leave, can I? I'm trapped. Imprisoned. Tied down," he said, the shivers overtaking him. "There's a noose around my neck and it keeps tugging."

"There's no noose," she said, threading her fingers under his. "Hawk, look at me."

His pupils were dilated, and his skin was losing color.

"I can't see you. My vision is red. I can't see you at all. Just the prison."

"It's not real, Hawk. Not physical," she said, hugging him close to share body heat. Spirit kept her warm, but she had no idea if he could feel that warmth.

"I can't go to asylum. No one helps. They just hide you," he whispered.

"I will take care of you," she promised. "Hawk, I need to find a way to send a message to my friends. You have to take me to the yard when we go back. Or you have to bring things back to the house. Do you understand?"

"Are you in?" he asked, putting a hand on the yoke. "Sky, we have to go."

"Hawk, you can't see. Let me fly."

17

Douglas lay in a nest of clothes on the floor of the hanger bay with Sky spooned around him. Her body felt so hot it burned his skin. He could barely make out her form, she glowed so bright. They'd huddled together next to the glider's engine, taking advantage of the heat radiating off it.

"I don't have medicine for this, Hawk," Sky said, running her warm hand over his neck, feeling his pulse. "If you're not walking in ten minutes—"

"I'll walk now," he said, sitting up. He felt defeated, having finally taken the glider up only to turn around and come back here. Sky wrapped the blanket around him, but he shrugged it off. "This stays here. It was hard enough stealing it the first time. I don't want it reclaimed for Rocan."

"So you acknowledge you're a thief," Sky grinned, helping him stand. They folded the blankets and stashed the extra supplies, ready for the day when he'd have the courage to leave. His shivers subsided once they started moving, and he sipped liberally from his hip flask until Sky looked human again. Caswell felt darker without her glow. They heard the faint gong of the clock tower in Qu'Appelle, and Douglas cringed.

"John was exhausted," Douglas rambled, swaying as they walked. "If we're lucky, he'll sleep through the morning and won't even know we're gone. He never gets enough sleep, so he crashes pretty hard. You tucked him in. Thanks. Thanks for making him lie down. He never takes care of himself."

"Calm down, Hawk. He's in better shape than you," Sky said, flipping on her flashlight to illuminate the road.

"It sneaks up on you, you know. Little things. They took Maman away because I couldn't take care of her," Douglas said, cringing at the memory of his mother being hauled from their home in restraints. John was nearly sixty and if anyone found out how often he suffered numbness down his arm or bouts of confusion, he'd be kept from work. He'd suffer as Kinley did, receiving basic resources. Food and water, but no medicine to fight the mental degradation.

"Hwan! I knew I'd find you here!" Celio Ferriera shouted, running toward them. Sky reached for a weapon, but Douglas charged at Celio first.

"Are you stalking me, Celio!" Douglas retorted.

"Half the town is looking for you two," Celio said, grabbing Douglas by the collar and hustling him back to the Qu'Appelle border. "You're lucky it was me who found you."

"I don't feel lucky," Douglas muttered, swatting at Celio's arms. His joints were stiff and aching, his vision getting hazier the faster he moved.

"Couldn't resist taking her to see your little project, could you?" Celio crooned.

Douglas clenched his fist.

"Hawk?" Sky whispered. She wasn't following the conversation, but she caught the sentiment.

"He knows my secret," Douglas whispered in Trade.

"Do you want me to kill him?" she offered.

Douglas' eyes widened, his vision going red. The claws clamped around Sky's body reached out, swiping at Celio.

"No, you can't kill him!" Douglas cried, waving his hand until the threat dissolved into smoke. "He's Celio! He's annoying! He's not dangerous."

"I understand Trade!" Celio shouted at the pair of them, pushing Douglas into the smoke cloud. "I found them! Tell the Constable, I found them!"

Douglas froze, unable to see, but able to hear the cacophony of shouts and running feet. Celio wasn't lying about the search parties and if the Constable retraced their steps, he wouldn't be as forgiving of the project as Celio. Hoarding resources was punishable by death, and the Intendant was angry enough at Douglas over the Coureur. He flailed his hand until he felt Sky take it.

"Is it too late for you to fly us past the mountains?" he asked.

"Too early," she said, kissing his knuckles. Then she let go, leaving him blind and helpless.

"Channing! What is wrong?" she called, addressing Constable Mace informally in Rocanese.

Douglas closed his eyes, focusing on the sounds.

"Oh, thank the gods," John cried, plowing past Douglas, nearly knocking him over. Douglas reached blindly for him, but John's muffled cries were directed elsewhere. "I'm sorry, I'm so sorry."

"It's not your fault," Sky whispered. "Hawk, tell him. Tell him."

Phantoms floated in Douglas' vision, creating vague forms from the shroud of darkness. Sky glowed red as before, but her light was eclipsed by John's shadowy form.

"What were you thinking, Hwan!" Constable Mace said, jerking Douglas' arm, jarring him from the cloud, back into the real world. "You've been missing half the morning. You're concussed, she's–well, we don't know what she is yet. Where have you been?"

"Concussed," Douglas repeated, falling against Mace's arm, barely able to catch his breath. The phantoms in his vision were from the injury; not dementia. He thought Sky had healed him, but it was just part of the illusion.

"They were on the running trail," Celio piped up. "Sky tried to leave the Dome."

"It wasn't like that," Douglas stammered, not sure why Celio would lie for him or accuse Sky. "That's not . . ."

Douglas' jaw dropped. John's sobs had softened to moans and kisses! He was kissing Sky. "John?" Douglas stuttered.

"You got a license for that, Harris?" Mace chuckled.

"We're not breeding. It's just a kiss," John replied, rubbing his cheek on Sky's shoulder.

"He's in love with her. He hasn't even asked how you are," Celio crooned, sidling next to Douglas, dropping his voice. "He'll give up your secrets to keep her."

"Shut up," Douglas growled, pinching his nose.

"You're not his child anymore," he taunted. "Are you going to cling to the past?"

Douglas grabbed the front of Celio's shirt and threw a punch. The other men were on him in a flash, separating him from Celio. The smoke returned and the world went dark. Then just like the day of the Coureur explosion, an angel descended into the flames, her touch cooling the heat of his grief.

"Don't make trouble," Sky whispered, pressing his face to her chest. "Can't escape the Sequestering if you're dead. Don't make trouble."

"It's not too late, Hwan," Celio smirked at Douglas.

Douglas' ears flushed, but then his body went cold. He scratched at his neck, feeling for the noose he'd been so convinced was there a few hours ago. There was no escape from

Rocan. He was Sequestered here. Sky's soothing tones echoed until they became noise. Celio was giving him a chance. All he had to do was surrender the glider's engine.

Douglas sat on the front porch, wrapped in a warm blanket, brooding from his latest mental lapse. The phantoms in his vision were starting to feel normal, and it scared him. Capping his flask, he tucked it into his shirt pocket, listening for the tap of the metal against the pebble he'd taken from his father's grave. It was the only proof he had that last night's adventure wasn't a dream.

Sky had insisted on a warm bath and hot tea, and while the bath did stop his shivers, he suspected she wanted him occupied so that she and John could slink away to the bedroom. They were unabashedly loud in love making and Douglas was tired of listening. He knew Sky had been flirting with John and he knew John was intrigued. But after so many years of seeing John deny himself, Douglas had not foreseen this turn of events.

"Mon Hwan!" a little girl cried, breaking away from her mother and charging up the street. Sylvie, a former breeding partner of his, called after young Noelle, but the toddler stumbled into Douglas' lap. Douglas hopped to his feet, cursing, and Sylvie grabbed the little girl.

"What did I tell you about jumping on other people? What did I tell you?" Sylvie admonished the girl.

"What did I tell you about bringing her to my home?" Douglas grumbled, plopping down on the step. He wanted to flee, but didn't want to go inside; didn't want to hear Sky and John going at it.

"We're not in your home. We're outside," Sylvie said, sitting next to him on the porch, keeping Noelle in a death grip until the girl's pleas to be let go reached earsplitting levels.

"I need to talk to you about this Exception," Sylvie said, attaching a leash to Noelle's shirt so the girl couldn't run too far. Noelle had Douglas' lidless eyes and Sylvie's fair skin.

"What's to talk about?" Douglas asked.

"I had requested you," she said. "It's my first breeding since Noelle was born and I wanted to be with you."

"I got blown up, Sylvie. I'm badly concussed. The Exception is not negotiable," Douglas said.

"You look fine to me," she said. "You've been getting around the city just fine."

"My doctor says I'm not cleared for breeding," he said.

"Then he's wrong. It's not a Level Four labor task. You just lie on your back for ten minutes," she scoffed. "Can't you get an exemption from your Exception?"

Douglas rolled his eyes and stood. The law allowed for almost any physical injury to justify an Exception, because if mental trauma were an excuse, no one would breed. Douglas was not about to pass up the opportunity to skip a call. "Thank you for coming by, Sylvie."

"No, don't cap this conversation, Douglas," she protested, grabbing his pant leg. "I want my children to have the same father."

"If you want your child to have a father, then get a love union," Douglas said, flicking her hand. "I am a breeding partner. And I want you to leave."

"I thought you were kinder than other men," she fumed. She could wish all she wanted, but she'd never have the luxury of all her children having the same father unless she was referring to only the ones she kept.

Douglas sank back to the porch step, put his head between his knees, and laced his fingers behind his head. He'd worried enough about passing his golden skin to his children, now he worried about their mental health.

"I got blown up," he apologized, not wanting to worry her with talk of phantoms.

"We are glad you survived," Sylvie said, taking Noelle's hand. "Noelle, give Mon Hwan his gift."

"Here, Mon Hwan," the little girl said on cue, handing him a crumpled portrait of herself, painted by an artisan. Every year, they took the canvas to have it updated, so that Douglas would have a picture of her. He had portraits of all his living children.

Sylvie's silence as they left did more to add to his guilt than any of her words, but she took Noelle's hand and left. It was unusual for a breeding partner to keep in touch with a non-custodial parent. Douglas couldn't decide if the connection with his child did more to lift his spirits or rip him to shreds. He stood, debating whether or not he should chase them. When Don Yale rounded the corner, the urge to run quadrupled.

"She wasn't successful," Douglas informed. "That's why you're here, isn't it? What is wrong with you?"

He ran inside and slammed the door. The grunts and sighs from the bedroom left little to the imagination, and he covered his ears, flopping into the chair. Don opened the front door, but stopped in the doorway.

"Can my Exception be repealed if a woman requests me?" Douglas asked.

"I don't want to talk about breeding," Don murmured.

"You figured Sylvie could pressure me on her own," Douglas snapped, kicking the wall.

Don flinched. A tear escaped his bloodshot eyes, but he wiped it away and backed out of the house.

"Hey, get back here!" Douglas said, leaping up and grabbing his sleeve. "Where do you think you're going? Are you here for Sky? You're not going to report them! She seduced him!"

"Let me go," Don whispered. His skin was cold to touch, his face pale, his eyes glazed. Douglas had seen that look a thousand times, and he knew someone was dead.

"No! I'm not letting you leave," Douglas said, dragging him back into the house. "I'm not—"

"Douglas!" John warned, running from the bedroom, shirtless and sweaty. "Stop picking fights."

"I'm not picking a fight!" Douglas protested. "Something's wrong."

"If you're going to break the law, Johnny, you might pretend to show a little discretion," Don teased, the fake laugh announcing that he was not okay. "I was never here."

"You're not leaving, friend," John said, pulling Don into a hug. "You lost a mother?"

Don nodded, his composure crumbling. Douglas swore, racking his brain to remember who was due this month. Life was so fragile. Douglas didn't want to think about dying women and he definitely didn't want to explain Don's tears to Sky. "Don, can you give me medical clearance to work?" he asked.

Don waved dismissively, his momentary burst of emotion dissolving into numbness. John laid him on the couch.

"Dr. Song asked me to take Sky to the yard to test her mechanical acumen. Can I take her with me, Don?" Douglas asked. It was the flimsiest cover for getting Sky into the yard, and Douglas felt bad for taking advantage, but he felt obligated to try.

"Stop, Douglas," John warned. "He's in no condition."

"Let her live as she wants," Don croaked. "She is more than a womb."

Douglas waited a beat for John to protest—to tell him to stay home, lie down, and take care of himself—but John was focused on his friend. Poking his head out the front door, Douglas whistled for a messenger.

"There's breakfast made. Already warm on the stove," Douglas said, getting a blanket for Don. "You should probably eat. You, too, John."

"Think you can eat, Donny?" John whispered, tucking the blanket around his friend.

"Do you want me to fix a plate?" Douglas asked, hurrying to get the two settled so he could leave. Sky wandered out of the bedroom, naked, blond hair askew.

"Sky!" Douglas laughed. "Where are your clothes?"

"Bath," she replied, pointing down the hall.

"Make it quick. We're heading to the yard in ten minutes," Douglas said.

"I'm ready now," Sky said, turning back to the bedroom.

"Not until you wash off that sex smell," Douglas said, snapping and pointing to the bathroom. "Ten minutes. The messenger has to get there first."

18

To Douglas, this week was about the upset and destruction of his sanctuaries. His Coureur was gone, his home invaded by visitors, his favorite bar turned into a crime scene, his sacred hanger exposed, and now he was bringing Sky to the yard.

"Don't look at me like that," Sky laughed, taking his hand.

The show of affection both calmed and confused him, so he pulled his hand free and wiped it on his pants. "You had sex with my father. The only other person who has ever been in his bed is Don."

"They're lovers?" Sky asked.

Douglas sighed. "Not every relationship is about sex."

"Douglas!" McGill Lefevre shouted, hustling out of the yard, phantom wings spread in anger. Douglas jumped, then forced a smile, shaking his head to clear the hallucination. "It's bad enough that you sneak in when you aren't cleared, but you can't shut down all our projects and bring a woman on site! The Intendant will kill you."

"Sky, meet McGill," Douglas said. "McGill builds conveyors for the processing plant."

McGill did a double-take, the redness in his cheeks spreading down his neck. "Whoa."

"Really? She's twice your—" Douglas stopped, looking from Sky to McGill. "Actually, I don't know how old you are. You look younger next to him."

"Age is a matter of perception," Sky smiled. "What he sees is the way I look at him."

McGill shuddered on inhaling, enraptured by the sound of Sky's voice, even though he didn't speak Trade.

"Then stop looking at him like that," Douglas hissed. That sound McGill made brought back memories of their past relationship.

"Jealous?" Sky teased.

"John would be, and if you hurt him . . . I won't help you anymore," Douglas threatened. Then he snapped his fingers in front of McGill's face and switched to Rocanese. "Is the floor safe, yet?"

"Women aren't permitted. I can't shut down fifteen projects Level Four for one sightseer," McGill said. He tried to sound snappy, but his mouth had gone dry, and he wanted Sky to stay.

"Of course I wouldn't ask you to do that," Douglas said, touching the back of McGill's hand, taking a page from Sky's playbook. "This town is in need of inspiration, and it starts here, today."

McGill looked at Douglas, surprised. His blue eyes sparked with hope. He moved his fingers to bump against Douglas again, but then shook his head and crossed his arms. Douglas did the same.

"Douglas!" a young female designer squealed, skipping down the street.

Sky tensed, her hand going for a weapon, but Douglas put her behind him.

"Douglas, Douglas, Douglas! Is it true?! Your message! Can I?

Can I really?" Zoe squeaked, breathless and jumping. Although women weren't permitted to be a part of equipment testing and refurbishing at the yard, several were schooled in electrical and mechanical design and actively contributed to Rocan's innovations. Douglas met with Zoe and the other designers regularly, and brought non-volatile parts from the yard for them to analyze.

"McGill, do you know Zoe?" Douglas asked.

"Only by her designs," McGill said, shaking the woman's trembling hand. "What brings you here?"

"To work the floor! To see my Coureur come to life!" Zoe exclaimed, dancing in a circle. "Please tell me this isn't a prank. The others didn't come because they said it was a prank, but Douglas doesn't play pranks. Not about something like this. Right?"

McGill exchanged a look with Douglas and Douglas nodded, confirming that this was his plan. Since he had to secure the yard to get Sky here, Douglas had sent messengers to all the Level One workers at the design lab, inviting them to the floor for hands on experience, open-ended until the engine tests began again.

"We're still finalizing preparations," McGill sighed. "But there might be more motivation to secure the place if you just come in now."

"Ramsey uses her work. She can apprentice with him," Douglas said. "Zoe, do you speak Trade?"

"No. Is that a problem?" she asked. "I can learn."

"No, I was asking for Sky. She's just learning Rocanese. She likes learning from women," Douglas said, leading Sky inside. Douglas didn't know Trade words for a lot of the machinery in the yard.

"They'll be here when they realize it's not a prank," Zoe

laughed, hesitating at the entry. This area had been forbidden to her for her entire life.

Douglas paused, his own nervousness rising. He'd taken a lot of liberties in interpreting permission, but Eddie had begged him to help Sky, and after their adventure with the glider, he knew it was beyond his ability to figure out what she needed on his own.

"Come," Sky said, taking Zoe's hand and smiling. Zoe grinned and shivered, but even Sky's persuasive smile couldn't override a lifetime of indoctrination about the dangers of Level Four facilities.

"Zoe!" Ramsey called, trotting down the stairs, picking up speed when he saw her. Zoe's feet remained planted until Ramsey embraced her, lifting her off the ground and spinning her around, setting her down inside the threshold. "Is it true?" he asked Douglas, tears in his eyes.

Douglas nodded, caught off guard by the elder man's emotion. "Conditionally. I would like you to mentor her. You are most familiar with her work."

"Our work," Zoe said, relaxing her embrace and leaning her head on Ramsey's shoulder. "You know he's my father, right?"

Douglas laughed and shook his head. "It does explain a lot."

Word of the mechanical yard's open house spread like wildfire through the community. Twelve more designers showed up within the first twenty minutes and more came every hour. People started coming from other backgrounds, not just the design studio. A few men normally restricted to Level One and Two jobs trickled in as well.

When Zoe first stepped in, it had stirred a ruckus among the men. Douglas had warned them to clean their stations for apprentices and close out any Level Four projects, but many of them still argued against the presence of a woman . . . until the next woman arrived and Douglas assigned her to a mentor. Now every new arrival stirred cheers. Most of the men were eager to train an apprentice. For the first time in a while, there was joy in his work and hope for progress.

Douglas sat on the stairs, overlooking the entrance to the yard, arms folded on the railing.

"What is that?" Sky asked, trotting from her work bench toward a roped off area.

Douglas glanced over his shoulder, reaching out for her, but lacking the energy to jump up and stop her. "That is where we test compression chambers. Very dangerous. We have twenty-two Level Ones on the floor today, so no one is going in there."

"Do you have any more of these recorders?" Sky asked, holding up a metal cube that she'd rooted out of his hobby box.

"Recorders?" he repeated, rolling onto his knees. "Is that what it is?"

Sky tapped the side, and the unassuming metal cube projected a tinny voice, speaking in Rocanese.

"How did you do that?" he asked, hauling himself to his feet. They'd found hundreds of these littered around Caswell over the years, and had only just determined they weren't explosive and could be handed over to the designers.

"I'll show you," Sky said, handing it to him, then heading back to the workbench. The table was neatly organized with wire filaments and metal tubes lined up, just as she'd done when she dismantled his kitchen. She'd also collected several broken and worn motor belts.

"What are you making?" he asked.

"A two-way communication device. Like an electronic messenger boy."

"Or a telephone!" Douglas grinned. "We have a few of those

around. The Chiefs of Law, Medicine, and Mining all have direct lines to the Intendant. There's some in the hospital too."

"I don't suppose you have one here," Sky said.

Douglas smiled. "It's amazing. Can you build more? Do you want to wire it into the system? The Constable has a telephone near his office."

"I don't need wires," Sky said. "This has a *transceiver*."

Douglas didn't know that word, but any system that didn't require wires to function would save resources. "If you're going to communicate, don't you need two to make it work?"

"When we get this to my *Bobsled*, hopefully we can get the power I need to respond to the message my friends sent," Sky said, sinking onto her stool, holding her flashlight glove next to the electronic device. She hadn't let Douglas take apart her toys. "As soon as I send a message back—"

"Sky, you can't talk like that around here," Douglas warned, twiddling the recorder between his fingers. "What we did—what you saw—it has to stay secret."

"They're coming!" McGill hissed, charging over to Douglas' workstation, wrinkling his nose at Sky. "The Intendant and Dr. Frank are coming and they look angry. Did you lie to me?"

"Relax, McGill," Douglas said, standing slowly, rubbing his aching head. "I'll—"

"What in the name of the gods is going on here?" Intendant Hubert bellowed, storming onto the main floor. Douglas put a hand on McGill's shoulder, then went to the catwalk, glad he was seeing people and not fireballs. Douglas was so scared of the phantoms he saw, he didn't dare pick up a tool today.

"Mons, please come into my work area," Douglas called, motioning him up the stairs. "The rest of you, resume your projects."

Frank sputtered, his double chin wobbling under his deep-set scowl. His bushy white eyebrows furrowed so hard, they blended together over the black eye that Sky had given him. Intendant Hubert raked his fingers through his thinning white hair, taking notice of the women on the floor.

"What have you done?" Frank growled, stomping up the steps.

"Making use of an asset before you destroy her through confinement," Douglas said, pointing over to the bench where Sky worked. "There she is. Working. Or she was until you hollered."

"Hwan, I agreed to give her a hearing. We don't terminate people for starting bar fights. If we did, the whole town would be dead," Hubert seethed, seeming to rise up the stairs on a cloud of anger. "You put her in danger by bringing her hear. You're the one who needs to worry about termination."

"We have a lot of new people on the floor today," Douglas said. "Once we made the place safe for Sky, it seemed only reasonable to bring in others who showed interest. You're always saying people are more eager to work when they feel inspired."

Frank sputtered, darting to the catwalk. He'd been so angry about Sky, he hadn't noticed the other workers. "You have women on the production floor?"

"Individually supervised," Douglas said proudly, leaning on the rail, then pulling back when he felt it give under his weight. "I've had to turn people away because I don't have enough supervisors. I thought I should get permission to skew the ratio beyond one-to-one. Would you—"

Hubert raised a warning finger and Douglas bit his tongue. "I appreciate your initiative, Hwan, reckless as it may prove to be. Is she skilled in mechanics at all?"

"Beyond skilled," Douglas laughed. "We take broken tech and we try to figure out how it worked. She just knows."

"Perhaps she has more bravado," the Intendant suggested.

"Do you know what that is?" Douglas smirked, showing

them the recorder. "I didn't. I pressed all of the buttons, I tried locating the power source. None of the words are legible, but after I determined that it was not an explosive, I deemed it safe for Level Two and set it aside to be dismantled. Then Sky picked it up." Douglas placed the device in the Intendant's hand and activated it, playing back a distorted voice on the ancient speaker.

"An audio device," Hubert breathed, holding it to his ear.

"We have so many of these tucked into scrap boxes," Douglas continued.

"Amir, listen," Hubert said, holding the box between them. A woman's voice specified the date and indicated that she was keeping a research log about a rocket program.

"It's over two hundred years old," Frank said, his eyes lighting with wonder.

"And nothing but scrap until yesterday." Douglas shut it off, not wanting to drain the power source, since he didn't know what was powering it. "I don't know how she got this to work. On the one hand, I want to open it up and see what she did—"

"No!" Hubert cried, cradling the device against his chest.

"Don't worry. I called a historian to transcribe the records first," Douglas assured. "Sky's intuition for technology is not like mine. She is trained with the knowledge of the Dome Builders. We have so much we can learn from her, and she is behaving now that she has had time to learn about us."

"Will the new Coureur be done any faster?" the Intendant asked.

"Maybe a little," Douglas shrugged. "We have such a free flow of knowledge today that other projects will benefit as well. Intendant, please don't divide our workforce."

"I don't approve of your methods, Hwan," the Intendant growled. "Take your builders to the design studio. Not the other way around. I want this floor cleared!"

"No," Douglas exclaimed. "This place has come to life today, and breaking down barriers is a part of it. We can fix every engine, we can build everything we need to survive. We will do it with or without your support, but our place is here! My place is here!"

The realization hit hard; it was the first time he hadn't felt like a transient in his own home. Celio was right. As long as he kept his glider, he would never take his place in Rocan. Sky would die trying to escape, and he couldn't let her. It was time for that dream to end. "My place is here."

19

The temperature dropped below freezing outside *Oriana*, and inside felt pretty much the same. The engines did not pulse and the air vents did not circulate heated air to counteract the chill. The heat of re-entry radiated away, and Corey's lifeless body grew stiff on the exam table in the infirmary.

Captain Danny Matthew's hands were numb, his mind in a fog. Corey, their pilot, had died in the night, but the rest of them still needed saving. Gravity weighed him down. After four days of weightlessness, his limbs were weak, and after losing Corey, so was his heart.

"You're obsessed with that stupid *Bobsled*," his brother Tray griped, stomping down the stairs into the cargo bay. Danny had limped the ship through the valley all evening, determined to find the source of the signal. "Why are you bringing it on board? Look at it! It's wrecked. And you followed it here. You damned us all!"

Danny shoved his hands into his gloves, gritting his teeth. He had been tracking the *Bobsled* for four days. It was a whim. A dream. A chance to reconnect with an old friend. He'd first received the *Bobsled's* signal when they were still on the moon.

With their own comms damaged, salvaging the *'sled* was their best chance to find help.

"You can tell he's eaten because he's talking to me again," he muttered to Saskia. His breath formed a cloud in front of his face every time he exhaled.

Saskia closed her eyes and leaned against the wall, tuning out the fight. She was a lean soldier, armed to the teeth. The collar of her black coat was pulled high and her dark hat low so that only her eyes were exposed. A pair of goggles dangled from her gloved hands, but she was waiting for Danny's order before she put them on.

"Make jokes all you want," Tray snapped. "It won't change what you did. Corey is dead because of you. Amanda is dead!"

Tray smacked the controls that opened the cargo bay doors and the icy air whooshed into the bay. "It's now or never. This is the only time the sun and shadows are in our favor for not dying. Not that the odds are ever in our favor with you in charge."

Saskia donned her goggles and was out the door before the ramp fully lowered. Danny shot his little brother a look, but followed her out.

"Is there any way we can get a brace on that landing gear? The front wheel is broken," Danny observed, trying to remain dispassionate as he circled the wrecked vehicle. Standing on tiptoe, he checked the cockpit for signs of a body. There were smears of blood on the controls, but no pools.

"It's so cold, I'd be surprised if any of the wheels still turn," Saskia said, giving the *'sled* a nudge to see if it moved. "I thought this was supposed to be lightweight."

"It is. We're weak," Danny said, angling himself under the nose and testing the weight on his back.

"Why don't you answer me?" Tray shouted, standing just

inside the bay. "Do you still have ears or have they frozen and chipped off? "

"You're just yelling to keep yourself warm!" Danny hollered back. "If you want us to move faster, get out here and help! I can't lift this thing on my own."

"I've been telling you for years to buy a grav-lift," Tray retorted, stepping carefully out onto the tundra. His work boots were new and had never been used for actual work.

"When we get back to Quin. First thing," Danny grunted, throwing his weight against the *Bobsled*. The back wheels were frozen into the permafrost.

"Keep going," Saskia ordered. "We don't need the wheels. Ready? Heave!"

With each of them at a wheel, they inched their way back toward *Oriana*.

"We could use the crane," Tray frowned, stepping back as soon as his wheel made it to the foot of the ramp.

"You couldn't suggest that a half hour ago?" Danny commented. Gravity sickness loomed and every ounce of exertion threatened his balance.

"I couldn't see the broken wheel a half hour ago," Tray said.

"Keep pulling. By the time we get the crane set up, we'll have the sun on our backs," Saskia said.

"We don't need the whole *'sled*. Just the transmitter," Tray griped, heaving again. "It doesn't look that bad. Maybe Chase walked away. Maybe someone found him and carried him away," he added, climbing around the *'sled* to help Danny pull.

"Back wheels in! Good enough," Saskia said, smacking the controls. The ramp shifted upward, dumping the *Bobsled* into the bay.

"Whoa! Whoa! Not out of the way yet!" Danny cried, yanking Tray's arm and tossing him clear of the *Bobsled*. Tray screeched.

Saskia groaned. They all lay on the floor of the bay, out of breath, dizzy from gravity.

"Everyone . . ." Saskia panted, rolling onto her side, clutching her head. The combination of cold and gravity sickness had warped her judgment.

Suddenly, Saskia scrambled to her feet and fumbled for her weapon. There was a scream at middeck and the hatch slammed shut.

"Amanda?" Danny called weakly, pushing up on his elbows. "Amanda, come back!"

"Amanda's dead," Saskia said, stumbling to the stairs. "Intruder?"

"Corey saved her," Danny replied. He'd found Amanda stashed in his quarters late last night, shortly after Corey died. Before that, they'd all assumed she had been ejected with the last escape pod. Danny thought he'd told them. He remembered mumbling something about it when he'd chugged his breakfast that morning. Time passed slowly, but the moments all coalesced into one overwhelming lump of grief.

The upstairs hatch opened again and Amanda aimed a pulse rifle at Saskia. "Guard!" she hollered.

"No! Amanda! Put the weapon down," Danny warned. "Put it down!"

Amanda's attention wavered and Saskia shot first, felling Amanda.

"Saskia! What are you doing?" Danny cried, pushing to his knees, the surge of adrenaline overwhelmed by the weight of fear.

"My job," Saskia said, using the handrails to steady herself as she made her way up the stairs. Amanda lay on the catwalk, either kicking or having a seizure. "Tray, get the stretcher!"

Danny sat on his heels, clutching his spinning head. He crawled over to his brother, new fears lapping over the old.

"Tray?" Danny asked.

Tray lay on his side, his arms wrapped around his torso, his eyes open, but distant.

"You're fine; thanks for asking," Danny prompted. That was what Tray said when he felt ignored.

"You dislocated my shoulder," Tray mumbled, the intensity of the whispered accusation stinging just as bad as his yelling.

"You were about to be crushed." Danny moved Tray's hand aside and reached under the coat, feeling the joint. Tray's eyes squeezed shut. He was recovering from Moon Pox, and his skin was rough with slow-healing blisters.

"It's not dislocated," Danny said, pulling his hand free. Tray's shoulder felt swollen. Danny shouldn't have guilted him into helping. "Let's get you to the infirmary."

"Not enough beds." They had two beds; Corey's body lay on one, and Amanda would soon be in the second.

"There's always room for—"

"I don't want to go in there," Tray said, pulling his coat closed, hissing in pain. His neck was raw where a rash was fading, and his eyes were bloodshot.

"Fine. Lie on the floor in the coldest part of the ship," Danny grumbled, flicking his brother's cheek.

"One of you get up here! I don't care which," Saskia shouted, dragging Amanda through the hatch to the heated galley.

"Is she dying?" Danny called. "It's not like I have the energy to carry her down here. We're all too gravity sick. We can't help her!"

A tidal wave of grief washed over him and he bowed over Tray.

"You're not going to cry on my shoulder," Tray snarled, kicking his feet. "This isn't the time. You pathetic, worthless waste of air!"

Danny froze, hearing the damning words of his stepfather in Tray's voice, a much older source of guilt creeping in.

"I hate you," Tray whimpered, pressing his cheek to the top of Danny's head.

"I hate me now, too," Danny said.

"Get off my shoulder. It hurts."

Danny shifted his weight, but kept his face close to Tray's, lingering in the embrace just a little longer.

"Are you really going to lie here?"

"I'm going to take a crack at the comm system," Tray sniffled.

"You're down two hands and a shoulder," Danny quipped.

"This one's okay," Tray said, holding up his burnt hand. His other hand was in a splint.

"The *Cadence* should be entering orbit in the next hour or so. Alex will be looking for us," Danny said, standing slowly, eager to get away while his brother was being civil. He wanted to say something comforting, but he couldn't make any promises about getting home. He didn't even know if they'd get through lunch.

"Dumbwaiter," Tray said.

"Enough name-calling," Danny huffed.

"Use the dumbwaiter to get her down here. She'll fit," Tray said. "Jackass."

20

Douglas paced in circles outside the hospital. Small, agitated, paranoid circles. In one hand, he worried the pebble he'd taken from his father's grave. He'd run out of the house early today to visit his mother, half-thinking he should just check into asylum.

The hospital was dark, except for the lights at the emergency ward entrance. There was a dim light from the window of the asylum's common area. If only his mother had a window. He would climb through it and visit all the time without having to justify himself to anyone. There wasn't enough privacy in that place to tell her all the wonderful things that had happened—that he'd been able to fly into the valley and lay his father to rest.

"Checking in, Hwan?" Celio's voice brought a chill to the air.

"Thinking about it," Douglas replied, feeling for his flask, needing liquid courage. His hallucinations had been compounding ever since he and Sky came back to Rocan.

Celio gave him a look, not knowing how to handle the sincere response. Celio was dressed in worn but clean coveralls and his dark hair was slicked back. He always looked sharp in the morning, but it took less than an hour for the mine to destroy that presentation. Most miners didn't bother.

"What are you doing here?" Douglas asked, abandoning his flask, instead smoothing his shirt to look more presentable like Celio. Like a proper member of society.

"You're not the only one with a mother in asylum," he said, his answer catching Douglas off guard. He looked up at the light in the asylum window. "Are you going in to see her? She was awake."

"Are you stalking everyone in my life now?" Douglas bristled, his chest tightening.

Celio glowered, and brushed past Douglas. Then he stopped and turned. Douglas clenched his fist, tensing for an attack.

"This secret project you're working on—is it for you or is it for everyone?" Celio asked.

"What does it matter?" Douglas growled, shifting foot-to-foot.

"What you did yesterday at the yard—that was for everyone. That helped everyone," Celio explained. "What you do in Caswell—if you're going to put yourself in danger, if you're going to put Sky in danger, then I need to know: is it for the good of Rocan?"

Douglas pumped his fingers, then took a breath. Conversation was foreign for them. All Douglas had to do was throw a petty insult and things would be back to normal. His fingers brushed over his flask again, but he decided that he needed a different kind of courage to succeed today.

"I thought it might be. But in the end, we'll still be trapped here," he confessed, his insides twisting at the revelation. "Sequestered in this valley. Sequestered in this Dome. The mountains are too high; the engine will stop working."

"Don't let it kill you," Celio jabbed, turning away.

"Celio, wait!" Douglas called.

Celio turned, fists raised, expecting a punch.

Douglas raised his hands, resisting the instinct to make a fist. As much as he enjoyed Sky's enthusiasm, the moment she said his glider would never make it out of the valley, he knew it was wrong to keep stealing from Rocan to fuel it.

"I want to take my place in this town." Douglas was shaking as he said it. He could bring back the engine first, then slowly leak the other resources into circulation so no one would notice.

"I'm listening," Celio said.

"We can't fly over the mountains, but we can drive," Douglas gushed. "We can find a mountain pass and drive through, if we finish the Coureur. And we could take more people and more supplies. It would be safer."

"What does this have to do with me?" Celio asked.

"I can bring the engine, and the consoles, and the wheels," Douglas said. "I'll finish the Coureur much faster."

"You're serious?" Celio asked.

"There's still time for me, right? You won't tell the Intendant."

Celio nodded, his lips parted, a hint of sadness in his eyes. "You're really giving up your glider?"

Douglas nodded. Something inside of him was breaking, but another part was coming to life. "The glider is selfish. It will never leave this valley. A Coureur might, and it would be for everyone."

"Don't be rash about this, Little Hwan. The Coureur is still in pieces, and you need to take time to get that engine out safely." With a hesitant breath, he looked to the clock tower. "I have a shift to run."

Douglas looked at the time, too. He'd have to be careful when he worked and how long he stayed away, but he had to act quickly before Sky realized what was happening. "But you won't tell," Douglas requested. "And you'll keep the other scavengers away."

"I will hold you to this, Hwan," he said. "If it comes to light that I knew and said nothing, we'll both be in trouble."

"Let me see you!" Saskia growled, wrestling Amanda into the galley where it was warmer. "Hold still!"

Amanda rolled onto her stomach, clawing at the deck plates for purchase, her sweat-soaked skin sliding off anything she managed to grip.

"Jo!" Amanda screeched, her body going rigid, then limp.

Saskia shivered and shuddered, bracing Amanda's trembling body against hers and checking for injuries. She'd had no idea what she was doing when she'd put Amanda into stasis, and she was sure Corey was equally ignorant in pulling her out.

"Somebody!" Saskia cried. She was trained as a soldier; Amanda needed a doctor.

"Guard," Amanda murmured, her head lolling, her body convulsing.

"We're not going through this again," Saskia said, pressing her ear to Amanda's chest, reeling at the rapid pace of the girl's heart.

"You'll break her! Saskia!" Danny cried, rushing into the galley and shoving Saskia aside. Cold air leaked in through the hatch, the sense of emptiness it invoked compounded by Tray's continued absence.

"The Guard is hurting me, Danny," Amanda moaned, grabbing Danny's shirt. "The Guard—"

"Saskia is helping you. Let her help," Danny coached. He motioned Saskia over, giving her an apologetic look.

"I don't want to sleep again. Don't make me," Amanda whined, slumping in Danny's arms.

"Shh. Don't work yourself up. We need to slow your heart," Danny said, massaging her sternum.

"Corey gave me bunna," Amanda whispered.

"We need to *slow* your heart," Saskia huffed, feeling for Amanda's pulse. "Captain, how did you find her? What state was she in?"

"Gravity sick. Immobilized," Danny said, his expression glazing, his body curling protectively around Amanda.

"Where did she get the pulse rifle?" Saskia asked, feeling Amanda's limbs, checking for breaks. She didn't know what else to do.

"I'm a thief," Amanda said, retracting her arms, balling her fists.

"Did you steal all the heat, too? I can't tell if you're warm or fevered."

"I wrapped her in the thermal blanket. Or tried to," Danny said. Amanda was in a loose, sweat-soaked t-shirt, and the shirt had bloody handprints down one side.

"Is this your blood or hers?" Saskia asked.

Danny turned Amanda's hand, showing a partially healed cut across the palm. Saskia had healed a nearly identical cut before putting the girl into stasis.

"She had a knife," Danny said.

"Have," Amanda said, bringing a leg up and reaching into her boot. Saskia braced Amanda's leg, relieving her of the weapon, unleashing a fresh wave of kicks and wails. Amanda scrambled out of Danny's embrace and tumbled into Saskia, knocking her back. Saskia's head hit the corner of the dining table with blinding force and the knife clattered away. Diving for the weapon, Amanda turned, brandishing the knife, holding the blade to her palm. "Galen!"

"Amanda, stop!" Danny shouted, grabbing her wrists. "Galen isn't coming for you. Galen can't reach you here. Put the knife away."

Amanda's face turned red and her eyes glazed. The knife fell from her hand and the blade nicked her cheek. "Galen," she whimpered, crying out to her Elysian abuser. She'd been captive for ten years, confined and starved. Her skin bore the scars of abuse, and Saskia didn't know if she was calling Galen for rescue or confrontation.

"Saskia, how's your head?" Danny asked.

"Spinning." Saskia retrieved a knitter from the first aid kit and sat in front of Amanda, but she was too nauseous to close the cut on Amanda's cheek.

"I'll patch her and get her to the infirmary," Danny said, taking the knitter. "Check on Tray. He might need a brace on his shoulder."

"If I braced every injury of his, he'd be in full body traction," Saskia commented. "He doesn't get gravity sick, Captain. And his injuries aren't that bad. If he's lying on the ground, it's grief."

"Just help him," Danny said, his eyes closing as his whispered plea became a prayer. Every hour lost to mourning lessened their chances of rescue. If Saskia could help it, they wouldn't lose any more people.

21

Felicity tugged her hand free of Reg's and trotted across the street to touch the white flowers growing in a corner garden. She looked back to him for a word, but he didn't know the name of the plant.

"Flower," he said. "If you chew on it, it'll settle your stomach."

She'd been alert and questioning all morning, so he'd decided on the walk to introduce her to the town. She held up her bandaged right arm, like she was about to ask something, but then she noticed the hospital and turned her attention back to the flower, shutting out the environment. Geneculture was two buildings over from the hospital, and seeing someone go inside made Reg cringe. Taking Felicity's hand, he led her into the Parliament building instead. They used to have a counsel of delegates, but now the chambers were used as a schoolroom for the older children. There was a fire in the school last winter, and they'd been lucky to only lose the building.

"Hello, Deputy," Intendant Hubert said, pacing through the lobby. His face was red, and he was huffing, as though he'd been running. "Have you come make a statement regarding Sky?"

"No, sir. What time does the hearing start?" Reg asked.

"Twenty minutes ago," the Intendant grumbled. "I sent the Constable to retrieve the woman. Dr. Louis indicated that Felicity suffered no lasting injuries from the incident at the Glass Walls. Did you need to amend that?"

"No. She's fine," Reg said, feeling a tug as Felicity went exploring around the lobby.

"Good. Good," Hubert nodded. "Sky has behaved. She worked two shifts in the yard yesterday. Hwan had a whole slew of women there. I never realized how much protection and oppression overlap when it comes to our handling of women."

"She'll adapt well, I think," Reg said. "She owes Felicity an apology."

"I will see that the little one gets it."

"Would it be okay if we stay? I want to see if Felicity speaks to her," Reg said, shivering as he made the suggestion. He and Colleen had fought enough about it, and they were never going to come to an agreement. But sitting in on the hearing, waiting to get Felicity's apology, seemed a fair excuse.

"Still silent, then?" Hubert asked.

"Not completely. Yesterday, she asked us who she was," he said. "'Who?' She knew that Felicity wasn't her name."

"And you think Sky knows who she is?"

"I don't know if she knows. She can help her remember, maybe," Reg said, losing his conviction.

Felicity came over with a jar and held it up to Reg. The Intendant chuckled at her, his face softening, making Reg remember for a moment that the man was also a father.

"I see you've found the candy jar," Hubert said, opening the top and pulling out a candied berry. "Would you like a piece?"

Felicity frowned at him, then at the jar. Then she shook her head and went to put it back where she found it.

"Wait, little one. Do you know what candy is?" Hubert

smiled, following her with the lid and popping the berry into his mouth.

"We're getting more yeses and no's out of her," Reg offered when Felicity ignored him. "This morning has been a lot of picking up things and asking for the words, but she's remembering them, not learning them. The language is in there somewhere. And it's Rocanese. Not Trade, like Sky's."

"Sky!" Felicity repeated, dashing to the middle of the room. The door opened, and in walked Sky, her arm linked with Constable Mace. Sky's flush skin and silky clothes seemed to radiate light and she chattered with Mace in a quiet voice, her words bringing a smile to his lips. Felicity watched for a moment, then she darted behind Reg, clutching the back of his shirt.

"Do you want to leave?" Reg asked, putting a hand on her head. His mistake at the Glass Walls had been carrying her to the hospital without asking or explaining. As long as he was getting responses from her, he'd vowed to ask.

Felicity shook her head, twitters of sound choking in her throat.

"Felicity, I won't let her hurt you," Reg said, squatting down to get at eye level.

"That?" Felicity whimpered, pointing past him to Sky.

"Sky?"

"Spirit," Felicity cried, dropping to her knees. "Stop! I mean to forget. I mean to forget!"

Reg had been hoping Sky would get her to speak, but he was startled to hear so many words coming out of his child. Worse was the terror in her voice. Colleen had said the two got along and were laughing about travel stories the other day.

"Don't forget. Don't forget, little one," Reg urged, gathering her in his arms, looking back at Sky. Sky seemed equally shaken by the encounter and wrestled against Mace, retreating out the door.

"Do you remember your name?" Reg asked, running his hands over Felicity's shoulder.

She nodded.

"What is it?"

Felicity clamped her hands over her ears, her wheezes choking off into silence.

"Darling, it's okay. It's okay, Felicity," he said, emphasizing the name they'd given her. He put her good arm around his shoulder, then gingerly brought her to her feet. Felicity bounced on her toes, letting him pick her up, and she cried against his neck.

"Felicity," the Intendant said, touching her fingers to get her attention. "You told Sky 'stop it.' What did you mean? I can't guess Felicity, I need you to tell me."

"Not Sky," Felicity sniffled, wiping her cheek on Reg's shoulder. "Her Sequesterer. It follows her."

"Constable Mace?" Reg gasped, his heart rate shooting up.

Felicity shook her head, and Reg breathed a sigh of relief.

"You called her 'spirit'," the Intendant pressed. "Did you mean to? Or were you calling to the Aurora gods for protection? Were you scared?"

"The gods," Felicity murmured, shifting in Reg's arms to get the pressure off her burnt side. "Innocent Sky. The goldens killed us, the magics protect us, but the gods will tear it all down and show us what is. Show us what isn't."

"Perhaps you've been listening to too many travel stories," Reg smiled, tears in his eyes. Colleen would be happy to know that Felicity had been listening, and that the words were coming.

"I mean to forget," Felicity groaned, squirming and yet

clinging harder to him. "Let me be happy. Let me be Felicity. Let you be . . . Papa."

The last word was forced, like she didn't want it to be true, but the fact that she'd said it at all made Reg's heart soar.

Spirit groped through the darkness, its claws scraping the back of Sky's eyes, making her dizzy. Heat rose in Sky's body, and Spirit welled, screaming and shrouding her in darkness. The next thing Sky knew, she was gasping for breath, body sweat-soaked and bruised.

"Sky? Calm down, Sky. You're safe." Edwige's voice cut through the darkness.

Felicity had looked right through her, the hybrid's penetrating gaze rousing Spirit. Sky realized that Spirit wasn't quelled by Mace; it was blinded. With Felicity there, either Mace was having no effect, or it was terrifying enough that Spirit couldn't be still.

"Sky, what happened when you saw Felicity?"

Sky touched her throat involuntarily. She could feel Mace next to her, and she sank into his arms, hoping the physical closeness would soothe the war raging inside of her.

"Are you having trouble breathing again?" Edwige asked.

Sky shook her head, but she felt Edwige's slender fingers sliding under her chin and down her neck.

"Take a breath in and out," Edwige coached.

Sky complied, feeling her body relax with every breath. That morning, she'd slept next to John with her eyes closed and her body nestled against his. Mace wasn't as warm or comforting, but she could close her eyes and breathe when he held her. The materials in Rocan weren't great, and she had no idea how long she'd be trapped her. But there were perks. Like sleeping.

"Why are you here?" Sky asked, forcing her eyes open. She was surrounded by people. No wonder the fog felt so strong.

"Dr. Frank and I were waiting for your hearing. We heard you screaming from the second floor," Edwige said, motioning to the other doctor scowling behind her. "Tell me what happened."

"I don't know," Sky murmured, feeling for her satchel, making sure she still had it. "She startled me. The girl."

The Intendant asked a question in Rocanese, and Sky shivered.

"Felicity called you 'spirit.' Do you know what that means?" Edwige asked.

A hundred nights of abuse flashed before her mind, some at the hands of spirit, others at the hands of those who knew she carried it. She slipped her hand into her bag, feeling for her gravity gun. "Don't you?" Sky choked. There were too many gathered for her to shoot her way out.

"Are you some kind of shaman?" Edwige asked.

Mace was a hybrid as was Felicity. The rest, Sky couldn't tell. And she didn't want to. She hated having a piece of that other realm in her.

"No," Sky whispered.

The Intendant asked something else. Sky recognized more of the words, but she was too nervous to rely on her own understanding of the Rocanese language.

"Felicity seems to think a Sequesterer still has a hold on you. That he's following you," Edwige translated. "Maybe he intends to take you back. Have you noticed anyone following you?"

"I don't know," Sky said, pushing off of Mace, testing her balance. "Can we do this hearing now? I need to get to the yard. I need to help Hawk."

Edwige translated for the Intendant, then took Sky by the elbow, helping her to her feet.

"This won't take long. Let's go inside," Edwige said. Sky hesitated. Thus far, Edwige was the only one that believed Sky wasn't a Sequestered, but at the moment, playing the part of a Sequestered was her best plan to invoke sympathy.

"Felicity isn't in there anymore," Edwige reassured. "I'll stay with you. I'll make sure you get to the yard today."

Sky nodded. She'd told Hawk the glider wouldn't make it over the mountains, but maybe there was a way through. It had been dark when they went up before. She needed to get to the glider.

22

With one hand sprained and his arm in a sling, Tray was useless for manual labor. Sitting outside while Saskia repaired the hull only reminded him how far from home he was, and sitting inside with Danny and Amanda reminded him of why.

Tray stood in the galley, surveying the available food stock, calculating how long it would last four people. The gravity made him constantly hungry, and the hunger made math difficult.

Tapping the Feather device on his ear, Tray opened a comm channel. "Saskia, are you coming in any time soon?"

"I want to finish this section before my hands freeze," she answered. She was panting.

"Anything I can do to help?"

"Can you make lemonade?"

Tray chuckled and scanned the fresh produce, but he already knew they had no lemons. They had never had lemonade on the ship. He didn't even know Saskia liked the stuff. "I might be able to make something with the raspberries and carrots."

"Sir, don't you dare feed me carrot juice," she warned.

"Yes, ma'am." A part of Tray wanted to laugh, but Saskia was scary, and she backed up her threats with her pulse rifle.

"If I'm not back inside in fifteen minutes, assume I froze to death and come get me," she said. *Was that a joke?*

Tray didn't know, but he made a mental note of the time, filled a bowl with carrots, and headed down to the cargo bay. Danny had extracted the comm box and set it on the bottom stair for Tray to work on. The box looked partially melted and partially frozen. A dim blue light indicated that the device was still transmitting.

Nibbling on a carrot, Tray removed his Virp from the glove mount and set it next to the box so he could use his one good hand to sync the devices, but he couldn't find anything to link to.

"Did you solder this together with a candle, Danny? I've never seen a beacon so primitive," Tray commented. Tray could only see Danny's legs, sticking out from under a propped open access hatch on the side of the '*sled*. Amanda was sprawled in the pilot's seat, looking like she'd been tossed there and hadn't bothered to move. The thermal blanket was tucked around her, cocooning her limbs, keeping her warm in the chilly bay.

"Danny, can I have your Virp?" Tray called.

Without a task to occupy his mind, all Tray could do was wallow in self-pity and think about his son waiting for him in Quin. Tray didn't have a picture of his boy, but then, he didn't even keep pictures of himself. Tray hated pictures. He resented them. More accurately, he resented that other people had them and he didn't. After his mother died, his father destroyed every memory of her. All the money in two worlds couldn't change that. Once, Tray had hacked into Quin's computer system to get his mother's photo-ID; he just wanted to know what she looked like. All he'd gotten was a corrupted data file, a night in jail, and a hefty fine.

"What are you doing?" Danny demanded. Tray sat up

straighter, but he slouched again when he realized Danny was talking to Amanda.

"Pressing buttons," Amanda answered, slithering around in her seat so that her face was close to his. She was playing, but Danny didn't notice.

"Stop, please."

"I'm scanning for music broadcasts," she smiled. Tray chuckled, thinking it might be nice to have music on the ship. It'd also be nice if there were any local broadcasts, but he'd made those scans earlier and encountered only depressing silence.

"There's no audio system on the *Bobsled*," Danny snapped.

"You don't know what all these buttons do."

Danny swatted at her hand as she pressed another button and she swatted right back.

"You haven't changed a bit. You know, I get enough lip from him!" Danny ribbed, pointing to Tray.

"I resent that!" Tray bantered, though he was glad to know he wasn't invisible.

"Stop before you press something that kills the system," Danny snarled, snatching both of Amanda's hands.

"You don't know what I'm doing."

"Neither do you. Now stop."

Ever since Tray had found his brother, Danny had been searching for Amanda. Tray figured they'd had some star-crossed romance, and once reunited, they'd ride off into the sunset on twin unicorns. He certainly never expected to see the two of them bickering. Amanda made a face and climbed out of the cockpit, nearly falling when her legs gave out. Danny caught her and carried her to the steps, sitting her down next to Tray. Danny didn't notice the way she smiled at him or how her touch lingered when he pulled away. Maybe he did, but his heart was stuck on Corey.

"Here, Tray. Make yourself useful," Danny said, pressing

Tray's head close to Amanda's. Tray flinched, both from the manhandling and his brother's cutting words. He offered Danny the bowl of carrots as a show that he wasn't completely useless. Danny took a few.

"Give me your Virp," Tray said, tapping Danny's glove. "That's the one you wore yesterday, right? I want to see how it linked to the *Bobsled*."

"Don't know why I'm still wearing it," Danny grumbled, peeling off the sweaty glove and dropping it on Tray's lap. Tray extracted the electronic component, and activated the interface projection. The main screen was nothing but errors from empty news feeds.

"Find her some proper shoes," Danny said, pulling the blanket across Amanda's shoulders, taking a moment to fuss. "I told you about Tray, right?"

"I don't remember," Amanda sighed. She leaned against Tray, slipping one arm around his waist, getting cozy like they'd known each other for ages. The day's excitement had taxed her body, and her legs twitched even when she was sitting. Tray shifted, discomfited by the physical contact, but he couldn't in good conscience push her away.

"In all your years knowing him, he never mentioned me?" Tray asked once Danny was out of earshot.

Amanda shrugged. "I don't remember a lot of things. I'm supposed to see a neurologist before I leave Terrana."

"You left Terrana," Tray reminded her. Amanda snickered and Tray laughed with her.

"I did?" Amanda murmured. She leaned more heavily and Tray winced at the pressure on his shoulder. Half his body was bruised from the fall during landing and he could see that half of hers was as well. There would come a point where neither of them could power through the injuries.

"Do you remember carrots? You should. You've lived on

Terrana your whole life," he said, offering her the bowl. "They don't grow these in Quin. The whole city has declared war on beta-carotene. It's a wonder they aren't blind."

Amanda looked at the bowl and looked at him. He wasn't sure if her reluctance was psychological or physical. He broke off a chunk of carrot and held it close to her face, just in case she was worried about controlling her hands, but she snatched it up. She sniffed the carrot, nibbled off the tip, and after a few chews, she spat it out.

"I declare war on beta-carotene!" she cried. "Danny, can't I help? If I sit here, Tray will poison me with his beta-carrots!"

"Sure you can help," Danny called back, not lifting his head from the circuit board he was extracting. "You and Tray can clean out that spare bunk so you can have your own room."

"Why can't she just sleep in Corey's bunk? It's already clean and Corey's not using it," Tray asked, regretting the words as soon as they'd come from his mouth. It was callous and disrespectful. Danny's fist clenched around the tool in his hand and he attacked the *Bobsled* with new fervor. The *Bobsled* retaliated with a loud, crackling shock that lit up the room and blasted Danny flat on his back.

"If I kept pressing buttons, that wouldn't have happened," Amanda deadpanned.

"Shut up," Tray snapped, running to his brother, and checking his breathing. Cradling Danny's head on his lap, he tapped his Feather. "Saskia?"

"I still have five minutes."

"Sorry to cut you short. Danny shocked himself again."

The hearing was the most formalized slap on the wrist Sky had ever received. There were ten people in attendance. She recognized the man Jude from the Glass Walls. He had a fading bruise on his cheek, and his view of the situation was that Sky was "perfectly agreeable until the little girl started wailing." Constable Mace spoke next, summarizing other witness testimonies. Dr. Frank gave an overview of injuries among the crowd, the worst of which seemed to be Hawk's concussion. Then a wiry, young bookworm-type rattled off a list of the resources that had been lost due to the disturbance. Edwige testified about Sky's health in general. The Intendant wrapped up the discussion with comments about Sky's mechanical aptitude, and he played one of the recorders that she'd fixed.

"Sky, we appreciate the balance of contribution you've made in such a short time," the Intendant summarized, addressing the compliment to the device in his hand. "It is the agreement of this counsel that you should be given a chance to adapt to life as a free woman. Going forward, you will be expected to obey our laws."

"What is the consequence if I do not?" Sky asked.

There was a murmur among the five white-haired men comprising the counsel.

"They don't need to be here for this. I just need to understand your laws and your system of punishment," Sky said. "As a punishment, am I made to sit out in the cold until I freeze? Am I forced into some undesirable form of labor? Am I beaten? Am I confined? Are my fingers amputated or my eyes gouged out?"

"If you present a danger to other citizens, you will be kept confined and isolated from the general population until you are rehabilitated or the terms of your punishment are met," the Intendant explained. "If the nature of your crime warrants death, then you will be put to death, but not in a manner as slow as freezing."

"What crimes warrant death?" Sky probed.

"Sequestering, abuse or neglect of a child or woman, causing injury to another that inhibits their ability to breed, hoarding of resources, intentional damage or destruction of resources," the Intendant said, trailing off as though the list of items physically pained him. "Your fight at the Glass Walls could have injured other breeders, Sky. You could have caused irreparable damage to the Glass Walls. Were it not for the mitigating circumstances of your mental health, you would have been put into confinement for at least three months. If it becomes apparent in the near future that you have taken advantage of our forgiveness, then you will serve this term in addition to whatever punishment your next crime bears."

"Then I will make amends by fixing as many of those recorders as I can," Sky offered. "I have more questions about your laws, but I would like to go to the yard now."

"Constable Mace will escort you," the Intendant said. The room cleared out, and Mace escorted Sky to the yard.

Sky was at the yard only a few minutes before she confirmed that Hawk wasn't there. Going to her workbench, she gathered the components she'd assembled to boost the power on the *Bobsled's* communication array. The glider itself would be her antenna. She was using the power source and audio circuits of some of the recorders, and she felt sad for disassembling those pieces of history, but her need was more pressing.

"Where are you taking those recorders?" Ramsey asked her when he caught her leaving.

"Design studio," she lied in Rocanese. "Intendant wants me working there."

She hustled across town to the hanger bay, and when she got there, the glider engine was in pieces.

"What happened here?" she whispered, setting her transceiver on the table. "Hawk, we've been discovered. How am I going to fix this?"

Sky felt a rush of heat and Spirit went into a frenzy. Two men appeared from thin air, the force of their arrival knocking Sky to the ground. The curly-haired one had enough bronze in his skin for Sky to recognize him as at least part golden. The freckled one had a hand pressed to his ribs and leaned heavily on his friend.

"You," Sky said, recognizing the freckled one. "You were in the tunnel when the Coureur exploded. You pulled Hawk away from the fire."

"My name is Kyrn Gate. This is my brother, Jotham," he introduced, wincing when he spoke. When Sky had run from the tunnel, she'd shot him with her grav-gun, and the blast had caught him in the chest. By the way he leaned, she could tell she'd bruised his rib. Both the men were scrawny and their dark coveralls sagged on their bodies.

"Is he the brother who Sequestered Felicity?" Sky asked, recognizing the name 'Gate' from Colleen's weeping.

"That was Thomas. And he's dead," Kyrn said. "Are you leaving finally?"

"Trying to," Sky sighed, pointing to the ignition switch lying on the ground. "Can you teleport me past the mountains?"

Kyrn looked at his brother, as though considering it. "That's beyond our ability."

"We assumed you could teleport yourself, spirit carrier," Jotham spoke up.

Sky shivered at the name, but these hybrids had unabashedly teleported in front of her. She'd never met spirit-kind who could or would do that.

"What are you? What is Felicity?" Sky asked. "Why are you the only ones who know what I am?"

"We're hybrids," Kyrn said simply, taking a step into the hanger. He marveled at the mottled body of the glider, then he gazed a moment at her, but he didn't look through her the way Felicity did. "We've never met a pure spirit before."

"The air burns around you," Jotham added. His oily hair hung around his face, and his eyes were dark with grief.

"But the others—Mace, Hawk, John—why don't they know what they are?" Sky asked.

"There are dozens of us that know, but hundreds more that have no idea," Kyrn said. He started to limp closer, but Jotham held him back.

"Why don't you tell them?" Sky asked.

"To protect the conjurers from knowing what *they* are," Kyrn said, his eyes crinkling like he was searching for the right words.

"Protect them?" Sky repeated. "This city has no resources. I'd imagine you want to find as many conjurers as possible. Can't a conjurer create whatever you need to get out of this valley? Isn't that what a conjurer is?"

"They conjure," Jotham said defensively. "Constantly."

"This whole section of the Dome was conjured by hybrids," Kyrn explained. "But it's not a perfect seal. They can see the border between the Moonslate and the patch, and when they see it, the seam grows into a crack. Then another one sees the crack and it becomes a hole. They change things, whether they mean to or not. That is why they can't know the truth."

"So John doesn't have any idea what he is, and if I tell him, the Dome collapses?" Sky repeated, raking her hands over her chest. She'd dreamed of taking John with her when she left, but now she realized that she couldn't.

"If he remembers how it was broken before, it will break again," Kyrn frowned.

"But you broke Felicity," Jotham accused.

"How? By talking to her?" Sky retorted, then bit her lip. "How broken?"

"If she can't recover, she'll become like us. A hybrid who is aware," Kyrn said. "We think. We don't know what her abilities are, but we know she was not supposed to speak, and you made her speak."

"But if she wasn't Sequestered, why was she burned?" Sky asked.

"An accident," Jotham said, his face getting red, his eyes watering.

"We think," Kyrn added quietly. "We don't remember who she was before. That's how deeply the conjurers' illusion is entwined with our memories."

"Thomas led the Constable to her, because he knew she wouldn't be found otherwise," Jotham insisted. "He was a good man. He didn't deserve to die!"

"Jotham."

"But why was she in a box? Why was the box on fire?" Sky asked.

"I wish I knew." Kyrn clutched his side, and Jotham took his weight, helping him get to the ground, whispering to his brother in Rocanese.

"Did you teleport all the way here to see me off?" Sky asked, going to the tool bench and pulling out what she needed to fix the glider.

"Can you heal my brother, like you healed Hwan?" Jotham asked. "The doctors won't give him medicine because he's Excepted from breeding. You have to undo what you did."

"I can't un-shoot him," Sky huffed, though she mentally ran through the supplies in her medicine kit.

"Can you heal him?" Jotham begged.

"That's beyond my ability," Sky said. "I'm working on a way out. When the time comes, do what you can to help. I'll try not to break anyone else."

23

Danny hissed and shivered as consciousness found him lying face down on the infirmary bed. He was hungry, but exhausted, and he wished his stomach would stop grumbling so he could get back to sleep. The ship was chilled, but the electric blanket tucked under his shoulders kept him warm.

His breath was humid against the pillow, and Danny buried his face trying to keep his mind quiet and convince sleep to return. Corey died in this bed. Alone. Danny lifted onto his elbows and scanned the room. Her body had been moved to the quarantine unit, taking up the only other bed, isolated from their air.

Rolling to his feet, Danny swooned and grabbed his bed for support. His headache had elevated to a piercing migraine. Keeping his eyes closed, he felt his way to the medicine cabinet and squinted through the stark lights to find an analgesic. It would take five minutes to work, but the migraine threatened to knock him off his feet sooner than that. Keeping one hand on the wall for support, he let himself into the quarantine unit. Cold air mixed with warm, bringing a cacophony of scents.

Folding back the sheet that covered Corey's face, he shuddered and bowed his head. Her brown eyes were closed forever now. Her dark brown hair was combed neatly, but the ends were singed from being electrocuted. The strangulation marks on her neck were more prominent now that her skin was paled from death. Her ear had been severed, as were two fingers—the marks of the torture she endured to save Amanda. Danny touched her cheek and slipped her left hand into his. Even with her fingers cold and stiff, her hand fit perfectly into his. He loved her, and now he would never know if their last night together was real, or if she had been coerced into seducing him.

"Danny?"

Danny inhaled at the sound of Tray's voice. It was soft and gentle, void of the hatred that had laced it earlier.

"About her body—"

"We will return it to her family in Quin," Danny said. He couldn't look at his brother right now.

"She has no family," Tray said. When he whispered like that, he lost his deep, mellow tone and sounded like their mother.

"Then we will be her family. Her ashes can rest with Mom's." Danny squeezed Corey's hand, wishing he could warm her back to life simply by holding her.

"We don't have the means to render her to ashes," Tray said.

Danny looked to the ceiling and murmured a prayer. *Zive, why her?* The echoed answer, *it could have been Tray,* made his heart ache. Forcing the grief away, Danny looked squarely at Tray, willing himself to see his brother. Living. Needing him. Danny had to keep it together.

"In the ancient days, before the Ritual of Ashes was established, the dead were arranged in positions of serenity and buried beneath the earth. The graves were marked with stones and epitaphs as a permanent marker," Tray said, pressing his hands and face against the clear walls of the quarantine unit.

Danny started to understand why Tray hated the view from inside these walls.

"I don't need a history lesson," Danny said. Tray crossed his arms and raised his brow. Danny shook his head. "You want to bury her in the ground? Here?"

"The earth will render the body to ashes," Tray said.

We will never find this place again! Never find her again! Danny shook his head, trying to pull Corey's hand over his heart, but her arm was stiff. "That was on the ancient world. The ground on Aquia is poisoned by decomposing human bodies. That's why the Ritual of Ashes was established."

"It used to be poison. Six centuries ago," Tray replied. "This is not the same world anymore. The life we brought with us thrives here. The plants and the animals that live outside the Domes—they don't have a Ritual of Ashes to protect the land; they join it."

Danny shook his head and leaned closer to Corey's face, promising her they would not leave her where she'd never be found and remembered. Kissing Corey's cool cheek, his composure crumbled. He shuddered again when he felt a warm hand on his back—Tray. Tray ran his thumb up Danny's shoulder blade, then he squeezed Danny's shoulder before letting go again.

"I'll keep trying the beacon. If we don't get home soon, her body will poison *us*. This is the best way to honor and respect her memory. I promise."

It was the kindest thing Tray had said to him all morning. Letting go of Corey, Danny reached out for his brother, but Tray had already left the room.

Douglas Hwan was so nervous he was biting his fingernails, and considering the layers of engine grease covering them, he was sure his lips were black. He wiped his sweaty palms on the front of his coveralls, circling over the myriad of possible excuses for just how he had stumbled upon a perfectly restored engine. Celio would hold him to it.

"You do stupid things when you're not drinking, Hwan," he murmured, raking his hands through his bright red hair, leaving black grease streaks behind. Things were going well at the yard. People were working hard. When Ramsey noticed the sweat on his lip, he asked if Douglas was ill. He even offered to walk Douglas to the hospital. Douglas leaned on the catwalk railing overlooking the yard, soothing himself with the sounds of conversation and laughter. The tape was peeled away on the fuel storage room, and he went to investigate. The area was off limits while Level One workers were on the premises, and they were in the process of expanding some of the safer projects to the design lab. He was relieved to find Sky in there.

"How long have you been here?" Douglas laughed. "Ramsey told me you took your telephone to the design studio."

Sky was dressed in mechanic's coveralls, and though grime covered the worn fabric, her white shirt remained unblemished beneath. Her blond ponytail swished side to side as she moved purposefully through the room, carrying a fuel tank to the storage barrel. The lights in the room were off.

"I need fuel," she said tersely.

"No, Sky. We can't," Douglas said, weaving between the work tables to get to her. All of the chairs had been taken to other workstations. "Things have changed. We can't be selfish. We need to think about the rest of the Rocan. No more joy rides."

"Not a joy ride," Sky said. "I'll contact my people, and I'll be gone."

"Gone where, bébé? You said we couldn't fly over the mountains."

"It's not safe for me in Rocan. Edwige said as much."

"Did something happen at the hearing, Sky?" he asked, wringing his hands. "I should have gone with you. We should have showed them your telephone. We could go back now."

"Transceiver," she corrected, turning her attention back to the fuel tap. "I installed it in the glider."

Douglas rubbed his hands together nervously. "When did you install it?"

"Hawk, your secret is out," she warned, her manner shifting.

"What did you say at the hearing?" Douglas asked, his body going cold.

"Nothing. But when I went to the hanger, the glider was in pieces," Sky explained. "Someone was there before I was. They were trying to take the engine."

So much for breaking it to her gently. "That was me."

"Why?" Sky cried, her chest puffing defensively.

"I've decided to bring the engine here. And the console, and the wheels. For the new Coureur," he said, his voice quaking. When he'd started extracting the engine that morning, he'd only gotten through it by ignoring the big picture—that his father's dream was falling to pieces. "We stand a better chance driving over the mountain. We wouldn't have to work in secret. We'll have the tools and the support of everyone here."

Sky fumed. "If you don't want the glider anymore, then you can dismantle it tomorrow. Today, I need to go up and see if I can contact my people."

"You never said you needed the glider to do that. You have the tele—transceiver," Douglas argued.

A silhouette appeared in the entryway, and Douglas froze.

"Hey, no one's supposed to be in here," McGill said, flipping on the lights. Both Douglas and Sky squinted, but McGill cocked a grin. "Oh, it's you two. Come on. This area's off limits."

"You heard him, Sky. We can't be in here," Douglas said,

keeping his voice low and his hand on the tap. "You're threatening the progress we've made."

"I'm not making trouble," Sky crooned. "I showed you how to fix the recorders. I showed you how to . . . Hay nah, Hawk. After all I've showed you, do you doubt that I can bring help to this valley?"

"No," he said, his stomach turning at the fear that Sky's friends would be more reckless than her.

"Douglas?" McGill asked.

"We may need the Constable," Douglas said, hoping that threat would be enough to make Sky back down.

"One more day, Hawk. Just one more day," she begged.

"Put down the fuel. Now," Douglas said firmly.

"I don't even know what I can tell you without cracking the Dome," Sky fumed. "I barely understand myself, but I know the city is in danger."

"What kind of danger?" he asked, stepping closer.

"I can't tell you. But if you let me go, it'll be okay," Sky said.

"McGill," Douglas ordered, motioning him out.

Dropping the fuel tank, she reached into her satchel, pulled her gun, and shot McGill. There was no projectile and no sound, but everything on the tables between them and McGill went flying, and then McGill collapsed.

"Sky, what have you done?" Douglas cried, leaping over the toppled equipment and falling on his knees next to McGill.

Sky ignored him and resumed filling her fuel tank. "I'm leaving."

"No. No, no, no," Douglas whimpered, cradling McGill's body against his. "Is he dead?"

"Shouldn't be. He's still breathing, right?"

Douglas leaned his face next to McGill's, and he sobbed with relief when he felt a breath. "Yes."

"Then he'll be fine," Sky said, closing the tap and sealing off her fuel tank.

Douglas didn't care about her or the engine anymore. It was one thing to be startled in a crowded bar and throw a punch, but she'd shot McGill for no reason. That violence was unforgivable. Hugging McGill to his chest, he scooted closer to the entryway. "Help! I need help in here!"

"Fool!" Sky raged, yanking Douglas up by the collar. McGill hit the ground and Douglas cried out. Then he felt her weapon pointed at his neck. "Take the fuel tank," she ordered. "Take it!"

"Sky, don't do this," Douglas begged. Ramsey came running first, but disappeared just as quickly, shouting orders to evacuate the women to a safe distance.

"I asked for one day," Sky hissed in his ear. "Why couldn't you give me one more day?"

24

John paced outside the Geneculture building, working up the nerve to go in and visit Don. The building looked just like every other building in the town—bland and russet, with only slightly less dust in the corners of the windows. No one ever painted murals on it, because no one liked being near it when they didn't have to be. Don's office was near the front, since he liked to greet all the breeders personally. John hadn't stepped foot through the door since his last breeding eight years ago.

Licking his lips, he tasted Sky's last kiss. They'd had a leisurely morning in bed, translating Trade and Rocanese for the body parts they kissed, and John had had an epiphany. He wanted to make some changes in his life; he wanted to make his last years good ones. Riding a fresh wave of confidence and resolve, he charged into Don's office and gave as casual a wave as he could muster.

"You're taking lunch out. Come with me," John said.

Don glanced up from the slate he was making notes on, looking pleasantly surprised at first, then confused, then reluctant. "It's too early for lunch."

"Come on, Donny. We're not skipping out," John smiled, pulling out Don's chair. "I promise, you'll get plenty of work done."

Don fidgeted with his slate and stared at the names he'd written. He was either assigning breeding pairs or counting the dead.

"Is this about Sky's hearing?" Don asked.

"Not at all," John answered, relieved when Don got up to follow him. He put an arm around Don's shoulders, giving him a squeeze, and leading the way outside. "I haven't been to the mine in days."

"I know," Don said, shrugging off John's arm, his pace lagging.

John walked backwards, facing Don. "Well, do you know what happened? Nothing. The world kept spinning. The men still brought home more potash than we know what to do with."

Don made a face. "That's great, Johnny. If more people had that attitude, no one would work."

"I'll work where I'm needed!" John said. "I could go to the commissary and learn how to make bread. I'll help serve lunch. I can go to the orchard to pollinate the blossoms."

"A Level One job?" Don criticized, kicking the dirt as they walked. John cringed. It was the same prejudice he'd felt as a young man that had compelled him to go to the mines to begin with.

"I'm tall enough to reach blossoms most of them can't," he shrugged. "And I can stand on a ladder. Do you know we don't pollinate the top half of the trees because Level One workers aren't permitted to climb ladders? I'm all for protecting the weak, but some Level One men aren't even breeders."

"I'm not the one to talk to about changing that policy," Don said.

John punched him in the arm and Don stumbled. "Will you

get your head out of your high-level government work for five minutes." He scanned the block, seeing if there was any place where they could work and talk. "Let's go to the juicing factory. Do you want to make juice or recycle bottles?"

"I have a job."

"So do I. And I've been dead inside for thirty years because of it. Today, I feel alive!" John smiled and put both his hands on Don's shoulders, hoping to squeeze some sense into him.

"Couldn't be the woman, could it?" Don said, trying for a tease but unable to force even a weak smile. "You're in love with her."

"I don't believe in love," John sighed, feeling the piercing pain in his heart mixed with the fire of yearning.

"Nonsense," Don huffed, bumping John's shoulder.

John quirked his brow, surprised at the tease. "You're as single as I am," he pointed out.

"I'm head of the Registry," Don shrugged, looking away and screwing his face unhappily. "Being responsible for breeding pairs does not endear you to anyone."

John's face softened into pity. John chose to remain single as a matter of principle and protest. He'd never realized Don was unhappy alone. "You've carried that weight a long time, Donny. Maybe it's time to pass the torch."

Don shuddered and clutched his stomach. "I wouldn't wish this on anyone, Johnny. And someone has to do it. Someone has to be despised. I'm perfect for it. I have no family. No children." He bent forward, like he was going to heave, and stumbled to the nearest garden. "I have never had a successful conception, and I judge other men on that same failure. The only use I have is to let others hate me so that our race can survive."

John knew that Don had no children. It wasn't his fault. If all men could breed, they wouldn't have Geneculture. John put a hand on Don's back. "That's not your only use. Honestly, Donny,

I'd rather our civilization die out with dignity than live another generation so obsessed with breeding that we all *want* to die."

"You don't need me now," Don murmured, hands on his knees, head so low John thought he'd pitch forward. "You have Sky. Get your license. Or are you afraid of losing face for breaking your vow?"

"Sky hasn't been my best friend since birth," John said, breaking off a stem from one of the plants, using the scent to soothe Don. "Sky wasn't there when Myung-Ki died or when I took in Douglas. When the Coureur exploded and Douglas was in the hospital, you stood by my side. Not Sky. You."

"And I'll take her from you when she's ready for breeding," Don choked, dry heaving. John pressed his lips together. This was why Don was despised and why John had refused a love partner for so long. John couldn't imagine hating the one person in the Dome that he'd always called friend.

"Remember when you had that mid-life crisis and decided to scale the Dome wall? Who was there to spoon-feed you applesauce while your arms healed?" John asked.

"You." Don shivered, dropping to his knees. John hadn't seen him shaking like that in a long time. He shouldn't have brought up the incident. In the silence, the frantic footsteps of a messenger boy echoed.

Please, pass us by. John reached out to put a hand on Don's shoulder, but Don retracted and sat straight.

"Mon Harris! Dr. Yale!" the boy shouted, running like his pants were on fire. Don was a picture of professionalism. He raised a stern eyebrow at the boy, intent on schooling the child in manners, but the red-faced boy wasn't interested in schooling. He waved at the two of them to follow him. "Madame Sky has gone crazy! She's taken hostages in the yard."

All Sky kept thinking was that she should have left yesterday. After talking to Edwige, she knew time was short. The transceiver she'd hacked together barely worked and Hawk had chosen now for a time of personal growth, self-sacrifice, and community involvement. He'd dismantled her plans from the top down, giving up his glider. Without an alternative to call for help, her flight instincts kicked in. Laws and culture be damned; she needed to get out of here.

The yard erupted in chaos. A few people had made it out the door, but the fuel storage room was near the front and when Sky came out, holding a gun to Hawk's neck, everyone fled to the rear of the building. There was a wall of thirty men and probably an equal number of women behind them, all begging for mercy in Rocanese. Hawk kept whispering to her, begging her not to hurt them. This was getting ridiculous.

"Stay here if you want," Sky said, snatching the fuel tank away and pushing him toward the other workers. If she shot the ground with her grav-gun, they'd keep their distance, but even Sky wasn't foolish enough to rattle this building. The dispersal on the shot that took out McGill was wider than it should have been, meaning the calibration of the device was off.

"Put the blasting gun down before anyone else gets hurt," Hawk said, holding out both hands.

"Give me a head start. I won't be back. I won't make trouble." Sky lowered the gun, but did not put it away.

"I'll go with you," Hawk said, glancing over his shoulder at the workers. "We'll go to the warehouse. We'll figure this out. If you fly off without me, I lose my engine."

Why can't I say no?

Sky motioned Hawk out the front door. She swept her gun, showing the workers in the yard that she'd hurt anyone who tried to follow; the whimpers and gasps were sufficient to satisfy her that no one was feeling particularly heroic. Aside from

Hawk. Holstering her weapon, she picked up the fuel tank. Hawk tipped open the front door, took one step outside, and froze.

"Go on," Sky said, giving him a shove. Then she saw what he saw—Constable Mace, Deputy Arman, Dr. Frank, and three other brutish men in black law tunics. Sky dropped the fuel tank, slammed the door closed with her and Hawk outside, then drew her knife and held it to Hawk's neck. She would fight her way out if she had to, and in this primitive culture, the blade showed that better than the gun.

Arman raised a pistol, but Mace did not. *Damn him!* Even in this tense situation, Mace mesmerized Spirit. Frank hollered something in Rocanese, pointing to her, and by the way the three lawmen moved to strike, it was not hard to guess what he'd said.

"Wait!" Hawk cried. His body bowed as his neck came in contact with the blade. His almond eyes watered, clouded with feelings of betrayal. "Sky, what can I do?"

"What you promised," Sky said. "Take me to the warehouse."

"It would be a lot easier to diffuse the situation if you didn't have a knife," Hawk said. He reached for her hand, but she jerked him hard, bracing his arms by his side. He was brazen because he trusted her not to kill him.

"If I put it down now, I get three months confinement. At least," Sky said, pursing her lips. "I'm not surrendering to that!"

Three more men rounded the corner, joining Mace and the others on the street. *John!* Sky's vision filled with spots. She could barely stay conscious with two spirit shrouds around.

"My Douglas! Do as she asks!" Don Yale called in Rocanese. He said more, but Sky didn't catch the meaning.

"Sky, let him go! Please!" John pleaded. One of the lawmen had to break formation to hold John back. The tussle drew an even larger crowd from the neighboring work sites. There was nothing John could do to help her. She'd dug herself too deep of a hole.

"You won't answer him?" Hawk challenged.

"You volunteered to come with me," Sky said. It was strange no one had asked her what *she* wanted or why she had taken hostages—no one but Hawk. "Show them the fuel tank. Pick it up."

Hawk leaned sideways to pick up the fuel tank, his breath hitching when he felt Sky's blade brush his chin. Raising his voice, he showed off the three-gallon tank to Mace. "This is full of refined ethanol. It's a Level Four dangerous explosive. Be careful with your pistols."

Mace shouted orders to his men, and within seconds their pistols were lowered, replaced by clubs. They formed a net around her, blocking every avenue of escape.

"Set the tank down. Sky, we can talk about this. Please release your *otages*," Mace said. He kept his Rocanese simple so that she would understand. She assumed the last word was hostages, but that wasn't the kind of vocabulary one found in a language primer. Sky could sense the overwhelming power in the spirit realm like a dark cloak, blinding Spirit and forcing it down. At least if she were knocked out, she stood some chance of surviving.

"Go back to your work, Channing. Hawk will return with treasures beyond your imagining," Sky promised. She'd never had qualms about turning on her hosts in other Domes.

"Douglas, are any of the hostages injured?" Don asked.

"Don't answer," Sky warned.

"McGill is unconscious," Hawk said, closing his eyes and tilting his head back, shuddering as though he expected that breath to be his last. Sky nicked his skin to show her annoyance.

"Any of the women, Hwan?" Frank said. Sky bristled,

thinking how good it would feel to shoot that man. She felt Hawk start to quiver.

"Dr. Yale, come forward," Sky said. The last time she'd taken hostages, it'd been much more organized. And planned.

Don and Mace had a hurried, hushed conversation, then Don stepped forward, ready to assume the role of negotiator.

"Remove your jacket. Empty your pockets," Sky said, making a small motion with her knife. Hawk took a breath when the blade left his throat, but he stopped breathing again when he saw the Dome light glint on the blade. Sky dropped her voice so that Mace and the others could not hear. "You may go inside and verify that McGill is not injured," she said to Don.

Don's eyes widened, and he looked back at Mace. "I'm not carrying a medical bag."

"I promise you won't need it. Stay inside until you get the 'all clear.'"

"If he's okay, why do you want me in there?" Don asked, his eyes fixated on the knife.

"To calm them."

"No one is calmed by the sight of me," Don said, his eyes crinkling. His fingers kept balling into fists. *Thinking how he can grab the knife.* "My Douglas?"

"I'm not hurt," Hawk said. "I volunteered for this. To save the others."

"Sky, please don't hurt him," Don pleaded, reaching out for her. Sky pressed the knife against Hawk's neck, slicing the skin.

"No!" Don cried. The crowd gasped, their overlapping murmurs crescendoing.

"Go inside or go back with the others," Sky said.

"I'll do it. I'll go in. Just don't hurt him," Don said, hands shaking as he hurried through the door.

"Donny!" John cried.

"I thought you wanted to talk, Sky!" Mace shouted over the

crowd. "Are we in a stand-off? Why did you send Yale into the building? Tell me why you have a knife to young Hwan's neck."

"No harm will come to him if you let us go!" Sky said. "Clear the road!"

"I thought you cared about me," Hawk taunted, his nerves showing now that she'd shed his blood.

"And I thought you wanted to escape," Sky hissed, flicking the blade and nicking his skin again. His body broke into a sweat, but the injuries only seemed to fuel his obstinance.

"I changed my mind."

"Get me to the gate. Then you're free," Sky growled.

"We'll find the men who Sequestered you," Mace tried. "Please know we want to help you. You must talk to me."

He believed his words. Unfortunately, he'd never believe that she came here from another Dome. Two more deputies emerged from the growing crowd, bringing Arman and the others new weapons.

"Those are tranquilizers, Sky," Hawk said. "If you don't want to wake up in asylum, surrender now."

"You said you would help me," Sky said.

"You shot McGill!"

"You should have kept your mouth shut," Sky snapped. "Now how are we going to get out of here?"

"You could start by putting the knife down."

"I don't see that happening," Sky said.

Frank yelled something in Rocanese—something about forgiving them. Mace hollered his agreement, but Hawk cringed at the words. John screamed and charged forward, his rage so fervent it took three men to hold him back. He begged and pleaded in mixed Rocanese and Trade. Hawk's body went stiff and a tear rolled down his cheek. She felt him leaning into her arm, getting closer to her blade. Something was about to happen. Flash bombs were distributed among the officers, and then Sky notice Jotham Gate at the edge of the crowd.

"I see our salvation," Sky said. "Close your eyes."

"I don't want to die," Hawk stammered.

"Come with me, and I'll keep you safe," Sky whispered. "Are you ready to escape?"

Pushing Hawk forward, she drew her grav-gun and shot the ground. The earth shook, the crowd erupted in panicked screams. A few of the deputies dropped their flash bombs and the square filled with blinding light and sound. Spirit awoke, but with the shrouds surrounding them, it was trapped. *Your move, Gate.*

25

The ship was finally heating up, but Tray refused to strip down. He'd taken off his sweater, but still wore a long-sleeve shirt to cover the scabs on his arm where the Moon Pox scarred his skin. Saskia had found a brilliant way to vent the solar heat from the Observation Deck. The ward room was sweltering and the galley slightly less so, but that was as far as the heat went.

Saskia had stripped down to shorts and a tank top, which looked amusing with her military boots and weapon holsters. Tray rarely saw Saskia's legs, and the fact that he was staring at them now, thinking they looked nice, told him it was way too hot in here. Saskia's calf muscles were lean and well defined. She stood on the countertop suspending electrical cables from the ceiling. Tray wasn't sure if he was supposed to be spotting her or ignoring her and fixing lunch.

"Amanda, do you eat squash?" Tray asked, picking one-handed through the sandwich materials, creating an assembly line for lunch. The heat in the galley was already making the leafy vegetables wilt.

"Is it like carrots?" she grunted.

"Have you ever had a vegetable?" Tray asked, holding up an orange squash for her to see.

After swooning and falling out of her chair three times, Amanda had conceded to lying on the floor, where she was currently doing leg lifts and humming songs in Lanvarian.

"You know, isometric exercises make so much more sense in full gravity," she said. Her face was beet red and she was sweating through her t-shirt.

"Don't push too hard. If your heart explodes, we don't have a backup," Tray quipped.

"I can't just lie here," Amanda said, her voice shaking, her legs dropping to the ground.

"You'll die there if you don't sit still," Saskia criticized, hopping down from the counter and wiping her boot prints off with the hem of her shirt. "I'll take her squash, Tray."

"We have plenty," Tray said. They were far from home, but there was comfort simply in knowing what Saskia liked to eat and being able to prepare it for her.

What does my son likes to eat? Tray's throat tightened suddenly. Had Hero even tasted a carrot before? Tray grabbed a cup and filled it with water, drowning the emotion before it crept too close to the surface. There was hope they'd only be delayed another half day.

"Power for the beacon," Saskia announced, threading one of the cables to the table. Tray had a Virclutch tablet linked to Danny's Virp, and the comm box from the *'sled,* and Saskia ran the cable to a power box they'd hacked together.

"Good. Now we can change the frequency of the pulse," Tray sighed. The frequency of the beacon's pulse appeared hard-wired, and the only way to shift it to Quin's distress frequency was through voltage modulation. Saskia made the adjustment and Danny's Virp vibrated on the table. A few seconds later, the ship echoed the Virp alert, and a distress siren activated.

Amanda screeched and clamped her hands over her ears.

"Nolwazi, silence the alarm," Tray ordered the ship's computer.

The alarm silenced, but a yellow light on the wall panel blinked to say the alert was still active.

"Are you okay?" Saskia asked, leaning over Amanda, prying her hands off her ears.

"I think my heart exploded," Amanda panted, wiping her cheek on her shoulder.

"What was that alarm?" Danny groaned, trudging into the galley, looking as haggard as Tray felt. "What is she doing on the floor?"

"I can talk," Amanda said, kicking his ankle.

Danny hopped over her, landing by her head. "Fine. Why are you lying on the floor?"

"I tried the chair. It didn't like me." Amanda made a face and hooked her wrists around Danny's ankles.

Danny looked accusingly at Tray.

"What?" Tray interrupted. "I offered her a pillow."

"Thank you, Tray" Amanda sang, arching her back to look at him upside down. Tray smiled at her, glad for the show of appreciation.

"I thought I told you to find her some clothes," Danny harped.

"He did. Then it got hot," Amanda said, jumping to Tray's defense. He liked that she wasn't afraid to talk back to Danny.

"We don't have any shoes that will stay on her feet," Tray said.

"Want to play cards, Danny?" Amanda asked, picking up a deck of cards and spilling half of them.

"Where did you get these?" Danny asked, his face going white.

"Your drawer," Amanda answered.

"I know where. Why?" Danny said, snatching the cards from her, counting the cards to make sure they were all there. "Why are you going through my drawer?"

"She needed clothes, Danny," Tray criticized, turning his attention to the Virclutch, since he lacked the energy to fight.

"Unlike some people, I have no clothes here!" Amanda carped, using the bench to pull herself up.

"Don't you ever—don't touch these ever!" Danny warned. The grief and rage that Danny had been storing erupted, but Saskia put up a warning hand to keep him from lashing out and breaking their beacon.

"They're hers aren't they?" Amanda groused.

Tray nodded. It was a special card game Corey had bought for Danny and the two never invited anyone else to play. Tray should have realized she'd picked them up; he should have watched her more closely.

"Do you have regular playing cards?" Amanda asked. "If I don't keep myself occupied, I'll start having flashbacks. Which is weird because I can't remember what . . . I remember. It's all swirly."

"Yeah," Tray murmured, helping Amanda up. Blocking out his brother's blubbering, Tray brought the sandwiches to the table. It was hard to think. Saskia let go of Danny and Danny sank to his knees, his tears splashing onto his special cards. Tray was at a loss. As much as he wanted to join his brother in a fit of despair, one of them had to hold it together.

"Looks like we're now transmitting on a standard distress frequency. Alex will know that we survived landing," Saskia said.

Danny's Virp vibrated and he crawled to the table, holding out his hand. Tray handed him the device, and Danny laid he head on the bench next to Tray, his face falling when the projection activated.

"Tracking's disabled," Danny reported, blinking tears from his eyes.

"What?" Tray asked.

"Tracking." Danny set the Virp on Tray's leg. "Transmitter's directional. If he's not in the line of the signal, he won't get it."

"You got it on Terrana, and tracked it four days," Tray argued, his lunch souring in his stomach.

"It was looking for my Virp. And it was attached to the '*sled*. The moment I responded, it locked on and followed me," Danny explained, lying back on the floor, covering his face with his hands, stomping his feet in anger.

"That's why your Virp vibrated first," Tray realized. "Dammit, Danny!"

"Chase installed this program," Danny sighed. "The '*sled* should be able to find him, too. We just have to get the box high enough to scan."

"As in take off?" Tray scoffed.

"There's a thruster damaged. Take-off will be lopsided if we don't fix it, and I haven't found a replacement for it in stores," Saskia said, sliding in next to Tray and taking a sandwich.

"Tray, is this squash?" Amanda asked, pulling her sandwich apart, eating the bread first, dividing the vegetables by color.

"It's tomato. If you don't like it, give it to Danny. He loves tomatoes," Tray said, tugging the back of Danny's shirt. "Danny, stop crying and eat something. We can use our comms to widen the beam, right? How broken is our antenna?"

"We don't have a position to transmit," Danny coughed, his body wilting on the bench. "The wider our broadcast, the harder it will be to pinpoint a source."

His fingers grazed Tray's arm, then he bowed his head, like he was praying.

Tray poked at his food, shaking his head. His hands hurt. His face hurt. His shoulder hurt. "Right now, I just want someone to realize we're alive so they don't stop looking."

———

For the second time this week, Douglas was waking up with a splitting headache that could have been avoided if he'd never met Sky. Maybe it was the third time this week. There was still that block of memory missing from when the Coureur exploded. It had been a long time since a flash bomb had caught him off guard and he'd forgotten how much it stung his eyeballs.

He was lying on the floor—a cement floor. This wasn't the yard, the street, or the hospital. They'd made it to the warehouse.

"What happened?" Douglas groaned, rolling onto his back, feeling for his hip flask, and taking a drink.

"Flash bomb," Sky answered, funneling her stolen fuel into the glider. All the work he'd done that morning was undone. The pieces were restored. A part of him felt whole again, but if he gave into sentiment, Celio would turn them in.

"Put that fuel can down," Douglas warned, grabbing a wrench.

"Make me," she deadpanned.

The blood rushed to his ears, the urge to avenge McGill rising. He raised the wrench and she drew her gun.

"How did we get here?" he asked, approaching his glider. He wanted to wipe off all the smudges and see it clean and perfect.

"At the risk of breaking you, magic," she answered, eying him, then looking up as through she expected the ceiling to collapse. "Magic is real. That story you told me of the goldens is real. We teleported here. We moved by magic"

"If you can move by magic, why stop here?" he sneered. The flash must have taken out all the deputies too. Her earth-shaking weapon had caught them all off guard. Or she'd shot her way out. Douglas felt his neck, but the cuts Sky had made with her knife had healed.

"I didn't do it. I hitched a ride with a local. And we brought you so you wouldn't get trampled," she said, capping the fuel can. "I told you I'd keep you safe."

"By taking me hostage?" Douglas charged her, using the wrench to knock the empty can from her hand. She grabbed him by the shoulders, throwing him on the ground.

"Before the flash, Dr. Frank said something to you," Sky said, squatting on his chest, pinning him down. "Something that upset you. Upset John."

Douglas lashed out with the wrench but Sky blocked with her elbow, then howled in pain. Grabbing his arms, she slammed his hand against the ground until he released the wrench.

"What did they say?" she asked.

"They said the gods would forgive me if I fell on your blade," he replied, deflating. She had destroyed his life. She created chaos and endangered the lives of fifty people— half of them women—and when she'd held a knife to Douglas' throat, his people had asked *him* to die! "You are a woman. To hurt you is a capital crime."

"If you come with me, I can take you places where no one asks you to die." Sky got off of his chest and picked up his flight jacket, running her fingers over the hawk emblem. Kneeling next to him, she covered him with the jacket. "Barbarians. How dare they? How dare they!"

"You're mad at them when you held a knife to my throat," he challenged, pushing up to his elbows.

"I knew I could heal you. Did they?" Sky said, touching his neck where she'd made the cut. "I thought they would protect you. I thought they'd let me go to keep you safe."

Douglas was stunned by her words. She kept muttering to herself as she moved to open the gate.

"Sky, daylight!" Douglas exclaimed, pulling her sideways as the gate swung open. The frosty air filled the room. When Sky didn't shove him off right away, Douglas checked to make sure he hadn't accidentally hurt her. Her crystal blue eyes gazed piteously at him.

"I can't get a signal down here," she said, as though she were explaining that heaven was a myth. "In the air, we have a better chance of contacting help."

Douglas shook his head, gazing at her with equal pity. "Sky, we'll burn in the daylight. We don't have protection for our faces."

"Then stay here," she said, her expression turning cold. "You'll be stuck here forever, you coward. You're not like your father. He at least had the courage to fly out there."

Douglas' nostrils flared. "And he's dead. You saw his bones."

Sky raised her chin, preparing to fight. Then, in the silence, he heard a faint chirping sound.

"What is that?" Douglas asked.

"The transceiver," Sky said, her eyes going wide. "Someone is calling. Someone is here!"

26

The afternoon sun was blistering and the glider's top wings provided little shade in the cockpit. Douglas knew he needed to keep his face shielded, but the world looked so different in the light of day that he couldn't help but stare. The land in Rocan Valley was more barren than he'd ever imagined, dead and lifeless, the dirt bleached and hard packed all the way to the mountains. Snow sparkled on the mountaintops. The Dome stood out, its pale grey slate alien to the environment. Sweat beaded on Douglas' face, stinging his eyes, and he removed his goggles, letting the frosty wind dry his skin.

The signal from the transceiver could have been a trick, but with the fuel stolen and the engine reintegrated, Douglas couldn't say no to one more ride. Closing his eyes, he imagined he was a child again and his father was in the pilot's seat. They hadn't been in the air more than two minutes before he felt Sky banking.

"There. Do you see it?" she said.

Douglas saw a black boulder. "That scorched rock? It was probably hit by lightning."

"That's no rock, Hawk," Sky said with a grin, circling again and going in for a landing.

"That's your home?" he asked. The lower they got, the easier it was to tell that the structure was manmade. It looked broken and burned, but it wasn't sun-bleached like the rest of the land.

"Not home; ship," Sky said delightedly. "That ship could eat mine for breakfast. In fact, I think it did. He found me. Chase found me! Four days. He must have sent help from Terrana the moment I crashed."

Douglas swallowed nervously. It was as though the story of the goldens had come to life, and he imagined people who looked like him spilling out, come to save and rescue those who had been stranded in Rocan. If they'd come for Sky, he knew it wouldn't be so, but for the first time, he could entertain the possibility that there was truth to the myth. Sky rambled in another language, but she landed the glider smoothly, rolling to a stop next to the monstrous ship. Her jaw was set and she got a vicious glint in her gaze. It was not the look of a woman going to greet friends.

The "ship" barely looked airworthy, but the resources it contained were vast. It was easily thirty feet high and the wings looked too small for the body. The markings along the hull were not in Rocanese or Trade, but the alphabet was the same. The hull plating was scorched and broken in places, and the windows were blacked out.

Sky charged the ship, pulling some new device out of her satchel. She placed the device on the ship's hull and a few seconds later, a door popped open. Douglas stared as she disappeared inside, then using his flight jacket as a sunshade, he dashed across the rocky land and into the ship.

The air inside was clean and brisk, and Douglas closed the door behind himself to keep it from getting any colder. He tested the latch, making sure he could open it again. There was an electronic panel next to the latch with blinking lights.

It took a minute for his eyes to adjust to the dim lighting. They were in a giant storage room, spanning at least half the height of the ship. Sky climbed onto something in the middle of the room that looked like a ten-foot silver bullet with wheels.

Douglas hugged his father's jacket to his chest, marveling at the sight. He'd believed Sky's desperation to contact her friends was selfish, but he saw in this place his city's salvation. They could escape the valley, find new blood. Love who they wanted. Let their children grow up without fear of breeding.

"Sky," Douglas croaked, stumbling toward the giant bullet. If he had this kind of raw metal, he could make a fleet of gliders. He could sneak his own glider back into Rocan without having to explain the surplus resources, too. "Sky?"

She muttered angrily in her foreign language. Climbing out of the bullet, she brushed past him to a dismantled metal box on the floor. Douglas couldn't keep his jaw shut. *The devices we have in the yard must seem so primitive to her.*

Hearing a loud clanging, Douglas spun about, searching for the source of the noise. Someone was coming! Going silent, Sky drew her gun and motioned Douglas to stay down. Not knowing what to hide behind, he cocked his fist and prepared to fight.

"Danny," Amanda hissed, shaking Danny's shoulder.

Danny lifted his head off the floor and wiped the drool from his mouth. It felt like the sandwich he'd had was still lodged in his throat.

"Ask Tray," he murmured, folding his arm under his head. Someone had put a blanket over his shoulders. They just let him sleep on the galley floor.

"I'm going to Disappear," Amanda whispered, pressing her face against his neck. "I remember now. I remember this feeling. This is what it feels like right before I Disappear."

"You're not going anywhere, sweetheart. You're stuck here with me," Danny said, patting the back of her head.

"A spirit is close. The spirit realm is bleeding," Amanda rambled.

"Where's the knife?" Danny asked, blinking away grief. He checked Amanda's hand, but there were no fresh cuts.

"I need it," Amanda realized, scrambling across the floor, looking for something to use as a weapon. She grabbed a frying pan from one of the drawers.

"No, you don't!" Danny cried, shoving the blanket aside. Amanda darted out of the galley and opened the hatch to the catwalk, letting in the chilled air from the lower deck.

"Saskia! You down there?" Danny called, grabbing the frying pan from Amanda and closing the hatch behind them. The cold air brought goose bumps to his skin.

Amanda dropped to a crouch, body tense, eyes alert.

"Let's go back to the galley. You're not dressed for the cold." With a longsuffering sigh, Danny linked his arm with Amanda's, but she hooked her fingers into the catwalk grating and refused to stand. Rolling his eyes, Danny trotted down the stairs into the bay.

"Tray?" he called. "Are you in the '*sled*?"

"Thieving, scavenging, deviant mongrels!" an angry voice cried in Lanvarian and Danny panicked. A white-clad woman charged toward him, gun in hand, fist cocked. *Should have kept the frying pan.*

"Who are you? How did you get in here?" he demanded, rushing forward and knocking the gun from her hand. Their last stow-away had appeared on their ship by some kind of spirit portal, and Amanda had sensed a spirit coming.

"You greedy vandal!" she screamed. Her accent was from Kemah or Olcott, but her fighting style was purely Pierce. She grabbed his arm and twisted. Still gravity-sick, Danny was overpowered, but he managed to shake her off before she ripped his arm out of socket.

"You've ruined my one good chance of getting out of here!" she accused, pointing to the *Bobsled.*

"You were in the '*sled*!" he realized. "Is Chase with you? Did he survive the crash?"

Suddenly, a red-haired man jumped out from behind the *Bobsled* and whipped Danny around by the collar. The man was smaller than Danny, but strong from a lifetime spent in Aquian gravity. He raised a gun like a club and whipped it across Danny's chin.

Stunned, Danny punched the guy in the gut, jabbed, and disarmed him. The gun felt strangely weighted, but the firing mechanism was clear enough. Danny pointed it at the two intruders.

"Hawk, get down," the woman ordered in Trade, taking a defensive position in front of the red-haired man.

Hearing a clamor on the catwalk, Danny saw Saskia positioned with a stunner.

"Danny?" Tray called, holding a shock-dart and coming down the stairs, leaving himself wide open. Danny held up a hand to show he had the situation under control and the woman used that opportunity to get in a punch. Her fist clipped his jaw and he stumbled. When he heard the whine of Saskia's stunner charging, he crouched instinctively.

"Saskia, don't!" he ordered, wanting answers before Saskia stunned the intruders into next Tuesday. Danny tasted blood, and his tongue stung, but he still had all his teeth. He held up one hand in surrender and tossed the strange gun up onto the catwalk out of the other woman's reach. "And you, stick to name calling, please."

"Scavenger! Depraved beast! Nomad!"

Danny got the sense she was the kind of woman who read thesauruses in her spare time . . . or wrote them.

"Captain, she's a National sympathizer. I recognize her! She's one of General Santos' people!" Saskia warned.

Danny retreated up the stairs, pulling Tray back and taking his brother's weapon. "Are you a bounty hunter?" Danny asked.

"Hay nah! Did you crash?" she exclaimed. "I thought Chase sent you to rescue me!"

"Chase and I built this ship. We followed its signal here," Danny said, pointing to the *Bobsled*. "What happened to Chase?"

The woman's eyes narrowed and finally she backed off, looking between Saskia's stunner to Danny's shock-dart. Heaving a frustrated sigh, the woman sat on the ground next to her red-haired friend. "Chase stayed in Quin."

Tray was damn sick of intruders showing up on his spaceship and threatening his crew. In spite of that, he was excited by the fact that these two had come from a Dome. If he played this right, they'd not only get a signal home, but negotiate some lucrative trade deals with a previously untapped market.

The woman, Sky, was more vocal than violent, though Danny would need an icepack for his chin. She was familiar with Quin, and that gave Tray hope that he'd be reunited with his son soon. The man she called Hawk hadn't spoken. He was backed against a wall, watching wide-eyed. His clothes looked older and more worn than Danny's, which was saying a lot.

When Sky stopped fighting and started talking more civilly, Tray approached Hawk. The man was frozen in place; his eyes fixated on the shock-dart Tray carried, getting wider with every step Tray took. With the wires coiled around the barrel, shock-darts looked scarier than stunners, but they were among the least dangerous weapons in the armory.

"Are you alright?" Tray asked in Lanvarian, since that was the language Sky spoke. Hawk's brow quirked and he licked his lips, but didn't say anything. His face was blistered from exposure to the sun.

"Do you want to sit down?" Still no response. Tray turned to Sky. "Is he deaf?"

"He's in shock. Hawk's people don't believe in aliens," she answered in Trade. "Or anyone living out here beyond their Dome."

Hawk looked to her, then back at Tray, mouthing the Trade word 'alien.'

"I bet I could make your head explode just by staring," Tray said, switching to Trade and grinning evilly. Hawk's lips parted, but no sound came out.

"Tray, behave!" Danny ordered.

Saskia touched Hawk's face and he jumped back, his grip tightening on the garment in his hands. Up close it looked like a canvas coat, not nearly warm enough for the weather.

"You're going to be okay, Hawk," Saskia said. "Do you hear me?"

Hawk nodded, strands of his bright red hair falling over his eyes.

"Do you believe me?"

Hawk shrugged.

"Hawk, sit down," Sky ordered, crossing between him and Saskia, posturing possessively. Hawk sat at the base of the stairs, staring at his knees. Tray resisted the urge to tease, since his first attempt at humor had only frightened the man.

"Hawk, look at me," Sky said, fussing over the burns on his face. "Can you see me?"

Hawk peeked at her, then ducked his eyes.

"You can go home whenever you want. You don't have to wait for me if you want to take the glider back now. Take it apart. Build your new Coureur. Whatever you want. I'm safe here," she said. "Do you understand?"

Hawk tucked his chin against his jacket.

"Take your time. Find your voice. These people are going to help me," she whispered, kissing the top of his head maternally, then turning back to Danny. "Are you going back to Quin or Terrana?"

"Quin first," Danny replied. "We're not space worthy."

"Only if we can find it," Tray said, biting back a curse.

"Maybe I could have found out if you hadn't dismantled my nav system!" The woman broke into a string of insults once more, not restricting herself to Lanvarian or Trade.

"And we're back to name calling," Danny said, throwing up his hands and heading to the infirmary.

Sky chased after him. "Wait! What do you need to get this thing in the air?"

"Nozzle's cracked on the starboard thruster," Saskia answered. "It'd be an easy fix if we had a replacement part, but we don't."

Danny, Saskia, and Sky huddled up, their conversation devolving into technical terms that Tray wouldn't have followed no matter what language they were in.

Glancing up the stairs, Tray saw Amanda still crouching in the doorway. She held her finger to her lips then slunk back into the corridor.

"Let's get you clean and get some medicine on those blisters," Tray said, turning to Hawk.

Hawk twitched and blinked, rocking back and forth with his jacket.

"Are you cold? It's warmer in the infirmary," Tray tried, standing and waiting to see if Hawk followed.

"You've been here the whole time?" Hawk asked. "You're so close. Why didn't you come visit before?"

"We just landed a few hours ago," Tray said. "Until Sky's signal, we had no idea there was anything or anyone here."

Hawk gave him a blank look, and Tray fidgeted, too angry about the circumstances to explain them in child's terms.

"Stay here. I'll be right back," Tray decided. It was better that Hawk not see the corpse in the infirmary.

27

Douglas hugged his father's jacket, worried he would drop it or it would dissolve or the world would end. Sky called them aliens. They certainly looked it. Danny had brown skin, darker than any golden in Rocan. Tray and Saskia were even darker. They all had deep brown eyes and black hair like him—like his natural hair. They spoke Lanvarian. History books never depicted Lanvarians as brown-skinned. Maybe they did and Douglas hadn't paid attention.

Saskia spoke Trade with the same accent as Sky. They were speaking to him, asking him questions, but he could barely make sense of any of it. He wanted to ask them about the blinking lights on the wall next to the door or the electronic box on the floor. But then, they gave up talking to him and started talking to each other again. Shifting to the edge of the stair, Douglas looped his arms through the railing, watched, and listened. They were speaking rapidly and technically. Sky had used a lot of those words in the yard yesterday, but he couldn't remember what she'd been referencing at the time.

Alien technophiles. Of course, it made sense that only technologically advanced aliens could make it this far. There were no phantom wings or clouds of smoke and magic. No talk of teleportation.

"The people here barely have motors. A rocket is out of the question," he heard Sky complain. She rubbed her forehead and crossed her arms. The interplay of men and women as equals was refreshing, like what he'd hoped for when he first invited Zoe to the yard.

"The old plant," Douglas said, finding his voice. "When the skies first cleared, we sent up rockets to broadcast our survival. Every year, they did it, hoping to draw attention to the valley. They did it until the rocket fuel ran dry. That's what the recorder said. The rockets are stored in the old processing plant."

He'd listened to the recorder devices telling the history of the rocket program over and over. Now he wondered if the goldens had been in Rocan at the time, or if perhaps their arrival had spurred the launches.

"The old plant," Danny repeated. "You can take us there?" He was taller than the rest—as tall as John.

Douglas cringed at Danny's intensity. Everything felt surreal and if he didn't help the aliens, Tray would make his head explode.

"Not if you're going to steal from us and leave," Douglas murmured. If the rockets went missing—if anything went missing—and Sky didn't return, Douglas would be blamed. "Just go in. Peacefully. Tell them you can help. Tell them you'll help them. Don't leave them to die."

"We won't leave you," Sky said with a congenial smile. "I'm sure this nice captain will give you a ride wherever you want to go."

"I have a place in Rocan," Douglas said, though the words felt hollow now that his truth had been shattered. There was a world outside of Rocan, just as his father had believed.

"Your people asked you to die," Sky reminded him.

"I don't want to leave my home," he whimpered. "I want to open it up to the world! You want to steal what little resources we have—"

"I will repay your generosity," Danny assured. "You have my word."

Douglas covered his mouth, hyperventilating. Tray knelt in front of him, and Douglas was sure his life was about to end. When Tray's hand touched his face, Douglas' skin felt instantly chilled.

"Breathe, friend. Breathe," Tray soothed, massaging a cooling ointment all over Douglas' face. It was different than Sky's medicine, but more effective than anything he would have gotten at the hospital. Once Douglas' face was covered, Tray squeezed a dab of the ointment onto the back of Douglas' hand, and rubbed it in. "Forgive my brother. We're eager to leave, but we are willing to trade for what we need. We can negotiate with your leaders if you think they'll listen."

Danny frowned and turned to Sky. "Can *you* get to this plant?"

"I know where it is," she replied. "We'll take the glider."

"We?" Danny repeated. "Given *his* response, I doubt I'd be well received in that Dome."

Douglas shrank back, frustrated that his first encounter with aliens was going so poorly.

"I don't plan on making my presence known. And if you think I'm leaving this ship without insurance, you're crazy," Sky said.

"This is an air ship," Douglas murmured, hoping the experience would seem less surreal if he said it out loud.

"No," Saskia said. "It's designed primarily for short distance space jumps. Aquia to Terrana."

"Terrana?" Douglas choked, his vision swimming.

"The gray moon," Tray explained.

Douglas looked incredulously at Sky. This was beyond alien. "Short distance? Long distance is an option?"

"It's not as exciting as you'd imagine," Tray said, capping the ointment and sitting back. Shocked, Douglas folded his arms and laid his head on the stair. It was getting hard to breathe.

As far as Sky was concerned, she was past plans A, B, and C. Her current plan didn't have a letter, but the sudden arrival of a spaceship willing to take her back to Quin was a stroke of good fortune that she'd be sure to thank Chase for later. The captain reminded her of Chase and she had a feeling she'd met him before.

Oriana was larger than the typical freighter, designed to haul water tanks and heavy moon-slate. Danny didn't seem to be using it for anything of the sort. What few cargo items Sky saw had been pushed to the corners to make space for the *Bobsled.* Those crates got shifted and stacked once more as they made space for the glider, bringing it inside so the rudders wouldn't freeze off in the weather. They would wait until sunset to go back to the city. Danny offered them food and drink, but Hawk just drank gin from his flask and sat in his glider in the frigid bay.

"You must be getting hungry," Sky said, stroking his hair, tucking it behind his ears. "Don't you want to see the rest of the ship? You can see the engine room. It's amazing."

Hawk blinked at her, still dazed and clinging to his flight jacket.

"Hawk, I need you to snap out of this," Sky said, snapping her fingers in front of his face. "If you go back to Rocan wearing that look on your face, people will know something's up."

He touched the yoke, then touched his jacket. “You let me believe you were a Sequestered.”

“No, I told you the truth. You didn’t listen,” Sky pointed out, tucking a blanket around his shoulders.

“Why?” he whispered, brushing his cheek on the blanket. “If they can go all the way to Terrana, why haven’t they come here before?”

Sky shrugged. She’d heard many excuses through the years. No fuel, no supplies, no landing strips, no communications. Hawk folded his jacket over his hands and touched his empty flask to his lips.

“Or is the myth true?” he mused. “The goldens came by rocket and destroyed the real Rocan . . . and we’re descendants of the survivors.”

“That’s not the myth you told me last night,” Sky said, taking the flask away. “I came. They followed me. This is the world as you dreamed it would be. You’ve found your place. This is your chance to save Rocan.”

“Save?” he repeated, focusing for the first time. “How?”

“There you are,” Sky smiled, pinching his chin. “Do you remember the device I used to heal your head, the medicine I got from Cordova?”

Douglas touched the ointment on his sunburnt skin. “You’ll take me there?”

“These people can get you there, if we help them.”

This was a bad plan. That was the only thought on Danny’s mind as he slipped out of his brown, leather jacket to don a shoulder holster. As much as he wanted a stunner, a pulse rifle was easier to conceal.

Bad plan. Grief was no excuse. He was going to get his crew killed by trying to save them.

Danny leaned against the ward room weapons locker, and took a deep, shuddering breath. He gasped when he felt Amanda's hand on his shoulder.

"Haven't Disappeared completely, I see," Danny commented, taking the bowie knife and freshly charged Virp from her hands.

"Sky tried to kill me," Amanda said, her voice distant and hollow.

"Sky hasn't been near you," Danny sighed. "It's me she tried to kill."

"She makes the air taste like ashes."

"She smells fine. She's riding with us back to Quin. You'll get bored if you hide from her the whole way," Danny said, pulling off his drained Virp and sliding on the glove for the fresh one.

"Spirit Sky," Amanda carped, giving him a look.

"Spirit Sky?" he asked. He'd dismissed the notion of Sky arriving by spirit portal when he'd seen that glider, but he couldn't deny that Amanda had sensed their arrival. "She's not going to open a portal to Elysia and bring in more of the Guard is she?"

"Spirit Sky doesn't talk to half-breeds like Galen," Amanda sighed. "She doesn't trust the human hybrids either."

Danny wanted to ask more, but he didn't think her answers would lead to clarity. Amanda tilted the spent Virp in her hand, watching the metal casing reflect light off the ceiling. Whatever it reminded her of, it made her smile. He closed his eyes in prayer.

"Listen to Tray while I'm gone," he said, giving her a nudge.

Amanda pressed her lips together and twitched. Her sallow cheeks held a faint rosy tint, and after a few moments, she turned her green eyes on him and frowned. "I think he should listen to me."

"Say something useful and he might," Danny quipped. Her gaze flickered and she didn't smile. She reached past Danny into the weapons cabinet, fingering a stunner. Danny closed the cabinet and locked it. Linking his arm with hers, he escorted her from the ward room down the stairs to the bay, leading her as far from the weapons cabinet as she allowed. He didn't force her past the hatch to the catwalk.

"The glider's as sky-worthy as we can make it, sir," Saskia reported, meeting him by the stairs.

Danny nodded, habitually checking his Virp for fresh news feeds, and cringing at the network error. Saskia handed him a long coat and gloves.

"We should be back by morning. Keep trying to contact Quin. If you don't hear from me, I'd appreciate a rescue," Danny said.

"It's not like I have other options. I'm on a broken ship in the middle of nowhere," Saskia shrugged, as if his rescue were already penciled in on her day's schedule.

"We could always set up a garden," Tray grinned. "Hang some curtains."

"Don't start," Danny warned.

"What else *can* I do?" Tray retorted.

"Stay here. Keep an eye on Amanda."

"Or you can stay and he could come," Sky suggested, leaning close to Danny's ear.

Danny cringed. Until she gave him a clear answer about how she wrestled the *Bobsled* from Chase, there was no way Danny was letting her take Tray anywhere. He half-expected to find his old friend dead when they returned to Quin. Amanda's warning that they may be contending with a hybrid only added to his worry.

28

It was easy to hate Danny when he was flying off into the darkness. Tray glowered at the vanishing glider then turned on his heels, stalking back toward *Oriana.* Danny had spent the entire afternoon with the strangers, and they were no closer to getting a signal to Quin.

"Come inside before you freeze to death," Saskia said, pushing him inside and locking the back door. Tray stumbled, his mind spinning, his breath freezing in front of his face.

"Did you see their clothes? They didn't even have coats. They barely had sleeves," Tray exclaimed.

Saskia hooked his elbow, dragging him up the stairs.

"They don't have rockets," Tray continued. "They don't have anything. Did you see that contraption they flew off in? It's scrap! They're going to come back with an army and salvage *Oriana* for parts. We're going to die here!"

"We are not going to die here," Saskia said. "The captain—"

"Is blind with grief. I never should have let him go," Tray interrupted.

"Sky—"

"She's going to betray him!" Tray finished. "You said it yourself. She's one of Santos' operatives."

Saskia slammed the hatch to the galley, sealing them into the upper decks, then she clamped her hand over Tray's mouth to silence his rant.

"She's not working for him now. She's a nomad. And right now, we're her ticket out of here," Saskia said.

"We? Or *Oriana*? She doesn't need me!" Tray retorted, flexing his arms like he was about to throw her off, but not daring to push. Saskia dropped her threatening stance and went to pour herself another cup of Terranan coffee. Her fifth today. Tray would have made a comment about rationing, but he planned to get rescued before it became an issue.

"It's been fourteen hours since we landed," Tray sighed, massaging his shoulder. "Alex wasn't that far behind us."

"As long as we can see Terrana, there's someone up there who can receive our message," Saskia shrugged between sips. "Is your shoulder hurting?"

"It's feeling okay. And we had intruders," Tray said. "I left the sling by the weapon's locker."

"I'll get it," she said, trotting upstairs. The upper decks had cooled a lot faster than anticipated and Tray worried what another freezing night would do to their morale. They should have braved the Dome in the daylight, met the people, and asked for help.

"If Sky was a Guard, that explains why Amanda doesn't like her," Tray said.

"Sky was no Guard. She was General Santos' mistress," Saskia scoffed. She stopped in her tracks when she reached the ward room. Tray bumped into her and the coffee spilled. Amanda sat at the console, wearing one of Corey's thick sweaters, her brown hair in a ponytail. For a moment, she looked so much like Corey that all Tray could do was stare.

"Turn that off. You're wasting electrics," Saskia carped, snapping out of the trance.

"What are you reading?" Tray asked, diffusing the tension.

"Rumors mostly," Amanda answered, hunching over and squinting at the words. "They're all about me. You spent a lot of time looking for me."

"Danny did," Tray confirmed, pulling a seat next to her. "He never gave up."

"Off," Saskia said irately, reaching between them and shutting off the screen.

Amanda rubbed her eyes, and leaned sideways against Tray. "He doesn't seem happy that I'm here. He did the first hour. I guess that's how long it took for him to figure out I was broken . . . or at least not who he wanted me to be."

"He's not disappointed in you, sweetheart," Tray said, patting her shoulder awkwardly. "He's grieving. He loved Corey and it's been a long time since he's let himself love anyone."

"Because he was searching for me?" Amanda asked. If Amanda hadn't resurfaced, they'd be in Quin right now. Tray could have left *Oriana* to be with his son, and Corey and Danny could have been together. *No matter how the dice fell, Danny and I were never going to be a family again.*

The glider was tight with three. Douglas wanted to fly, but he let Sky do it because his hands were shaking and his stomach growling. He was bringing an alien into his city. Douglas was squeezed into the back seat of his glider, his body pressed tightly against Danny's. He leaned his ear against Danny's back, enjoying the vibrations as Danny and Sky conversed in their foreign tongue. Danny smelled like an alien, and it was intoxicatingly savory. His clothes were fresh and clean in a way that clothes in Rocan never got. And he was warm.

Sky landed smoothly just outside the Caswell gate and Douglas' pulse raced. His heart and mind warred. That afternoon Sky had had a knife to his throat, and now she offered him a chance to save his children from breeding. He had to help. This was for his children. For all of Rocan.

The pressure against Douglas' body eased as Sky and Danny extracted themselves from the cockpit. Douglas slouched, then carefully folded and tucked his father's jacket under the front seat. The gate closed, the room warmed, and the future he'd dreamed was finally arriving.

"I thought I'd find you here," Celio clucked, leaning against the warehouse door. Douglas' face went pale and he ducked into the cockpit instinctively, but he knew it was too late to hide. Sky was in trouble for taking hostages, and the plan had been to avoid anyone finding her.

"Celio, I can explain," Douglas said, climbing out of the glider. His fingers were so cold, they ached. "When I told Sky the story of the goldens, she realized it was safe to share her magic with us."

He turned in a circle, looking to Sky for confirmation, but both Sky and Danny were gone. Black smoke oozed from his fingers just as it had from his father's bones. A new panic took hold—the fear that he'd dreamed the whole thing.

"Danny? Sky?" he called, circling the glider, his heart sinking.

"Are you ill?" Celio asked, his voice tainted with malice.

"Yes," Douglas whispered, wringing his hands.

"You and Sky disappeared from the yard. Harris is worried sick. I nearly told him to look here for you."

"You told him about this place?" Douglas squeaked. "You said there was still time."

"You said you were going to bring home that engine. You haven't even cracked the casing."

"I started to, but then Sky undid it," Douglas murmured, touching the engine hood, cringing at the heat rising off. "Celio, what are you doing here?"

"I didn't know where you were, so I came for the engine."

"Celio—"

"Your face is red."

Douglas touched his cheek and the alien ointment rubbed off on his fingers. Or maybe it was engine grease. "We can take it as soon as it cools."

"Cools?" Celio touched the glider, grimacing. "Did you take this thing outside the Dome, Hwan?"

"Yes, but it's not what you think," Douglas said.

Celio charged him. "Where is Sky? She's not holding you hostage now. Is she out there—outside? Is that why you stole the fuel?"

"No," Douglas said. "She's not from here. We used the transceiver she built to get a message to another Dome! Sky tell him!"

Celio looked around, waiting for Sky to jump from the shadows, but nothing happened. Douglas was afraid to move. There weren't any places to hide in the warehouse; she and Danny had effectively disappeared.

"Are they invisible?" he asked. He didn't know what kind of alien powers they had.

"Hwan, there is no such thing as magic," Celio grumbled. "Tell me the truth."

"There were aliens with brown skin," Douglas said, panicking as the smoke coming from his fingers clouded his vision. "They came on a spaceship from Terrana! They came for Sky to take her back where she belongs and—"

"Are you listening to yourself?" Celio interrupted, grabbing Douglas by the elbow, hauling him out of the warehouse.

Douglas was listening, and he didn't believe it himself. The walls between dream and reality were crumbling, and he wasn't sure of anything anymore, except the woman he'd promised to protect had held a knife to his throat and caused the ground to shake. Her medicines could have made him hallucinate the rest.

"There were aliens," Douglas repeated, clinging to Celio's arm, terrified that he was losing his mind.

"You were abducted by aliens?" Celio repeated. Douglas nodded, tugging Celio's hand, pointing back to the warehouse, but Celio slapped him across the cheek. "Listen to yourself Hwan. Listen to what your obsession with this flying machine has done to you."

"No, it's true. It's true!" Douglas cried.

"Come with me," Celio snarled, grabbing him by the elbow again and dragging him back to Qu'Appelle. "You're burned. Look at yourself. You're completely sunburned, wind-burned, frost-burned. Did the first Coureur really explode or was the fire a ruse so you could hoard that engine too!"

Douglas couldn't even look Celio in the eye. The whole afternoon felt hazy. "They had brown skin. Dark. One of them almost black. They want to take me with them. To save our children."

"Right now, I'm less worried about the children and more worried about you," Celio said, putting an arm around his shoulder. It seemed so unnaturally brotherly that Douglas thought he was still hallucinating.

"I have a place here," Douglas whispered, clinging to Celio. "I have a place . . ."

"Yes, you always have," Celio said. "Little Hwan, you have an extraordinary gift. Unless you want to spend the rest of your life locked in the asylum with your mother, you won't tell anyone about these aliens."

Whining wretchedly, Douglas buried his face in Celio's

shoulder and let himself be led back to Qu'Appelle. His body trembled, overwhelmed by fear and physical pain. Celio's scent soon replaced Danny's. He smelled comfortingly familiar, like the mines of Rocan, and despite his muttered disapproval, he seemed to want to help.

29

A gust of icy air blasted Danny's face, and the dim lights of the warehouse were replaced by dimmer lights of twilight in the cold tundra.

"There's no Dome. Hay nah, I broke the Dome," Sky murmured, clutching his elbow, pressing her cheek to his shoulder.

Danny turned, looking for the glider. They were outside the Dome, several yards away. "It's there," he whispered, turning to show Sky.

"Oh, good," she exhaled, taking his hand and running toward it.

A stranger moved to intercept. He wore thick, ragged layers of blankets, and his face was shielded, but he didn't appear any warmer than Danny.

"I thought you were leaving," he accused, waving his arm at Sky. "Now you bring more strangers?"

"Danny, Jotham," Sky said, her teeth chattering as she huddled close to Danny for warmth. "Jotham, Danny is my ride out of here, but his ship is having some mechanical difficulties."

"You are wanted for assault and injury to over thirty men. I cannot keep helping you," Jotham protested.

"Can we talk to Kyrn?" Sky tried. She smiled at Danny. "Kyrn is the reasonable one."

"Kyrn can barely walk because you broke his ribs. He went back into the hospital this morning," Jotham said.

"Did we teleport?" Danny asked. They had been in the warehouse. He got out of the glider. He was just about to call for Hawk when the cold hit.

"Yeah. Keep up," Sky smirked, biting his shoulder.

"We teleported," Danny affirmed. And Sky had broken a man's ribs. That didn't bode well.

"He's not spirit-kind?" Jotham balked.

"No."

"Spirit-kind?" Danny repeated. He'd barely accepted that the Disappeared had been affected by some kind of alien, supernatural intervention, but to see humans wield that kind of power was frightening. He now knew what Amanda meant by 'human hybrid.'

"Apparently, this town is littered with hybrids, but most of them have no idea what they are," Sky whispered. "Jotham and his merry band keep it that way."

"Oh." Danny nodded, numbness coming from inside and out. "The spirit realm is bleeding. That's what Amanda said when she felt you coming. The spirit realm is bleeding."

"It does feel that way when you sense the approach of an unbridled power," Jotham agreed. "Kyrn and I—we can move, but we are blind to the other realm. We see what humans see, but we know when a conjurer breaks. We protect them."

"Ok." He had so many questions, but his mind was in turmoil.

"We need to get to the old processing plant," Sky said.

"I'm not letting you back in my city," Jotham said, starting to cross his arms, then realizing his clothing was too thick.

"We can't leave until we fix the nozzle. Hawk said . . ." Danny trailed off, looking for the boy. "Where is he?"

"I barely had the energy to carry two of you," Jotham said. "Besides, he belongs in the city. He's not wanted for crimes of violence."

"Poor kid's going to be scared out of his mind," Danny realized.

"And into asylum," Sky added.

"No thanks to you," Jotham accused.

"Jotham, it's freezing. Take us back," Sky demanded. The two stared off a moment, then Sky added: "We're not leaving until we get what we came for."

"Gate's that way," Jotham said, pointing left. He vanished and Danny stared at the footprints left on the permafrost.

"Process inside," Sky said, yanking his elbow. The gate wasn't hard to find, and when they went through, they were back in the warehouse. The Dome air felt sweltering, but Danny was shivering too much to unzip his coat.

"Hawk? Hawk!" Sky called, leaping onto the glider's wing and checking the cockpit. Not finding him there, she slid back to the ground, circled the warehouse, then went to a door leading out to the street. Danny came next to her, just in time to see a man put his arm around Hawk and the two of them walk around a corner.

"Damn it," Sky hissed, ducking back inside. "One foot in asylum already."

"Stop them," Danny said, pushing past, but Sky kept him back.

"He was on the fence about leaving as is, and taking him hostage again isn't going to help anything," Sky said, slipping into the street and motioning Danny to follow. "We'll get what we need and come back for him if we can.

"If?" Danny repeated. The streets were deserted and freakishly quiet. Quin was densely packed through and through. Even Terrana never had more than a few abandoned houses on any street. This city had only a single Dome and the population didn't even fill it. "Hawk took a risk bringing us back here. We should make sure things are right before we go."

"You're going to tell a Dome depleted of resources that you have a spaceship sitting three miles across the tundra," Sky sneered. "We fibbed a bit to Hawk to get him on our side, but you know how Quin feels about charity cases. That's why Terrana opted for independence and poverty to begin with."

"Terrana and Quin have a long, political history," Danny argued. "Finding human survivors in another Dome . . . it'll change how they see the world. Maybe they'll send people some place other than up."

"It's a lot more fun to travel the world when you don't have the government breathing down your neck demanding you turn a profit," Sky chuckled. They approached a makeshift barrier, beyond which the houses had lights and there were people on the streets, dressed in drab, conservative garb. Sky's white clothes seemed to glow in comparison.

"You stole my *'sled* to get here. But someone had to pay to build it," Danny retorted. "I can't believe I followed you here."

"I didn't tell you to come!"

"You didn't tell me not to," Danny huffed. "I thought if Chase were here—"

"He's not. I am," Sky said, pressing her lips together. She grabbed his collar and pulled him into the shadows, and Danny followed her lead. He hid behind Sky, waiting for danger to pass. Her closeness was intoxicating, and Danny's hips pressed to hers.

"There's no one around," she said, sliding her hand up his thigh. "Do you want to—"

"Do not finish that sentence," Danny panted. He didn't want her; he wanted Corey, and it was too late for that.

"I'm sure I can be more entertaining than that girl you have locked in your quarters," Sky crooned, sauntering closer and running her hands across his chest. "I can tell you're not married."

"You don't know anything about her," Danny said, clenching his teeth to keep from succumbing. Sky dropped the seduction, moving across the barrier to the populated side of town.

"You have the freedom to choose your companions, captain," Sky said. "But if I find out that girl being kept against her will, I will castrate you and set her free."

"Thanks for the heads up," Danny said, smiling despite himself. It was the first thing Sky had said all day that made him want to trust her. "She knows you from Terrana. And she's hiding from you."

John rolled the dice, but he was too distracted to concentrate on the game. Don wasn't paying attention either. They'd forgotten the score five times in the last hour.

"No more," Don moaned, lying down on the couch. His head touched John's leg and John jumped up.

"Pillow?" Don whispered, stretching out to take the whole couch.

John paced to the bedroom, getting Don's pillow and blanket. Then he sat on the bed and cried.

Fall on her blade, Hwan. The gods will forgive you. John would never forgive Dr. Frank for those words. His son could have been murdered in a public square; a lot of people could have. John couldn't believe he'd allowed Sky into his home—into his bed. He was sickened by the thought of her.

"Aren't you tired?" Don asked, stumbling into the room, setting the pillow and nestling under the blanket, leaving space for John to lie next to him.

"I—" John stammered. "You know how you feel after a breeding, when your partner just goes out of her way to make you feel . . . vile?" He shivered, his skin crawling so much he could barely stay seated.

"Take a long soak. Get her touch off your skin," Don suggested, his eyes closing.

The thought had crossed John's mind, but it was a tainted thought. "She kept refilling the bath over and over. When I thought what her Sequesterer may have done to her, I didn't question. She was in my bath. She was in my bed. I want to burn the whole house down."

Don's breathing settled, and John tapped his arm.

"You're supposed to make me feel better," John groused.

"Your heart's broken. You're not going to feel better today," Don sighed, not even opening his eyes.

John shook his head. "For a moment, I believed I'd missed out on some great part of life. I thought things could be so much better."

"Me too." Don turned his face to the pillow, fresh tears streaming. Their unfinished conversation that morning opened up old wounds, and Douglas' disappearance only made it worse.

There was a knock at the door.

"Oh!" Don writhed, rushing to dry his face.

"I'll get it. I'm expected to be a mess," John said, wiping his face.

There was a messenger at the door—a young boy, not ten years old. "Mon Harris, Mon Ferriera sends word. He's taken Douglas to the hospital."

"What? What?" John stammered, clutching his chest. "Thank you. Um."

"Do you have a return message?" the little boy asked, fidgeting and tugging his oversized, green shirt.

"Um. No. Thank you," John said, his mind spinning.

"Goodnight, sir."

"Donny!" John hollered, grabbing his shoes, running back to the bedroom. "They found Douglas. Donny, let's go."

"Douglas doesn't want to see me," Don said, his chest rising and falling like he was talking in his sleep.

"Douglas loves you. He'll be glad to see you," John insisted.

"He attacks me every time—" Don was cut off by his own sob. "I can't be around people in this state."

"Donny, you being in this state is exactly why I can't leave you alone," John said.

Don shrugged out of John's embrace the minute they left the house. His tears dried and his posture stiffened. John hated seeing him like that. He kept a hand on his friend's sleeve, knowing he'd need strength, feeling guilty because Don had so little to give.

Constable Mace met them in the lobby, shaking John's hand formally.

"Ferreira found Little Hwan wandering the streets," Constable Mace explained. "He's been out in the sunlight, and Dr. Louis says that may be affecting his mind. He certainly has a tale to tell."

"He's been committed?" Don asked.

John's throat went dry, realizing they weren't going to the emergency ward, but rather to the asylum.

"No, he's with his mother," Mace answered. "Dr. Louis

thought that would calm him. He says he's built himself a glider like his father's. He told Ferriera that it flies, and by the windburn on his skin, it's plausible."

"That's amazing!" John breathed, stunned. "That must have taken him ages."

"The hoarding of resources is a damning claim. Are you saying you knew?" Mace challenged.

"No." John felt queasy. There were times when the Intendant seemed narrow-minded, and John yearned for new leadership. Then there were times when hours of whiskey and debate led to the conclusion that leadership was not the problem. The Dome Builders had condemned them centuries ago when they chose to build this Dome around a mine in a frozen desert.

"Did you find Sky?" Don asked.

"Sky wasn't with him," Mace shrugged. "We think she's with this glider. That she ditched him when she no longer needed a hostage. He says she disappeared. Ferriera is leading a search of Caswell, in case she's also there hiding. Dr. Frank will evaluate Hwan's mental health within the hour."

"Frank?" John repeated. "No! Frank told Douglas to kill himself. He is not going near my son."

"Harris—"

"I want another doctor to do the evaluation. Donny can do it."

"If he'll talk to me," Don muttered. "There are plenty of doctors who are qualified."

Mace held up a weary hand. "They all report to Frank, and ultimately it's his call. Unless resources are allocated for Douglas to stay in asylum, I have no choice but to take him into custody for the alleged hoarding."

"No choice?" John gulped, feeling a shooting pain in his heart. They didn't have much use for prisons in Rocan. Men who didn't behave were terminated. Women who didn't behave were kept in asylum through their breeding years and then terminated. "There is a choice. I will take him home. I will watch over him."

"He's a flight risk. Literally." There was a hint of pride in Mace's voice on the last word. "Although I hope Sky did steal the machine and fly into the mountains. So long as it's never found, he'll never be convicted."

They reached Kinley's door in asylum and Mace paused outside. John could hear his son's voice, and he closed his eyes, listening. He caught tidbits about the brown-skinned aliens and their spaceship. Douglas' voice hitched, like he was upset.

"I would rather not distress his mother," Mace said. "Will you bring him out?"

John didn't know if he was being offered a kindness or not. To spare Kinley, he had to arrest his own son. "Can I talk to him first?"

"Twenty minutes," Mace said.

The time seemed so short. John hadn't expected more than five minutes, but he wasn't sure any amount of time would help him build the nerve to hand over his son to Mace.

"Donny?"

"I will talk to Dr. Frank about performing the evaluation," Don said, excusing himself from the group.

John knocked on Kinley's door before entering. He was surprised to see Douglas and Kinley on opposite sides of her bed; he'd never found them so far apart. "Hey."

"Run!" Kinley shouted, standing up on the bed, holding a pillow like a bat. "Run far! Run fast!"

"Maman, it's just John!" Douglas exclaimed, diving behind the bed to protect himself from her outburst.

"It's me, Kinley!" John said softly, keeping eye contact with Kinley as he stepped toward Douglas. Kinley screeched and swore, bouncing on the bed. Douglas shuddered when John hugged him from behind and John could feel the heat rising off of Douglas' burnt skin.

"I'm having déjà vu." John quipped. John hadn't been called to the hospital this often since Douglas had experimented with roller skates in the third grade. "Are you okay?"

Douglas wriggled in John's embrace, crossing his arms, closing himself off. "I don't know," he answered.

"Where's Sky?"

"I don't know."

John frowned. "What happened to you after the flash bomb at the yard?"

"I don't know." This time, Douglas' voice cracked. "Sky Sequestered me. She took me. She showed me all these amazing things, and she promised she would help, and now she's gone."

"Let him open his eyes!" Kinley screamed, throwing the pillow at John's face. "Sequesterer! You can't keep him here! Let him go!"

"Kinley, sit still," John begged.

"What's going to happen to me, Papa?" Douglas whispered, his body shaking. "I don't want to be crazy like Maman."

Chills raced up John's spine. In ten years, he'd never heard Douglas call his mother crazy. People that called Kinley crazy in Douglas' presence usually got punched.

"I want things how they were," Douglas whimpered. "Before Sky."

"Did Sky do something to you?" Her name was bitter on John's tongue, but Mace was going to ask, and John wanted to be prepared for the answer.

"She cut my neck," Douglas said, kicking until he was backed against the wall. "I don't know what she did to me. I told her not to go out in the sunlight."

John could see the glazed, stricken look on Douglas' face—he'd seen it on Kinley's face a hundred times.

"I should have fallen on her blade," Douglas moaned, touching his neck.

"No. No, it was wrong of Frank to ask you to do that," John insisted, squeezing Douglas' hand.

"Was it?" The sincerity of Douglas' question sickened John. "I'm lost. I'm nothing. I'm so far gone, even Celio was nice to me."

"Believe it or not, Celio is a nice man. He knows you don't belong in asylum. You had a rough week, but we'll get through it." Holding his boy didn't seem to be enough. They *had* broken him—Sky, Frank, everyone. Douglas quivered, clinging to John. It felt like he was saying goodbye.

"Run! Run far! Run fast! They don't need you here!" Kinley shouted, retrieving her pillow and chucking it at them again. "Crazy man! Crazy! Go back to your spaceship!"

"Kinley!" John cried in frustration.

"She won't listen," Douglas said, wincing as a tear rolled down his cheek. John guided Douglas out of the room and once in the hall, Douglas buried his face in John's shoulder and sobbed.

"They found me," Douglas wept, his voice muffled by John's shirt.

"Your family found you. You're okay now," John soothed, pulling his fingers through Douglas' wind-tangled hair.

"I'm sorry I didn't tell you about the glider."

"I understand why you couldn't," John said. He would hold onto Douglas for as long as Mace let him.

"How many times have you flown it?" Mace asked.

Douglas craned his neck, realizing that they weren't alone. He fisted John's shirt and pressed harder into the embrace.

"How many?" John prompted.

Douglas looked up, but kept his cheek against John's chest. "Three times."

"Where were you going, little Hwan?" Mace asked. "Not over the mountains."

Glancing at Mace again, Douglas shrugged and rocked foot to foot. "I buried my father." With one deep breath, Douglas' body relaxed. The emotion of his embrace shifted from terrified to comfortable. John was glad to be able to give Douglas the comfort his mother couldn't tonight.

"Little Hwan, can you tell me where Sky went?" Mace asked, creeping closer, his tone gentler than John had ever heard it. "Douglas, I am in charge of keeping people safe. She may have other hostages."

"She took me. Only me." Douglas lifted his head. "But she came back. She brought the alien here."

"Alien? Where?" Mace asked. "Can you show me where you where before Celio found you?"

"We have to find them. They can help us—the aliens. They can take us to Cordova." He turned eagerly back to John, touching his neck. "Cordova—it's a city to the east. A city with medicine. Sky healed my cuts with the medicine. They're gone. Look at my hands. Look!"

"I see," he said. "And I'm curious what kind of medicine could heal you so thoroughly. Did she take you out of the city, to that place of medicine?"

"Douglas, you don't have to say anything else until your mental evaluation," John said, worried that Douglas was digging his own grave with those words.

"They can help our children," Douglas insisted.

"Tell me where the aliens are," Mace said.

"He has a right to the evaluation," John snarled, stepping between Douglas and Mace.

"Papa, it's okay," Douglas said. "They are aliens. Sky said they are. They came to steal a nozzle for their rocket. Their home is automechanical, but it's broken," Douglas murmured, like he was remembering a dream.

"Douglas," John pleaded, grabbing his boy's hand. Even talk of stealing resources was dangerous. Mace shot him a look and John knew his time was up.

"Thank you, Harris," Mace dismissed, putting an arm around Douglas and walking away with him. "I believe you, Little Hwan. Tell me where their home is, so we can send help."

"They're only a few miles journey. It's cold, but it's not far," Douglas said. "If we tell them what we need, they'll find help for us. They can do that."

They went down the hall together, walking and talking. Douglas shuffled along, looking trustingly at Mace—something John had never seen before—and his boy never looked back.

30

Constable Channing Mace heard the gong of the clock tower, marking the hour before first shift. He'd sat up half the night, mulling over Douglas Hwan's story, hating that he'd taken the man from the asylum, where he so clearly belonged. Dr. Frank had allocated basic resources, which was just short of a death sentence for a man.

The Constable came to the mouth of the tunnel that led to the Hudson mine, pausing when he saw the Intendant kneeling in prayer. The aurora was bright, casting a pink glow over the tunnel, and the Intendant was not the only one who had come out to acknowledge the light of the gods. Mace waited for the Intendant to stand, then quietly stood beside him, observing the silence. The Intendant glanced at him, then backed away from the tunnel wall, heading into the light of the Dome.

"Tell me it's more than boredom that draws you into the valley," Intendant Hubert said, clasping his hands behind his back. His was of the oldest generation in the Dome, and this early in the morning, he lost a few inches of height to a stooped back. His legs were stiff from kneeling.

"It is more than boredom," Mace assured, walking beside his

leader. "Sky told Douglas of a city to the east called Cordova. They have medicine and medical devices. And we know that clothing Sky wears was not made in Rocan. I do believe there is something out there."

"But a place we can walk to?" the Intendant argued. "Nothing on any map has indicated a Dome that close. We've seen nothing from the height of the Dome. The recorders tell us that in the entire history of the rocket program, no signal has ever been detected. Just that cloud of ancient satellite debris that rains down constantly on the sky and distorts everything."

"Sky arrived at the mine first. Douglas said she came by spaceship," Mace pointed out.

"The device she built to find this spaceship—he didn't bring it back," the Intendant argued. "No one else had detected any kind of signal or interference."

"The men are meeting here at first light. We'll relay one up the Dome ceiling and if we see the ship, then we'll go toward it and meet these visitors. We can post a watchman with a two-way radio. Ramsey says as long as this ship is within five miles, the watchman can direct us and not lose contact."

"You can take ten men," the Intendant said, crossing his arms, scowling.

"We have twice as many coats in resources."

"We don't know that you're coming back," the Intendant snapped. "You'll each be given a flashlight and compass. You'll have two flares, a beacon, a portable shelter, food, and water."

There was a squeak behind them, and Mace reached instinctively for his baton. Felicity stood in the middle of the road, her blond hair damp with sweat, her cheeks red.

"Little one, what are you doing so far from home at this hour?" Mace asked, getting down on one knee. He reached out, but Felicity took a step back, shaking her head.

"Sky," she whispered, cradling her burnt arm.

"If you've come to see her, I'm afraid she's not here," Mace said, scooting closer to the girl. "Come here. I don't want your parents to worry."

Felicity shook her head.

"Are your genetic parents out there?" he asked, nodding to the side. "In Cordova? On the spaceship?"

"I don't know my genetic parents. I was born here. Adopted here," she sniffled, rubbing her eyes.

The Intendant raised one eyebrow, then looked skeptically at Mace. "Are you sure these untold resources are worth the trouble this woman brings?"

"Hwan said there were other women on that ship," Mace said. If it weren't for the consistency of the story, Mace would have dismissed it.

"The boy is stricken with madness. His word can't be trusted," the Intendant countered.

"Don't look for the cracks," Felicity whined, charging into Mace, squeezing the air from his lungs. "They aren't there. Don't believe they're there. You must forget that you've ever seen them."

"Then deny us the resources to go," Mace challenged the Intendant, prying his arms free so that he could calm Felicity down.

"Deny an adventure?" the Intendant huffed. "Something new, something different, something helpful?"

"Don't let him go. Please, don't let him go," Felicity begged, turning on the Intendant.

"Calm down, little one," the Intendant said, lifting her in his arms. "He will be given everything he needs to survive the day's journey, and he will bring his men home. Have faith. Now let's get you to your mother before she worries too much."

"Felicity," Mace began, then hesitated. He wanted to reassure her, but he didn't want to silence her or dismiss her past experiences. They didn't know enough about what had happened to her. "Can you tell me why I shouldn't go? Do you know something about what's out there?"

"Use your words, Felicity. Don't make us guess," the Intendant added.

"Sky isn't there. She's here. And you should stay here, too," Felicity whispered, laying her head on the Intendant's shoulder, bringing her bandaged hands to her lips.

Mace shivered. He had men scouring the town for Sky. The clock gonged once. It was quarter past the hour. The men would be gathering soon.

Don Yale was numb. Sadly, it was not a change from the norm for him. There was a notion of rage, fueled by news that young Douglas Hwan had been imprisoned, but even that fire was encapsulated by numbness. Douglas had hoarded resources and was slated for death. Rather than storm to the Bastien Law Office, Don trudged, medical bag and supplies in hand, his heart aching.

Douglas lay curled under a blanket on the floor of his prison cell, clutching his empty gin flask. The cell was worse than Don had anticipated—cold, cement floors and cinderblock walls. Dirt and lint crept in from the corners, and the air smelled of sweat and body odor. It wasn't used often enough to be kept clean, and it was an awful place for keeping a burn patient overnight.

"No bed?" Don asked the deputy on duty—a rookie named Breaux. He lay on one of the cleared desktops, feet tapping the floor idly, a teacup balanced on his chest. "Get up. This isn't a social call."

"It's not a breeding call," Breaux grumbled, giving him a

dirty look. Breaux would be summoned for his first breeding next week, and he'd been bitter toward Don since the first consultation. Like most young men, he'd expected to woo his first breeding partner and come away with a prized love union, but she had other interests. He stood just long enough to open the cell, then shuffled back to his desk.

"Good morning, my Douglas," Don said, setting down his supplies. At first, Don thought Douglas was wearing a shirt, but then he realized it was just the outline of a shirt on Douglas' burnt skin. The sunburn was worse on his face, neck, and arms, but even the skin that had been protected by fabric was red. The skin on Douglas' jaw was peeling off.

"Breaux, where are his clothes?" Don asked.

"He had three layers of stolen clothing on when Mace brought him. The Resource Manager took all of it," Breaux replied. "They redistributed everything for the trek to the 'spaceship.'"

Stirring, Douglas mumbled incoherently, then he held out his flask. "More?"

"No more," Don chided, taking the flask, and filling a cup with water. "Drink this. The sunlight has dehydrated you."

He was glad when Douglas complied. The man sat up and drank, letting his blanket pool in his lap.

"How do you feel?"

"I don't know," Douglas mumbled. Don wished they had a better relationship.

"Does this hurt?" Don asked, sweeping away Douglas' sweat-soaked hair to get a better look at his neck. Douglas shrugged and Don frowned. "It looks painful."

Douglas touched the burnt skin. "The alien—" he began, then deflated and rubbed his cheek.

"What about the alien?"

"I don't know," Douglas mumbled.

Don touched the reddened skin, but Douglas didn't flinch. The skin was hot to touch, but there were patches of mild frostnip on his ears and hands. "Did Sky put medicine on your skin to dull the pain or did you drink it away?"

"I don't know."

"How long were you outside?" Don's frown deepened when Douglas didn't answer. Frustrated, Don prepared a bowl of green tea leaves. He'd come here to treat Douglas' burns, whether the boy knew he was in pain or not. Tea leaves were a free-resource remedy from the medicinal garden. When the tea was ready, Don dipped his washcloth in it, then he dabbed it on Douglas' skin and Douglas hissed.

"That hurts?" Don asked. Not meeting his eye, Douglas shrugged and curled into a fetal position. Don was familiar with that broken look—in his line of work, he saw it often, though for different reasons.

"Do you want something to eat?"

Douglas nodded.

Finally! A definitive answer. Hopping to his feet, Don motioned Breaux over.

"My Breaux, please order a breakfast from the commissary?"

"Why?"

"Your prisoner is allocated basic resources. That includes all meals," Don growled. "And clothes. Get him clothes. Go!"

Breaux grumbled, but went outside to flag down a messenger.

Douglas curled under his blanket again, cradling his cup of water to his chest. Pulling the blanket back, Don resumed his treatment of the burnt skin, but he didn't make Douglas sit up. The cool stone floor probably felt nice.

"Where is Papa?" Douglas asked, touching his nose to his cup.

"At home. Resting. He misses you," Don said soothingly.

"Can I go home, too?" Douglas whined, tugging the blanket up to his ears, smearing dirt on his skin.

"Soon, I hope," Don said, dipping a fresh cloth in his brew, and spreading it across Douglas' neck.

"Can I go to work?" Douglas asked. "The Coureur is just starting to come together. I have an engine all ready."

"Not today," Don said, wincing at the pout on Douglas' face. "Is there a message I can get to McGill for you?"

Douglas shook his head. "Is he okay? Is McGill okay?"

"Yes, he was on his feet . . . all afternoon, looking for you and Sky," Don said, a lump rising in his throat.

Breaux returned with a bowl of potato casserole, steaming hot, and after realizing that he wouldn't be able to pass the bowl through the bars, he opened the cell and set the food on the ground next to Douglas. There was no beverage, no napkin, and no utensils. Douglas was either tired, drunk, or starving, because rather than complain, he started eating the casserole with his bare hands. The hot food burned his fingers, but Douglas didn't bother wiping away the tears of pain and shame.

"I'd like to move him back to the hospital," Don said.

"Before the Constable gets back?" Breaux stammered, stealing glances at Douglas. "I don't know if I'm allowed to do that."

"Figure it out."

"Donny, I don't want to go to asylum. Maman doesn't want me there," Douglas spoke up, licking the potato from his knuckles. Breaux looked even more uncertain.

"At least get him a clean blanket so his wounds don't get infected," Don snapped.

Embarrassed, Breaux went in search of something cleaner. His anger dissolving, Don rooted through his medical bag for a spatula or anything that Douglas could use as a utensil. He jumped when he felt Douglas tapping his chest—or rather, the pocket into which his empty gin flask was tucked.

"More?"

"I'll get you a refill," Don promised, patting his hand. He'd need it for the pain. "Hopefully you won't be in here too much longer."

"I know I was bad. I thought I could make it better," Douglas said, stirring the potatoes with his fingers. "She promised to help."

The darkness lasted nearly sixteen hours and the sun rose late over the mountains. The solar cells deployed over *Oriana's* wing were finally bringing sufficient charge so that Saskia could recharge the electrics. She worried that the intense UV radiation would melt the power cells, but for the trade-off of climate control, she had little choice. She lay sprawled on the floor of her quarters, directly under the air vent, contemplating whether her hair would freeze if she took a shower.

Hearing a loud crash in the hall, Saskia grabbed her stunner and steeled her nerves. The door to one of the vacant crew quarters was opened and the room overflowing with the various sundries that had been stored in there.

"Captain wasn't serious about the curtains, Tray," Saskia said, checking for sharp edges and broken glass around the fallen shelves before she entered. Tray's black hair was powdered with dust and he hacked when he tried to jump out of the dust cloud he'd kicked up.

"Just making a place. Unless *you* wanted to bunk with Sky," he taunted. "We didn't need these light tubes, did we?"

"What are light tubes doing in here?" Saskia asked, stepping around the mess of linens. The captain had a nearly eidetic memory when it came to how and where things were stored on the ship, and Saskia hadn't ever figured out the logic of it. Tray occasionally tried to organize, but had discovered it more effective to simply label things as he found them, so the captain wouldn't yell.

This room had turned into a supply closet a few months ago. Both of the bunks were folded against the wall and storage containers were packed three crates high. It looked like Tray was trying to organize rather than simply clear out.

"Did you get Amanda to sleep?" Tray asked, wiping his face on the inside of his shirt.

"Unfortunately no, but at least she's lying down. She's reading," Saskia replied, twisting her long, black braid into a bun. Amanda had a subcutaneous medicine capsule delivering antipsychotics, but between the microgravity and the stasis pod, there was no way to know if those medicines were still potent.

"More rumors?" Tray asked, switching on their heavy duty vacuum to clean the shattered polymers.

"No, we had some novels in the database. I thought something familiar might help," Saskia said. Once, Saskia had witnessed a man's heart explode from exertion, and she would use every resource at her disposal to keep that fate from befalling Amanda.

Tray kept up idle conversation as they cleaned. He and Danny had been tense at each other since landing, but the anger Tray had been wearing like a shield had given way to worry. The captain had been gone all night, and hadn't made contact since the little plane crossed the ridge of the valley. There was something beneath Tray's worry, though—an intense fear. Tray was usually better at shielding his emotions around her, so Saskia pretended not to notice and just nodded along as he prattled on about the history of light tubes.

"We should take these mattresses outside and beat the dust out," Tray griped after ten minutes of vacuuming.

"There will be shade by the back door for another hour," Saskia said, wiping the caked dust on her cheek.

A siren sounded and a red light in the crew hall flashed—a proximity alert. Saskia had rigged it after the unexpected arrival of the glider. They didn't want any more surprises. Dropping her dust rag, Saskia dashed from the bunk and climbed the forward ladder to the bridge with Tray hot on her heels. He silenced the alarm as she called up the external view, ready to open the hatch for the returning glider. Saskia swore under her breath when she saw a hand carried tent shielding at least ten men from the rising sun.

"What is that?" Tray asked.

"Rocan sent us a welcoming party," Saskia said.

"Danny," Tray murmured, his face going pale.

"No reason to assume he's been captured."

"Well he's not with them!"

Saskia studied the new arrivals. They were underdressed for the weather and even with the tent, the two men on the eastern side were exposed to the sunlight. The remaining men were huddled together for warmth. Saskia could easily incinerate their tent with a shock-dart, but for now, the shelter was keeping the enemy contained. They didn't seem to know where the door to the ship was, but they began circling, systematically testing the hull.

"Maybe we should pull the curtains and pretend no one is home," Tray said, lowering his voice as though they might overhear him.

Saskia nodded. Then she saw a little, yellow light blink. The personnel door in the cargo bay had opened. Amanda Gray stepped into the blazing sunlight, raised a pulse rifle, and fired at the Rocanese men.

31

Tray couldn't stop swearing as he bolted down the stairs, self-consciously wiping the caked dust from his face. He detoured through his quarters, grabbing a warm coat and a washcloth. He wasn't useful in firefights, and the more presentable he looked, the more likely he'd be able to smooth this mess over with diplomacy. What would he say? *Sorry she shot you. She's a little crazy.* What if they started shooting at him? When the chaos erupted, Tray hadn't taken the time to see what kinds of weapons the Rocanese men carried.

The sounds of men shouting carried into the bay from outside, and Tray could hear the agonizing cries as their visitors were struck with stunner and pulse rifle blasts.

"Danny, if you get this message, we've been boarded. And there's shooting," Tray relayed via Virp, removing his Feather and hiding it in his coat pocket.

The bay door faced away from the rising sun, and the daylight leaked in along with the chilly air. If they didn't resolve this within an hour, they'd lose the long shadow of the ship and they'd all get burned.

Peeking outside the door, Tray could only see Amanda,

rolling on the ground, diving for cover. She had socks but no shoes, a sweater but no coat. Tray hadn't even stepped outside yet and his fingers were freezing. Amanda hollered in Moon-speak, shooting erratically, sometimes grazing their visitors, but mostly firing wild. Ducking out, Tray tried to spot Saskia. He yelped as two men grabbed him from behind.

"Tray!" Saskia shouted. Tray counted ten men total—six lying on the ground, moaning. Two had him and two others were closing in on Amanda. They all seemed to be shying away from Saskia.

"Sorry, I should have stayed inside," Tray choked, swallowing as he felt a blade against his throat. The man holding him shouted something in his ear, but he didn't understand.

Amanda shot one of the men nearest her, but the second one jumped on top of her, knocking her pulse rifle away. Tray winced, worried her bones would be crushed, but Amanda kept struggling, kicking and screaming. The man holding Tray shouted again, pressing the knife more firmly against his throat.

"Amanda," Tray called. "Sweetheart, calm down."

"They're attacking me!" Amanda protested, switching to Terranan, eyes glazed, face red and glistening with sweat.

"You're the stealthy one who came outside and shot them," Tray retorted.

Saskia approached Amanda, but the man holding Tray shouted and waved his blade threateningly. The other man aimed a crude pistol at Saskia.

"Help!" Amanda cried, her vicious screams turning into pained sobs. Her body convulsed as her attacker pinned her arms and legs.

"Do any of you speak Trade?" Tray asked. "Anyone? We mean no harm."

A young, red-haired man that lay groaning just a few feet from Saskia rolled over and grunted a few pained words, but not in Trade. Either he'd given an order or he'd translated, because the man holding Tray relaxed just a hair. His grip was still tight enough to bruise.

"Amanda!" Tray called out, switching to Terranan for her. "Sweetheart, stop screaming. You're turning purple."

The man who had stolen the pulse rifle shouted harshly in response to the language switch, but his threats were barely audible over Amanda's keening.

"Saskia, help her!"

"He'll kill you," Saskia hissed, trying to keep all three of the still-standing men in her line of fire and stay within the boundary of their slowly shrinking shade. They exchanged a helpless glance, then Saskia took another step toward Amanda. The man with the pistol shouted at her, then fired. Saskia shot back, rapidly felling him and the man pinning Amanda. Tray felt the trickle of blood on his neck as the man with the knife shouted again.

Amanda didn't respond to Saskia any better than she did to the stranger. She shouted 'Guard!' and scrambled toward Tray.

"Amanda," Tray called desperately. "Calm down and let Saskia help you."

"Help," Amanda cried in Terranan, collapsing on Tray's feet and hugging his ankles. The man holding Tray tripped over her, nearly slicing Tray as he fought for balance. He was burly, and freckled, and he had some kind of metal shield on his uniform that indicated rank. He was the last of his people left standing, although some of those hit earliest were starting to move around.

Moving carefully to keep his throat from being slit, Tray knelt with his captor and gathered Amanda in his arms. The man with the knife followed Tray's lead, withdrawing the blade when Amanda reached up to grab it. Tray caught Amanda's hand, barely keeping her from slicing her fingers.

"We'll help you," Tray promised, cradling Amanda's chin, trying to tell if the purpling on her cheeks was from injury, exertion, or weather. "Saskia is your friend, remember? She's not a Guard anymore."

"Lie still," Saskia ordered, holstering her weapons and kneeling next to Amanda. The man with the knife barked and gesticulated, but Saskia ignored him. She touched Amanda's cheek, making a quick assessment as well, then turned to the red-haired Rocanese man. "Water?"

Those simple words spurred a few of the Rocanese men to action, and those men translated for the others. Tray tried to remember which, besides the redhead, responded to the Trade.

"Their wings rustle. I don't want to Disappear. Something spirit is touching me," Amanda whimpered, clawing at Saskia's hands.

"We're on Aquia, Amanda," Saskia said. "People don't Disappear on Aquia."

One of the Rocanese men offered a canteen and Saskia snatched it. "Drink," she ordered, pressing the canteen to Amanda's lips. Amanda drank slowly, sputtered, and shook. She'd started this mess and they'd probably all be hanged for it. This culture looked primitive enough to still practice hanging.

The man with the knife stepped forward and demanded something in Rocanese.

"I'm sorry, we don't understand," Tray said, leaning protectively over Saskia and Amanda, flaring his coat to share the warmth with them.

A few of the Rocanese men argued with each other. Four were upright now. Tray wished they could stun all the men, move the ship, and let them all think they'd dreamed this encounter.

"You will speak only Trade?" the redhead asked Tray.

"Not only—but I guess, yeah," Tray shrugged.

"I am Officer Blayze," he said. Then he motioned to the freckled man with the knife. "This is Constable Mace of the Qu'Appelle district in Rocan. We have come seeking Cordova."

Tray straightened up, but didn't let go of Amanda. "I am Tray Matthews of *Oriana*. This is Saskia Serevi and Amanda Gray." He stroked Amanda's face when he said her name. "Sorry about the fire fight. The women don't like strangers."

Saskia glared at him.

"This isn't Cordova?" Blayze checked. "You did not come with medicine?"

"Um. No," Tray replied.

"You will come with us to Rocan," Blayze said.

"We'd rather not, thank you," Tray said. "We're hanging curtains."

Blayze cocked his head and spoke to Mace; Mace took the news badly. Humor never translated. Mace dropped to one knee and yelled in Tray's face, but Saskia smacked him across the cheek.

"The spirit realm is bleeding!" Amanda screamed, flailing her arms. Her face was turning purple again and then she clutched her chest.

"Are all alien women this aggressive?" Blayze demanded.

"All the ones on this ship," Tray smirked, catching Amanda's hands and rubbing her fingers to warm them. "Why don't we invite our guests out of the cold and talk this out?"

"Tray," Saskia growled.

"Do you want to freeze?" he retorted.

"How many are with you?" Blayze asked, pointing toward the ship. Tray gave Saskia a look, then tapped his Virp to open the bay doors. The loud groan startled the Rocanese men, and they clustered into a defensive position.

"There's no one else on the ship. Come out of the cold and see," Tray invited. He and Saskia took Amanda by the shoulders and knees, moving her into the ship. They'd only been in full gravity for a day, and after this much excitement, he couldn't carry his own weight back to the galley.

The Rocanese men hesitated, but a gust of chilly wind seemed to convince them that they belonged inside. Unfortunately, that same gust took a lot of heat out of the bay. Tray closed the ramp behind them, inciting a wave of panic.

"Why do you Sequester us?" Blayze demanded.

"Just keeping the cold out. You can leave at any time," Tray said, opening the inset door to demonstrate. He waited for Blayze to translate, and although Mace was wary, he motioned Tray to close the door and keep the cold out.

"You're here looking for medicine?" Tray asked, kneeling next to Saskia and Amanda.

"And a spaceship with aliens," Blayze said, holstering his pistol, taking his first look around the bay, gravitating toward the *Bobsled*. "I assume you're the aliens. Have you really been to the moon?"

"We just came from there," Tray acknowledged, shrugging out of his coat and putting it over Amanda.

"How do you get through the debris cloud?" Blayze asked. "We see the meteor showers day and night."

"Did you see the pockmarks on the hull?" Tray commented. "We come from a Dome somewhere south of here. A place called Quin."

"And you brought these resources for us?" Blayze asked, moving on to a stack of cargo crates.

"No, we found this place by accident and we're trying very hard to leave," Tray said. "But now that we know your city is here, we can perhaps work out some trade."

"Don't bring your women," Blayze said, dropping his voice. "In the future—"

"Why? Because they're aggressive?" Tray remarked.

Mace caught the tone and glowered before asking a question of Blayze.

"We are also looking for a woman called Sky," Blayze translated. "She is wanted for crimes of violence against our people."

Tray swore under his breath and exchanged a look with Saskia. "She's already left."

"Douglas Hwan has testified that you conspired with her and intend to steal resources from Rocan," Blayze continued.

"I will explode his head so hard," Tray muttered through clenched teeth, then he put on his diplomacy face. "We were afraid of how we'd be received if we came right out and asked."

"Then you admit to attempting theft?" Blayze asked.

"I admit nothing," Tray huffed.

"Amanda needs a doctor, Tray," Saskia said quietly in Terranan. "A real one. Her heartbeat is erratic and her blood pressure rising. Even if their medicine is primitive, they may have something that can help."

"Hawk thought our aloe mixture was magic. Amanda's crying spirit. We don't know what's there," Tray protested. Surely they had something in their infirmary that would keep Amanda from dying.

"Do you deny that you're in conspiracy with Sky," Blayze continued. "Have you sent agents to the city?"

"I'm going to forgive your horrendous interrogation tactics, since Trade is not your first language and you don't seem to be getting my sarcasm," Tray began. He looked uncertainly at Saskia. In his five years running trade missions on *Oriana*, Tray had been included in a number of stupid plans, and this would be no different . . . except this wasn't a business transaction, and aside from Saskia's weapons, they had no advantage over these people and nothing of value to offer. "Do you have medicine? Amanda's heart is weak and she needs a doctor."

When Blayze translated, Mace knelt next to Amanda again, this time looking concerned and gentle. It didn't help.

"What are you?" Amanda screeched, grabbing his shirt.

"Amanda," Tray said in Terranan, clamping his hand over her wrist.

"What is it? The darkness you carry. You're blinding everyone," Amanda wailed, then devolved into Moonspeak ramblings.

"He's a man," Tray said, taking Amanda's fingers and guiding them to Mace's face. If she couldn't make out faces, she was worse off than he feared. "Constable Mace wants to take us to the city. He won't hurt us. Danny's going to kill us."

"The Captain will thank us," Saskia grumbled at Tray. She reached for Mace's hand and held the man's fingers against Amanda's neck, letting him feel her racing heart. "She's hypertensive. She needs a doctor," Saskia said in Terranan.

Tray gave her a quizzical look. He translated as best he could, but medical jargon wasn't his strong suit in Terranan or Trade. His first language was Lanvarian.

"It would be better if Amanda doesn't walk," Saskia said.

"I can't carry her. If we put her on a stretcher, they're going to keep it. I don't want to bring any coats or gloves into their city either, but I also don't want to freeze to death," Tray commented. "You think we can just roll the ship closer? We've been rolling around the valley all night looking for the *Bobsled*."

"How are we going to keep them contained? How are we going to defend the ship?" Saskia argued.

"That's your job. I'm just trying to save her life," Tray said, rubbing his forehead.

"I can hear you," Amanda groused in Terranan, flicking beads of sweat off her cheeks. Tray wondered if her use of Moonspeak was a psychotic thing or simply a preference, like when he swore in Lanvarian. They'd never treated Moonspeak like a language for the sane, but Amanda slipped in and out of it naturally.

"That's good, sweetheart," Tray said, dabbing her face with the hem of his jacket sleeve. "Do you want to weigh in on this vote?"

"I want to know what he is," Amanda said, running her fingers over Mace's cheek. She pulled her hand away, studied him for a moment, then touched his face again and gasped. "I'll figure out how it works."

It wasn't a vote, but at least she seemed to have calmed down. She started speaking Moonspeak again, then stopped and touched her ears.

"The Constable asks what's wrong with her," Blayze translated.

"There's no gravity on the moon, so her heart is weak. There's a touch of schizophrenia," Tray began. He didn't know enough of Amanda's story, and they didn't have time to discuss it. Bracing his hands on his knees, he stood slowly, putting a hand on Saskia's shoulder when he felt dizzy.

"Are all your men on their feet?" he asked Blayze. "We're going to a slightly warmer part of the ship. You're going to sit down, strap in, and we're going to roll our way back to the city."

"Roll? Isn't this a spaceship?" Blayze asked.

"I don't know how far you think you walked, but going back to Rocan by way of space would be a waste of fuel," Tray said. "Not to mention, we can't get off the ground," he added under his breath.

32

The ship moved and Mace gasped. His men were crammed into a tight space with seven folding chairs and an equal number of beds. Half of the men sat on the chairs or next to them. Mace sat on an out-turned bed slab, cradling Amanda against his chest. There was a pillow for her head, but no mattress. He could feel her body pulsing against his. When he'd first touched her, he worried her skin would burst just from the pressure of lifting her up. The redness had faded from her cheeks and her skin was pale. Her eyes went glassy on occasion, and she murmured to herself in a language Mace didn't recognize.

The black-striped blanket Tray put over her was the warmest and thickest Mace had ever felt. Tray and Saskia had only allowed Blayze to accompany them to the ship's control room, and the rest were ordered to stay here. Inside the ship, their radio couldn't reach the watchman, but Tray assured them that they would get a signal on the bridge to inform Rocan of their peaceful arrival.

At least now Mace understood why young Hwan was raving

about brown-skinned aliens. The dark skin on Saskia and Tray was unsettling to look at.

"These restraints are fabric," Deputy Reg Arman said, tugging at the harness over his chair. "Sturdy and new."

None of the men in chairs had applied the restraints, despite Tray's assurance that they came open at will. It was kind of the aliens to offer them shelter from the cold, but mutual trust had yet to be established.

"Can you imagine Felicity leaving a place like this?" Officer Miller mused, circling the room, tugging at every handle that looked like a cabinet or door, finding them all sealed. "No wonder she wants to forget."

"She didn't grow up out here, Miller," Arman sighed. "She speaks Rocanese. She was Sequestered by someone in Rocan. These people don't speak our language at all. It is as Douglas said—they are from another world."

"Even their Trade is weird. You should feel these seats, Constable," Grimes said, laughing as he wriggled against it. "The man apologized for them being old and worn out, but I want this cushion in my house. Can you imagine the luxuries they cast aside?"

"This girl doesn't look like she's seen much in the way of luxury," Mace said, stroking Amanda's cheek. She looked emaciated, very much like a Sequestered he'd rescued in his youth when he'd first joined the force.

"The hinges on these look new," Grimes added, kneeling in front of the chair, moving the seat up and down.

"This part looks like it's meant to be a shower!" Miller called, poking his head out of the only door he'd managed to open.

"He said it didn't work anymore," Grimes called back. Mace gave him a look and Grimes shrugged. "I understood the Trade, I just couldn't come up with the words fast enough to speak it."

Amanda's head lolled against Mace's shoulder, and she

poked his chest hard with her finger. He'd guessed her a teenager when she first attacked, but now that he saw her up close, he wasn't so sure.

"Yes?" Mace asked, tickling the back of her hand.

Amanda's lips moved and her voice croaked.

"Arman, water," Mace ordered, shifting the girl in his arms to get her in a better position for drinking. Arman brought his canteen and together they helped the girl drink. She cleared her throat and poked Mace's chest again. Then her eyelids drooped and she started singing. Kinley Hwan and other Sequestereds who landed in asylum sang to self-soothe. He hoped Amanda had a better future to look forward to than that.

Amanda repeated the song, poking his chest every time there was a chorus of "solay, solay," if those were even words. She prompted him at the chorus until he joined in. When he made the sounds, her face lit up, making her look younger. By the third chorus, she was back to sleep.

"Arman," Mace whispered.

"More water?" he asked.

"No, look. Precious girl," Mace said, scooting out from under her and lying her down on the bed, covering her with the blanket. "She sang herself to sleep."

"More than that, sir. She got you to sing," Arman grinned.

"These women are so reliant on Tray Matthews, it may be difficult to separate them once we're in the city," Mace murmured, more to himself than Arman. The travelers had agreed to come to Rocan because Amanda needed a doctor. That meant they didn't have one of their own. He didn't trust their promises, but he could see the value in being diplomatic, given their resources.

"He's not a Sequesterer. At least we're not fighting that possessive mentality," Arman offered. "Saskia Serevi is his equal, and at times, she appears to be the primary decision-maker of the group."

"Then we must find a way to speak her language without using him as an intermediary," Mace said. "If she knew Trade, she would have spoken to us."

"Sky might know the language," Arman said.

"I don't believe Sky is on our side anymore. We're not on hers," Mace sighed. "Where these travelers fall in the mix remains to be seen. Hwan said their intent was to repair the ship and leave."

"If we wait in here, Sky may return," Arman suggested.

Mace nodded. "Are we doing the right thing, allowing their ship this close to the city?"

"I'm not sure we had a choice," Arman said.

"They may have shown more of the ship to Hwan," Miller said, joining the conversation. "May have felt more control with just one visitor."

"I will demand the Intendant pardon him." Mace sighed. "The man is a great asset to his generation. Why did he have to be mixed up in this?"

Arman snorted. "In recognizing what this situation is, sir, there's no one else who could be."

"Danny, if you're getting this message, we're taking the ship to the city. Going by a different entrance, though. Our captor wants us to park by a Pagoda. Wherever that is. And before you get angry, it was Saskia's idea," Tray hummed, speaking Lanvarian in case anyone in the city was eavesdropping. He was strapped into the captain's chair, and had Blayze next to him, getting directions from their man via radio. "How are we doing?" he asked Blayze, switching to Trade.

"There will be a greeting party at the Pagoda," Blayze replied. "They will confiscate any weapons and escort us to the hospital."

"Swell." The closer the Dome loomed through the front window, the less Tray liked this plan. "Let's make one thing clear —no one will be permitted on the ship. Your people were brought out of the cold as an act of mercy."

"You may find resistance," Blayze warned.

"Then when I drop you off, I'll drive right back into the valley," Tray replied. "If your people want help from mine, respect our sovereign boundary."

"I am just a translator," Blayze shrugged.

"Then translate."

"We're here," Saskia announced in Terranan. They pulled up next to a stone, domed gazebo-like structure.

"Oh. Pagoda," Tray said, studying the wing-tipped layers accentuating the roof. The sides of the pagoda were freshly painted red and gold, but the stone itself was chipped and cracked. "That's what that word means. Is it?"

"Go gather our guests. I'll try to contact the captain once more," Saskia said.

"Blayze says no weapons," Tray said, handing her his shock-dart so that Blayze could see he wasn't bringing it. He didn't expect Saskia to enter the city unarmed, but for the sake of diplomacy, he made the show. Donning his coat, he motioned Blayze to follow him to the lower deck.

"We've arrived at the Pagoda. Bundle up everyone," Tray announced, doing a quick count to make sure none of the men were hiding. None were seated, but they didn't rush the door either. Blayze translated, and they started dressing.

"Hey, sweetheart," Tray whispered in Terranan, kneeling next to Amanda's bed. "How are you feeling?"

Amanda stirred and groaned. Her body tensed and she

braced her feet against the bed. "Hybrid made me sleep," she moaned.

"I think you passed out on your own. Your heart needed rest," Tray said. "We're taking you to a doctor."

"I'm supposed to see a neurologist before I leave Terrana," she whined, her body twisting.

"You'll see one in Quin. Come here," Tray said, scooting her into his arms, grunting as he lifted her. The blood rushed from his head and he swayed, nearly dropping her on the bed again, but Constable Mace intercepted, catching them both and taking Amanda. She squirmed and whined, kicking against him.

"What's going on? What happened?" Saskia demanded, forcing the men aside and rushing to the bed.

Tray sat on the bed, panting, and it wasn't until he felt Saskia's hands on his cheek that he realized the question was to him.

"I tried to lift Amanda. I got dizzy," he explained, bracing his hands on the side of the slab. "Did you get through to Danny?"

"Yeah. He was abducted by a hybrid and Hawk got arrested," Saskia reported, feeling Tray's face for fever, then peeling his eyes open.

"We should be going," Blayze insisted. "The Intendant is eager to meet you."

Tray took a few slow breaths to quell his nausea.

"No quarantine. That's not good," Saskia murmured.

"Sounds good to me," Tray smirked. It hadn't occurred to them that they might get trapped here by disease.

"The Moon Pox is barely out of your system, and you're prone to secondary infection," Saskia reminded him. "I think you should stay on the ship."

"Leave Amanda?" Tray scoffed. "Danny would kill me."

"So will new diseases," Saskia huffed.

"We demand you release us!" Blayze said more forcefully, stamping his foot to show he didn't like being ignored.

"Sorry," Tray responded. "We were concerned about the possibility of contracting illness here. I supposed it's a little late now."

"Do you carry illnesses with you?" Blayze asked.

"Nothing contagious that we know of," Tray said.

Blayze spoke to Mace, who didn't seem concerned by the content of the conversation. The other man rocked Amanda in his arms, like he'd discovered a long-lost daughter.

"You will be kept isolated from the general population," Blayze translated. "We ask that you not wander."

"Fair enough," Tray agreed, pushing off the bed. Saskia took his arm, giving him support. "I'm okay. Really."

"I don't want them separating us," Saskia whispered. "We have to show them that you are our protector and sole translator."

"We should have closed the curtains," he mumbled.

33

The air was colder in the shadow of the Dome, but it was a short walk to the Pagoda. Tray would have run the distance, but his joints seemed to freeze almost instantly, and he wouldn't have stepped out of the ship at all were not he pushed out by Saskia. They were relying on the tundra to shield their ship from invading forces, and Tray didn't like it.

The Constable carried Amanda into the Pagoda, and Officer Blayze held the door while the rest of them followed. The inside was even more colorful than the outside. There were benches and tables, and a panoramic mountain view. The space was barely large enough to accommodate ten people, let alone the five additional armed officers and med-wagon waiting to greet them. The Constable laid Amanda on the wagon, and she moaned.

"Tray, help!" Amanda screamed, her face turning purple. Tray hustled over, squeezing into the wagon next to her. Saskia sandwiched her on the other side.

"Amanda," Tray whispered, wincing as she nuzzled against his sore shoulder.

An older man approached and Mace stepped aside. "My

name is Dr. Yale," he greeted, his Trade about on par with Hawk's. He had only a thin coat and no gloves. Tray felt over-dressed in his custom-woven, tailored suit. "This is the young woman in distress."

"This is Amanda," Tray said. "Her heart is racing."

Yale applied a stethoscope, but when he tried to use it, Amanda smacked his hand and shrieked.

"Also mentally ill. And she doesn't speak Trade," Tray added. He held one of Amanda's hands and Saskia held the other, while Yale listened to Amanda's heart. She groaned and arched her back, but calmed when she felt the cool metal listening device on her skin. When Yale pulled back, she motioned for the stethoscope, holding it to her heart again, listening to her heart-beat, seeming soothed by the sound.

Yale reached into his bag and injected Amanda with something.

"What is that? What did you give her?" Tray asked.

"It's a temporary fix for high blood pressure," Yale explained. "Dr. Louis will meet her at the hospital to give her a more comprehensive evaluation. He doesn't speak Trade either. They'll be a good match."

"I'm staying with her," Tray said. Amanda held the end of the stethoscope to his wrist, listening to his pulse.

"You may walk behind the ambulance. It is important we transport her with the utmost speed," Yale suggested.

"You're going for a ride, Amanda," Saskia explained in Terranan, taking the stethoscope from Amanda and handing it back to the doctor. "Hold tight. We'll see you on the other side."

"Don't leave me alone with him. He makes me different," Amanda whimpered, stretching, then contracting.

"Who?" Saskia asked, lying her down, tucking her blanket around her.

"The man who carried me," Amanda said. "He makes me

sing. He makes me sleep. But it's not me. He conjures what soothes him. I become what he sees."

"What is wrong?" Yale asked.

"Um. I'm not sure," Tray replied.

"Galen," Amanda moaned.

"Galen. That's the man who held her captive," Tray told Yale. He leaned over Amanda, stroking her sweat-soaked hair off of her face. "Galen's not here. It's me and Saskia, and this nice doctor. Doctor Yale."

Amanda lifted her head. "Human. Human. Human."

"I really should stay with her," Tray told Yale.

"I'm inclined to agree," the doctor nodded.

He gave the order to the men pulling the wagon. Tray felt motion sick almost as soon as the rickety wagon started.

"Human, hybrid, human, human," Amanda murmured, laying her head on Saskia's lap, looking out the back of the wagon.

They entered the city through a long tunnel that was shaded, but poorly insulated. A few people were waiting just inside the Dome gate when they arrived, and the crowd of gawkers grew quickly. When Tray saw the brown walls of the decaying city, he cringed. Some of the walls were painted, but all were crumbling. The Dome lights were dim and out entirely on one side. Even the slums of Terrana had more resources than the people here. The crowd pressed in, a few of them reaching out to touch Tray and Saskia, ogling at them like they were artifacts in a museum.

Mace shouted an order, then organized his men to clear the path. They reached the next building, and the wagon stopped. A bed was waiting for Amanda, as was a portly, middle-aged man who introduced himself as Dr. Louis.

The Rocanese men that had come to *Oriana* were directed down one hallway to be treated. Tray, Saskia, and Amanda were taken in the opposite direction to a hospital observation room with a high ceiling that had windows on the second level. The glass was streaked from age, and Tray could see a few people already standing on the other side, watching them. The bed they'd wheeled Amanda in on was the only one in the room, and what few machines there were looked more dilapidated than *Oriana*. All this way, and there still wasn't a bed for him.

Tray surveyed the countertop, looking for anything he could use as a weapon. With only Mace, Louis, and Yale in the room, Tray figured Saskia could fight her way free with her bare hands . . . if she were at her best. If she felt half as bad as Tray did right now, she'd need his help.

A new man entered the room, this one white-haired and hunched over. His sleeves were rolled up, and his hands bore the bruises of a laborer.

"Greetings," he said in heavily accented Trade. "I am Alain Hubert, Intendant of Rocan."

"Human," Amanda murmured in Terranan.

"Tray Matthews of *Oriana*," Tray replied, ignoring Amanda.

"Are you aliens?" the old man asked.

"No," Tray smiled, backing up so that he could lean on Amanda's bed. His father would have told him to stand straight, but his father wasn't recovering from Moon Pox, gravity sickness, motion sickness, and a slew of other ailments.

"You look strange," the man said. It was an odd comment, but Tray chose to take it as a cultural miscommunication rather than an insult. "Do you know where Sky is?"

"I do not," Tray said, looking down at his Virp, longing to call his brother.

"But she came to your ship with Douglas Hwan," Hubert pressed.

"Yes," Tray said, pursing his lips. "We followed a signal here, but we expected to find someone else on the other side."

"I see," the man crooned, crowding closer to Tray. "So you didn't come to trade with us?"

"We didn't know there was someone here to trade with," Tray said, pushing off the bed, crowding the man right back to show he wasn't intimidated. "But we would gladly negotiate including Rocan among our trading partners."

"I see," he said again. "How old is your civilization? Were your historical records destroyed? Were you originators of Trade, or like us, did the language persist for academic reasons?"

"Intendant, if I may," Yale interrupted. "Dr. Louis requires an interpreter to communicate with his patient. She is in distress and Mon Tray Matthews is the only one who can speak to her."

"I look forward to speaking with you later," Tray said, turning back to Amanda.

With a grunt, Amanda twisted and kicked, floundering like a fish out of water as both Yale and Louis tried to hold her down. Mace came in from the foot of the bed, but Amanda rolled out of the two doctors' grasps and dove over Mace, sliding headfirst to the floor.

Tray danced around the Rocanese men, leaping sideways to catch Amanda before she hit the ground. She crashed onto his chest, knocking the wind out of him, and Tray fell onto his back, his head knocking hard enough against the concrete floor to make him see stars. Tray wrapped his arms around her, whispering her name, pleading with her to stay calm. It was all he could do to stay conscious. He heard Saskia calling his name, and he felt her fingers probing the lump on the back of his head, checking for blood. Tears came to his eyes, but he didn't let them fall. Tray hoped Saskia wouldn't mind if he passed out.

The observation room above the Sequestered's hospital room

had restricted access, so when Mace came through, the crowd of curious interns pretended to be engrossed in other things. Yale stood by the observation window, taking notes. Arman was by the window as well, cradling his left arm against his chest, barely keeping hold of the blanket he'd been given. They should have taken more layers of garments when they'd gone outside. When Yale saw Mace, he gave up his chair and made Mace sit down.

"My Constable, you need treatment," Yale fussed.

"I walked four miles through the tundra to find these people. I want to see that they're cared for," Mace said, crossing his arms, wincing at the wind-burn.

"We can care for all of you," Yale frowned, touching Mace's head on his way out of the room.

Mace sat forward in his seat, watching from above as Saskia attended to Tray, checking his wounds. She unwrapped the splint on Tray's left hand, delicately probing the injury. Mace winced empathetically, pressing his own broken wrist against his thigh. Saskia made herself at home in the exam room, finding the supplies she needed to treat Tray. She had treated Amanda with similar diligence, never letting Dr. Louis near, only occasionally presenting him with a medical issue that had her stymied, communicating with sounds and hand signals.

The interplay was intriguing. Like Sky, they had a firm grasp of language, it just wasn't a useful language. Mace didn't like being so far removed given Saskia's temperament, but Louis had insisted, and the thinning of the crowd had lessened the tension in that room by equal measures. Once satisfied that Amanda was stable, Louis excused himself to come up to the observation room. As soon as he'd left, Saskia tried to follow, and she kicked the door when she realized she and the others were locked in. It was an isolated burst of rage, after which she went back to the bed, and colluded with the other aliens.

Tray sat up, untangling his limbs from Amanda, then pulled a shiny, silver slab out of his pocket.

"Arman," Mace said, thinking it was a weapon. Tray peeled away the silver shell, broke the slab inside into three pieces and distributed it to the group, and they ate. "Huh. It's food. In wasteful packaging."

"Fascinating," Louis said, arriving in the observation room with Yale and going straight to the window. He rubbed his hands together, wiping off the powdery residue left by his gloves. "They behave like a family unit. Look how Saskia cares for the other two."

Dr. Yale put a blanket around Mace's shoulders and handed him a glass of water. "She's never given birth. Neither woman has," Yale added. He could tell by looking at the shape of their hips.

Mace cringed. After speaking with young Hwan, he thought he knew what he'd find out there. Now, he was confused. 'Brown-skinned aliens' was as apt a description as any.

"Amanda shows signs of neglect," Yale said.

"But also signs of recovery. I noticed that, too," Louis said. "She is recovering from starvation."

"So what changed?" Mace asked, studying the trio. Tray seemed content to sit on bed, but both Saskia and Amanda were on the move as soon as they finished eating. "Are these two really her rescuers or were they simply bored of torturing her?"

"Rescuers," Arman said. "Her trust in them is too innocent and tentative. It's the same way Felicity looks at me."

The mention of Felicity made Mace's hand ache. Sky and these others were nothing like Felicity. Felicity was Sequestered—born in Rocan and abused by someone here. "But their languages. We've heard them speak three distinct languages. Is it possible they didn't come from one place, but from many?"

"All those travel stories Sky told," Yale smiled. "How many do you think are real?"

Tray pulled another one of those silver-wrapped food pieces out of his jacket and munched on it. The young man sat straight, like a bureaucrat. His clothes were so new and clean, they practically glowed.

"The two darker ones—do you suppose their skin condition is a side-effect of sun exposure?" Louis pondered. "We know that some bronzing can occur in natural sunlight, but theirs seems severe."

"I tried to examine Tray Matthews privately, but Saskia would not allow him to be separated from the group," Yale snorted.

Saskia moved stealthily about the room, but she lacked Tray's finesse. Fixating on one of the broken machines, she traced the sensor leads and tried to get Amanda to sit still long enough to hook up the sensors.

"I've been begging McGill to fix that machine for months," Louis groused. "Oh, kerf!"

Saskia pulled open the back of the machine, exposing the wires.

"Someone who speaks Trade go tell her to stop before she hurts herself."

"That would be me," Yale sighed, rubbing his face.

"Wait," Mace said. "She's fixing it."

Mace watched, amazed, as the machine came to life. Some of the lights were out, but the monitors still worked. After seeing their ship, he shouldn't have been surprised.

"Oh God, I hope those numbers are wrong. I thought we fixed that blood pressure!" Louis said, charging out of the observation room.

Mace took another drink of water and slouched in the chair, weariness overwhelming curiosity.

"What about Hwan, Constable?" Arman asked. "He was, in fact, abducted by aliens. Isn't it time we get him the help and counseling he deserves?"

"Waiting for the law to catch up," Mace shivered. Hoarding resources was a capital crime.

34

The sunlight had made Deputy Reginald Arman's skin freckle. Reg hadn't had so many freckles since he was a boy, and it had taken fifteen minutes of painful poking to convince Felicity that the spots weren't coming off. His brown hair was streaked with blond and his ears were red and peeling. Where his clothes had protected him from the radiation, his skin was waxy with frostbite. He lay on the couch, cradling his napping daughter against his chest. His blistered left arm rested tentatively across her shoulders, and his new empathy for her severe burns turned his stomach. If she could smile through the pain, so could he.

Reg stroked her hair, debating with himself over whether to move. The painkillers he'd been given at the hospital had worn off hours ago, and every time he sat up, he felt nauseous. He needed water or whiskey, and he didn't have the heart to wake Felicity and ask her to wait on him, nor did he expect her to understand the requests.

The front door slammed, and Reg lifted his head. Colleen leaned against the closed door, face buried in her hands.

"Good morning, my love," he greeted. When Saskia's weapon

had left him paralyzed and lying on the frozen tundra, he'd felt certain he was going to die, and all he could think about was his family. Were it not for Felicity sleeping on him, Reg would have run over to get kiss his wife.

Colleen stayed silent, brooding. She'd been quiet the past two days, avoiding Felicity, and coming home from work upset. Reg worried that she blamed herself for putting Felicity in the middle of that brawl.

"It's afternoon," she finally said, dropping her hands, her body sagging.

"Good afternoon, then," he said. "Can you get me a drink?"

Colleen made a face and crossed to the kitchen. Her muscles tensed before she hit the swinging door, and she held back a rage-filled shove. Two breedings ago, she'd torn the door off the hinges, and they'd had to scavenge for days to find replacements. Now she was more careful. The fact that she had to be worried Reg.

Colleen disappeared for a few minutes and returned with one glass of brandy and one of juice. She leaned over and kissed him, but there was bitterness to it and her skin felt flush. Maybe that was his skin. It felt like he was on fire and even the slight brush of her lips against his stung. He caressed her face, but she shuddered and pushed his hand away.

"Did you meet the aliens?" she asked.

"They're not aliens," Reg said, shifting uncomfortably and taking the brandy glass. "They're human, like us. They just look a little funny. They were pleasant enough after the initial encounter."

"Like Sky?" she muttered.

"Very much so. Recklessly violent."

Her hands trembling, Colleen reached toward Felicity but didn't touch her. "Did she have lunch?"

"We ate early. I made chili for you." Reg smiled, but Colleen's distant expression didn't change.

"Not hungry," she murmured. *Turning down her favorite meal!* Reg was a hairsbreadth from calling a doctor for her. Then her hand brushed absently over his bandaged arm, putting pressure on the blistered skin. Crying out in surprise, Reg jerked away from Colleen, jostling Felicity in the process. Felicity squirmed, her restless movements sending more pain through Reg's body.

"Careful!" Reg whined, straining as dark spots filled his vision. He looked desperately at his wife, but Colleen's eyes watered and she ran away. "Colleen?"

Concerned, Reg rolled off the couch, gingerly extracting his left arm.

"Uh-ah?" Felicity wheezed. The grunted sound caught him off guard.

"Papa? Are you trying to say Papa?" he asked, combing her hair back, waiting for a coherent word. Her silence was fine before, but now that he knew she could understand him, he was desperate to reawaken her voice. "Will you talk to me, little darling?"

Felicity stood on the couch and pointed after her mother.

"You know you're not allowed to stand on the couch," Reg said, pushing her down. "Stay here, little darling. Drink the juice Maman brought you."

Reg chugged his brandy, hoping the alcohol would counter the physical pain and nausea. Colleen sat on the floor, resting her head on the toilet seat, flushing away a bowl full of vomit.

"Oh, Colleen," he said, sitting next to her, rubbing her arm. The sight of this sickness was too familiar. "Breeding sickness is hitting later this time."

"Breeding didn't take," she said. "Verified twice."

Reg smiled sympathetically, kissing between her shoulders.

"Darling, you need a third opinion because I believe you are pregnant."

"I can't be," she moaned, a tear rolling down her cheek. He gathered her hair, holding it back as she vomited again. "I don't want Felicity to see me like this."

Reg lifted his arm, wanting to point out that he wasn't at his best either, but he decided to hold back the remark. "I'm sure the sickness will pass. Last time, ginger tea helped. I can make you some."

Colleen nodded almost imperceptibly. Her body quivered and she traced little circles around her belly with her middle finger. "The sickness was always a blessing before. I resented the child for it; it made the separation easier. I don't want to hate our baby."

"Ours?" Reg repeated, stunned. He'd never heard her talk about an unborn child like that. It was exhilarating that she might give him another child, but he was cautious. His heart had been broken by too many breedings already. "Felicity will understand if you don't want to keep—or if you do—"

"I wasn't even thinking of giving it up. What if our baby dies? Reg!" Colleen hacked and spit into the toilet bowl, then laid her head on her folded arms. "Reg, the breeding didn't take. This isn't a breeding pregnancy."

Reg tensed, the tiny ray of hope he'd felt crushed by fear. "Did something happen at the bar?"

Colleen whimpered, her cheeks flushing. "Kerf, Reg! It's ours. Yours and mine." Leaning forward, she brushed her lips against his. Her body went stiff like she was going to heave, but she held it in.

"A love child?" Suddenly, Reg thought he would be sick. He put his head on his knees, squeezing his wife's hand. After all these years! It was everything they'd always wanted, until Felicity. They'd promised each other they would stop trying once they took her in. "Promise me, if this child survives you will still love Felicity."

"I will love her more," Colleen said. "She never made me sick like this."

35

Tray chewed on another protein bar, but the food did little to sustain him. He needed a square meal, a real doctor, and about a week of sleep. Amanda worried over him, and Tray felt even more pathetic for wanting her to keep fussing. It was more attention than Danny ever paid him. Tray hoped they got home soon. This place had no computers, poor lighting, shoddy clothing . . . Tray would walk back to Quin if that was what it took.

The door to their little hospital room opened and both Amanda and Saskia went on the defensive. Amanda dropped to a crouch and moved predatorily to one side. Saskia cocked her fists and placed herself squarely between Tray and their visitors —Blayze and Louis. Easing off the bed, Tray's stomach contracted and he swallowed hard to keep from vomiting. He placed a hand on Saskia's shoulder, but she did not back down.

"Mon Tray Matthews," Blayze said, speaking the name like one long word. "Doctor Louis would like to take you to a private exam room so he can properly catalog and treat your injuries."

Tray had swindled enough men in his life to recognize a duplicitous look, and Blayze was a bad liar. Ten years ago, Tray wouldn't have been scared at all. He knew the laws of Quin well enough to weasel out of anything. Then he'd gone to Terrana and learned how fuzzy the law could get before society degraded into anarchy. He squeezed Saskia's shoulder, taking a step closer to her, but staying behind her, trying to appear submissive.

"I should go with him," Tray said, feeling a shiver go down his spine. If he cooperated, maybe they wouldn't torture him.

"No! We can't be separated!" Saskia hissed, pushing Tray away from Blayze until he was flat against the wall.

"They'll force us apart eventually," Tray said.

"This is survival, Tray, not some aristocratic detention center," she snapped.

"We have to trust that they won't hurt us."

"They won't hurt *us*!" she countered, motioning to herself and Amanda. "They will hurt you!"

Tray had never seen Saskia so intense outside of a fistfight. She was the stoic warrior, unaffected by everything. It was all he could do to get her to laugh at a simple joke. "They're not going to kill me, Saskia."

"They're not going to catalog your injuries," she glowered. Tray took her hand and pressed his Virp against hers, careful not to draw attention to the devices.

"I'll keep you apprised," he assured, stepping sideways to get around her.

"Tray!" Saskia snapped, cutting him off. She stood ready to fight, but Tray had made his decision. After a brief stare-off, she yielded. "If they take you out of the hospital, ask to be taken to Hawk."

"To jail? Why?" Tray scoffed.

"One less stop for me to make while I'm rescuing everyone."

Tray grinned at her. "Maybe this time, I'll rescue you."

Saskia snorted and rubbed the bridge of her nose, hiding her smile with irritation.

"Danny loves you, Tray," Amanda said, snaking her arm around his leg and leaning her cheek to his knee. "He'll come for you."

Tray nearly jumped out of his skin, he was so surprised by her touch. Amanda was still a stranger to him, but in the last two days, she'd treated him more like a brother than Danny ever had. "He loves you more," Tray said, choking back emotion. "He'll come for you first."

Douglas Hwan lay on the cold, stone floor of his jail cell, shivering despite the clean, warm blanket that covered him. His stomach rumbled, and no matter how many times he ran his finger over the empty bowl, there were no scraps of food left. The guards had rotated, but Mace hadn't come in and Don hadn't returned with his flask. His skin burned where Don had washed it; the cool lotion the aliens had put on it had wiped away. If he stayed perfectly still, he could keep the blanket from grating against his skin and shooting fire through his body.

The door to his holding cell opened and Douglas lifted his head. His jaw dropped when he saw Tray strut into the cell. *What have I done?* His breath quickened, and Douglas pressed his eyes shut, pulling the blanket over his head. By the time he'd finished talking to Mace, he was convinced the visit to the alien ship was a dream and he belonged in asylum. People don't just disappear, and Danny and Sky had done that. But Tray was real, and he'd come to avenge his brother.

"Hawk. Come on, alien boy, talk to me," Tray said, yanking the blanket away from Douglas' face. "What happened when you came back to the city?"

"I don't know," Douglas cringed, pressing his hands to the sides of his aching head. "They were there and they were gone."

"Were they hurt?" Tray persisted.

"Can't you tell?" Douglas asked, cowering under the blanket. "I didn't see. I just looked away for a second."

Tray reached out again, but Douglas jerked away, bringing his knees to his chin. "Where did they go, Tray? Why did they leave me?"

"I don't have the answers," Tray said, testing the perimeter of the cell, searching for an escape. "I can't say I've always been an honest man, but my general rule of thumb has been don't get caught. This is a pretty lame jail."

Pulling a gadget from his coat pocket, he chipped away at the window frame. He had no respect! Rocan was suffering enough decay without his vandalism.

"This isn't a jail," Douglas shivered, pulling up his blanket. "It's a waiting room. They're going to kill me."

"What about me?" Tray asked.

"You're going to disappear, just like they did."

"I wish I could," Tray sighed, putting his hands on his hips. "Do you think they'll kill you tonight or wait until morning? All we need is a few hours to escape, find the others, fix *Oriana*, and be on our way."

Have I been here that long? Douglas crept from his corner and when Tray paced past, Douglas reached out and touched his leg. The material of Tray's pants was soft and thick; the leg was solid and lean. He didn't dissolve like the hallucinations or vanish like Sky and Danny. Tray nudged back with the tip of his shoe.

"You can't disappear?" Douglas asked. Maybe this was the trap his mother had fallen into, but Douglas wanted nothing more than to go back to that spaceship and fly away from here. That fantasy was better than being executed.

"Are you going to help me get out of here or not?" Tray asked.

"I betrayed you."

Tray frowned and Douglas covered his head, worried Tray would make it explode.

"I know this has been a really lousy day for you," Tray said. "This may go down as one of the worst in your life. But I'm getting out of here, and I think you should come with me."

"What would I do?" Douglas asked.

"You built that glider yourself, with no help from your city. I know plenty of shops that would be glad to have a mechanic like you. I'm not leaving you to die in this place. Danny will just come back and save you later," Tray said, turning his back and trying to pry open the cell's small window. In all likelihood, the thing was rusted, not locked. "Tomorrow's a new day. You'll start a fresh new life away from this creepy *hollenloch*."

"I don't know that word," Douglas murmured. He sat back on his heels, looking uncertainly between Tray and the deputy on duty; the deputy watched him suspiciously.

"It's not important," Tray continued. "Tomorrow is a new day. Every day is a new chance to get things right. That's why our ship is called *Oriana*. It means new dawn."

"Why not just name the ship New Dawn?" Douglas asked, inching closer to Tray.

"Because that's a cheesy idealist's name for a ship. Danny is a cheesy idealist, but I . . . I had to fill out the paper work. Come on, alien boy. Let's break out of here."

"The window is rusted," Douglas said, hefting to his feet. He had nothing left to lose. The blanket dropped and his skin stung, but he grabbed the bars of the window and yanked with all his might. Then he felt the sting of a tranquilizer dart on his back.

"Dr. Louis?" a young nurse beckoned, knocking on Louis' office door.

Louis jerked awake and rubbed his eyes, wondering what fresh hell had warranted waking him from a much-needed nap. There were a few lingering patients from an incident in the orchard. There was a mild sexually-transmitted infection circulating through the young teen population and he'd yet to find patient zero. He'd had to de-allocate resources for a few older patients and send them home to die.

"What time is it?" he asked, shaking the numbness from his arms and tucking his pillow under his desk.

"Quarter after," the nurse replied, shying back. "Sorry to wake you so soon, but I thought you should know: Dr. Frank separated Saskia and Amanda for examination. Amanda's anxiety is rising."

Louis groaned and banged his head against his desk. "Where is Dr. Frank?"

"Ultrasound room."

Louis wanted to punch the old doctor. He rushed to the ultrasound room, surprised by the quiet inside until he saw Saskia passed out on the table.

"Louis, come look," Dr. Frank said, waving him into the room.

"What are you doing?" Louis demanded. Saskia's clothing had been pulled back and her upper body was covered with a sheet. "You self-entitled kerf! She'll never trust us now."

"You never finished your evaluation of her. She has a scar on her hip," Frank said, ignoring his tone and pointing to the old, healed injury on Saskia's skin. "I did a resonance image and—just look."

Louis glanced at the scan and did a double take. There was

extensive scar tissue through the pelvic region. "She couldn't survive that. The machine must be acting up again."

"That's what I thought. Which is why I began an internal inspection," Frank said.

"You have no right," Louis growled, pulling him away and covering Saskia's lower body. "You have no right to do this without her consent."

"It's difficult to get consent when she doesn't speak our language. I'm not waiting for her to learn Rocanese before I evaluate her allotment," Frank said. "We've been wasteful enough since their arrival."

"We can afford to be charitable until they are well enough to negotiate trade with our city," Louis countered. "There are more women than men in their tiny clan. Can you imagine having a thriving female population again?"

"This one is hardly a woman. Look! Look inside. There's nothing there!" Frank bellowed.

Louis punched his chin and Frank cocked his fist, but suddenly Saskia leapt from the bed and tackled Frank from behind. She spun him around and slammed his body against the table, twisting his arm behind his back.

"Get her off of me!" Frank cried.

"You speak Trade. She doesn't understand me," Louis sneered, massaging his knuckles, tempted to hit Frank again. He wanted to see Saskia take revenge, but she didn't strike. She patted down Frank's pockets, then reached into one and pulled out the glove that she'd been wearing earlier. Then she released him.

"Did you steal that from her?" Louis asked. Saskia kept an angry eye on them as she dressed herself, her limbs twitching and shaking from the residual sedative in her system.

"It's more than fabric. It could be a weapon," Frank said.

"You . . . hoarder!" Louis hissed at him. "Saskia, I'm so sorry. He just wanted to understand."

He pointed to the image readout and Saskia glanced at it, then went back to what she was doing. She couldn't understand his language, but she understood his intention.

"I'll take her back to Amanda," Louis said, putting a tentative hand on Saskia's shoulder. He repeated Amanda's name and motioned to the door. Saskia took a step, then she glanced at the image again. Her hand ghosted over her hip and her face paled.

"That's right. That's you," Louis smirked, looking over his shoulder at Frank. "I wonder if she has interest in medicine. She did take point in nursing the other two."

"If you can get her to speak," Frank grumbled.

"For her knowledge, I will devote the time to teach her," Louis smirked. "We already know she's a mechanic. Their ship has more working technology than our entire city! We have the medicine they need, and they have a way for us to escape this valley."

Frank sighed and rolled his eyes. "Fine. Give them the medicine they need. But don't be wasteful. Don't give them more than you would a Level Two laborer. And let's do a scan on Amanda and make sure she hasn't been gutted as well."

"It can wait," Louis snarled. "She was stressed enough by the separation."

Saskia sniffled, her hands ghosting over the image of her scars. If he could get her to speak, he could figure out how she'd survived such a devastating injury. They could save so many with her knowledge.

36

The moment Louis brought Saskia into the room, Amanda's already heightened anxiety went through the roof as she worried over her friend. Amanda ushered Saskia to the bed and made her lie down. Leaving the women to calm each other, Louis trudged up the stairs to the observation room, not trusting Frank far enough to risk sleeping.

Yale was there, watching by the window. "She seems like the mythological walking water lily," Yale commented.

"Amanda? I think the term you're looking for is walking fish,'" Louis chuckled. He'd noticed how Amanda tripped on her feet, like a child who had undergone a recent growth spurt. At times, she flailed, like she didn't understand how her own limbs moved. "How long have you been watching?"

"Not long." Yale turned, showing off an infant boy in his arms. The roundness of the boy's cheeks suggested he was a few days past birth. "We were getting some air. Do you need to talk?"

Louis nodded and sank into one of the chairs, catching Yale up on Frank's findings. "Saskia's not even making hand signals at me anymore," he said, rubbing his face.

"Give her time. She may not have realized the severity of her injury before now," Yale said, his words solemn but his tone bubbly for the benefit of the infant. The infant gurgled and flapped his arms.

"Is that the boy with the heart murmur?"

"He's the one," Yale said, kissing the boy's nose. Yale turned the infant toward the window and pointed out the ladies, telling a story about dark-skinned aliens on spaceships coming to save them. The infant wriggled until Yale had no choice but to cradle him close again.

"He should be in the nursery where it's sterile," Louis chastised.

"They get healthier if you hold them. Let them see the world," Yale said, nuzzling the boy. "If the heart defect was going to kill him, it would have done so days ago. Everyone said he wouldn't survive the night and he's survived the week."

"Because you held him?" Louis griped. "He's not out of the woods yet." Louis wasn't a pediatrician or a pessimist, but he knew the statistics. The young ones were fragile at this stage.

"He deserves to be held," Yale countered. "He deserves to see the sky and hear laughter. I have a family all picked out for him. Wonderful fathers—"

Louis tensed. "You've spoken to them?"

"Of course not." Yale rolled his eyes, then smiled at the boy again. "I have hope for this one, though. He'll make it. One of them has to."

In previous generations, they had informed adoptive couples of a coming child while the birth mother was still pregnant. As the stillbirth rate rose, they began waiting until a few days after birth. Now they waited two weeks before they even allowed official names to be given. It was possible Yale had marked several babies for this couple in the past, and none had survived. It was better that no one knew. Adoptive parents would not have been able to handle the truth of the process—knowing how close they came and how often they lost.

"Have you ever considered taking in one yourself?" Louis asked.

"I'd be a terrible father," Yale said.

Louis chuckled. "Yale, you are everyone's father."

"Ah. No wonder they all resent me," Yale commented.

Louis stiffened. He and Yale weren't close friends, but they shared a stressful job. Every doctor faced resentment and shouldered blame beyond what they could possibly be accountable for. "Do you need to talk, Yale?" he checked.

"I'm fine," Yale dismissed, though his smile was a little more troubled than before. "Let me take my little boy back to the nursery, and we can see to my Douglas and our new Tray Matthews."

Mine. Ours. No one else used words like that. Yale was everyone's father.

"Almost there," Jotham coached, linking his arm with Kyrn's, helping him sit at one of the hospital's cafeteria tables. Kyrn scrunched his face, keeping one hand clamped to his side, but he was determined not to spend the morning in a hospital bed. Jotham checked to make sure his brother was balanced before getting the food. He opted for the stuffed shells, because he figured Kyrn would spill the soup

"You exposed yourself as a hybrid," Kyrn nagged, scratching his fingers against the back of his hand, looking at the fork. He was hungry, but in too much pain to eat, and so he'd chosen to berate Jotham again for his reckless teleport.

"You exposed us first. You told Sky," Jotham countered,

loading his brother's fork. He waited to see if Kyrn moved or needed to be fed.

"You teleported a man," Kyrn hissed.

"How was I to know he was a mono-kind?" Jotham whispered back. "I don't have the sight in that realm. I just wanted them out before they ruined everything."

"Everything is ruined." Kyrn reached for the fork, then decided against moving his arms. "The question is do we suffer it or do our children?"

Jotham didn't have an answer. Knowing how fragile the illusion of safety was, he'd been hesitant to bring children into the world, but given the nature of breeding laws governing his generation, he didn't have much of a choice.

"It isn't fair," Jotham muttered, holding Kyrn's chin steady and bringing the fork to his lips. "Hwan's engine explodes. You get caught in the blast. It's not fair that he gets medicine and you're left to suffer because he happens to have a breeding record."

"I don't want a breeding record," Kyrn smirked. He had a child hidden from Rocan, but he wasn't an evil Sequesterer. As merciful as his protection was to his child, things would have been different for Kyrn if Rocan knew about the boy. The message sent by their leaders was clear—a man with no offspring was not valued in this society.

"You sensed Sky coming to Caswell. Would you be able to tell if Sky was in the hospital?" Kyrn asked.

"You're asking if I feel the spirit realm bleeding?" Jotham smirked. After Sky's first flight in the glider, he'd learned to feel the difference when the spirit was in the city or out, but he could only see her coming and going if he teleported atop the Dome. "Can you?"

"I can," a small voice whispered behind them.

"Nadia," Jotham said, feeling a shiver go through him at the appearance of the missing hybrid child.

"Don't call me that. That's not who I am anymore." Felicity stood by the table, cradling her bandaged arm.

"I'm sorry. Felicity," Jotham corrected, shaken by the schism in her appearance. For a moment, he could see who she was, and what the conjurer's illusion made her to be. Her burns looked worse in her natural state. "Why did I call you that? How can I see that face?"

"Someone's in the hospital," she whispered, looking over her shoulders. "Someone new."

"Yes, the aliens were brought here," Jotham nodded. "Is there another spirit carrier? Can you tell?"

"She has eyes to see what the conjurers are changing," Felicity said, peeking under her bandages. "I feel like I can see through her eyes sometimes. I see dead people walking the streets because the conjurers want them alive."

"That can't be," Jotham said, pulling the girl into a hug. She used to play with his daughters, with the protected children, and he felt the overwhelming urge to protect her again, but she needed Rocan's medicine. "What you're seeing is wrong. The conjurers can't bring back the dead."

"But they can kill," Kyrn shuddered. "One wrong word . . ."

"She speaks another language. The conjurers don't understand her words yet," Felicity said.

"A conjurer's connection to the spirit realm is not verbal. If they catch an image of the world as she sees it, even in a stray thought, the way you have, things will change," Jotham reasoned. Hybrids weren't telepathic—not all of them—and given how fragile the minds of conjurers could be, he didn't know what it would take to break one.

"Where is this new person?" Kyrn asked.

"A tall room?" she said. "I was taken there, when they first rescued Felicity."

"Felicity! There you are. You can't run off like that, little one," Colleen called, bustling into the cafeteria.

"She's all right, Madame," Jotham assured. "Came for a story, I think."

"Help me," Felicity whispered, squeezing his fingers. "Close these eyes."

37

Kyrn's bruised ribs were killing him. It was the third time this week that the pain had gotten so bad as to drive him to the hospital to beg for help, and still, there were not enough medications allocated to ease his suffering. The strangers from outside the Dome had suffered no such inconvenience. He didn't know why he tried to hide his bitterness from Jotham. Someone bumped into them as they shuffled down the hall, and Kyrn fell to his knees.

"Hey, watch out!" Jotham cried, catching Kyrn, righting him gingerly so that he could breathe again.

"Sorry, I didn't see you there," a young boy said, kneeling next to Kyrn. "I'll get help."

"Don't bother," Kyrn gasped, clutching his side.

"Where are you off to in such a hurry?" Jotham demanded. Kyrn grunted to get his attention, warning him to back down.

"I have clothing for the aliens," he said, nodding to a pile of clean clothing and freshly soled shoes. "I hear they have magic powers. They can burn you alive just by looking at you."

"Why don't you let me deliver the clothing," Kyrn said,

turning his palm, but keeping his arm plastered to his side. "Maybe they won't hurt an injured man."

"Or maybe they'll eat you alive," the boy said.

"Doesn't matter. I'm not a breeder," Kyrn sighed, tears of bitterness in his eyes.

"Kyrn, you can barely walk. You're not going in there," Jotham argued, taking the package. "I'll go."

"Thank you so much!" the boy said, zipping away, knocking into other patients in his urgency to flee.

"I'm injured, pained, and delirious. I have better reason to be wandering in than you," Kyrn argued.

"Then we'll go together," Jotham said.

"Two product runners of the mine delivering clothing in a hospital," Kyrn smirked. "If I get in trouble, you need to be free to help them later. To help me. It's okay, brother."

Taking the package, Kyrn stumbled on, pushing through the pain. He was doing this to help Felicity, and to protect his son.

"Gate," said the deputy on guard. "What are you doing here?"

"Hello, Officer Miller. Resources have been allocated," Kyrn replied. "I am to retrieve their old garments for inventory."

"You?" Miller said doubtfully.

"Can't run product in this state. I have to remain useful," Kyrn said. It was getting harder to hide the fact that he shouldn't have been standing at all.

"Well they don't speak any language we know. The dark woman is a fighter, but she's more likely to attack if you approach the other girl. Maybe you should wait out here," Miller offered.

Kyrn stiffened. He needed to be in there alone. "Are they afraid of you?"

Miller smirked and pushed open the door. He seemed ready for a fight, but none came. There were two women in the room:

a fair-skinned one asleep in the bed, and a dark-skinned crouched on the floor, her body coiled for attack.

"This is Saskia and Amanda," Miller said, pointing to each in turn as he said their names. They were alien names to match their alien faces.

"I have clothing for three," Kyrn said. He didn't sense anything supernatural about them. Jotham would have been able to tell.

"There was a man. The Intendant entrapped him so he could confiscate the ship. Now he's incarcerated for trying to break out of a prison he never should have been in," Miller said. "It's a shame, too. He was the only one who could translate what they were saying into Trade. The Intendant was wrong to separate them."

Kyrn looked back in surprise and Miller's eyes widened.

"But you didn't hear me say that," Miller amended.

"Of course not," Kyrn agreed. He approached Saskia, holding the clothes out as an offering. She rose slowly, showing herself to be taller and stronger than him, her right hand clenched into a fist.

"I have clothing for you," Kyrn said in Trade, hoping she'd respond. She glanced at the clothes in his hand, then back at him.

"Wait, you speak Trade?" Miller asked. "I thought only academics did that. You're wasted as a runner."

Kyrn smiled, then clutched his aching ribs. Saskia rushed forward putting her hand on the injury.

"No, don't touch." Kyrn whimpered, dropping the clothes.

Saskia spoke rapidly in another language, then turned to Miller. "Louis. Louis," she hissed, repeating the doctor's name. She turned back to Kyrn, gently coaxing him to sit.

"What does she want?" Kyrn asked, his head getting foggy.

"Go with it, Gate. I think she's concerned about your injury," Miller said. "She wants to help."

"Really?" Kyrn said, his chin quivering. Saskia looked into his eyes, speaking soothingly as she moved his arm over his head and lifted his shirt. Kyrn clenched his teeth, crying in pain, so close to passing out that he barely heard Miller swearing.

"Louis!" Saskia repeated, snapping her fingers at Miller. She hopped up and went to a counter on the opposite side of the bed.

"Where are you going?" Kyrn asked in Trade. She looked at him like a person. She touched him like she intended to help. And she came back when he called. Her fingers trailed up his spine, tracing the point where his ribs connected, and then he felt a pinch and his skin burned.

"What is that!" Kyrn cried, feeling the sting of an injection.

"Saskia, stop!" Miller ordered. "These medicines aren't allocated for him!"

"What did she do?" Kyrn asked, feeling his skin go numb, and then his side. The pain in his body finally subsided.

"Gate!" Miller shouted, dragging Saskia back. Saskia pressed into the pull, slamming Miller against the wall, then slamming him onto his back.

"I'm okay," Kyrn said, speechless at the mercy this stranger had shown him. Jotham was right to want to help them. "Thank you, Saskia. Thank you," he said in Trade.

"Water?" she asked, pointing to a cup on the counter.

"For me?" he asked, getting more and more light-headed. "Officer Miller?"

The other man groaned.

"Do you understand me, Saskia? Come closer," Kyrn said. He tried to stand, but his legs felt like jelly. Saskia laid him on the ground next to Miller.

"I can get you back to your ship," Kyrn said, touching her face. "Be waiting tonight. I will come back. Do you understand?"

There were people observing this room, but hopefully, he could dismiss his statements as the desperate ramblings of a drugged man. He took a deep breath—the first he'd taken in a while.

"Saskia. Saskia?"

Saskia wiped the tears from his eyes, leaning her face close to his. She mouthed the words 'I understand.' Her eyes darted toward the door, and she retreated to the bed spreading her arms protectively over her sleeping friend. The door burst open a few seconds later, and Kyrn lay on the floor while doctors and policemen stepped over him, giving priority to those who mattered.

Tray's hands were bound to the bars at the front of his jail cell. He'd been smart enough to remove the Virp from his glove and hide it in a pocket, but now he couldn't pull it out and tell Danny the latest developments. He'd tried the voice activation, but the device was designed not to respond to accidental activation when pocketed. His shoulder ached. A fresh rash itched on his neck. His wrists were scraped raw from the rough rope wrapped around them. He could slide his hands up and down the bars of the jail cell, and had been tied such that he could lie down if he wanted, but the position forced his shoulder into an awkward position and made his hands numb.

Hawk was tied to the bars on the other side, his bright red hair peeking out from a thin blanket pulled over his head. He'd woken once since the tranquilizer darts hit, and whined in Rocanese for half an hour before Constable Mace talked him down. The Constable didn't speak Trade, and he pretended not to hear when Tray spoke to him.

"Hawk?" Tray whispered.

"I'm not talking to you," Hawk muttered.

"They're not going to use explosives to break into the ship, are they?" Tray asked.

"No," he replied. "If it's as close to the Pagoda as you say, they wouldn't risk it. Rocan may be primitive, but we understand how volatile fuel can be."

"Okay," Tray murmured. "Are they still going to feed us in here?"

Hawk didn't answer, and Tray leaned his head against the bars. He was going to get very sick very soon if he didn't get something to eat. "Can you translate something for me?"

The door opened, and the smell of food made Tray's chest ache, hoping for sustenance and fearing that the food wasn't for him. Don Yale had two plates with him, and he showed them to Mace, nodding toward the door. Dr. Louis was a step behind, carrying a medical bag.

"Yale, are they safe? Saskia and Amanda," Tray asked, sliding his hands up the bars as he stood, despite the weakness in his body. Mace nodded, then rapped at Tray's knuckles, forcing him back to his knees while he opened the door, much to Louis' chagrin. The doctor hurried over to nurse Tray's bleeding fingers.

"Amanda? Is she okay?" Tray asked again.

"The women are being cared for," Yale acknowledged, setting a food plate down within Tray's reach. Kneeling beside Hawk, he peeled back the blanket and released the ropes around his wrists.

"He says you brought him here to die," Tray said. Louis detached Tray from the bars, but didn't unbind his wrists. Tray held out his hands to Yale, but neither doctor seemed willing to untie him, and so he picked up the dull spoon they'd brought for him and found a way to eat. He nearly gagged when the food touched his tongue.

"That's not decided, yet," Yale said, petting Hawk's face, bringing a drink to his lips. "I do hope that both of you will be freed shortly. There are many of us on your side."

"I asked to speak to him, not to join him," Tray said. "You said you would help me. That you'd catalog my injuries. Instead you've tied me up like an animal!"

Louis put a calming hand on Tray's chest, and spoke to him in Rocanese.

"He wants to know about Saskia. How did she get that scar on her hip?" Don translated, motioning over his pelvis.

"You wouldn't believe me if I told you," Tray said.

"Yesterday, I didn't believe there were dark-skinned aliens hiding in a spaceship in the valley," Yale said. "Tell the truth as you know it."

"She was in a war before I knew her. We only met a few years ago and . . . she came with the ship," he shrugged, stirring the slop that looked like a chowder. It was remarkably flavorless, despite the bright purple color. Tray kept his posture straight, taking small, clean bites, letting his captors know that they could not humiliate him by leaving him bound.

"Saskia will fight you in every way she can," Tray warned. "She can make a weapon out of a grape stem, which is handy if you're stranded in a vineyard with her. She will kill you to rescue me."

Yale's expression turned grave. "It's not wise to repeat that. She may be forced to join you here."

"Amanda," Tray began, then pressed his lips together. "She has only recently become free and we don't know what was done to her." He wanted to give these people as much information as possible, so they wouldn't trigger her psychosis. "I don't know why she attacked your people. She didn't know who you were or where she was. She can't hold on to the memories. I don't know how she got a weapon. You've seen the condition of her heart; she was supposed to be resting—hey!"

Tray jerked away from Louis' prying hands and yelping as his bonds cut against his wrist. "You can have my clothes when you take them off my corpse!"

"He is curious about your skin condition," Yale apologized, finally loosening the bonds on Tray's wrist.

Mace growled a warning in Rocanese, drawing his tranq gun.

"I had a sickness called Moon Pox that caused rashes, although I think my newest one is a reaction to the filth of this place. I'm not contagious," Tray explained, although the new itching on his skin worried him.

"The sickness caused your skin to heal this dark?" Yale asked.

"All my skin is dark brown, if that's what you're asking. It's not a condition; it's a natural skin color," Tray said, backing away from Louis. "If you want to examine me, take me back to the hospital. Take me back to my friends."

"Hello again, Mon Tray Matthews," Intendant Hubert said, making a sinister entrance. He lingered by the door, letting the Dome light cast a silhouette around him.

"Intendant," Tray greeted, his nostrils flaring. "Why have I been locked in here?"

"You came here to speak to Mon Hwan," the Intendant crooned, sauntering up to the bars, staying just out of reach. "And within minutes coerced him to damage the building and break out of prison."

"You trapped me in here with him without cause," Tray countered, keeping his tone as even and smooth as the Intendant's while rising to his feet. "You cruelly keep me from my son."

The Intendant exchanged a look with Mace, and there was a murmured translation. Hawk had said this town prized children, and it seemed Tray's bait was having the desired effect.

"You have a son?" the Intendant asked. "The Constable said there was no one else on the ship."

"My son does not travel with me," Tray explained. He didn't want them breaking in to mount a rescue. "He's in Quin. My home city. And I need to get back to him. That's why we were hesitant to make contact initially. We were in a hurry to return home."

"I see," the Intendant murmured.

"I see," Tray mocked. "Do you?"

"My Trade is out of practice. Perhaps there is another word," he said. His previous arrogance was clouded by the news of the boy.

"Let us talk about what Quin can do for Rocan," the Intendant tried.

"I won't negotiate while I'm being held captive," Tray sneered, stepping toward the bars, but keeping his distance so that Mace wouldn't rap his fingers again. "Take me back to my friends or we'll break more than the bars on the window as we make our escape."

"You're Sequestering him," Hawk murmured. "Sequestering us both so we can't escape. You think he won't help us? Was I wrong?"

Yale hugged Hawk, rocking him like a child. Tray had heard the word 'Sequestering' before, but he didn't know enough to use it to his advantage yet. The Intendant seemed displeased by the accusation, though.

"This boy is your genetic son?" Yale asked.

"Yes, my genetic son. Why is that important?" Tray asked.

"And is his skin dark like yours?" Yale asked.

"You sure as hell don't get black babies from white parents," Tray said, his stomach contracting as Louis reached out again.

"But the color can be diluted, if you mix parentage," Don reasoned.

"Why?" Tray asked. "Why do you ask?"

"It will make breeding easier if they can be assured a child will look normal," Hawk spoke up, his chest muscles rippling at the last word. It was the first time Tray really noticed how different Hawk looked from the other people he'd met. He'd assumed there was a mixture of skin tone here, just as there was in Quin, but Hawk was darker than all of them.

"I look perfectly normal," Tray growled, backing away from the doctors. "And no way you will be breeding any of us. Let me free, or you will regret crossing us."

"Don't look at him, Intendant," Hawk whimpered, hiding his face in Yale's shoulder. "He can make your head explode just by looking at you."

Tray bristled. On the ship, he'd meant it as a tease, and he'd never expected Hawk to repeat the threat.

"Stop your yammering, Hwan," the Intendant sneered. "If he had the ability, he'd have done it already."

"He's not well, sir," Yale spoke up. "He belongs in the hospital. You have no evidence of resource hoarding beyond his word, which is clearly compromised. It is time you released him."

"But Mon Tray Matthews saw the glider. Didn't he?" the Intendant crooned.

Hawk shrank back. Tray knew he was meant to understand the accusation, because it was made in Trade.

"Three times you flew, correct? That is what you said when you confessed to the hoarding?" the Intendant sneered.

"I was going to give it back," Hawk said, his voice high-pitched with fear.

"You promised our city's resources to this man and his accomplices. To Sky who put thirty women in danger yesterday," the Intendant continued.

"We are not accomplices," Tray spoke up, though given the circumstances, his position was difficult to argue.

"You can have the glider, just let them go. Let them bring help," Hawk begged.

"Take me around your ship," the Intendant smirked, turning his burning gaze toward Tray.

"Take us to Saskia and Amanda, and I will consider it," Tray countered, squaring his shoulders.

"Us?" the Intendant asked.

"Hawk says you brought him here to kill him," Tray said. "Since you have no use for him, I will take him with me. That's the deal. And if you enter my ship without my consent . . . I will make your head explode."

38

Spirit shivered and Sky turned to see who was coming. The street was crowded with people headed for the cafeterias and taverns for the afternoon meal. They didn't seem to notice Sky, but somewhere, someone's psychic scent had sent Spirit into a rage. Then the screaming in her mind quieted.

"Sky, what's wrong?" Danny asked, standing between her and the crowd.

"Hide," she warned, ducking into the nearest doorway. The silence had its own scent. *John.* Sky slammed her shoulder against the door, breaking the jamb, then she shoved Danny inside.

"You came back," John seethed, jogging to the bottom of the porch steps, steel pipe clutched in his hand.

"Yes. For you," Sky said, backing away slowly.

"Do you know what happened to my son because of you?" John said, crowding her into the house. Sky stumbled into an empty room that smelled of dust and urine. John's nose wrinkled, but his face was hard and threatening. "They're going to kill him."

"What for?" Sky asked, keeping John's eyes on her and off of Danny.

"What for? What for!?" John screamed, raising the pipe up.

"John, I can't help him if you don't tell me what's going on," Sky said, motioning Danny to stay back.

"It's all your fault. He was fine before you came!"

"Fine," she scoffed. "He has been drunk since I got here! He can't stand living in this place. I don't know how he got tricked into giving up his glider."

"He was not tricked. He knows they are going to find that glider and take it from him. They're going to destroy it and with it, everything good left in him. Then they'll kill him." John dropped the pipe, his face falling. He clutched his chest, his body quaking. Sky stepped closer to comfort him, but suddenly John made a grab for her wrist. She barely managed to dodge.

"And you will die with him!" John snarled.

"I can save him, John," Sky said, dodging as John feinted toward her again.

"You took him hostage," John said, stumbling to one knee.

"I was protecting him! Your own people asked him to die."

"They found the alien's Coureur," John croaked, muddling through the Trade words, pressing his hand to the side of his face as if he were trying to hold his thoughts inside. "They found the others."

"You found the spaceship we travel in. That's how we'll escape," Sky explained, searching for words that he would understand. "John, I promise you, I meant him no harm."

"You slit his throat!" John screamed, lunging at her, and catching her across the chest. Startled, Sky curled her body protectively, and rather than throw him off, she pulled his arm around her. John tried half-heartedly to drag her from the house, but Sky planted her feet and held him tightly, rocking her body against his in a soothing rhythm. He wasn't soothed. His breathing calmed, but his attempts to drag her out became more forceful.

"By morning, we can be gone forever. All of us. You can come, too. Stay with me," she promised. John locked his arms and he swept her body around to face the door. Danny blocked their path, pulse rifle raised.

"Tell me what happened to the others they brought from my ship," Danny growled. John scrambled backward, pulling Sky with him.

"Is this him?" John asked, a low, threatening hum in his voice. "Your friend?"

"New friend," Sky said. "He's not even an old friend; he's just my ride. I called for help and he came to take me home. Compared to him, you and I go way back."

"We can help," Danny said, keeping his pulse rifle raised. "We can find a cure for the disease that kills your children."

"You lie," John cried, snapping Sky's body against his so hard she saw stars.

"It's true," Sky choked. "Cordova is a city to the east, and they are rich in medicine and they have diagnostic tools you can't imagine. And women. There is no shortage of women there."

John's breath quickened. "There was nothing out there besides your ship."

"Not this side of the mountains. We will go out as ambassadors on your behalf," Danny promised. "If you help my crew escape."

"Escape?" John repeated, his arm constricting around Sky's neck.

"Hawk agreed to help me and I will help him in return. I can't do that without my crew."

"If you could really heal my people, you would go straight to the Intendant and demand your crew's release."

"John, you're hurting me," Sky whispered.

John shifted his grip just enough to let her breathe. She could feel his tears sliding down the back of her neck. "Don't let them kill my son."

"Let her go," Danny ordered, aiming his rifle at John's head. "This is your last warning."

Sky wasn't used to exhaustion. Exhaustion was for common mortals, not for spirit-carriers. Not that she would have minded mortality, but now was a bad time for exhaustion to consume her. This was John's fault.

"I'm trusting you, Sky," John whispered in her ear, his breath tickling her skin. Sky relaxed into his arms, fighting to stay awake.

Then he shoved her.

Sky's face slammed against the door of the Bastien. John hooked his arm through her elbow, dragging her into the small room that served as the law office. Her thigh slammed against one of the four desks crowding the room and she bit back a curse.

"Constable Mace, I'm here for my son!" John bellowed.

"John?" Hawk murmur. Sky had expected the Bastien to be bigger, but it barely spanned a room. There was no way to break the others out without Mace seeing.

"Mon Harris, you know I—Sky!" Mace exclaimed. Mace jumped up from his desk, his chair scraping against the cement floor. With John alone, Spirit maintained a restful silence, but with the two men together, the void was painful.

"Channing," Sky whimpered, playing the victim. John pushed her to her knees, and Sky gasped. When they'd discussed this plan outside, Sky had imagined a lot more acting and a lot less violence.

"Release my boy or she dies," John said, jabbing Sky between the shoulders. This was not part of the plan. The plan was to keep Mace's attention while Tray and Hawk climbed out the window. The small room wasn't the only hindrance to Plan A. Hawk and Tray were bound and tethered to the bars at the front of the cell.

"Channing, help," she whispered.

"You don't want to make threats like that Harris," Mace warned, approaching cautiously.

"You've condemned him for nothing," John said. "Sky manipulated him. He's the victim."

Sky brought her Virp to her lips. "Captain, switch to plan B," she whispered, hoping the captain was more adherent to plans than was John.

"Harris, let her go. You do not want an injured woman on your record."

"She is not the victim!" John seethed, yanking Sky by the hair. "Tell him!

"Channing, Hawk's innocent," Sky said, trying to keep her eyes on Mace and avoid drawing attention to Danny's face peeking through the cell window. "I forced him to help me escape."

Charging forward, Mace punched John and pulled Sky off the ground. Barely fazed by the blow, John ran to the cell and reached through the bars to touch his son.

"Harris!" Mace shouted. Danny barely dropped out of sight in time.

Untie him. Untie them, Sky coached mentally.

"Don't be seduced by her, Constable. She's evil! She cut me; she burned me; she made me do things I didn't want!" Hawk screamed. His lips dry and cracked, his face and hands blistered.

"Harris, step away from the bars. Step away!" Mace ordered. Mace's arms were around Sky and he carried no weapon, but strangely, John heeded his words like he was under a spell.

"John, don't let go," Hawk whimpered.

"Good," Mace said, his voice deep and intoxicating. "Now find a messenger to summon Arman and Breaux."

John's fingers twitched and his gaze flickered toward Sky. He looked like he did not want to follow Mace's orders, but was powerless to move on his own. "My son comes with me," he begged, his voice cracking.

"You will die beside him if you do not leave now," Mace snarled.

"Do as he asks, John," Sky begged. "I'll make this right."

Every time John looked at Mace, he took a step away from Hawk.

"Don't trust her!" Hawk shouted, tearing at his bonds, shaking the bars of the cell. "Don't do it! She lies!"

The frustrated look on Tray's face told Sky that Hawk had lost his marbles long before she had entered the room. Tray knew his moment was coming and he was ready to run.

"Douglas," John whispered, quieting his son with the simple word. "We'll be together soon." With that, John dashed out of the Bastien.

"John!" Hawk screeched. "Don't go! Papa!"

"Channing," Sky whispered, cupping her hand behind Mace's head and pulling him into an embrace. She needed to keep his eyes off the cell. In mixed Trade and Rocanese, she begged him for protection. "I'm scared. Get me out of here. Take me some place safe."

"Help is coming," he said, his eyes darting around the room. He didn't believe her innocent anymore.

There was a noise as Danny pulled open the window.

"It's a trick! Mace!" Hawk screamed, kicking the bars and

howling when he saw Danny climbing through the window. "They're here!"

Mace made a dive for the tranq gun on his desk, but Sky shoved him, knocking the gun onto the floor. He fought back, though he was unwilling to unleash his full strength against her. Using that to her advantage, Sky slammed Mace against the wall, dazing him.

"Hawk, shut up and help!" Sky shouted. None of her plans accounted for Hawk switching sides. Danny cut Tray loose first, then he clamped a hand over Hawk's mouth, putting Hawk in a full body lock so that Tray could sever his bonds.

"Keys?" Danny asked. There was no way they could take Hawk through the window.

"Where are the keys?" Sky asked Mace, pinning him to the wall and searching his pockets.

"Who is that man, Sky?" he asked. "Is he forcing you?"

"Stand back," Sky said to Danny and Tray, drawing her grav-gun. With a single blast, she rendered the lock to dust, crumbling the bars around it in a two foot radius. Hawk's face went red as he screamed and struggled to get free. Danny and Tray wasted no time getting Hawk out the front door and Sky waited until they were clear before releasing Mace.

"Sky!" Mace called, grabbing his tranq gun, but not raising it.

"I don't have a choice, Channing. I have to go with them."

"Why?" he asked. "Who are they? Where did they come from? Where did you come from?"

Smiling, Sky sauntered to him, pushed him to sit on the desk, and straddled his lap. "Darling Channing, there is so much that I can't tell you. You can't imagine how safe I feel with you, but I know that safety is just an illusion conjured by you," she said, caressing his face with her gun and kissing him tenderly on the lips. She closed her eyes, reveling in the quietness of Spirit, wondering how many more in Rocan possessed his calming gift. She could live a normal life with someone like him around.

"I am so glad I met you," she said, relaxing in his arms. Then she pistol-whipped him, knocking him out cold.

39

Amanda crouched on the hospital room floor, huddling next to the door as Saskia desperately tried to trip the lock. Despite the blanket wrapped around Amanda's shoulders, she shivered. They'd been at it for twenty minutes and no one had come to stop them. They were locked in. Trapped.

Amanda heard a raspy voice behind them and jumped, knocking the wire out of Saskia's hand. Ever since Sky had come, memories had been leaking through her mind, straining her grasp on the present. It was worse now that they were in the city, surrounded by the hybrid energy. There was no one behind her. She felt the pull of the spirit realm—the tingle that came right before she Disappeared.

"Amanda!"

"Jo?" Amanda moaned and rolled onto her side. The past and present were patched together and her brain couldn't force a logic onto either.

"You're on Aquia!" Saskia snapped. Her temper had been short since the Rocanese doctors took her. Even though her vision was fuzzy, she could tell that Saskia was scowling.

"I'm on Aquia," Amanda repeated, rubbing her aching chest.

The texture of her clothes was wrong. This was Corey's sweater. "What did you do to me?"

"Stabilized your blood pressure," Saskia said.

Amanda's nose wrinkled, seeking form for the memory that came with the charcoal smell of this room. Saskia rolled her onto her side and injected her with fresh medicine. Amanda felt a tingle and a whoosh of air. A man asked a question and Saskia whipped around, fist cocked.

"I didn't hear the door open," Saskia said.

"He didn't come through the door," Amanda whispered. A wiry, hybrid man stood over them. He was fuzzy in her spinning vision, his wings coming in and out of view as her sense of the spirit realm flickered. His eyes glowed and his frail body was hunched. "You can travel through it, can't you? You can take me to Galen!"

"His name is Kyrn. He is here to help," Saskia explained, taking a package from the man. "Put on your shoes."

"How are those things shoes?" Amanda griped, toeing the worn sandals she'd been gifted. Curling on her side, she slid the shoes onto her feet. She felt a light-headed, but it was nothing compared to the dizziness of this morning's gravity sickness.

"No! Off the bed. He needs the bed," Saskia said, grabbing her by the elbow. Amanda jabbed and screamed.

"Quiet!" Saskia growled, crowding Amanda into a corner. Kyrn lay face down on the bed, his eyes closed, his body limp. "Flashback or hallucination?"

"Flashback," Amanda said, climbing Saskia's body until she was standing. She was somehow on the other side of the room. "Losing time, too."

She touched Kyrn's back, feeling the warmth of his spirit presence even through the darkness that pervaded the city. He didn't make her see strange things or become strange things, but he was hurt. It wasn't only his physical form, but his spirit form seemed to be damaged, too, carrying the lingering ashes that surrounded Sky.

"As soon as his meds kick in, we have to move. Can you walk?" Saskia asked.

"I'll manage," Amanda said, hiding her face in Saskia's shoulder. "My feet are heavy."

"But the shoes fit?" she checked. "You can run in them?"

The man said something and Amanda jumped. Kyrn rose to his full height, unfurling giant wings. She knew what came next. Amanda hugged Saskia and held her breath. There was a chill and then heat, and then Kyrn's protective wings fell away and he collapsed on the ground.

"What happened?" Saskia gasped, rolling onto her back. "We teleported?"

"He's hybrid. We've moved," Amanda said, looking around. "Galen?"

"We're in the hall. We're still in the building," Saskia said.

"Oh, God. He's bleeding. He's bleeding!" Amanda cried.

"He's not bleeding," Saskia said, rolling Kyrn onto his back and checking his breathing.

"He tastes like ashes," Amanda said, kneeling beside him. His pain radiated through the realm like fire.

"He's not dead," Saskia hissed. "Let's get out of here."

Amanda shook her head. "Doesn't *he* need to get out of here, too?"

"Are you going to carry him?" Saskia retorted.

"He carried us." She knelt next to Kyrn and lifted his heavy arm over her shoulder.

"No! His ribs are broken. You could puncture his lung carrying him like that," Saskia said, yanking Amanda to her feet. "If we leave him here, a doctor will find him. If we take him with us, he's an accomplice. Let's go!"

Saskia started them running, and when Amanda couldn't keep pace, Saskia carried her.

Danny's shins were bruised from Hawk kicking and fighting, but it was still easier than pinning down Amanda, because Danny wasn't worried about crushing Hawk's bones to dust. The poor kid was burning up, the sweat dripping off his skin making him both sticky and slippery. Danny couldn't tell if he was screaming for help or crying out in pain, but when they rounded the building to where John stood waiting, Hawk's body went stiff.

"Did you call a messenger," Sky asked, taking a look-out position.

"Of course not," John answered in thickly-accented Trade.

"Do it, now."

John ignored her, focusing his attention on Hawk instead, bending his knees slightly so that he was face-to-face with his boy. He whispered something in Rocanese, then pulled Danny's hand off of Hawk's mouth. Loosening his grip, Danny let Hawk's body slide down his so that his feet touched the ground.

"Papa," Hawk whimpered, nuzzling John's hand.

"John, messenger. Now," Sky snapped. "Mace needs to think you're on his side."

John shot her a look, but then took a breath. Tenderly, he brushed his thumb across Hawk's cheek and whispered to his son again. Hawk shook his head, sobbing, but John shushed him and kissed his temple, offering assurances. Then Sky nestled in, pressing against John seductively.

"Please, John. I want you to survive this night, too," she whispered in John's ear, letting her lips brush John's skin. The color rose in John's cheeks, and he leaned into her.

"You know, an hour ago, he was ready to kill her," Danny

remarked, rubbing Hawk's shoulder. Hawk's body sagged, and he quivered as he clung to Danny's arm, whispering to himself in Rocanese.

"He's a liability," Tray warned, massaging his splinted wrist.

"We can't leave him to die," Danny said. He cringed, seeing the rope burns where Tray's bonds had cut into his skin. Danny brushed his fingers against the hem of Tray's jacket, pushing the sleeve up enough so that his brother knew he saw the wound.

"Not my fault," Hawk whimpered. "Mace—he makes me see things differently."

"Amanda said that about him, too," Tray said.

"He's definitely got that hybrid magic," Sky agreed. "He seemed to have this power over John. He just gave orders and John obeyed."

"He said you weren't real, and I believed him," Hawk whined, backing into Danny's arms. "I thought I was crazy, but I'm not. I'm not crazy."

"You're not crazy," Danny affirmed, giving him a hug.

"But you disappeared," Hawk whispered.

"Why were you with him?" Danny asked Tray. "You were supposed to protect Amanda."

"They were going to separate us eventually," Tray shrugged.

"So you left voluntarily?"

"I wasn't going to submit to a cavity search with the girls watching!"

"Hey!" Sky snapped, slapping them both on the cheek. "I will shut down this rescue and make you two walk home."

"Don't ever hit my brother again," Danny warned, aching for a fight, but finding it work enough to keep Hawk contained.

"Are the girls already on the ship?" Tray asked, straightening his suit.

"Haven't rescued them yet," Danny replied. His brother gave him a confused look. "What?"

"You really came for me first?" Tray asked.

"No, we came for Hawk first," Sky said. "He knows the layout of the hospital. Come on!"

Tray ducked behind a bench next to one of Rocan's many roadside gardens, and checked the foot-traffic at the hospital's entrance. It was the only public building on the street that still had lights on at this hour.

"We were in an observation room," Tray said. "The door was locked from the outside."

"Make yourself invisible again," Hawk murmured, laying his head on Danny's chest.

"We weren't invisible. We . . . teleported. I'm sorry we scared you," Danny said, squeezing Hawk around the shoulders.

"Then do that," Hawk said, squeezing back hard. "Show me what you did."

Tray's lips twitched, his jealousy surging. Danny wasn't letting go of his new charge, no matter how much trouble Hawk got them into.

"Still nothing from Saskia," Tray reported, checking his Virp again.

"Maybe they're tied up, too," Sky said.

Frustrated, Tray scanned the building for alternate entrances, since there would be no way to sneak past the nurses' station at the main one. Every one of them was far too recognizable for the wrong reasons. *Maybe a window—*

"Oh, no! There's why she doesn't answer," Tray smiled, pointing to two shadowy figures scaling the side of the building. He looked at Danny and they laughed together. Tray felt another twinge of jealousy when Danny immediately turned and tapped Hawk on the shoulder, pointing to the women.

"Neither one of them has any patience," Danny chuckled. He was looking away when Amanda slipped.

His heart leaping into his throat, Tray charged across the street toward the building. Saskia had thrown her body sideways, catching Amanda, but she barely had a grip and until Amanda found footing, the two were stuck.

"Give me a boost!" Tray cried when Danny overtook him. Between instinct, years of cargo hauling, and one too many ninja flickers, Danny knew exactly what Tray meant. Cupping his hands, Danny caught Tray's foot and hoisted Tray over his shoulders. Finding a ledge, Tray shifted his weight off Danny's hands, scaling inch by inch until he reached Saskia. *I'm wearing the wrong shoes for this.* The pressure on his wrist was agony, but it was too late to back down now. Tray bent his knee, pressing his weight against the brick wall, feeling it scrape his skin through his pants.

"Hey," Tray greeted, taking part of Amanda's weight off Saskia and letting her stabilize. "I warned you I might try to rescue you."

Saskia didn't respond to the joke. Her sweat-soaked limbs made her grip tenuous, and her fingers trembled. Sliding down to the ledge, he tried to take a little more of Amanda's weight.

"We left him," Amanda whimpered. "We should have carried him."

"Dig your toes in. We need to climb a few more feet, then Danny can catch you," Saskia ordered.

With a few more directions, the three of them worked together and lowered Amanda into Danny's waiting arms. As soon as the weight was off, Saskia nearly fell, too. Her fingers were bleeding. They inched down the wall until Danny could reach her ankles. Tray made sure Saskia was down safely before he jumped. The impact knocked the wind out of him. Saskia bowed over, looking ready to vomit, and Tray pulled a handkerchief from his jacket to dab the blood from her fingers. He kept his injured wrist cradled to his chest.

"Fancy meeting you here," Danny said.

"Trying out a new doctor," Saskia deadpanned. Tray chuckled, glad for Saskia's dry humor.

"I picked this up for you," Tray said, handing her the stunner Mace had confiscated. He swore her eyes misted as she took the weapon. Then she looked sick again and bent over, taking slow, concentrated breaths. "Saskia?"

"She's been hurting ever since that doctor took her," Amanda groaned, wedging herself under Danny's arm.

Saskia shook her head. "Gravity," she whispered, rubbing her chest. It was a transparent lie, but Tray wasn't going to challenge it.

"How much farther?" Amanda asked.

"Go ahead and rest a moment. We allotted twenty minutes for this rescue, so we're ahead of schedule," Tray joked.

"This isn't some romantic picnic," Sky hissed, emerging from the shadows, dragging Hawk, keeping her hand clamped over his mouth. She pointed down the street where Deputy Arman was barking orders to a handful of Rocanese men.

"You killed them. You killed them all," Amanda said, her eyes going wide.

"Amanda," Danny said, tightening his grip on her.

"You killed your entire family," Amanda whimpered.

"Captain, you had better put a lid on her," Sky warned.

"I'm not talking to you!" Amanda hissed, smacking Sky in the face. The force of the impact didn't hurt Sky, but it sent Amanda reeling backwards. Releasing Hawk, Sky grabbed Amanda's shirt and cocked her fist.

"Help! John, come back!" Hawk screeched. Tray dove forward, tackling him and covering his mouth.

"Sky!" Danny warned, lifting Amanda off her feet and

blocking Sky. "She's schizophrenic. She doesn't know what she's saying."

"How convenient for her," Sky smirked.

"You choked them all. Choked the life out of them!" Amanda cried, shaking loose and running off.

"Get them to the glider. I'll catch her and meet you there," Danny ordered, taking off after her without a glance back.

Laying his body prostrate over Hawk's to keep him from running, Tray muttered, "Sure, I'll just take care of everything else."

40

Danny prayed hard as he charged into the darkness after Amanda. It was bad enough that she was having flashbacks, but now the dark street and stench of decay was taking him back to Terrana as well. Danny had only been in the tunnels a handful of times and each venture landed him in a Terranan interrogation room, beaten senseless by the Guard in the name of the law.

Zive, help me.

Amanda was fast, but every time she tripped, he gained ground. As soon as Danny was close enough, he leapt through the air, tackling Amanda. She attempted a dodge, but he caught enough of her body to topple her. They landed hard on the broken pavement and Amanda screeched in Moonspeak.

"Amanda," he said, repeating her name desperately as he struggled to hold her. She flailed and jabbed, agitating the bruises Hawk had given him earlier. Scooping her into his arms, Danny kicked open the door to the nearest building and dragged her inside. Finding a switch, he flipped on the lights. The police might find them faster with the lights on, but there was no way to win Amanda's trust in darkness.

"It worked. You came!" a man laughed. Jotham Gate sat in the middle of the floor, legs crossed in a meditative pose.

Amanda dropped into a crouch, putting one hand on the ground for support. They were in the lobby of some kind of office building. The reception area fed into several hallways, none of which held obvious secondary exits.

"Amanda," Danny said, dropping to one knee and reaching out a hand. "It's okay. It's me."

Amanda's eyes were fixated on Jotham and his eyes on her. She scampered a few feet closer to him and cocked her head.

"Jotham. You have to help us? We need to get back to the hanger," Danny begged. "Or the ship. Can you get us to the ship?"

"What are you?" Jotham mused, rolling to his knees, crawling toward Amanda. "Not hybrid. Not human. But you heard me."

"She is human; she's just sick," Danny said.

"You showed Felicity the . . . the things you see with spirit eyes," Jotham said, hesitating on the last word. "What's your name?"

"She doesn't speak Trade. I'll hold her down if you help us," Danny warned, edging between them.

"Hold her down?" Jotham repeated, pausing, then sitting back and making space.

Amanda ripped at her hair, muttering in Moonspeak, and Jotham touched his ears, his face getting pale.

"No, don't start this," Danny said, closing the gap enough to touch Amanda's sleeve. "Sweetheart, we are so close to freedom."

"Where is my brother?" Jotham asked her. "Kyrn helped you escape. I can feel his blood on you. Where is he?"

"She doesn't understand you, Jotham. Will you listen to me!?" Danny pleaded, wrapping his arms around Amanda. She seemed entranced by Jotham, and they had yet to break eye contact. Amanda jerked her head back, smacking into Danny's jaw.

"You left him to die. Is that what you're saying?" Jotham asked, covering his ears.

"Don't read into it. It's not a language," Danny said.

"Is my brother dead?"

"I never saw him," Danny said. "He never came out of the hospital."

Jotham tipped his head to the side, then vanished.

"We left him!" Amanda said, writhing in Danny's embrace. "His brother came to help us. We used him. We left him."

"He'll find his brother on his own. Just breathe, sweetheart," Danny said, cradling Amanda to his chest. "Don't run away from me again."

"There are hybrids here," Amanda whispered, pressing the door shut and leaning against it. She repeated the words over and over, hitting her head softly against the door.

"Yeah, we just saw one. You scared him away and now we have to walk," Danny said. "I need you to trust me. Come with me back to *Oriana*."

Shivering, Amanda nestled into his embrace, fighting for breath and lucidity. She made him feel so helpless.

Tray hadn't seen much of Rocan, but he hadn't liked any of it so far. The residents took no pleasure in little things like sweet dessert or the pretty gardens planted along the streets. They weren't miserable; they were dead inside. When Hawk had first come to *Oriana*, Tray knew the man's hope was fragile. Something awful happened to him in that prison, and he'd died too.

"Come on. We have to find John," Hawk hissed, hooking his

arm under Tray's shoulders, and pulling him through a doorway to escape the pursuing deputies. It looked like they were in a cafeteria, but it smelled like they were in a cardboard factory. Hawk guided him behind a counter and Tray sat on the floor, wheezing. He swore he'd start working out more as soon as they got back to Quin.

"We should split up," Saskia whispered, risking a peek over the countertop to see if they'd been discovered.

"The glider needs more fuel if it's going to fly again," Hawk panted.

"John is getting it," Sky said. "He's meeting us at the hanger."

"You told him to steal for you?" Hawk murmured, tugging the roots of his hair. "Sky, why?"

"Have you forgotten that we could just walk to the ship?" Tray pointed out. "We parked right next to a Pagoda."

"They'll be guarding the main gate," Saskia said, shaking her head. "If they haven't found the glider yet, then that's the gate we need to exit by. Let's hope the cold has created enough of a deterrent to keep them inside the Pagoda."

"I have a coat, and even I don't feel equipped to run that distance in the cold," Tray argued. "Saskia, I'm sick. Amanda's sick. The ship's broken."

"All the more reason for us to sneak back to it rather than storm the main gate," Saskia said. "You can ride back in the glider."

"I hate flying," Tray groaned.

"Let's meet at the hanger," Sky decided. "Hawk, with me."

"Sky!" Saskia hissed. "You and Hawk are the only ones who know the way back to the glider. Hawk, with *me*."

Tray gasped when Saskia squeezed his shoulder. He wasn't expecting the contact, and it certainly got his attention. They exchanged a look, then she motioned Hawk to follow her. Before Tray knew it, he was alone with Sky. He could feel his pant leg clinging to his bleeding shins and his socks grating against his blisters. They weren't under siege, and Tray was not ready to move yet.

Sky didn't rush him. Glancing over the counter, she watched Saskia and Hawk make their escape, then sat cross-legged on the floor and studied him smugly. "Captain went after his girl toy, Saskia takes Hawk, and you're stuck with me. Your crew doesn't like you much, do they Skipper?"

"Not really," Tray said, his chest tightening at the unwitting confession.

"Ooh. Did I strike a nerve there?" Sky teased. "You're so much like your brother."

Tray glowered. "I'm nothing like him."

"Oh?" she crooned, her tone shifting. She crawled closer to him, straddling his lap and leaning close to his face, teasing her fingers against his cheek. "So if I solicited you, you'd take advantage of the offer?"

Tray smacked her hand. The only woman he'd ever been with was his wife and he didn't like strangers getting close. "You think I'd want you after seeing you kissing a man twice my age? You're a greedy, selfish double-crossing—"

"*You* are expendable," Sky retorted, closing her hand around his throat. "That's why your crew left you with me."

"Not true," Tray said. Sky was not from Rocan; she was from Quin, and Tray understood her threats better than the accusations of the Rocanese. "Saskia doesn't care if you are greedy and selfish. She looks at you and sees a warrior—someone capable of fighting, winning, and bringing me home safe. She has taken your friend under her protection and she expects you to take me under yours."

"She's a fool," Sky spat, her fingers flinching, agitating the bruises on Tray's neck.

"Is she?" Tray challenged. They stared off, but Tray grew

weary of the standoff. He had a child waiting for him in Quin, and he'd be damned if he'd die here. "Okay then, forget all that honorable warrior crap. We owe you a ship. If you get me to Quin, I will get you that ship."

Sky considered him shrewdly, then smiled. She was from Quin; when she looked at his suit, she believed he could deliver on such a promise. Her hands played down his chest, smoothing his jacket apologetically, and then she rolled onto her feet. "Come on, then, Skipper."

Sighing in exhaustion, Tray trotted after her. The street was vacant, and Sky strolled along, setting an easy pace for him to follow.

"A working ship, right?" she asked, sounding like a child inquiring about a birthday present.

"Better than that *Bobsled,*" Tray said.

"Airship?"

"Spaceship."

Sky made a face. "I had a spaceship once. So much work."

"Fine. Airship," Tray said, rolling his eyes.

"Single pilot ready?"

Tray threw his hands up. "I don't have anything picked out. Show me what you want and we'll talk."

"How about money?" she asked, her tone sweetened by hope.

"Whatever," he agreed. Tray figured that she didn't want to get to Quin so much as she wanted to get away from it again, and he'd pay anything to see her leave.

"You're awfully accommodating."

Tray thought of his son and forced himself to stay calm. "I just want to get back to Quin. Alive."

"Oh. Alive?" Sky grinned. "That'll cost extra."

41

Tears stung John's eyes as he shoved supplies into the glider's small storage hatch. When John looked at the glider, the aliens, and their weapons, he understood why Celio had taken Douglas to asylum. He didn't like it, but right now, the aliens were the only ones who could save his son. Douglas' glider was breathtaking. Aesthetically, it could not hold a candle to Myung-Ki's glider, but this one flew. Safely. Whatever Douglas had scavenged and stolen to make it happen, it didn't justify an execution.

A pound of compressed, raw potash, a few ounces of refined fertilizer, bottles of gin and buffalo berry juice—John could barely make it all fit into the plane's tiny storage compartment. The glider was meant to carry supplies for a few hours of exploration, but the world outside needed to know what Rocan could offer. John would have stowed cargo in the seats, but Captain Matthews said they needed space for three flying back.

"John!" Douglas cried, running into the warehouse.

John nearly fell off the glider's ladder, but he hurried to the ground, catching his boy in his arms. There was a woman with him—definitely a brown-skinned alien—but no sign of Sky or the others. John grunted as Douglas squeezed him hard and John squeezed back, burying his face against his son's neck.

"John, we have to go. We have to get out of here," Douglas rambled, trembling.

"I know. I brought you a coat to keep you warm," John said, rummaging for the coat. "Open the gate."

"What?" Douglas' face went ashen. He backed against the wall, horrified. "No. No, we have to—what are you doing?"

"Making sure we have something to trade when we get to Cordova," John answered, tossing the coat at Douglas. Douglas let it fall to the floor.

"You stole all this? John, you'll be guilty, too," Douglas said. Fighting to get John away from the glider. "You have to look innocent, Papa. You have to stay and take care of Maman. What if they lie? What if they disappear on us? Papa!"

"Douglas, I'm already guilty," John said, hugging his son. "Kinley told us to open our eyes. Run far, run fast. I think she knew this was going to happen. She wants us to go."

Amanda dove for cover behind a crooked porch, and Danny swerved in, rolling beside her. He peered over the side of the porch, scanning the empty street.

"Help, now," Amanda gasped, hooking her arm across his shoulders. They'd crossed the border to Caswell a few blocks ago, and she could walk no further on her own.

Pulling Amanda's legs around his waist, Danny lifted Amanda and carried her piggyback, running top speed the final few blocks to the warehouse. The interior lights leaked through the doorframe, making it visible from halfway down the street.

Bursting into the warehouse, Danny wilted in frustration. The gate was still closed and the glider parked inside. Danny released Amanda's legs, letting her slide to the ground.

"Where's Tray?" Danny asked, his throat closing. Danny briefly flashed to Corey's body lying cold in the infirmary. Would he even have Tray's body?

"We split up," Saskia said. "Sky is with him."

"You left him with Sky!" Danny cried.

"Thanks for the vote of confidence," Sky carped, trotting into the warehouse and slamming the door.

"Saskia, I need my coat," Tray said, rushing past Danny and going for his food stash. Danny checked him over for fresh injuries, but Tray chomped on his protein bar, putting on a brave face. He knew they weren't out of the woods yet.

"The glider's loaded," John said, cinching his coat.

"Hawk, I need you flying," Danny pointed from Hawk to the glider.

"Papa, you're not going!" Hawk insisted, hanging on John's arm, knocking him back. Their arms tangled, and John whispered in Hawk's ear. It reminded Danny of the day he'd told Tray he was leaving Quin. Tray was eight and he had begged Danny to stay.

"If you two aren't coming, I need to know now," Danny said.

"They are coming," Sky insisted, pushing Hawk toward the glider. "Hawk, he deserves to see the world as it is. So do you."

"Amanda can't walk the distance. Tray, how are your feet?" Danny asked.

"I'm not getting in that thing," Tray said, bundling his coat, pulling the collar high. "Just go, Danny. Fix the ship."

"Not a chance!" Sky protested, jumping onto the wing. "You are not leaving without me."

"Ride on the wing if you want. We're not taking off. It's less than a quarter mile to the Pagoda," Danny said, lifting Amanda into the second seat. "We're about to be discovered here. If you know the glider controls, you can take Hawk's seat."

Sky glowered, and Danny pressed his pulse rifle into her hand. There was no time to argue.

"You bring my brother home or I'll send you back for him," Danny said.

Channing Mace groaned and clutched his head, rolling onto his back, still too groggy to join the hunt for the escaped aliens. Arman and the others were patrolling the street. Blayze formed a militia, gathering men. Mace didn't know how to prepare his people. Sky's weapon had dusted the bars of his only prison cell. Their town was under attack and Mace had literally carried the evil through the gates.

"Constable!"

Fighting the urge to heave, Mace forced himself to sit, cradling his broken hand to his chest. When his vision cleared, Celio Ferreira was kneeling next to him. Celio was young, with eyes as dark as the mine he oversaw, but he was dependable and loyal. Mace had petitioned the man to train for law, but Celio's heart was in politics. In twenty years, Mace expected to be calling him 'Intendant.'

"Ferreira, the militia is organizing near the hospital. You should go there," Mace grumbled, pulling away from Celio.

"I know where the aliens are, sir. I know where they'll be," Celio said, his eyes darting around the room.

Mace was on his feet so fast the room spun. "How?"

"When I found Hwan yesterday—he was by the Caswell gate. That's how he's been taking that glider in and out. Constable, I believe they're stealing more than an engine."

Forcing back nausea, Mace grabbed Celio's arm and dragged him to the door. "Show me."

42

John tucked his hands under his armpits and pulled the collar of his shirt over his mouth to fend off the chill. The last moon was setting, the temperature below freezing, and he kept slipping on the tundra. His vision was riddled with black spots and he veered sideways, getting woozy. A faint, red light glowed ahead of him, and he aimed for that, but then out of the darkness, a monster howled and snapped its teeth. John's body jerked so hard, he fell backward.

"John? John!" Sky cried.

The demon swooped closer, stirring clouds of red smoke, choking his screams. The light grew brighter and John closed his eyes, hiding his face. The chill of the ground seeped into his bones.

"John, what's wrong? What's happening? Talk to me," Sky urged, lifting his face off the ground, warming his cheeks with her hands.

"Sky?"

Images flooded his mind—childhood memories and monsters, long since repressed. Spirit things he'd tried desperately to escape.

"I've got you," Sky said over and over. "I've got you. Come on, we have to run."

John opened his eyes and screamed again, blinded by red glow, sure that his eyes were bleeding out.

"Quiet," she said, stroking his cheek.

She was next to him. Close enough to touch. "Sky? Is that you?"

Memories seeped into his mind. It wasn't a nightmare he'd forgotten—it was a whole realm.

"On your feet," she said, hooking her hand under his shoulders. "Hypothermia is making you delusional. Just hold on to me."

He stumbled a few steps, arms clamped around her waist, but then he felt a strain in his body, like a physical tether pulling him back to the city. The darkness overhead pulled back, and he saw the rain of meteors against the atmosphere. There was a shield over Rocan—over the Dome—and he knew he was a part of it. He could see the seam in the wall where the old Moonslate met the conjured rocks.

"I have to go back," he said.

"No, John. It's too late for that. You're already guilty," Sky reminded him. "You have to come with me. With Hawk—Douglas. Your son."

"Douglas," John repeated, his heart skipping a beat. "Tell him . . . tell him, I had to stay for Kinley. No. For Donny. He'll believe that."

"John, no. We are so close to the ship. So close, just stay with me," Sky begged.

She dragged him a few more steps, but his tether to the city grew taut. Then, like tugging a thread in a tapestry, it began to unravel, and the cracks spread over the Dome.

"John! You're going to freeze if you lie there," Sky whimpered, catching his head before it hit the ground. "Help. Help!"

John studied the darkness. His chest tightened, his mind overwhelmed by the energy required to keep the Dome in view.

"Sky, the darkness you feel when you're with me, the darkness that puts you to sleep," John said, reaching through the glowing, red cloud to find her. "I understand now. It's me. I'm a conjurer, and I help make the world look this way. I make Rocan whole."

"Rocan will be fine without you. There are plenty of others," she whispered, laying her head on his chest.

"You're glowing as bright as Caldori," he said, tucking his cold fingers around her to share her warmth. "But I saw you as human, and so you became."

"I am human."

"You're more than that," he said.

"So what?" Sky cried, hauling him up. "You're going to go back to Rocan and tell everyone my secret? I won't let you."

"The moment I remembered, the changes began. I have to change it back. If I step out, I don't know who else will be exposed," he said, tearing up. There were words, memories, and knowledge of that other realm flooding in, and he was afraid to see with those eyes again—those eyes that Kinley was always hounding him to open. "I chose this. I chose to forget. To not see."

"It was a bad choice. You can know the truth and still conjure the protection. Expose us, please," Sky said. "I feel so alone, thinking there is no one like me. No one who will understand how it hurts me. No one who will protect me. If there are people like me in Rocan, pretending that they're human is not the same as protecting them."

John touched her face, his freezing fingers moving clumsily.

"I can't see your lips. I can't see you as I did before," he said, closing his eyes. He felt her lips touch his, and he held her tight, kissing her hard. Her hot tears mixed with wind and turned to ice.

"What's going on? John!" Tray asked, limping toward them. His dark skin made him almost invisible, but his clothes seemed to shine in the moonlight. John pushed Sky toward him. Tray was human.

"I have to go back," John said. "You're coming back with medicine, right? Someone has to explain so you're not shot on arrival."

"No," Sky said.

"No time to argue," Saskia said, taking Sky's elbow. "Come on!"

"John, wait," Sky called, jerking free and reaching into her satchel. "Give this leaf to Felicity. Tell her to use it in a warm bath. It will prove that we have medicine that Rocan does not. That we can heal wounds; not just hide them."

Tray slid a slender device from his pocket and handed it to John. "Take this. It's a communication device. We'll let you know when we're near again."

"Take care of my boy," John said.

"I promise."

Celio worried Mace wouldn't make it to Hwan's warehouse. The man kept a quick pace, but he swooned as he ran, fishtailing through the streets. Even Celio's firm grip on Mace's arm couldn't keep them moving in a straight line. The first patrol they passed, Celio told the deputy to get word to Arman and gather the troops by the Caswell gate. Celio had crossed this border a few dozen times in the last six months, never on official business. He'd happened upon Hwan's warehouse by accident, and at the time the glider had still been in pieces. Celio had kept his mouth shut because he knew that Hwan's final product would be infinitely more valuable than the raw materials. That's what he'd told himself. Now the product was complete and Hwan's time was up. He just had to convince the Resource Manager not to destroy it. They rounded the corner on the last block leading up to the warehouse. The lights were on inside and the aliens were making no attempt to conceal their presence.

"There," Celio said triumphantly, running toward the warehouse. Mace yanked Celio's arm, pulling him into a doorway a ways down from the warehouse.

"They have powerful weapons. You're not armed," Mace said, pressing his lips together and studying the warehouse door.

"You intend to let them steal an engine from us," Celio countered. "And Hwan—they'll take him too!"

"Hwan will die either way," Mace murmured.

Celio froze, aghast. It couldn't be true. Douglas Hwan was important to this town—vital. Hwan brought machines to life. More than that, he'd brought a whole industry to life when he'd integrated women into his workforce. His abilities were special enough that he was able to circumvent laws and expose the foolishness of their class system. Without Hwan, Celio feared their world would change for the worse.

The world trembled around him and Celio dropped to his knees. Arman and the militia had arrived, armed with clubs, tranqs, and flash bombs.

"Do we mean to take them alive, sir?" Arman asked.

"Yes!" Celio cried.

"I give the orders, Ferriera," Mace growled.

Anger surging through him, Celio jumped to his feet, squaring off with Arman and Mace. "They have an engine and fuel. If you throw a flash bomb in there and Hwan is handling the fuel, this whole block could go up in flames." Thinking fast, he pointed to Arman's pistol and held out his hand. "Let me go in. Hwan trusts me. Sort of."

"Or these aliens could abduct you. He was Sky's hostage voluntarily, but after what they did to him, they had to drag him from the Bastien kicking and screaming," Mace snapped, brushing Celio aside. "You are staying here."

Celio braced for a fight, but he didn't get a chance. The street erupted with the roaring sound of the glider's engine. Mace and Arman dashed for the warehouse, and Celio followed hot on their heels. Ducking to one side, Celio scouted the area as the warehouse filled with militia. *Is this a trap?* The gate was open; the glider was gone. Mace's men ran out into the cold, night air.

"There are some on foot!" one of the men shouted. Without a thought toward provisions or even flashlights, a dozen of them took off into the darkness.

"It's too late! Fools, it's too late!" Celio called after them.

This can't be happening. Shaking in disbelief, Celio stumbled to the gate and stared dumbly into the darkness. He could just make out the lights of Hwan's glider, trundling on ground. Then he saw someone collapsed a few yards from Caswell gate.

"Harris?" Celio called, dashing out into the cold and dragging the man inside. John was limp, offering no resistance, but murmuring his son's name over and over. By the time he got John into the warehouse, the other man was unconscious, and Celio was seeing spots.

"Out here! Bring him out here!" Mace ordered, waving them onto the street and sealing the door behind them. "Let's hope others have the sense to come back, too."

"They're taking the glider to their ship."

"In Qu'Appelle, I know. Stay with him. There are messengers coming with blankets and coats," Mace said, feeling for John's pulse. "We can set up a secondary triage in the Pagoda. I had the lights turned on so that the men find their way there."

"This is my fault. I should have given him more time," Celio said, lying next to John to keep him warm. "Where will he go now?"

43

Douglas saw two worlds. He saw phantoms and smoke and lights in the darkness. Then he saw the Dome destroyed, and the people inside walking around, oblivious. It wasn't a hallucination or the onset of dementia, it was the intertwining of the magic world with the real, and he could see them both now. His mother always told him to open his eyes, and this was what she wanted him to see. Not the world his father imagined—but the world as it was. The world he needed to repair.

"Why did you have to get John involved?" Douglas murmured, looking over his shoulder. "He was innocent. I did everything to keep him innocent in this."

"He came looking for us. For Sky," Danny replied, putting a hand on Douglas' shoulder. "He came to kill her."

"I don't believe that. He wouldn't," Douglas said. They were too far ahead to see Sky's light anymore.

"Why are you so worried about him coming?" Danny asked.

"Because I don't think he'll survive." He closed his spirit eyes, willing himself to see only the safety of Rocan and not the broken Dome. "Why did he have to fall in love with Sky?"

"The heart doesn't follow rules, son," Danny smiled.

Amanda echoed the sentiment in her own language, and Douglas laughed at the tingling feeling her voice left on his ears.

"Kerf, we have company," Douglas said, firing up the glider's engine and blasting the lights. "Sit down, we're about to take a ride."

"Where are we going?" Danny cried in his ear.

"Into the imagination!" His red hair whipped around his face as the glider took flight. He laughed, feeling free for the first time. He wasn't worried being found out. "They'll be on our side when they see the glider fly. They'll know why I did what I did. It's for them. It's all for them!"

A thin wisp of aurora threaded over the mountains.

"Tray!" Danny hollered, fighting to be heard over the roar of the wind. "Did we draw them from the gate?"

"Please don't shoot us down," Douglas murmured under his breath. He jumped when he felt Danny's hand on his shoulder.

"Hawk, fly into the valley, where you first found us. The others will get the ship and rendezvous with us there," Danny instructed.

"Good-bye, Rocan," Douglas whispered. "Stay safe."

The further Sky got from John, the stronger she felt. Spirit seethed and prowled, creating an invisible fortress around her body, protecting her from the cold. Saskia kept loose hold of her hand, making sure she kept moving forward. The path back to the ship was barren, and there was nothing save the curve of the Dome that kept them shielded from their pursuers. Both moons had set and it was darkest in this hour just before dawn, but Spirit knew the way.

Sky heard a dart whiz past her ear and dove left, firing back into the darkness. Danny's pulse rifle was different from her grav-gun. It gave her more control over whether her shots were fatal. In the darkness she couldn't tell where the enemy was, so she aimed low. Saskia fired next, and the pained screech that followed let them know her stunner shot had connected. A light from the Pagoda shone on *Oriana*, showing a small, armed militia.

Suddenly, the valley filled with light so intense, Sky's eyes burned. *Flash bomb!* Momentarily blinded, Sky tripped and fell to her knees. The tundra chilled her legs, the force of the impact making her ears ring. Spirit's hands slithered up her body, closing around her throat. The light faded to darkness and Sky's eyes could not adjust through the bleeding, choking, red. Strong arms hooked under her shoulders, dragging her body. At first, she let herself be carried and focused on breathing. Then she realized the two people carrying her were speaking Rocanese.

"Help!" Sky kicked and screamed. Saskia fired her stunner and the two men fell to the ground. Blinking and sweating, Sky searched the darkness for *Oriana's* light. The battle looked unfamiliar, and the weapons too advanced for Rocan. In the darkness, she saw what Spirit wanted her to see. Two more people grabbed her and Sky screeched.

"Sky!" Hawk shouted, clamping his hands on her cheeks and forcing their eyes to meet. "Breathe, bébé."

It was a difficult order to follow. Stranger, still, this was real Hawk, not a spirit vision. "How?" she wheezed.

"Teleport," he laughed. "Don't look so surprised. You're the one who told me the magic is real."

"Find Tray," Sky shuddered. Tray was her ticket to freedom.

"I'm the one holding you up," Tray said, hefting her to her feet. "And thanks for asking."

She was so much taller than him that she folded over his shoulders. Sky heard another dart whiz by and Hawk pitched into her arms. Catching him as they fell to the ground, Sky turned and fired her pulse rifle at the attacker. The Rocanese were close enough to fight hand-to-hand, but they didn't seem willing. They were dying from the cold.

Trying to keep her head in the current battle and her eyes on the light from *Oriana*, Sky dragged Hawk toward the ship. He moved groggily, pushing with his legs, not willing to surrender to the effects of the tranquilizer dart.

"Saskia!" Tray cried.

"We're surrounded!" Sky cried. "Come on, Hawk. Wake up. We need you to teleport."

They were going to be captured again!

"Make the ground shake," Hawk said, his voice sluggish from the tranquilizers.

Reluctantly, Sky drew her grav-gun. *You had better not kill me, Spirit.* Aiming away from *Oriana*, Sky fired at the ground. Then she curled into a ball, grabbed onto Hawk, and tried to keep her eyes open, but shielded. She didn't know how many flash bombs went off, but the blinding light persisted for several minutes, and her lungs closed.

"We're going to roll first. Roll into the valley, pick up the glider, fix the thruster. Then we fly," Danny instructed Amanda. He had her in the pilot's seat. "Don't fly, and if you do, don't crash."

"You set the bar pretty low for what constitutes a safe landing," she teased.

The ship shook and the sun blinders on the front window engaged automatically.

"Hawk," Amanda murmured.

"Be ready on my signal!" Danny cried, dashing to the lower deck, pulse rifle in hand. The bay door was wide open and the whole valley glowed, the fading embers of the light sources lying on the ground next to fallen Rocanese militia. A few people were moving, and Danny couldn't find his brother among the fallen. The Rocanese weren't dressed for the cold or the soon-rising sun. *It's their own fault for trying to kill us!* Even so, Danny grabbed a few tarps that had been covering the cargo crates. He dropped his peace offering when he saw Hawk running toward the ship, Saskia slung over his shoulders. Just a few steps behind, Tray and Sky hobbled together, their bodies tangled to the point where Danny couldn't tell who was holding up whom.

"She needs oxygen!" Tray shouted.

Danny rushed to find the emergency tank. Half the pressure had drained from the canister due to age and lack of use, but it would get them to the infirmary. Tray grabbed the tank as he passed Danny, and he and Sky collapsed a few steps into the bay. When Tray pressed the mask to Sky's face, her eyes bulged.

"Where's John?" Danny asked.

"Not coming," Tray said.

"Captured?" Hawk asked, putting his head between his knees.

Sky rolled onto her side, sobbing into the oxygen mask.

"You're sure, Tray?"

"Not captured. Just turned back. A hundred percent his choice. I gave him my Virp so we can contact him when we bring Hawk home," Tray said.

"Hawk, get back," Danny said. Kicking the few tarps he'd gathered for the Rocanese clear of the door, Danny closed the bay doors and sealed the ship. "Amanda, we're on. Get us out of here."

"Going," Amanda replied. The ship rumbled as she fired up the engines.

"What about the beacon?" Tray asked. "Once we're above the mountains, we should be able to scan for Quin."

"Then get it ready," Danny ordered. "Hawk, what happened to Saskia?"

"Tranquilizer," Hawk slurred. Hawk's pupils were wide and black, and his shoulders sagged. "We're moving."

"Sit here with Sky," Danny said, lowering Hawk to the ground, laying him next to Sky.

"You teleported?" Sky asked, touching his face.

Hawk shook his head.

"It was the Gate brothers. They were worried I'd leave without you, so they brought us back," Danny chuckled. "Once you're mobile, tack down the *Bobsled*. Don't want it sliding out the back door when we take off. I have to make sure Amanda stays grounded."

Sky nodded and scooted closer to Hawk, seeming more comfortable now that she knew he wouldn't disappear. Danny trotted back to upper deck, slowed by his concern for the crew. He cut through the ward room where Tray had every networking gadget available, waiting for them to rise above the mountains so they could get a signal from Quin.

"Is the beacon dead?" Danny asked, keeping one hand on the wall and looking over Tray's shoulder.

"Dad always says 'don't put all your eggs in one basket,'" Tray murmured, his face ashen, his chair rattling, he was shivering so hard.

"Yeah, but if you divide your attention too much, nothing's going to work," Danny remarked.

"Nothing *is* working!" Tray cried, tossing a Virclutch aside and moving to a monitor. "You were so busy flirting with Sky, giving her tours of the ship, you never fixed the tracking on the beacon. You never attached it to the Vring!"

"I didn't realize we'd be leaving in such a hurry!" Danny said. "It'll take at least twenty minutes to replace that thruster nozzle. You have that long to attach the beacon yourself."

"Danny!" Tray cried through clenched teeth.

"What! What?" Danny asked, leaning on the center table of the ward room for balance.

Tray sucked in his cheeks and ducked his head. "Go. Just go."

"Are you hurt?" Danny asked, dropping his voice. Danny wanted to touch him—wanted to lift his brother's eyes.

Tray covered his scabbed hand. "Yes, but—"

"You fix supper, I fix the ship," Danny said, chuckling at their oft-repeated mantra. "We have what we need to fix the ship. We're out of reach of the enemy. We'll make it. Even if we have to limp along the coastline of the entire continent. I think that's Sky's plan."

Tray nodded and Danny ruffled his hair. His skin was burning with new fever, but waxy from frost-nip.

"Oriana," Danny whispered.

"Oriana," Tray repeated.

44

The ward room on *Oriana* felt pleasantly warm. The temperature was five degrees cooler than Danny would have liked, but the room was filled with his crew, healthy and alive. He felt the occasional pang of guilt for feeling content with Corey so freshly dead, but at least he hadn't had to lay anyone next to her.

"This is Tray Matthews to Quin Port control. Can you hear me?" Tray murmured into the transmitter he and Sky had hacked together. Tray was curled into one of the chairs, his legs draped sideways over one of the arms, his body twisted to face the table. Every now and then, he would transfer something from his Virp to his Virclutch. Tray was freshly bathed and bandaged, his hair tamed into ringlets. The casual, blue sweater he wore told Danny that his brother felt safe.

"Tray, just set up an automated signal," Danny groaned, tired of seeing their calls going unanswered.

"Why? Is there something better I can do with my time?" Tray sighed. "Quin, this is *Oriana*."

Amanda sat at the table in the middle of the room, playing Solitaire. Every fifteen or twenty minutes, she'd zone out or start murmuring in Moonspeak, but Danny could bring her back with a gentle backrub. He wanted her to go to sleep, but she didn't want to be alone. She'd flown well for most of the day once the new thruster was installed, but let him take over the landing. *Oriana* was not designed for air travel.

"We should stow the solar panels before we take off tomorrow. They're causing unnecessary drag and I don't want to lose them," Danny was telling Saskia. They'd been running numbers on fuel consumption, trying to figure the best way to balance their new cargo against dwindling fuel and food supplies.

"We could do that now," Saskia said, crossing her arms and glaring at the numbers on the screen. Her hair was wrapped in a tight bun, her coveralls zipped to the neck, and her stunner holstered by her side. Saskia did not feel safe. She'd recovered slowly from the flash bombs and hypothermia, and had woken up in the infirmary after they'd been in the air nearly half an hour.

"There's no rush to leave," Danny shrugged, hoping his lackadaisical attitude would rub off on her so she could relax enough to sleep tonight. "There's enough ozone here, so we can work by daylight."

"Are you feeling better?" Tray asked.

Hawk swayed in the doorway. He had fallen sick shortly after supper, and though he was less green now, he still looked pale. His oily red hair hung limply around his face, and the old sweats Danny had given him to sleep in were rumpled. Hawk seemed childlike, clutching that flight jacket like a security blanket.

"We've stopped moving," Hawk murmured, leaning on the doorframe.

"For now," Danny said. "You just noticed?"

"Were you motion sick?" Tray asked. "We have meds for that."

Hawk frowned, like he didn't know how to process Tray's question. "Where are we?"

"Come on, I'll show you," Danny invited, putting his arm around Hawk's shoulders. He remembered his own first trip outside the Dome—his mother took him from Clover to Olcott. At the time, it felt like a long trip, and the two cities seemed so different from each other. Now, everything in Quin looked the same. Danny guided Hawk to the ladder leading up to the Observation Deck. The foot of the ladder was near Tray's workstation, and Danny caught Tray peeking over his Virclutch.

Sky was already on the Obs Deck, lying on the floor, staring at the stars. It was a cramped space, not designed for crowds. With Hawk and Sky inside, Danny couldn't do more than stand on the ladder and poke his head and shoulders through the hatch. The view was beautiful. The sun was low on the horizon, painting the clouds pink and orange. Caldori was setting as well, but Terrana was high in the sky. The mountains of Rocan were distant, tucked behind a huge array of lakes and rivers. The land had patches of grass and small shrubs.

"We've gone a few hundred miles," Danny said. "It took a while to find solid ground to land on with all the lakes. I hope we don't sink in the night."

"It's all water?" Hawk murmured. He crawled into the room, laid down next to Sky, and mirrored her posture, from the way she peaked one knee to the way she pillowed her head. He laid the flight jacket over her like a blanket, then pulled a flask from the pocket, took a drink, and handed it to Sky. Sky drank and handed the flask back. Neither seemed to care about the view. They were in mourning for John.

"I suppose I should finish clearing out that second bunk," Danny said.

"I don't need a bunk," Sky said. She shifted, like she was

standing straighter even though she was laying flat. Hawk did the same thing.

"You can't sleep up here."

"She can share my bed," Hawk said.

"I don't *need* a bunk," Sky growled.

"Tell me about the water, bébé," Hawk whispered, nestling closer to her.

The change was sudden and stark. In a single word, Hawk shifted from the protected to the protector. Sky relaxed immediately, and scooted closer, resting her head on Hawk's arm. She pointed to the lakes and started talking about fish. The two of them were fine together.

With a relieved smile, Danny climbed down the ladder. Tray appeared engrossed in his project, but Danny could tell that the frown on Tray's face was aimed at him. Saskia fiddled with power relays. Amanda had zoned out again, and she kept flipping over cards without seeing them. Taking the seat next to Amanda, Danny rubbed her back.

"Can I play?" he asked.

Amanda's eyes focused, and she nodded. "Please, help."

"Tray? Saskia? Cards?" Danny invited.

Tray tried to look casual, but he couldn't hide his delight at the invitation.

Saskia slid into a seat across the table. "What are we playing?"

"Do you know how to play Pierce Pitch?" Tray asked. "It's something I learned in school."

"Teach us," Danny said, smiling at his brother. They were alone out here, but they had each other, and that gave Danny hope.

45

In the end, Constable Mace wasn't sure what they had been fighting for, but he knew they'd lost. It had been nearly two weeks since any of the militia men had been able to work. Between burns and frostbite, infections were rampant. The aliens' gift of fabric had saved their lives. Their losses were severe, though, and Mace closed his eyes, his body going numb as he listened to the Intendant recite the list.

"Theft of refined ethanol fuel. Theft of an engine. Theft of clothing resources," the Intendant droned as he stood importantly behind Mace's desk in the Bastien. John Harris slouched in the jail cell, eyes half-closed, hand over his heart.

"Theft of metal resources and metal tools. Theft of refined potash. Theft of medicine and medical resources." The Intendant paused to glare at John and take a breath. "Conspiracy to commit theft. Conspiracy to Sequester. Injury and loss of three women—"

"One confirmed unbreedable," Dr. Frank piped up. He sat in Mace's chair, flanking the Intendant, his medical bag prominently displayed. They weren't here to heal John; they were here to execute him.

"Those women are not dead," Mace growled, his fist clenching. Dr. Louis had removed the cast from his hand that morning, but he was already imagining the fight for John's freedom.

"They're not here," the Intendant sneered, his upper lip curling.

"They're not even Rocanese citizens. They came on a spaceship!" Mace snarled back. "These people have resources and technology like we've never seen! These charges are ridiculous!"

"This is not a trial, Constable. This is a formality," the Intendant said, crossing to the cell, staring down at John. John didn't react. The lock was dusted, but John wasn't trying to escape. "He's an aged man with physical defect, unable to work, beyond breeding obligation. He was part of Douglas Hwan's crimes. He confessed to loading stolen goods into the glider."

"This punishment is wrong," Mace insisted. He knew something bad would happen if John died. "They ran because we attacked them without cause. They weren't invading. They were willing to help! We could have flown over those mountains a generation ago—"

"Let's not drag this out. Some of us have work to do," Dr. Frank complained, resting his chin on his hand.

There was a shout outside the Bastien, and Mace hesitated, not wanting to come back and find Harris dead. But he figured he could trust the Intendant to finish the formality of the execution procedure, and the shouts resolved into cries for help.

Tearing open the door, Mace nearly plowed into a body. Two bodies. Don Yale hung from a rope suspended from the Bastien roof. His body twitched, and Deputy Arman had him by the knees, pushing him upward to get the pressure of the rope off his neck.

"Dr. Frank!" Mace called, helping Arman get leverage. Frank leapt to his feet, but John moved faster, galloping to the doorway, then pulling the noose off of Don's neck.

"Donny," John whimpered. His voice was hoarse, his skin waxy from frostbite.

"The idiot!" Intendant Hubert ranted. "Don't help him. He chose this."

Yale had threatened to do something drastic if the Intendant didn't release Harris from custody.

"I'm sorry," John whispered, taking Don's weight, cradling his head as the three of them lowered Don to the ground. "See you on the other side."

"Don't waste your energy on him, Amir," Intendant Hubert groused.

"Alain, I did not become a doctor to watch people die," Frank retorted. Mace was surprised to hear the men call each other by first name. "Even non-breeders have value."

Mace could see by the flush in Frank's cheeks that the flimsy excuse was for the Intendant's benefit. They'd all seen Yale's pain growing for years—the man who created families, even though he never had one of his own.

"Intendant! Intendant!" Colleen Arman hollered, running to the Bastien with Felicity in tow. She saw Don on the ground and stopped dead. "Mon Kerf!"

"Felicity, don't look," Deputy Arman warned, rushing to his daughter, covering her eyes.

"Oh, no!" Felicity squeaked.

"Don't look," her father warned again, pressing her face to his shoulder and lifting her off the ground.

"Deputy, get that child out of here," Frank ordered.

"Let's take him inside," Mace suggested. Their presence in the street was drawing spectators.

"I'm not moving a patient with a neck injury. Move the child," Frank said, brushing his thighs as he stood.

"No, but look," Colleen said. "Look at Felicity, Dr. Frank. She's healed. Her skin is healed!"

Mace did a double-take as well. Felicity's skin was soft and pink, smooth all over, free of the burns, scars, and black patches that had once covered it.

"By the gods," Frank murmured, brushing a hand over her ear. Her scalp was smooth and white, a shadow of blond fuzz signaling new hair growth. "Little darling, how did this happen?"

Felicity pursed her lips and shook her head, and Frank nearly cracked a smile.

"How?" Mace asked.

"That's what I came to tell you—before I found him," Deputy Arman panted. "What Sky said about Cordova—it has to be true."

"The next person who mentions Cordova," the Intendant warned.

"Cordova!" Felicity shouted at him.

"Shh. Felicity," Arman said, covering the girl's mouth.

"Let her speak," Colleen said, pulling his hand away. "Darling, tell them what you told me."

Felicity wriggled out of her father's arms, and took a tentative step toward Don, but the Intendant stepped in front of her to block. She looked up at him, furrowing her brow, then she showed the Intendant the smooth, healed skin of right arm, wriggling the fingers that only days ago she could barely control. "Mon Harris gave me a leaf—it was a gift from Madame Sky. It made the skin grow back and the pain stop."

"Why you?" the Intendant challenged her. "Why only you?"

"Because she saw me hurting," Felicity said, shrinking away from him.

"But who are you to her?"

Felicity cocked her head, like she didn't understand. Then she backed up until she reached Arman, and pulled his arms around her. "I'm Felicity. Felicity Arman."

"Harris," Mace called.

John lay on the ground next to Don, their faces close, their breathing slow, like they planned to die together in their sleep.

"Did you know that Sky could heal Felicity's burns?" Mace asked. The Intendant shot him a look, but Mace raised his brow and crossed his arms.

"She gave me the leaf for Felicity," John croaked. "She healed my son with the same medicine."

"She did," Frank realized, tracing Felicity's fingers in amazement. "When the Coureur burned, young Hwan did not; but he vividly remembered being on fire. And an angel healing his skin."

"Intendant, even if they cannot heal our worst ailment, they can help us," Arman spoke up.

The Intendant frowned, not liking the challenge to his authority, but not willing to appear unreasonable. "Mon Harris, do you have any way of communicating with these aliens?"

John nodded. "A device. It will alert me when they are near again."

He could barely get the words out, but those were the words that would save his life.

Colleen buried a grateful sob against Arman's chest, and Arman embraced his family. The Intendant squared off with Arman, his scowl deepening. He poked at Felicity's perfect, rejuvenated skin, and she peered at him defiantly.

"Your healing is a miracle, little one," the Intendant said. "Let us hope your friend comes back to save the rest of us."

"Douglas Hwan did not leave us; he only went ahead of us to the other Domes," Mace said. "His place is out there beyond the mountains, but his heart is here. He will come home."

COMING IN JANUARY 2018
TRADE CIRCLE
The New Dawn: Book 3

TRADE CIRCLE

PREVIEW

The fresh morning dew glistened in the dappled sunlight that reached the forest floor of Fox Run. Vivid green resurrection fern, revitalized from the previous evening's downpour, covered the wide-reaching branches of the ancient trees. The constant, fresh rains had prompted an early spring and colorful blossoms dotted the banks for the streambed bordering the Drava's nomadic camp. Wild turkeys grazed for insects along the game path, safe for now since the Drava hunters had achieved their weekly quota days ago.

Sky reclined on the upper branch of one of the old trees, watching the turkeys. She didn't believe the Drava should have let the turkeys go by. Five other nomadic tribes regularly passed through this land. Their hunters weren't nearly as skilled as the Drava and food was the best currency in the nomadic barter system.

A scream sent the turkeys running and Sky's eyes turned to the large supply tent at the center of the Drava camp. Scouts had returned just before moonset with a young woman in chains. It was an anomaly. The Drava were egalitarian and did not keep slaves or prisoners. Those they did not want in their camp, they exiled, and those who refused to stay away were killed. In all the months she'd been flitting in and out of their society, she'd never once seen that rule violated. The prisoner hadn't made a sound all night, and though she was alone in the tent, guards had been posted along all four sides of the structure. The woman's cry went largely unnoticed by the camp. The guard posted at the entrance peeked inside, but was presumably satisfied that the prisoner did not require any additional attention. Sky disapproved of captivity and was formulating a plan to sneak in and set the woman free.

Three hundred feet away from the screaming woman, Sidney Kassa, son of Marius, crawled out of his private sleeping tent and scanned the forest, smiling when he spotted Sky in the tree. Sky acknowledged him with a wave and leaned back against the trunk, letting one leg dangle teasingly out of his reach. Sky preferred a certain type of man, and Sidney fit the bill; he was a strong, young trade ambassador, a son of the Drava's Trade Master, and a good lover. He never wore a shirt outside of the Trade Circle, and Sky figured the world was better for it—at least her world was. She was similarly opposed to wearing shirts, though most societies she visited requested her to.

Kneeling by the stream, Sidney splashed water on his face, then he climbed the tree, lithely straddling the branch and facing Sky. Since most humans had retreated into the Domes four hundred years ago, the trees of Fox Run were aged and untouched by industrial society. The tree branches were strong enough to build houses in, rather than simply make houses from. The branch Sky and Sidney sat on was thick enough to be a tree in its own right. By comparison, most other forests Sky had seen were filled with mere saplings.

"Another sleepless night, Adita?" Sidney asked, tilting his face so his eyelashes tickled her cheek. The Drava didn't kiss with their lips, but Sidney's other caresses assured her they were missing nothing. Sky's reputation as a thief among the other nomadic tribes had prompted the alias. Although most of the nomads in this region spoke Lanvarian, the dialects had diverged over the years. Acceptable slang phrases used by one tribe might be interpreted as vicious slurs by another, so when Sky had met the Drava, she'd kept quiet until she had a handle on the nuances. Marius had called her Adita because of her golden hair. To the Drava, it was a mesmerizing feature. They were a brown-skinned people with iridescent black hair, so her fair skin was a novelty to them. She had accepted the name, not realizing until later that Marius had wanted to cut off and buy her hair from her. Sidney had saved her. He was more adept at languages than most of the traders and had waded through the various Lanvarian dialects until they'd found a common one.

Sky nodded toward the supply tent. "The Drava have a prisoner."

Pursing his lips, Sidney scooted forward on the branch, hooking his legs over hers until their bodies were pressed together. It wasn't a comfortable position, but his creativity in coitus was part of what drew her to him, enticing her to visit the Drava time and again. Sky arched her torso, wrapping her arms around his neck. Were it not for the disquieting presence of the prisoner in the supply tent, whose muffled screams had elevated to shrieks, Sky's shirt would have been on the ground.

"Why do you have a prisoner?" she whispered in his ear, the heat of her breath sending shivers of excitement rippling through him.

"It's not human," Sidney murmured breathily, sliding his hands under her shirt and lifting. "Not anymore. An Aquian spirit possesses the body now. We have a Seer."

Sky breath hitched, goose bumps rising on her skin. She'd never met another Seer. Retracting her hands, she tried to pull free of Sidney's embrace, but their legs were laced and she was pinned against the trunk of the tree. "Seers are myth, Sid. No one can see the future."

Sensing her discomfort, Sidney pulled her into a hug and reclined, lying backward on the branch and pulling her with him. Two days ago, they'd made love on this branch and their height off the ground had been exhilarating. Now, all Sky cared about was whether she could jump to the ground and if she'd make it clear of the camp before Sidney caught up.

"Adita, lover, you're not afraid of the Seer are you?" he chided, nuzzling her face. "There is no danger. The Spirit is trapped in the vessel; we need only harness it. Can you imagine the time it would save—telling our hunters which field the game is running through, or our scavengers which cities are building wagons?"

"The Drava don't believe in mysticism," Sky said tightly, unable to get comfortable lying atop Sidney. She had to escape before they figured out what she was.

"The Drava also don't believe that a water planet was devoid of life before humans arrived in this system," Sidney laughed, stroking her hair, determined to comfort her. "There is sufficient evidence for past organic life. And present non-corporeal life, even if our scientists can't put it into an equation. The Nayak harnessed a Seer spirit, and their numbers have grown three-fold in the last three years. The Chanti traded two of their best hunters just to possess the Seer's eyes."

"They cut out her eyes!?" Sky gasped, no longer caring about appearances. Scrambling away from Sidney, she swung off the branch. He caught her wrist as she fell, but only to help lower her safely to the ground. As soon as her feet hit the dirt, Sky took off running, and Sidney chased.

"Adita! Adita, be calm," he called, capturing her in his arms, and tackling her sideways into the brush. The twigs and brambles scraped at her skin. Sky cried out, hoping he'd let go, but his embrace tightened and he whispered soothingly in her ear.

"The human was dead when the spirit took the shell. The vessel has no need for eyes, and the leave it to Nayak to prey on Chanti mysticism. They needed the hunters with all those extra mouths to feed."

Sky's vision blurred with tears. Her Spirit was her most closely guarded secret, and this was why—her lover wouldn't even believe her human! "You cannot keep a spirit. If your prisoner dies, her spirit will kill you all!"

It wasn't an idle threat; it was the reason Sky had left her own family. She planned to die alone and take Spirit with her. Sidney wrestled Sky into his lap, combing the leaves from her hair, shushing her. Her knife was sheathed at her calf, and a surprise attack might buy her enough time to escape. Sidney was a trader, not a hunter, and a stab wound to the leg would keep him from chasing her without killing him. The scent of his blood would alert the hunters, though, and they'd track her. *Don't raise their suspicions; don't make them hunt you.*

"I'll take you to see her. You'll see that there is nothing to be afraid of," Sidney assured, hugging her tightly, flexing his chest muscles in a way that normally made her laugh. Sky's body was rigid, ready to run. She had to remind herself that while danger was near, it was not so imminent that she'd die in the next few minutes. In another hour, Sidney would start his daily tasks, and she could disappear into the forest. She'd done that often enough, leaving the Drava for weeks at a time, never stealing so much that they wouldn't welcome her back.

Sidney prodded her toward the supply tent, but Sky planted her feet and shook her head. She had no intention of getting near another Seer. One spirit was enough to contend with, and she didn't know if the other spirit could identify hers.

"You have considerable sway with the Supply Manager. She

listens to you," Sky said, facing Sidney and lacing their fingers together. He leaned into her touch eagerly.

"I don't need you to stroke my ego, Adita," he growled in her ear. "I have other parts I like you to stroke."

Using their joint hands, Sky dragged her knuckles over his pelvis, hoping the temptation would make him compliant. "Then ask the Supply Manager to let the Seer keep her eyes."

Sidney's body tensed and he squeezed her hands. "The eyes inhibit the spirit."

"Because the human part of her isn't dead!" Sky snapped, ripping her hands free and turning to run.

Sidney hooked his arm around her waist, lifting her off the ground. "What do you know of these spirit-carriers?" he demanded.

"Let go!" she screamed, kicking her feet and struggling to get loose.

"You've seen a Seer before, haven't you? You know how it can be tamed," he said adamantly.

"It can't be tamed! That psychopath spirit killed my family," she whimpered, bowing her body, trying to reach her knife. The spirit that possessed Sky had killed half her city within a year, including two of her aunts and three cousins before taking her. They had been too selfish, wanting to stay home with their families, trying to live a normal life, but they had been fools and each one had condemned the next. Sky condemned no one but herself.

"That is why you wander," Sidney realized, releasing her and running beside her, no longer urging her to stop. He chased her to the forest edge, then grabbed her hand, keeping her from breaking into the open. Jerking and kicking, Sky hissed at him to let her go, but he covered her mouth. "The Chanti are hunting in the plain. Adita, you'll be killed!"

Seething, Sky crouched within the forest borders, trying to

catch her breath. The Drava hadn't discovered her secret, but they might. She wondered what would happen to her if they gouged her eyes out. Would she finally be able to sleep at night? Would the visions and dreams Spirit plagued her with fall into order? All Spirit ever showed her was confusion. She experienced pain and fear every time she closed her eyes. If the Drava took her eyes, would all that was 'Sky' be gone so that only 'Spirit' remained?

Feeling Sidney's arms around her, Sky collapsed against him, trembling. Maybe the reason her Spirit was so cruel was because it wanted to drive her out of her own body. The light she saw let her hold on to herself. Maybe she was the selfish one. If she were truly selfless, she'd have sacrificed herself to kill Spirit long ago.

"Don't take her eyes," she begged, touching her face, imagining her crystal blue eyes strung up on a line and displayed in the Trade Circle for all the tribes to bid on.

"I'll ask," Sidney promised. "For you, Adita, I will ask."

To hear more about Trade Circle and other upcoming novels by this author...

Subscribe to her newsletter:
www.valeriejmikles.com/contact.html

And follow her on social media: www.facebook.com/vjmikles

Made in the USA
Middletown, DE
26 August 2018